I0778391

UKA BUKA

Book 1 of

Written by Efren Stat

CHAPTERS

PROLOGUE

Imagine our Planet Earth as a Goddess, able to create life, grow ecosystems, and tinker around in scientific properties to make miracles happen. Imagine that, obviously not too far off from our reality now. In a world where imagination grows wings and flies amongst realistic ideals, here is the unheard story of this voluptuously spherical Goddess, imbued with a natural essence of manifestation and flowing with the evolution of life's creations.

The key to unlocking the destiny of souls and transferability of consciousness into other Galaxies never seemed so near.

Long, long ago, the Earth Goddess created six daughters to help guard the planet from whatever may threaten her lifesource. Like their Mother, these six daughters, the Sky Sisters, angels of our world, could not be fully conscious and awakened for the millions of years the planet has to live, so they too, created their own guardians for when they slumber. Their chosen, the trees, also rejoice in their slumber, even though they have a more prominent appearance on the surface of the planet.

Nevertheless, with such going right in the world; Sky Sisters in harmony with the wood, the wood rooted back to the Earth, and the Earth Goddess able to sleep with her babies made comfortable on her belly, the Universe has a tendency to balance itself out.

Madness began to bleed out of one Sky Sister because of the vastness of their serenity. This separation between Sisters concluded in a massive war between the six of them, causing even their Awakened, the magical Treants, to slam their ancient woods against one another.

After the fall of the mad Sky Sister, her spirit arose mightier than any physical form, and she haunted Mother Earth and its children, bringing souls of unrest and darkness to the otherwise old world of sunlight and tranquility. Earth Mother had no way to protect her planet from such a haunting. Dark clouds rolled over erupting volca-noes, high seas broke away cliff faces, and tornadoes uprooted forest lands. The storm of the dead clashed relentlessly with the Garden of the living.

This catastrophe led to a most significant discovery. All sciences, astronomical star charts, and spiritual essences were compounded to coalesce into one intensified pathway to a galactic afterlife.

Our spherical Mother called on her Father, the Sun, to reach out for a solution to this dread haunting, and the Sun twinkled its flare out into space with an entirely other Galaxy, a Galaxy flipped amongst the universal laws of living. A Galaxy with no laws and with no living. Having a galactic bulge of pure chaos at its center and a holy ring of peaceful light on the outer rim. This was the Galaxy of the Dead.

Finding such a magnificent marvelment, The Sun, the Moon, and the Earth created a holy trinity of power to make two portals on Earth; one that allowed entry into the Galaxy of the Dead and one to receive the dead back. The Universe's compromise was a balanced warp portal or no warp portal. These portal openings then needed guarding just as the planet needed watching over. The Sky Sisters imbued epically powerful trees to act as Charons to the Galactic Afterlife. Those two trees, burdened with such a soul-charged duty, evolved two more guardians of their own to help deal with the immense flow of transitioning spirits.

This is the story of the Earth, the Sun, and the Galaxy of the Dead. A journey which rides on the coattails of Toko Tuki and Uka Buka, the yin and yang of earthly spirits.

DAWN

A dark eyed flat cheeked Japanese-American 4th grader sat biting his pencil. He liked the feel of his teeth slowly sinking into soft wood and leaving hungry little indentations. *My Mark*, he thought.

Slouched into his desk so his teacher wouldn't notice a distracted student, he held the marked pencil up to the sun. The pencil eclipsed the sun and the sun haloed the cratered wood. Some dints were smooth and deep, some jagged and shallow. Curving shadows amongst holy light, a light everlasting. He gestured a nod of gratitude toward the orb of power and light, for it was the sun that had blessed his mark.

He would use this pencil for as long as his fingers could hold it. That was his little youngling religion, zero fucking waste. A religion that will be belittled by living in a society that shits out plastic bottles, greenhouse gas emissions, and more shit. Straight from the bum of Don't Give A Fuck.

His eyes slid down the pencil, the blue sky, the misty blue islands, and dark blue sea, to yellow sand, pale buildings, and vibrant green trees, all the way back up the green and gray mountains to the rocky sleek shelf of an old stone face. *My Land.*

The bully sitting behind him, Frank, a dense white kid with his eyes too close to his nose, kicked the mused child's achilles while he was bobbing his knee up and down, tendon fully stretched.

"Tree Hugger," the chubby kid maliciously whispered while drinking out of his plastic water bottle.

The 'Tree Hugger,' otherwise known as Ki La'dori, kept his pained gaze away from the sickly looking fart behind him and continued looking out the window. His daydream of being outside above the city and under the sun was interrupted, but reality held some secret gems as well. For not perched in reality, fantasy would struggle to be awakened. An open mind lends new paths towards creativity.

Ki gazed out at the nice lawn and a large willow tree with its branches shrouding the exterior world. *Ah, Tree Hugger,* he pondered its meaning.

Ki had his ear pierced, a metal water container, and a short fuse for ignorance. Ignorance couldn't mean much to anyone younger than a teenybopper, but it did to Ki, he knew of it too well. He knew he had no real sense of the world, except for what ten years gave him, yet through public school he knew all these children were very different. Some were calm, some excited, some romantic, some angry, some funny, and some more ignorant and stupid than what fell into the toilet.

Other kids just saw him as the new kid with clothes his hippy 'Mommy' made for him, and 'Mommy' was always said in a long and drawn out torment.

"Calculated by an Ecologist, a person who studies communities of plants and animals in all kinds of different environments, there are about 3 trillion trees on Earth, but there is still room for 1.5 trillion more. Organizations like the Billion Tree Campaign are working hard to find areas to plant environmentally native trees for a very important reason. Can anyone tell me why we want to plant more trees?" The lady's voice was harmonic, soft, and sweet.

A little girl in the front row raised her hand. One finger had a vine wrapped around it as her ring. "To save the planet!"

"Ah, yes Millie. Trees sequester or absorb vast amounts of atmospheric carbon, which is an element depleting our planet's atmosphere and causing Global Warming, the topic we lectured on yesterday. Trees, plants, and most natural procedures try to help the planet during its new age of mass pollution-"

Ki peered out at the Willow like it itself was giving the lecture.

Because he didn't want to disappoint his mom further than he had already, being kicked out of his last public school just a week earlier. He made a choice. He liked the trees around this school and liked what his teacher had to preach. Sticking his foot up Frank's ass would most likely get him expelled again. So, he would take his mom's advice and try to write down his thoughts after an altercation with a bully. Then all he had to do was give the bully what he wrote.

Ki would feel great if he had his other way, the way of the Gorilla, the way of the sun, power and light.

The tip of his nose itched at the thought of dealing with a situation without physical violence. His thumb swiped his nose as if brushing a chip off the shoulder.

The next day Ki handed Frank a small piece of parchment with 14 lines. While doing so he realized his mother held some cool wisdom in this subject, because by the look in the bully's twitchy eye and the rattle of his cheek, Ki knew then that he liked to use poetry as a slap enhanced with words.

Frank's Sonnet
A hill of green weeds in a wild stance against the yellow sun.
A blue icy ring around the moon of gray.
A steady breeze on orange poppies within an indigo hum.
A pale chubby nimwit calling people gay.

For Earth needs acupuncture.
Sharp points leaving smooth ends;
And the point you need kid,
Is, never hit me again.

No threats no problems,
Have the guts to be new.
The fight is much deeper,
Then a tree loving screw.

Learn from me I am the Keeper,
Of an older day, much much sleeker.

Frank tore the poem in half, revealing his eyes that showed madly with hate, and then he kicked Ki's nuts that halved him against the gate.

"You, bastard Frank, you'll… never get it." Ki breathed out in a weeze.

As time went on Frank stopped bullying in general and Ki grew up with little to worry about. He was always in the garden and always helping his happy hippy mother around the house. From 4th grade to 9th, he was mostly left alone, except for a little group of girls that quizzed and examined his extraordinary green driven mind.

The girls never hung out with Ki, however, they would run up to him and ask questions about what he thought about climate change, how a plant identification app on their phones worked, or his thoughts on how he would cultivate a garden. The litany of questions made Ki have to dig and study up before divulging the correct answer thoroughly during the next day's lunch period. This Q&A process escalated his knowledge and passion for the planet, however. Living wasn't just about having two arms, two legs and a head, it was everything around them, breathing, living and dying in their own way. Most things died with an essence of ease and inevitability. The acceptance of the cycle of life embedded into their being. To be or not to be, frequently resonated through his head.

It was a contrast to the loud and dramatic lifestyle Ki saw on the chaotic playground and engrossing world news. Everyone went so fast that it seemed like they meant to create a diversion of peace. A declaration of conflict. A breach in atmospheric noise.

When those girls ask Ki, "Key, how many different kinds of birds are there?" or "Key, are all seven oceans the color blue?" Those questions gave Ki his peace. He felt security and warmth even if he didn't know the answer. Actually more so if he didn't know because it gave him a wonderful subject to ponder on all day. Ki liked taking a step back in the present space to absorb the elements and her kin, flowers and nature among them. A peaceful world was comforting to him. A natural world felt right.

His body and mind still needed a world of peace of its own. The bobbing knee was his forte. He liked to stay busy. Nothing zealous, just content, steady productivity. Whenever he slowed down his senses came attune with how the contemporary world really was. Declarations of conflict, drama, waste, dishonor, and lackadaisical mental disorders. Things that pushed him back into the garden, digging into the soil to be left alone six feet under, buried next to the pulsating roots of his Mother.

Alas, his friends brought him back to the surface, for living is to be out in the sunshine realms of exploration. Within his focus he gained a solid group of surf groms in his first year of high school. A blonde, blue eyed Adam Vander and a deep tan Hawaiian broda with brown eyes, Kavika Pinederosa.

He gained even more positive acquaintances who actually looked up to him after he created a school group, Zero Waste, Love Your Place. Ki would agree the name was a little hooky, but it had a fine ring to it when he and a couple other nature geeks would rally around the lunch hall. They would stand with their Zero Waste signs right in front of the trash cans and inform the students what was recycling, which was compost, and what the school faculty could do to cut down on wasteful products.

Signs read, Clean your Recycling, Plastic Murders the Soul, Refuse - Reduce - Reuse - Repurpose - Recycle, Improve Refill Centers and Condiment Dispensaries, No more waste! Compost = Creation of Enriched, Anaerobic Soil. Then there was a sign that was more of a banner, Ask Mycelium! Containing an image of an academic worm conversing with a studious mushroom on top of planet Earth.

Aside from enraged youngsters dubbing Ki and his group of attention seekers as an annoyance to their school, Ki received his first good nickname, a name that stuck. His friends called him Z for Zero the Hero, and his foes, his bullies, called him Zero for less than one. Ki loved both sides. He didn't want to really be anyone, so Zero was perfect. As for Z, that was the last letter of the alphabet, and to him there was something cool about being last, as if it meant he was the ultimate overseer. If he saw all, he could change all.

Later in his Sophomore year, there was this one girl in her Junior year, completely composed, confident, smart, and mostly character-ized as a 'hottie' in the student's eyes. To Ki however, she was a well balanced, integral standing, thoughtful, respectful, and smiley little sweetheart.

One day, before the second period, groups of California high school kids were around their outdoor lockers, chit-chatting as groups do. Some were playing with balls and doing piggyback rides, some dabbing on their phones as if that were the new way of abut-ting communication, and one group of Juniors and Seniors were talking, the old school way, about Friday night football and where the after party will be held. In that group was the dark haired girl with the everlasting smile.

She was watching Ki lounge on the lawn, reading the innards of some worn-out book cover. Troubled eyes followed her as she started away from her popular linebacker meathead boyfriend and straight to the slanted lawn area where Ki was reading, cross legged with his baggy pants made of hemp.

"What are you reading?" She asked, smiling, her dark hair illumi-nated by the sun.

Ki looked up at her, then around, and finally met the smoldering eyes of her boyfriend. Ki knew trouble was brewing but was also very delighted by an older girl's interest and grace.

"I… I mean, this is The Marchers of Valhalla," Ki said, waving the book around like it was just to pass the time. "It's quite brutal. Bunch of wanderlust, majestic Vikings venturing over the Bering Strait. Not my usual read, but I'm definitely into it." Ki looked her up and down and smiled.

"What do you usually like to read, hmm?" She was smiling too as she asked the question. She was patient and at ease. Within Ki's fanciful imagination, she stood as a fairy would stand, Tinkerbell proud and with the grace of a forest angel. Right here and now, Ki examined the trait of her patience, and he saw the immense stability in focusing on one thing while zoning out everything else.

They shared an exhilarating silence that pumped Ki's blood to the point of massive back shivers.

"I like to read philosophy, historical fiction, or tragedies written in older times, like Shakespeare, and of course fantasy and science fiction for pleasure. Ahpmh, it's all pleasure." Ki was blabbering. Being so close to this Tinkerbell Dreamgirl everything really was wonderful. He would have said his Chemistry book was a good read if the bell for the second period hadn't rang.

Lexi began to walk towards her class and twiddled her fingers goodbye, then Ki said in a slightly louder voice, "I like your freckles on your nose!"

Lexi turned around with an element flowing through her blouse, "And I like Shakespearean Heroes." She was almost too far away at that point to hear her, but it sounded to Ki like she said Shakespear-ean Zeros.

When Ki got his emotions running he used poems to dump his emotions out, and this was a perfect time to write a poem, because this time the receiving end might not kick him in the balls. This time the receiving end might be a tad gentler.

Ki got home that day and ran into the kitchen to make a vegetable sandwich with avocado, bell peppers, onion, pickles, and a hunky slab of cheese. He filled up his water canister, went into his room, laid on the short red leather couch, and began writing. He wrote about boobs and mountains, freckles and sun rays, and finally tits and twisters.

His computer closed unsatisfied, but he gazed up at the ceiling, still happy where the day left off. A girl, he thought, a real girl that I could hold, and perhaps bring down into his dugout earthy hovel of motherly roots and just be with. A girl. Awe buzzed throughout his body and tempurpedic nova bursts of glee amongst the awe made a rare smile curve onto his lips. The thought of their first date being in a perceived grave also made him laugh.

Later that night, Ki walked into the kitchen and greeted his mother, who was coming back from work. His mother Leia, was a Wilderness Ranger with a Geology degree.

Ki told his mom about his day as she chopped up vegetables from the farmer's market and sprinkled cheese onto a tortilla in a skillet. Leia then told Ki about her day as she threw the rest of the veggie skins into the compost bin, put the leftover vegetables in the now empty tortilla bag and whipped the dishes down with a quick stream of water.

Their unwinding period on this night was sewing clothes and listening to music until the hooting of owls put them both to sleep. Not every night was like this, however. Some nights were spent watching their favorite television series together, some were spent reading by candle lights, some nights were of talking strategy on finishing up a gardening project, and some they would both retreat in solitude for the pure introverted merriment of independent energy regeneration. The world was their oyster.

As Sunday rolled through, Ki became restless at having another encounter with this new girl, Lexi. It was in the middle of the night, Monday morning at around 3:11a.m. the believed witching hour, where words and inspirations flooded through his literary subconscious. Words destined to be will be. Just need the right moment for vocab summoning.

Ki thought about it and used the 3:11 calling to piece his silly majestic words into a poetic manner.

Monday slowly melted away. Ki was more pleased to not have run into Lexi because his anticipation was too high, too extreme, and he knew that would make him too rough and regrettably too pathetic.

Then just as suddenly as four rising moons, his whole week went by in a flash, and he never got the right chance to give Lexi this handwritten poem. With time being the holy liquid in the sun's spherical chalice, Ki became desperate, giving him a feeling he needed to depart with his poem and embark into the next phase of life, whatever that may be.

That Friday morning, Ki put his poem in the twelfth page of Shakespeare's The Tempest and went off to relieve himself. The school was cold on this mid-November Friday, and people were all bundled up, chatting and joking around with each other. Ki went to his locker, grabbed his binders and went straight into the group of cool kids.

Lexi's boyfriend, a tall stud named Brock, threw his empty water bottle in the trash with a crisp smirk, readying himself for the entertainment of geek Zero. Ki's painful wince lasted longer than he intended, giving Brock the time to crack his neck and roll his shoulders. Unabashed Ki swung his fluttery eyes over to Lexi.

"Hi Lexi, I thought you might want to read this." Ki's smile was stolen off of Brock's face, lucidly thinking about Lexi's freckles on her nose and cheeks.

Lexi surprisingly, to all of her group, was happy to see Ki and brightened up on his bravery to walk over.

"Thanks Z-" The last period bell rang. It seemed like Lexi was going to say more, but she left it with, "Thanks Ki."

Ki waved and walked away, happy enough to skip.

***

Later that night, at a post football game party, Brock asked Lexi for a lighter so he could smoke his blunt with all of his buddies. Lexi was braiding her girlfriend's hair, "There are a couple of lighters in my bag, babe." Brock grabbed her book bag and rifled around looking for her lighters, but then he hesitated and pulled out The Tempest.

"I'm 'tempted' to see what this book is all about." Brock looked at the cover, showed his buddies, and returned to diagnosing Lexi.

"And why would that little brat give you a storm book from Shakespeare? What does he think, he's Romeo, and you're Juliet?" The girls in the room giggled and Brock breezed through the pages. During the flutter between pages, Ki's little note fell out.

"Ohhhh, I see a secret Poem!" Now all the boys laughed, and the room's energy rotated quickly. Upbeat, a trill of something new, an entertainment that'll live past the party and into next week's school session. Lexi stared, starry eyed but frightened at what Brock might do with it.

Brock hushed the room and read.

DAWN

"Lexi's Sonnet
Our morning radiance settled along the clouds maturely.
The darkest of cracks illuminated by repetitive dawn.
I see strength in thine nature surely,
As I, the hundredth pawn.

Whisper your secrets of thy Grace,
For we have come to a paradoxical place.
You, a Miss with fragrant lace;
I, a lad that loves taking in your face.

Though we meander around in different worlds tonight,
Swindling dreamful eyes still watch thy lady,
As amongst the other fringe, thou eyes closeth at new heights;
Thy exploration and adventure present more than minds gone shady.

Our destined future lies within stories and codes.
Giving warmth to the grass of which we abode."

"Ooh Yes, what a terrific rendition of a true romantic lover boy," Brock said, obviously at ease with Ki's words.

Lexi stayed her tongue and peered at her girlfriend's hair as she worked the intricate Viking braid, of course reminding her of Valhalla, a place where death is honorable and romantic.

"So, you like him Lexi? You like living in codes and secrets eh?"

"Brock he didn't really say much. Plus, it could have been an old bookmark poem. I see those all the time." Lexi said in a level and untroubled tone.

"Or, he is just a friend who gave me a book of Shakespeare and was playing around with Shakepearean lingo with me. I like Shakespeare and he probably likes me, there is no secret in that… What is the big deal?"

"The big deal? The Big Deal is the little nature punk is hitting on Brock Zendolini's girl. That is disrespectful babe…" Brock waited for a response and didn't receive one. He huffed, turned around and told his boys to head out with him to the backyard. Seven of them went, and five of them left their red solo cups half filled with beer. Never to return for them and if so never to remember whose was whose.

***

Crash, and the trunk locked down on Ki. A minute earlier, Ki was walking home from school and a black Subaru Impreza with a racing spoiler in the back, drove by with five horny muscle boys ready to spring. Ki kicked one in the shin and popped one in the nose, but that's as far as those things go sometimes. He was slugged in the stomach and the trunk of the Subs locked down on him. At least it was quite comfortably spacious.

Ki wasn't scared, he knew it was coming. As soon as those red swindled eyes of Brocks locked in on him that Monday morning, he knew.

They drove for a good twenty minutes with a heavy Nirvana playlist blapping loud as hell. The trunk popped open and Ki was thrown to the dirt. Lingering dust hung in the air around him like a fog of war. He was thinking about how cool it was that during such an exhilarating moment time slowed down and gave him a chance to remember, to enjoy this moment of raw living.

There was some kind of off smell about the place that Ki couldn't pin exactly, something that dug at him more than the kick at his ribs. He didn't get much of a chance to access his surroundings because all that was around him were five muscle heads yelling at him with an occasional stomp and punch.

Ki didn't know what made him so disoriented, so deep in the depths of these guys' game plan that he couldn't even move, but Ki's anger was swelling up like the puff around his eye. Almost blind from the swell of both, he was then completely buried in stank trash. Three of their lads just dumped trash load after trash load of waste over him.

"Don't mess around with my girl Zero," Brock held his hand in an O shape above his scarred eyebrow.

"Nobody fucking cares about what you got to say." He paused, and his eyes turned from swindle red to lightning rod green; he relaxed, his job was done, vision complete.

Ki pulled himself out of the trash as the boys wiped their hands on their trousers and jumped into their Subaru. He bent down on his haunches and pulled his shirt over his head, wiping sludge and grease off his skin with the clean side of his navy blue Island Snow T-shirt with Japanese writing on the back. Looking around felt tranquil to him. The wind calmly shifted through the valleys of landfill mountains. Wasted at the waste zone.

He walked on, sucking the moment in with dark euphoria. A sense of duty overcame him, an urge to go certain lengths and to fulfill an honorable destiny. Ki previously felt like destiny meant the end, a lifelong quest to fulfill. But this felt like the beginning like the infinity snake eating its own tail and pouring its venom into itself. Beginning or end, it didn't matter. What mattered was the venom coursing through his veins. He hated waste.

Ki turned a corner of the trash maze and saw the landfill gate. As he walked through the gate, he kicked the bars, making them rattle, and he looked up to the clouds of a gorgeous puff of white blue that told you there's no better place than home and sunset orange to tell you you're on the right path. If destiny were a religion, it would have the banner of the Sun.

***

Ki got home and entered through the side gate where his mother was dumping organic food scraps into the compost bed and mixing in plant foliage. She saw him, sprinkled coffee grounds in the compost crater and covered it with soil. The blue streak in her hair bun matched the Celtic tapestry behind her, hanging over the house's stucco.

"I'm goin' take a shower Mum," he said as he walked past her and into the house through the kitchen.

Later on that night Ki ate most of an ice cream bin and a couple of cookies. His eyes were fixed in inner thought. He desperately wanted to think clearly, but his emotions filled him with instinctual thoughts. His gut, his instinct wanted redemption, but his deeper self knew he could take this redemption further, make it mean something, something good for the planet. Settling in with his basic thoughts, he decided time was the tool he needed not just for healing his body, but his mind as well.

The next day Ki went surfing and played with his puppy around the coastal parks. Her name was Zoo Za'mara, ZooZa for short, lil Z for shorter. She was a shepherd mutt pup that followed Ki anywhere and everywhere. They had an instant companionship of love, loyalty and understanding. Almost as if the couple of months of knowing each other had created an unbreakable bond. Ki the wolf and ZooZa the human.

Acquiring a fresh culture of truth and serenity after a fulfilling day of waves and puppy play, Ki finally began to feel clear headed. He decided on the big picture, the true quest, a fate that would lead him into becoming Zero the Hero.

It was easy for him to ditch school; his mother left for work very early in the morning and sometimes stayed at the National Forest Ranger's Station for three or four days at a time. Easy as it was, one ditch was all he needed for a little natural regeneration. The ocean water reduced the swelling around his eyes and the sun soaked into his bones. With that solar power and elemental therapy, he was ready to face his peers.

Ki's high school, at the base of the foothills in the Central Coast-line of California, was shaded by tons of Blue Gum Eucalyptus set in the middle of a wealthy college town. On good days, the town of El-lipsis bloomed with colorful flowers, art and open highways. On bad days, rival gangs battled, tourists complained, and homeless trashed the neighborhood. Like most towns these days, this one had potential for more.

Walking up through his usual garden path to his high school hangout spot, Ki saw his two brazen buddies staring at him like he was Johnny Knoxville in the flesh.

"Whoa there guys, just a reef bump. Don't get too excited." Ki held his hands out to try and contain his friend's billerbustery.

One of his mates rolled his eyes in complete realization, "Ahh, reef shiner."

The other mate, Kavika Pinederosa, Pineapple for short, Pines for shorter, had another look about him, much more troubled and a little defiant. "I heard you got trashed by some trashheads…" His hair was always spiked up in a pineapple-flared fashion.

"Yep, well… that happened too," Ki said, smiling. "I'm off, I gotta hand my late assignment into Mrs. Girard before class starts."

Ki slapped a couple high fives and took a venture through the school. He felt proud, happy, and untouchable. He reached his locker, tick click click click, tick click click and the lock opened; he took his binders out and turned his chin to those wondrous eyes. Eyes of hate, eyes of curiosity, eyes of lust. Brock chugged his plastic water bottle and tossed it into the trash can next to their group. Ki walked over with his right hand retrieving something from his back pocket and whipped it out quick-like, hoping to create a flinch or glitch in the matrix. Brock didn't flinch however, he never even blinked, his face really did look chiseled from rock. Nevertheless, Ki revealed a trash bag in his right hand and pulled Brock's plastic water bottle out of the bin with his left.

Lovingly he looked at the girls of the group and told them he was starting another club, a new radical recycling slash waste reduction club.

"Waste Not, is the new club, because plastic ignorance and conscious planet trashing is now on the zero tolerance agenda." Ki was almost in his Junior year, it was time to get serious.

He looked over to Brock and his boys before he left, "No more Pollutants in my town." Ki was obviously referring to the dicks in front of him as the Pollutants. He pointed at a water canister one of Brock's buddies had, "Try drinking out of something like that."

Ki walked away and into his favorite class, Mrs. Girard's History. He enjoyed past history for more reasons than one, but the big reason that really stuck out to him on this day was that less than a hundred years ago, there was no plastic. Even though he was mad at Brock's crew, he didn't charge them with the full responsibility of wastefulness. It was the times they were in, their leadership, their society.

He wanted the Queen of all Squader, the heart of all wasteful creation.

***

Senior year was a breeze. Actually, all of Ki's high school went easy peasy. Ki was primarily found in the school's new garden or surrounded by cute little hippy student waste management supervisors, even though most of the time Ki was perfectly content with being alone. He created ten compost influenced garden beds with four compost piles that got turned over with school kitchen scraps twice a week. Every senior professor was the director for one garden bed, where they treated their students as democratic advisors on what to grow next. The school grasped Ki's ideas because he didn't wait for acknowledgment or permission; he just made it happen, and suspending a kid for actually helping the school grounds instead of vandalizing it was difficult for the faculty.

Once he got his driver's license, Ki's mother bought him a little pickup truck and from there he hauled in whatever scraps and dirt he could find around town to make his ideas possible.

College was never a hard push on Ki. He was seen by the school board and students as an accomplished gardener. He kept his mouth shut and finished highschool while wrestling with what he thought the world needed. On the other hand, his present girlfriend Lexi, Brock's old girlfriend, got accepted into a prominent university in Northern California, and being the love birds that they were, Ki was pulled into this new chapter of college as well.

Yes, Ki actually won over Brock Zendolini's girl, and he actually wasn't enrolled in college, but the University Library became his playground. He attended the large lecture halls of Lexi's courses, which he was interested in. He joined the Rugby team on campus, and later on Lexi and Ki adjusted into the late night college scene. He became lost, cradled in instant pleasures and dazed reliefs, granted conditions of love and beautiful everythings for no cost. They simply lived and absorbed what life had to offer during this Spiritus Mundi, the spirit of the time.

Other than rugby games, crashing classrooms and late night poetry slams, Ki followed his own zero waste traditions along with his meditating sky praising religion. His world was so neat, green and simple. It felt like rolling down a beautiful grassy hill, yet a slight itch made him feel like his old world somersaulted further and further away. The simple life stole his big dream. Love eclipsed his hatred for all things wasteful and convenient.

***

Ki sat in a tent deep in the woods. BUMP, BUMP, BUMP music gave him an unconscious, restless rhythm in his vibing leg. His chest thumped with the festival bump, and his heart raced with his mind laced. First time being opened up by this sort of thing. Hallucinogens bonded with his soul and gave his mind wings, fluffy furry wings. Lexi, his loyal girlfriend for four years now, gave him three mushroom caps and four stems. As the ecstasy of the psilocybin hit, he had to run from the outdoor nook of a concert area and have a moment of bodily release.

Feeling lighter, he stopped by their groovy little camp spot. It had streaming lights, bubbly tapestries, and a parade of pillows. Lexi's friend Krista was there, amongst them. Submerged, entangled, cocooned within the fluff. She waved Ki over to her.

"Lay down," she motioned to the fold next to her. A long body pillow propped up Ki's head. The slight rotation of her body wafted a flowery trace, causing Ki's nostrils to organism and eyes to flip into his skull. She gently mounted him and slid her hand between the buttons of his shirt, feeling his beat.

"This is Unicorn Spray Z. It will balance you out and relax your body." And before he could tell her he was already so relaxed that he almost pooped himself. She gave him two sprays under the tongue. As Ki's mouth theatrically closed, she pushed his cheeks together with her thumb and index finger, putting another spray into the hole of his pursed fish lips.

She retreated feeling that was sufficient, but hesitated in her lucidity and gave him one more spray. Krista popped up and twinkled away amongst the fairy lights, giggling like a newborn angel.

Ki rubbed his cheek and stretched for the long journey ahead. Destiny always put him in a good head space. He went into his tent to find a coat. The acid, the shrooms, the weed, it all felt right; it all felt like the sun was setting inside his chest. He looked out his tent flap and watched the tip of the sun splinter away amongst the dense pine forest. With a strong belief of chasing destiny, he chased the sun into the pines. He ran, he walked, he looked up and around, only to be accompanied by tall historic heroes darkening evermore by the night. The tale of the mystic giants was simple, yet very valiant and steadfast. They spend their growth pulling carbon out of the air to store and build upon themselves. A handshake with photosynthesis. Carbon Dioxide or other humanly-driven gas compounds left unchecked in the atmosphere absorb infrared radiation, which then sits there trapping heat inside the atmosphere, an occurrence that modern human leadership does not give an F about. Trees build biodiverse ecosystems to protect the planet while humans completely destroy them. Heroes and villains rise and fall in every tale.

Ki, wide eyed and super high, went to them, thinking of that day in 4th grade when he was first called a tree hugger. "Ah, Tree Hugger. That makes sense." He whispered as his fingers worked around a stuffy knot.

He spent a good time saying hello to the forest and clasping his hands together in a namaste fashion. When it was time for his good-byes, the latitudinal shadows blended with the universal cosmos of night. The wind howled, and he followed. Traveling with the spirits that rode the element of air. Tree spirits, human spirits, dreams of all beings taking flight, he really didn't know, but something rode with Ki as he wandered, lost but happy he was not alone. It whispered to him of a balance. It imbued him with the power of the Earth. A force that expected a sacrifice for leading him home. A small sacrifice to keep nature grand and Mother whole.

that expected a sacrifice for leading him home. A small sacrifice to keep nature grand and Mother whole.

Cliff Dwellers

Ki was on his twenty-fifth pull and strained for every inch up. His eyes reached above the noble branch that rubbed against his nose.

He was in the middle of a foresty dog park along the shoreside cliffs of his hometown. Muscles ripping, tearing forth, mind allowing every bit of struggle to soak into his body. He needed to relieve the pain from the fight he had with his high school sweetheart the night before.

Ki's eyes passed the branch to see the gnarled oak engulfed in a leafy canopy. He dropped from the branch and picked up his phone.

'I'm at the airport and headed to Spain.' Read a text message from his now ex-girlfriend, Lexi. He believed once he lost a love like her, he'd lose all faith in long-term relationships, except for one. Ki's religion was with the Sky, the Air, and the Earth. It was the only fabric of reality that held absolutely true to him. He would vow to love, live, and die for this… and only this.

Ki went to his note tab and moved his thumb over the digital keyboard, M, O, T, H, E, R…

Mother's Sonnet
Mother, what must I do to honor thy past?
Floods flow but hath no taste.
Dashing towards our stars to feel free at last,
Ritual'd my life in a gathering of haste.

Let thee sing a ballad of harmony,
That lifts the stems of wildflowers,
With a prance like dance in the Willow Tree Ceremony.
Summoning a bloody brand in seismic powers.

One love has fallen into a den of lemming loves,
Gaia's own creation churned for more than a heartbeat's worth.
Conditioned beings burn for a multiverse of doves,
Driven towards protecting our Mother's continental birth.

I hath loved, I hath written, drugs hath impeded, drugs hath smitten.
The truth of thy chaos hence scribed as renewed nativity amongst
sin.

Ki looked up through the canopy of tree limbs above him, wondering why more people don't worship something so beautiful, so clear, so right there, under your toes, warmth on your cheeks, a breeze in your hair. True divinity of elements that scientifically keep us alive and evolving.

A fluffy little black shepherd dog brushed through Ki's legs like a kitty with her tongue strung out. Ki ran his hands over his buzzed Japanese head and picked himself up from a massive root protruding as a bench, and headed home. As they meandered through groves of trees, he found a still nicely intact half rolled joint in his board shorts pocket and lit that baby up.

Back at his mother Leia's house, the joint continued its chu chu of smokey billows during the process of gathering his spirited gear. He wanted to ultimately enjoy a humongously needed good time at his old high school buddy's house. No more girls, no more rules, just quest to quest, leafy step to leafy step.

He grabbed his element rings, his hair clippers, toothbrush, Zoo Za'mara's food, fake blood canister, an old plastic cheese bag full of trail mix, a couple oranges, a jar of weed, and his tequila. Then once his arms were completely burdened with his spirited gear, he grabbed a backpack, threw most of that stuff inside, along with a change of clothes, ball of twine, and a book he was almost finished reading, Treasure Island.

ZooZa jumped into his rumbling pickup truck, and Ki felt an inner relaxation and allowance. His girl wanted a change, and that was completely understandable. Ki knew he scared her off with his aggressive attitude. Emotions like exhilaration, hunger, thirst, lust, the anger, rage, pain, ecstasy were energy novas erupting through his heart and the veil of his soul. Whatever feelings came they seemed like they came from the center Shakra. The quake zone. Fragments of himself breaking apart like tectonic landslides.

The drive to Kavika Pines' house was nice. Ki took a side route through the foothill woodlands. A quieter party for him and lil Z before the louder party with their old friends.

When they made it to Kavika Pinederosa and Adam Vander's house, Pines sat Ki down and shaved some twirl designs and a sunrise in Ki's buzzed head, creating a powerlink between him and his elemental environment. The unique haircut drove parallel with a spirit ritual. The scentless candles, the Yoga Master Tunes 999 playing on the radio, and Adam Vander recycling old bullets into new shells in the corner of the garage. ZooZa played with their black cat under Vander's feet, and Ki's heart slowly pieced itself back together in watching an instinctual bond between beasts.

The following day, there were beer cans on the roof, Vander's motorcycle still in the house after burning rubber, with tire or weed smoke lingering in a corner, which was probably not very healthy for the good-sized white orchard trying to stand its ground. There was dog food in a blender and weed in a mug, and yet everything felt just right, just like old times.

Before Ki left the house, early morning around sunrise, he tossed a ball of twine he brought into their garden bed, grabbed one last beer sitting inside a self made disc golf basket, and headed out with lil ZooZa at his heels.

Driving back home he felt the sun envelop his left side from chest up. The power of the rays felt more violent now than when he was younger. It was an angry heat, ready to fry holes in the meager skin of humans. Skin that holds the bones, that holds the heart, that holds the soul of our essence. Violently frying the skin that holds the minds of our society that evolved into using Nitrogen Oxides as Earth's Atmospheric murderer. Ki rotated his arm to really grasp the integral feeling of life and the feeling of the sun. He chose the side of the sun. He chose the side of the sky. Never meeting his father, he now chose to be the Son of the Sun.

The highway mellowed out over the hill next to a great coastal cliffside bracing the Pacific. Ki pulled over on the apex of the cliff and exhaled a long breath. He got out of his truck and watched two hawks pleasantly flying nowhere in the strong breeze westward. Ki wondered about their prey, wondered what they must have been eyeing, and followed their gaze down to see pure trash. Plastic bags, cans, shit, fucking everywhere.

Ki halfway rolled up his truck windows so lil Z could be somewhat of a participant but not a distraction. He grabbed a couple black trash bags from his back seat and walked to the edge of the cliff. The Surfliner railway cut right under the cliff's edge and the waves crashed hard against the sea wall. He felt the sun in a different manner at this moment, a feeling of support, like a family member holding your hand in the hospital bed, giving you that loving warmth to keep you fighting for life.

Ki took this feeling into his chest. He was the Son of Sun. He was native to this land, born to these grounds, conceived by this sky overhead, held in the hands of this sun at birth.

The little camouflaged huts of trash looked like oceanfront living stations for the homeless. Homeless that obviously lost faith in the world, and felt that their brothers and sisters have exiled them to the fringe. They have lost faith in Gaia, and a terrible reckoning wobbles into their existence. Ki, the Son of Sun, was just beginning to believe his place in this world. As its preacher, or now more than likely, its Juggernaut.

Ki looked into the wasteland, where the heaps of trash could easily fly right into the ocean with a gentle breeze. The sun was now a burning orb, placing the time to be around seven in the morning. He had time to breathe, time to decide his next move. Ki thought of calling the city and working with the council members to bring a couple of dump containers and hazmat suits to clean this up; however, he felt his duty was more than waiting for hesitant and precautionary minds to make a decision. His duty was to inflict retribution immediately, to clean up the drag immediately, as the sun is his witness.

Wrapping the plastic trash bags around and through his belt loop, Ki felt his stomach flutter excitedly. The trash bags were Plan B. Ending the horrendous blasphemy at its primary source was Plan A. He wanted the Queen of all Squader, the heart of all wasteful creation.

He skipped down the cliff, hopping from ledge to ledge, to finally reach the plateau of a campground disguised with trash. There were five huts on this plateau, really only visible from the ocean, or of course, if you were right above them like Ki found himself to be. He kept in mind the love of his friends and family and his father, the sun watching overhead.

He walked to the closest hut and swiftly opened its oceanfront curtain of mold.

"Yo, it's time to clean up your shit!" His voice vibrated like a growl. He had no interest in watching them clean or no apprehension that they would do so.

The smell of that first hut was unbearable and seemingly inhabitable, underlined with a welcome matt of garbage.

A voice from the Northern trash hut, with more trash heaps than any, came up against the Southwest wind. "Get outta here you FUCKER! Or i'll kill you, you-" The rant of cursory continued and invited other hut dwellers for the harsh negatives. It was like setting foot in a den of witches rather than a cliffside of low socioeconomic individuals. Little did they know he was the one with snake venom in his veins.

The witches waved their clubs, pots and knives at Ki like he was the intruder. He pulled the molded curtain off the empty hut in front of him and went forth towards the knife wavering man.

"YOU intrude on the Sun's grace!"

The man went for a knife jab and Ki threw the curtain over him, much easier than imagined. The man struggled in it, the knife creating tears before it was pulled off completely, and right as the man gained his vision, Ki kicked him off the cliff, feeling delightfully like Leonitis and his Spartan warriors.

There was a scream, or maybe a couple, while the man fell with tumbles here and there. The knife wielding man reached the bottom with his right arm sprawled across the tracks. Ki didn't care if he hit his head, broke a leg, stabbed himself, or fucking died. Anyone who consciously let pollution cascade into his ocean deserved the worst. Which led to the other camp occupants still madly screaming their hysteria. They wouldn't learn this morning's lesson. They would continue to damage the planet, as well as become a barrier and threat to Ki's future. Ki threw two more dirty scum off the cliff, one a young bald headed shit and the other a raging monster lady. There was one more standing in horror and keeping their mouth closed. Ki pulled a bag from his belt and handed it to her.

"Clean. Up. Your. Fucking. Trash." Ki said calmly, "Do not follow me, you understand?"

The lady nodded and stood there looking at Ki and then over the edge at her friends squirming below.

Ki snapped his fingers together, "Start cleaning now!" The lady began to weep heavily, picking up her waste seemed worse than being thrown off the cliff.

Ki bear crawled up the plateau's edge and reached the highway pullout. ZooZa was wagging her tail frantically and she gave one loud bark with a big smile that split her face. They drove outta there with the sun bright in his rearview mirror.

On the way home, Ki thought hard, still with adrenaline venom fully pumping through his veins. He hated having to deal with the lowest of the low. A thirty-foot drop was a wicked play, but he was a man on fire. He needed to cast his heat where darkness dwelled too long. He reminded himself there were greater foes that would give him more honor in taking down. Relinquishing oil company board members from their positions. Getting rid of mass plastic creating CEOs and shithead politicians that believe stripping the planet's resources and billowing out power plant emissions was right for the people… right for their fucking wallets, maybe.

He decided to leave the blunt force of homeless waste enforcement to the city and politicians. He wanted big redemption, in the fiery eyes of the Sun, his Father, his God.

Ki rubbed the hair indentations on the back of his head. A rising sun and swirling winds. For now, he needed to get away and there was no better place than the Mountains to cool things over. Today was Friday. Today was a great day.

UKA BUKA Mountain

During his drive up the mountain pass later that day, Ki rhymed his own words to a thump thump instrumental beat that played on his solar powered speaker.

A Sonnet of the Sun
Aye the breeze of a blazon ray,
Let float, a belly of plundersome weight,
To tarnish the wreckage of the once worrisome reap day.
Bring forth the light shall we end up on winter's hate,

As ignorance and wellbeing both make kin weak.
The angle of the transcendent Sun, peeps, mayhap for weeks,
Whence thy own chunder doth drag feet to go meekly,
A crisp mess of moony leaks.

"There!" A being calls, "the son to Sun arises in the smoke,"
Curious looking, "we hope they all don't choke."
But the Sun knows things, it hath the spectrum of heat;
It grows wealth, whether be veggies or meat.

The Sun can't run, the Sun won't hide,
The Sun never hesitates in an up and down stride.

Up and over, weaving in and out of earthly patterns of the forest and valleys, rigid boulders and sumptuous clouds held the space. Ki pet ZooZa on top of her head, fluffing it up and flapping around her ears. He felt rewarded with this mountainous reclamation. A natural gift given to Earth's unforeseen thug. He also felt bad and mean, a little evil, but for all the right reasons.

For this, Ki said to himself, looking around at the beautiful valleys of trees and the long blue lake far out into the distance.

He pulled up to the Trail Closed sign, turned around and went up another dirt path a couple minutes back. At the end of this trail there was another Trail Closed barrier, however it was more of an inconspicuous place to leave his truck. He opened his tailgate, gave his nose a thumb flick, and started organizing his gear. He spread the map out and penned in where he was and his expected path. His backpacking pack with all his food and shelter lay against the wheel well. He just had to load up ZooZa's food, his knife, compass, and the map.

Around high noon, they took off. Pure joyously willing struts up the windy incline. He was comfortable with his muscles contracting and relaxing. It was a reasonable trade, getting lost out in the wild for a little sweat and exercise.

At sunset they reached a snowy fork in the road with a sign pointing to their destination campsite. Mckinley Springs 1 mile. They finally arrived after a seven hour hike and commenced their camping sequence. Test the water, set up a tent in the twilight, fire, food, fire again, water again, tent in the end. The elements were here. The elements that filled his heart back up with love. Running springs, fire made by the stroke of a stone, earth under their feet, wind whistling through the sky and tickling through their lungs, entertaining the hair on their brow.

Ki lay there under the stars with lil Z snuggling his left leg. The bite of the cold reminded him of his unconditional endearment to this magical world. He decided to let his mind run free with the elements and capture his thoughts with his pen on the pages in the back of his book, Treasure Island.

Element Sonnet
This is yer treasure, the spirit of thy tree,
Ethos of thy spring that hence drip in yer dreams.
The Anima of a breeze that tickles your knees.
Soul of a spark, scorpiously brought into wild dancing flames of leans.

Fire of thy heart, burning quite readily at the shrine.
Water whence the tongue spit rhythms and hymns.

Wind of blown contortions, frazzling the hair and lifting the mind.
Earth art thou dense? For ye connect a planetary torso of vines.

My Lady… She hath green at her bosom.
Blue weaves to thy ground and around thy toes,
Bottoming a shelter of orange hues in comfortable, tranquil, om's,
Whence swirl the gray rune marking of time drifting flows.

Thy Elements hath ever changing radically unique beings.
A face in nature, giving truth wings.

The campfire outside flicked in fathomless elevations and angles, his eyes only able to see her core. The front of the tent flap froze in unrepeatable crystallizations. The sound of the wind blew differently in seemingly infinite worldly environments because of the infinite shapes and lengths of Earth's trees, rocks, and topography. Infinite was a galactic characteristic, however the mind can only wonder so far.

Our planet tells us so much simply based on its being. Let us embrace the blissful perfection of a beast's mentality. Beasts symbiotic with the land. Grounding souls closer to our Mother. The heart of all beings. Being, being subjectivity within objectivity. All this being and not being could be the void of nothingness, the transcendence into the cosmos being subjectively knowing the truth. The truth is in our spheres of galactic proportions. The Sun, the Moon, the Earth.

Earth is a clever maiden that riddles round rhymes. Into the void and around the back to the light we may journey. An orb of never ending paths.

Ki stretched the frost away from his awakening bones and zipped the rest of the tent open for a rush of faithful air. The small trip to the mountains renewed his spirit and gave him clarity on his next venture. He packed his gear while ZooZa ate her kibble. The illumination into the next chapter of his life gave him quick movements of efficiency. He wanted things to start rolling, gathering momentum before they blinked out of existence. At least that's how he felt. Get it in, get it out, quit fucking about, Yo Ho, Yo Ho, Yo Ho!

Yesterday Ki prepared for a weekend getaway and now he was ready to race down the mountain to begin the rope-a-dope for environmental wellbeing. Disillusioned, bored and playful, Ki began playing with his nickname, Zero.

Zero time left, Zero waste projects, Zero false prophets, Zero to Zero, meaning radical movements of destruction. Creation of many Zero Heroes. Heroes ready to perish for the cause, which is no matter, because Zero is their name. Zero power willing to endorse a walloping Zero to the bad guy's functionality. Zero shits. Zero waste could be good for all Zeroes tattered around the globe. Numbers just haven't done the job. Beasts never used numbers except for counting their young. Beastly thoughts of survival and legacy drawing saliva to Ki's fangs.

The wind blew hard on the way back to his truck. He had about five more hours of regular hiking; however, with the wind pushing them back, he felt like two hours would add to it. ZooZa was leashed to him and walking the snowy ridge line because Ki didn't want her flying away in a gust. The tumble on either side of them would have been way too painful and troublesome to risk.

The flowing symbols of wind circlets rushed through the high sky like tremendous translucent labyrinths. To whom the maze's difficulty would stifle any but dancing wind spirits, for they have eyes not like our own.

Once taut on his buzzed head, Ki's hat blew straight off and down a gully. His favorite hat with the logo of Penguin's Veterinary Hospital, Central California, a cute chubby little Penguin leaning on the V with a dog pawed belly button.

Ki watched for a moment where the hat settled, deep down the gully, where Earth's darker presence lingered. In the shadow with a little broken canopy of light shining through a grand pine tree, his Penguin hat dangled on a twig of a fallen branch. He thanked the Mother's Joy she'd caught it and found that the tree next to the fallen branch was more than intricate.

He eyed her up and down and found the look of her intoxicating. Something more was driven into this Pine's knotty bark. A face he recollected from Hawaiian tribal illustrations and books of neutral pygmy camps. The totemic look of the tree's face made Ki shiver to the point of an inward quiver.

The Uka Buka of his dreams. A long lost island idol that Ki always cherished as a protector of natural territory. Uncle Uka Buka was here, staring Ki in the face. I have your hat boy. Would you dare risk taking it back from the forest's depths? He imagined it saying.

Ki tied ZooZa to a woody little bush, took his pack off and took another winceful glare at the increasingly more ghastly Uka Buka. The long wooden face was there without question. He watched it cautiously as if it may pop out at him during his descent. He tried reassuring himself how elements were always made so differently and this was just another example. A lonely tree in the shadowy woods.

He swiped at his nose stubbornly and went down to retrieve his hat, looking up occasionally at the squinty eyed Uka Buka, mouth slashed at an angle and face wide with long ear lobe bark knobs. Ki looked down and around where his hat had lain and found that it was caught up by an engraved fallen branch with swirly decorations on every inch of its wood. He pulled on what he could see and slowly revealed out of the foliage of leaves, a long worm engraved staff. Ki stroked it in awe. It was so straight, so perfectly reasonable in its length, hard, seemingly unbreakable pine wood, and now it was made lovely and totally unique with worm teeth, probably the little disciples of Uncle Uka Buka.

Ki put his hat on backward, gave the Uka Buka a moment of respect, and turned his back on the tree. His next twelve steps up the grade were happy. Lost in his own grateful mind of the awesome gift he had received, however, the thirteenth step had fallen him into a trench that bent his ankle in two.

ZooZa barked from above as the Uka Buka face flashed with fiery eyes and large blocky teeth. Stunned, Ki watched the face within the tree, deciphering whether or not his imagination took a realistic turn into a dark reality. He shuddered and slowly took off his left boot. Whenever you're not paying attention, boom, bang, out a foot.

Ki impaled his boot onto his new worm staff and crawled up the leafy hill to lil Z. The wind still blew hard, but now it blew as if time was caught in this storm, as well as him and his little doggy. The sky darkened gray and became pattered with dark clouds, forming a night with no undoing.

Ki had little choice but to camp in the closest clearing next to the Uka Buka. The thoughts of spirits and ghosts drowning his positive memories. He sat in the middle of his tent with Zoo Za'mara under his arm, being the only thing of any real comfort.

Why did I watch all those scary movies? Ki rubbed at his temple to try and create a courageous genie that he could use to wish the Uka Buka away. But the night grew darker, clouds blocked out the stars, the wind diluted all sounds but a persistent howling of wolves. The whistling and screaming of air gusts rushed through the neighboring trees. ZooZa flipped one ear up and pinned one ear back. Even inside his tent he could have sworn an invisible force knocked his trail mix bag on its side and unraveled his leftover bandage wrap into a loose coil.

Spirits grumbled haunting curses, while wind blew with furiosity. Ki shook off the scary thoughts and decided to find a way to fight back. He gathered the light he had left with his headlamp and searched for his pen.

The light dimmed evermore from the dampening of a shadowy veil and Ki threw up his hands. The situation was amazing. If he ever thought back on it in the future, he would most likely believe hallucinogens were a kick starter. He giggled some of the darkness back, laughing off the demons.

ZooZa took the laughter as an emergence into playtime and she picked up Ki's new staff and wagged it back and forth. Ki played with ZooZa for a couple minutes, definitely being the best couple of minutes of the night, then sat back and looked at the engraved stick during his lounge. He watched and wondered, what if? What if he took something that belonged to the Uka Buka? What consequences lay ahead for taking a fallen branch now magically engraved in symbols from disciple worms.

Ki tapped the staff on his head in thought, and after each tap there was a shot of light. Blink, blink, blink. Resembling an angel blinking into existence from an inner-dimensional heaven. He looked again at the staff huddled in the darkness of the night's shadow and then he took his headlamp off and held it to the staff. Light pushed back the irregular veil of darkness and the charge revitalized Ki's blood. It seemed the headlamp battery fully charged itself. It was warm again. Strength filled up his body and he sat back in triumph.

This is an enchanted twig. So enchanted it gave off power and light. So then why would it be next to Uka Buka? Unless there was another, more benevolent tiki child, or perhaps Uka Buka was a child of light and Ki's mind was just twisted from old fairy tales that he saw Uka Buka as a demon. But, he knew what he felt, and his gut was crucial to follow.

Ki started to get his feeling back. He wasn't so numb from the integral everythingness of the darkened night. He massaged his ankle while he thought, tracing a thumb along the intricate engravings of the staff.

Wards of the forest were a mystical brilliance, scary at the moment yet this whole experience was invigorating. He began to form light inside his mind, driving out the shroud of darkness. He pictured stars popping out from the clouds, lush green hills over alluring blue waters. Ki laid back to rest his head only to have his skull thud onto an old t-shirt. He squirmed back from the dark and ghostly corner, wrapped himself in his sleeping bag with ZooZa and grabbed his backpack for a pillow.

Who was Uka Buka's Nemesis? The little patches of hair around Ki's mouth twisted in his deep searching thought.

He scratched at his inner thigh and suddenly everything popped. His right eye slightly rolled back, pupil fluttering into a vibration of mind ecstasy. Sometimes your past seemed like it was lived by another. The best thing about ink on your skin was that it held portions of your story, documenting your traveling soul. So you never forgot, even when your mind was completely gone.

Toko. My brother.

Ki grabbed his enchanted light staff and uncovered his legs from the sleeping bag. There was my tribal mark! Ki couldn't believe it. How he'd forgotten the age of Tonga, rugby, and a simpler life of peace. He welcomed Toko Tuki, his good luminous spirit, rather than Buka's haunting and mischievous shadows. He welcomed his past for it was brutal, strong, and full of light.

ZooZa started to snore and wheeze while dreaming between Ki's bowed legs. Ki grabbed his pen again and began to fight back. Headlamp lit by the power of Tuki's Branch.

Sonnet Toko Tuki
Tuki, a mark of elemental functionality,
Sentenced to few repeated blurps of thy legacy and title.
Hung in rainbow feathers on top of ye planked face of mortality.
Never wilting in flotation nor written on Tuki's bridle.

Storms thy give prismatic energy, once circling the halo'd name.
When mountains rumble and winds gust,
When oceans roar and fire erupts.
This is the storm of rainbotic hovering lust.

A vortex keeping thy Uka Buka lineage thin.
Blizzard in thy mind, a tsunami falling down on thy body;
Quake in thy soul, forgiveth the reasons for thy sin.
Worthy in God's eye, but Uka sings with no grace in his rhapsody.

Patterns of nobility broken by a duki.
The fabric of thy jungle, protected by chants of Toko Tuki.

Uka Buka's hauntings and mischievous shadows had less effect. Tuki was here now. Whether in Ki's mind, heart, or true summons, he felt better. He studied over the ink lines making out Toko Tuki on his inner thigh. The tiki face was smiling with a colorful headdress, kind eyes, and strong tribal marked cheeks.

He laid back and closed his eyes, letting the wind do as it liked. He grasped enough spiritual fury for one night. Images popped up in Ki's mind. Memories of the sweet chubby cheeked faces of his old rugby mates. They were always cracking the funniest jokes and they were so fresh and cuddly. Ki couldn't help but feel like he was a part of the Tongan family. They took him to Hometown Buffet, and Noodle House, and Lin Quins Buffet Table, and the Smoke Shack. Protected him anywhere they went and smashed with him out on the rugby pitch. Ki naturally dropped into their family when he started playing rugby while Lexi carried on doing her college stuff. Lexi…

The game was brilliant, enabling players to play by their true characteristics; kicking, smashing, twisting, thinking, it was all a part of the vast game of rugby. Ki's play style was loved by the Tonga boys, and as their second season took off so did Ki's relationships with them. Lexi…

The main three Tongans that held the team together were real brothers, so Toko was always a part of their pigeon slang.

One day after a hard fought game, the family was at an aftergame house party and their team was drinking Kava, as usual. Their taped up sausage fingers were either wrapped around kava cups or beer cans for the most part. The quantity of tape, the amount of broken fingers, showed how deep a rugby team was in their season.

Lua, the oldest of the brothers, grabbed Ki by the shoulder. His whole hand seemed to be held together by a mass of tightly wound white tape.

Lua moved closer to his ear and whispered, "Toko." Ki knew this meant brother, but he wasn't completely sure how intimate it was until Meka and Michael's eyes met his from across the party's circle. They nodded appraisal and affirmation, and then Lua whispered again, "You are a Brother, much love wey."

Ki remembered finishing his Kava Root and swinging his cup around on his index finger, feeling the best he had ever felt. The whole rest of the season Ki felt more protected and loved than ever. He invited his Mother, Leia, to every event with them, to show her how great his new family was.

However, the venture North only lasted until his girlfriend graduated from college, and then they had to leave his Northern Tonga family and travel back home. Oh Lexi… my heart.

Before he left town Meka did an at home tattoo job for Ki. Meka created Toko Tuki exactly as Ki had imagined a Toko idol to be. Ki only added the Tuki behind the Toko. The whole tattoo was a tiki face with its name Toko Tuki between its teeth. Meka asked, "What this, Tuki? Not another Puki, ehhhh?" The family laughed, and the needle settled into its work.

Ki believed Tuki was his little elemental guardian angel, who took the form of a charismatic plank face tiki idol. Even though mean looking and worn, Tuki's image always had powerful colors, orbiting loyalty and brisk honest mannerisms. Ki simply enjoyed the look of him, and named him what he believed a spirit guide should be named, Tuki. Brother Tuki. Toko Tuki.

Kintsugi of Suga Duka

The walk back to the truck was difficult. With most of the day spent limping or dragging his injury around in the dirt, Ki was moving away from the Uka Buka den and towards the Toko Tuki pitch. He'd go home, talk with his mom, dig out his rugby boots, and join the local squad. He'd send out multiple letters to the City Council and fix that bum waste zone on the side of the cliff. He'd do things the right way, the way of the light, the way of the Sun.

If Ki could transform the town into a place like the mountains, at least by creating somewhat of a zero waste environment, he'd honor back the spirit of Gaia, the worm engraved staff, the mountains, the wind, the forest, even Uka Buka.

On the way home Ki turned on his truck radio. He was deep in wilderness territory so his favorite stations were static. He eventually found one station at least that had harmonic melodies and a smooth reception.

Zoo Za'mara was passed out on the seat next to him and Ki started to daydream about how he would approach the City Council with the logistics of his operation. The windy road interwove his thought frequencies; coming in, going out, moving forward, sliding back. Many ideas probably wouldn't fly, but he had to start digging, he had to start with something, and he liked the idea of having backup.

The nice melodic tune ended and a commercial popped on.

"Coca Cola. Celebrate the Heroes in Your Life, and share the Magic of Coke this Holiday Season."

One of Ki's eyebrows went up while the other went down. Coca Cola, a big company with a fundamentally insane amount of waste production.

Ki fell into his thoughts with a hypnotic daze as he wove his truck through the roads like a blind seamstress weaving her needle and tread with the warmth of the Sun as her guide. Everyone had their bloody cause nowadays… Everyone had a 'right' to do what they wanted, because they thought it was right. But what if that thought was skewed. The history of human error tells us that a basic mind in a grand population mistaking their reality isn't too far fetched. What if their focus on doing the right thing was for the wrong reasons? Hurting things that they 'thought' were lifeless and inanimate.

What if there was an integral study on the importance of one 'unconscious' thing compared to a thinking mind. It'd possibly show that this mindless thing was, in fact, filled with more importance and preservation for the planet's wellbeing than the mind of a selfish human being of relentless consumption and pure ruinous impulses. Of course, for this to be true we'd have to define what the most important thing on the planet was. Could the answer possibly be the planet itself? Without the planet there would be… nothing? So the 'cause' to save the planet would be the most paramount belief. Yet powerful entities that do the exact opposite are bringing our planet to ruin, and the masses are following. Keeping themselves alive by advertising their brand as magical and heroic. Pulling most of the simplistic thought processing minds to buy into these false realities simply because they have the freedom to do what is easiest for them. So let freedom ring and the Earth burn around its liberty bells.

Ki didn't exactly know the cultural attributes of other countries, but he knew most Americans would choose to do the easy thoughtless way before the more rigorous, more thought provoking honorable way of doing things. This was the time to make the right decisions. Ki felt like the fork in the road was approaching, and he had to be prepared.

Ki pulled up to his mom's house late that Winter Sunday afternoon. The dust hung in the air from the old gravel driveway. Now far away from solitude and Uka's embrace, he began to understand Uka Buka more. He understood the totem spirit tiki idol and its foreboding terror. Uka Buka scare the dumb dumbs off Mountain.

The front door was open and the welcome mat was crooked. ZooZa took the lead in entering the shady abode and Ki gingerly strutted in after her.

Ivy vines ran along the exposed joists and beams on the ceiling, pinned up in places to create a path of fluid curves for the meandering plant. In every corner of Leia's house were a bunch of plants and flowers all huddled together like they were gathered for a little green party. Ki looked outside through the huge eight foot by eight foot kitchen window to peer into the jungle outside. The plants and trees totally enveloped the terrace, creating amazing shade in the concealed environment. He turned on the faucet while searching for his mom and poured himself a glass of water.

Ki would enjoy moving back in with his mom. It would help his cause. It fit with his dreams. He didn't need to prove his independence anymore. He didn't have a girlfriend… Then suddenly a blade was put to his neck.

Ki splashed his water all over the counter before stabilizing his unsuspecting body. The first thing he thought of was who would invade a pleasant La'dori household? Surely the cliffside bums didn't trace… His second thought came from his nose. A fragrance of dirty vegetables mixed with orange blossom shampoo. A smell that told him everything would be alright. Even in an unknown void a soul can find bliss with a familiar sense.

Leia, Ki's mom, turned him around by the shoulder and took a bite out of her knife. The bright orange carrot was shaved down to create an edge.

T'was a carrot shank. Her blue streak in her hair hung loose now and they laughed at Ki's reaction and of Leia's forged veggie blade.

A short time later they made a nice leek, potato squash soup and chatted about Lexi's departure and his weekend. He solemnly went over the end of his year and what happened with Lexi, crunching together juicy details to get to the really juicy elements of the weekend. He loved Lexi but that was in the past. Now in his present and future life stood a quest to oversee.

Skipping the part about the cliff dwellers falling to their doom, he scrupulously went over his Uka Buka experience and revealed to Leia the Toko Tuki staff.

She walked Ki through the garden at twilight afterwards. There were twinkle lights strung out above, and Hawaiian plank faces hung around as guardians of the garden: two on the fence, one on a terrace post, and one facing the main gate. She brought the one down from the terrace post and it sort of had a heart contour to it, perhaps a heart with a flattened chin.

Leia went on. "This is you, your heart, your Suga Duka." She seemed pleased with the name, a new creation or not. After a moment of looking the heart shaped tiki face over in her hands, she dropped it and smashed the face in half with a solid boot stomp. Ki cringed and put a grievous hand out for the loss of a tiki just to make a point.

"That has to have some kind of bad juju, or unlucky repercussions mum."

She smiled and waved him to follow her to the outside of her shed.

"Only if you allow misfortune hun, will it drift over you like a dark cloud. That tiki, Suga Duka, or whatever you want to call them, is just a totem of our creation. See how easy it was for me to pick up and smash her to pieces. We have the power, Love."

Leia lifted some vials of goo, measured and mixed some into another container and searched in cobwebs for something else. She looked like a little alchemist, at least what Ki perceived one to look like. A potion pouring magician.

The fairy twinkle lights were taking greater effect as twilight settled into the atmosphere, "I prefer things broken a little, gives them character, gives the possibility to turn a new leaf down a barren road, if we so choose… and we need more leaves like that Ki. We need to change what's broken, to give our world the beauty it deserv… Ah, here it is." It was another mason jar, but smaller than the rest, and full of little gold flakes.

"Kintsugi is an old Japanese tradition of mending broken things. We don't always have to fear what is broken." She looked at her son, eyes full of sentiment and love.

"Don't throw this away, Ki. Use it to make a better future." Leia pushed her fingers into Ki's chest and smiled. Ki was overwhelmed with a new powerful motivating emotion while his mom mixed the epoxy with the gold flakes and created a jar of liquid sunshine.

They walked back over to Suga Duka, a tiki head tribal member, and Leia set Duka's halves on her workbench and gently brushed the gold epoxy over both cracked ends.

"Suga," She gestured with her left, "receive Duka" She gestured with her right. Then Leia pieced the two broken halves together, creating a golden line between the heart like face.

"I'm sorry about Lexi Ki, but everything will work itself out if you let it… Now as far as going back into rugby, I'm not exactly sure how to mend broken bones as I do broken Suga Dukas."

The Council

After a morning tending the garden and flipping his compost piles, Ki drove over to the City Hall building in the heart of town. The time on four wheels to get from the base of the mountain to the tide of the sea took around ten minutes. With all of society's nic-nacks in between it was a quick town to get from one place to another. Sky dawning the days of college students, retirees and tourists, Ellipses always seemed to be bustling with life. The town name, defined as an untamed grammatical pause in time.

This close to Christmas, Ki knew the City Council would have a very busy agenda for the end of the year, so he wrote them a sonnet and an inquiry letter just in case he didn't get a chance to speak during their Tuesday meeting. He tucked the sonnet and inquiry letter in an envelope. His prepared riddles ready to be read by analytical minds. The queasy, empty vortex in his stomach made him feel like it would be a wasted rhyme.

Walking up to City Hall, Ki admired the old sandstone carvings and masonry of the building. Stone guardians protecting and beautifying the building gave it a stoic feel of importance. The massive overhanging Oaks and Christmas lights also added to the magic of the headquarters. As he strode inside he palmed the stone lion's mane and peered at the carved dolphins above.

The Mayor and ten Council members were sitting in the high seats of the chamber overlooking the crowd of social workers and older Ellipsis citizens. Even though it was in the middle of the day the room held a dewy darkness to it, as if the fluorescent lights themselves brought a depression.

A man pushed past Ki on his right. He didn't want to be in anyone's way, yet he didn't know where to go exactly. Last was best for the overseer, so he headed to the back. As Ki looked around to make sure he didn't bump into another lumbering citizen, he froze in amazement.

Uka Buka was there floating right over his shoulder. A wooden head suspended in the air, looking right back at Ki, completely indifferent to the crowd around them or their quarters. Ki looked around at the people and the council table and discovered no one else could see what he was seeing. He swiped his nose and headed for a seat.

Everyone began settling down and the meeting slowly commenced. Safe in the back of the building now, Ki risked another look at the floating Tiki.

"Uka Buka." The tiki face grumbled nonchalantly at Ki, then finally looked away from him and at the Council table where the Mayor was now speaking.

Ki stroked his sprained ankle from his mountain expedition this past weekend. Uka Buka really followed me? He thought while rubbing at his buzzed head. He felt like a madman, like one of those lost souls he kicked off the shoreline cliffs. Was this his Karma? He thought he was doing right… He quickly reconceived. This maybe more of a blessing than a curse. A floating plank faced companion, a gift from the Earth Mother herself.

Whatever it was, Ki didn't like feeling flustered and insane. He took a breath and tried tuning back into the Council meeting.

The Council spoke for a solid thirty minutes about Moki's Tribal Stewardship for their National Forest wildfire relief plan, their Police departments undergoing audit, and environmental based events, businesses and ideas.

Ki noticed a burly red headed Sheriff in the corner growling at a City Council member who was drilling the new Police Commissioner about her policies and fresh ingenuity that blended in with the modern era of today. She answered the Council member's arid questions thoroughly and confidently, however her informal remarks made it seem like their police department needed help. Bringing up on side notes that their Police Officers had regular wages in a town with an extremely high cost of living and real estate, which minimized their numbers and reduced the quality of their Police Force.

After the awkward berating, a Councilwoman spoke of renewing a transient homeless family shelter. This jolted Ki into hiccuping. His natural instinct was to interrupt and tell them the matter of the Cliff Dwellers. At least while they were on the subject.

His thumb pressed into his forehead and he side glanced at Uka Buka still floating there with a flat yet absorbing gaze. No frowning, no smiling, no emotion, just listening and waiting.

"We will take outside questions and concerns now… Mrs. Marsanta?" The Mayor asked.

Little old lady Mrs. Marsanta, with patches and wisps of hair, went up to the podium and approved the meeting's digest that the Council already went over. The Mayor went on to the next civilian speaker. This young man began overly grateful for the Council's service to the town, but then turned it around and pelted the Mayor and the Council for last year's dispersal of funds. Calling them wrongdoers and conducting town leadership with no financial sense. Another lady after him argued against that man's opinion and applauded the Council. More people came up with inquiries and they all had their three minutes of fame, and everytime those three minutes were over the Mayor always looked up from her notes and said the same exact thing, "Who's next?"

A man named Thunder Claw came up to the podium in flowing rags and a dark stank to him. He scratched the crack of his ass while he brown-nosed the Council members, but really all that came out of his mouth was gibberish and nonsense that annoyed the Hall. Annoyed Ki.

He found that his awareness of his annoyance finally put some emotion into Uka Buka. Uka Buka rose high into the building's terraced ceiling and dove at Thunder Claw a handful of times. As Thunder Claw was wrapping up his jabbered commentary, Uka Buka floated right in front of his face and bore out a deep, bellowing laugh. Its blocky teeth inches from the man's nose.

Yep, other people definitely aren't seeing what I'm seeing, Ki thought with remorse.

Ki raised his hand and was then given his opportunity to speak on the podium. He walked up and Uka Buka slowly descended down right in front of his face. Its eyes studied Ki's own as if it knew Ki had something inside of him, something Uka wouldn't laugh at, something Ki didn't even know he had.

He closed his eyes to block out Uka and spoke. "Council people and Mayor…" Ki bowed his head and opened his eyes to clearly see the Council table. Fortunately, Uka Buka drifted off to the side to watch the room.

"A few days ago…" suddenly it clicked, telling the story of the cliff dwellers around the Sheriff and the Police Commissioner wasn't a good idea. They'd suspect he was the gungho spartan that kicked those people off the cliff.

"During a windy afternoon, I witnessed heaps of light garbage and plastic bags blowing into the sea off our rigid coastline. I wanted to propose a few clean up days each month to clear out all catalysts for trash collectives along our unpopulated beaches. It's the coastlines out of sight that gather an abundance of transient waste." Uka Buka floated more prominently into Ki's view and a different fiery passion rose inside of Ki, a rage like a wave crashing down with all the power of the water gods.

His flat cheeks grew more and more fiery and his voice vibrated with a grit of mirth. He led on, now not caring if they suspected him.

"I propose a plan to make an activist group of passionate naturalists and enforce the brilliance of clean natural locations. If the homeless want to trash our most majestic sanctuaries they can walk back through the paved streets that birthed their planetary disposition and live in the landfills. Maybe a new activist enforcement group and our local police department could help relocate these uncaring transients to landfills, where they could live happily in cumulus amounts of waste of their liking. Get the homeless off the preservations and into the landfills! We could even pay them to separate and consolidate recyclables that are mixed in with the trash." Ki noticed the Sheriff straightened, yet the Council table continued to hold an apathetic pose.

The Mayor did not look up from her notes. "Thank you. Are there any more inquiries or concerns?" The Mayor tied up the meeting and Ki felt an aloof political static. Did no one actually care about anything? Or were their agendas so important they needed to keep focus and sequester questions and ideas about our inquiries for the next meeting?

It didn't matter to Ki, he needed more than a slapdash 'Thank You,' so he ran up to the first available Councilman after the meeting and asked for a resolution. The Councilman responded in all umms, ahhs and I don't knows. It was the same Council member that berated their new Police Commissioner with stupid questions.

Eyes filled with calm apprehension glossed over Ki and the Councilman as Mayor Patricia Force walked out of the Hall.

"Mayor, may I have a word?" Ki leaned into her, but the burly red headed Sheriff blocked his advance and sort of snickered in his success. The Sheriff and the Mayor proceeded to the parking lot with their heads close to one another on seemingly important matters.

Ki's backup backup plan was to send his letter and sonnet to the Council Members. The inquiry letter was if the reader was an analytical left brain thinker, and the sonnet was if the reader was a creative and emotional right brain thinker; however, after witnessing their meeting, he had little hope for his written word.

Ki washed off the City Council politics with an icy plunge into the Pacific. The town seemed too busy to take care of their Mother, and it's always been easier for Ki to do things himself. The ocean refreshed him with clarity and transfused him with powerful planetary ideology. With the cold water, he finally felt like his ankle was just strong enough to run on as well.

He grabbed his boots, which were half buried in the sand, and went off to the rugby pitch. The rugby team's training ground was held at a park overlooking the ocean. All training sessions were held at night from 7:00 to 9:00 with tall thirty foot floodlights that lit up the pitch. He walked up with his penguin veterinary hat on backward and too short of shorts tight around his bum. The full moon brought an additional flush of light to the new faces, either putting their boots on in the bleachers or stretching their legs while passing the ball.

A slim man with a funny accent and salt and pepper hair came up to him and shook his hand. "Oei, come to join the Grunion did ya?"

"'Too late for another Skallywag to join your ranks?" Ki knew what rugby boys liked to hear, and he also knew it was mid-December, one month before the main 15s rugby season started up. Plenty of time to join the team with open arms.

"Yes Sir. I'm Safa. I see you have your boots and you look fast. We will start you off in the backline." He gave a bigger than life smile and clapped Ki on the shoulder.

"Ah, wait a minute, Stank Dick." A bigger player with groovy slicked back hair and a little strand hanging in his face got up off the third row of the bleachers and held his hand out to Ki, his index and thumb squeezed together like he was passing an invisible joint. Safa, A.K.A Stank, was still smiling vibrantly.

"Our Captain tries to recruit every quick foot to his backline, but you are a forward, I can see it in your eyes." The big guy looked back down at his hand. "This is our team's secret handshake, it's a fish kiss. When you kiss back we both say 'Mer'."

"Mer," They said simultaneously as their fingers kissed.

"Alright Bags, but I'm keeping the Aussie brothers Mate."

"Keep em. You'll need someone in the backline that can catch the ball." And just like that, Ki joined his new family.

After training Ki and a handful of the players went out to their local pub, Unluckies, the team's beer sponsor. He loved how they drank out of only glasses and metal steins, and finished kegs instead of smashing cans. It was the perfect sport for Ki. As far as waste went, there was none, you only needed cleats and shorts. Minimal waste, minimal material with maximum fun.

Ki started catching a heavy buzz his first night out with his new mates, and began loosening up around them. There were eight of them tucked back into their own little corner of the pub. It seemed like they were a rainbow of humanity. Two white guys, a South African, an Australian, a Polynesian, a black guy, an Irish man and Ki, the Japanese guy. A little over half a pitched rugby squad.

"How'd you guys get your names?"

The thick muscled Irishmen with red hair and freckled cheeks slowly peeled his pint glass away from his lips. "We ask the questions around here, Rookie." He growled. His free arm sprawled across the table, as if the table was only there to comfort his gingered junk. Ki barely recognized him because he was out of uniform.

The table giggled and Bags smoothly answered Ki's question with storytelling behavior.

"We can start with the hard hitting Irish Lug, Sheriff Worden. The Sheriff has always been very disturbed with drug dealers lacing their goods with the drug Fentanyl. And because he has that, 'I'll WHAP you on the side of the head' attitude, we call him Sheriff Fentawhap or Whap for short." The Sheriff gave a sly smile and slid his arm off the table to rest on top of the booth's brown ridge.

Bags thoughtfully looked around. "Safa, the South African, our beloved Captain, had a horrible plumbing problem that made his room smell exactly like Stanky Dick!"

Safa raised his stein and winked.

"Quiet Pena over there, who can spin out of any grapple, also loves to smoke the marijuana like the Aussie's love talking funny. So we call Pena, Mokes, short for Smokes. His last name is also

Mokalua." Mokes took a swig of his margarita and tucked a freshly rolled joint above his ear. His shell necklace and brown skin gave him away for the islander.

"The Grunion are paying the Australian Madden brothers to play for us so they don't get a nickname." Everyone around the table continued the roar of laughter during the nickname refreshments, but with this last one, good looking blonde haired Cam Madden almost rolled on the floor with hysteria. He found any American joke the joke of the century.

Bags kept his cool and continued. "The big guy with the spectacles is Wino. He never whines on or off the pitch, but he makes wine in the valley and sets up most of our fundraising events." Wino tilted his glasses down on his black nose and took a sip of his deep red wine while eyeing Ki. He looked wise and geeky.

"Wino's our prop, so take it easy on him eh." The Irish Sheriff gave him a heavy punch in the arm and Wino looked abashed that he spilled his precious wine.

"Fish here, got his name by simply drinking like a Fish." Fish pounded his beer and grabbed Mokes' beer and finished that one too.

"I'll grab a couple more pints for ye laddies." Fish's face twitched a little as he got up and went to the bar.

"And I'm ... Ooh! Buffalo!" The big white guy with the groovy hairdo pointed at Ki with his elbow. "Finish your beer Sir. We only drink with our left hands here. No one wants to shake a wet right."

Ki downed his pint.

Bags rang out right before he was done, "Over the head!"

Ki tipped the empty glass over his buzzed head.

"Very impressed," Bags professed, "Finished every last bit of your beer. Not one drop left. Zero wasted. Pretty fucking good brother."

Ki blushed, still working out the beer running through his body. "You are Bags because?"

"I am Baggans of the Shire because one, my real last name is Backens. And two because that guy over there gave me my name. Smeagol, the oldest player of the Grunion." Baggans pointed again with his elbow at a young guy with a scar that ran from the top of his lip to his nose.

"Ya, I remember him at training. He keeps the ball like it's his Precious. Agile as fuck, no one can catch him." Ki mused, still amazed and staring at the small guy. At that moment, Smeagol was sitting in his chair with the backrest in front of him and chatting it up with a geeky looking cutie pie.

"Fucking exactly. That's Smeagolstein. Able to tackle the biggest Tongan props that run at us. Most of the other guys have names too, but they're not here so where's the fun in that… That leaves you now Ki, and Key is too good of a nickname. Sounds too golden, like you're our pivotal player." Baggans sat back and gulped at his freshly handed pint from Fish.

Fish continued to fill everyone's glasses with the pitchers, while also starring at Ki.

Stank Dick giggled out, "Let's call him Zero. He bloody drank every drop of that pint and Zero is a horrible name."

Fish set down the pitcher and held his pint out for Ki to Cheers, "Aye, and we can call you Z for short!"

The guys started to get more rowdy and rambunctious, spilling their beers as much as drinking them.

Baggans had to yell for the boys to hear him now, "It's funny because we all have our positions, 1 through 15, but your fucking Zero. that fucking wild!"

Destined to be Zero, Ki felt like he was on the right path.

EARTH DAY

A year and four months went by. The moons waned and waxed, the sun rose and set, the drinks spilled in and out. Ki got sucked into another family squad. United as one vein supporting Earth's nexus. Walking amongst her plains with a zero carbon footprint. Ki not only respected this way of life, he enjoyed it, and loved being a part of a group that wanted to help the Motherland, not burden her.

The time spent adjusting after dispersing retribution on the cliffside trash trolls, kicking them over their trash cliff, and happily watching them fall to whatever destiny Earth had planned for them was time Ki needed to understand his true self.

He had time to search for his spirit, his quest, his Toko Tuki. Only to discover that Toko Tuki simply resembled his family, his brothers. Toko Tuki was a character he created in his mind out of love, however eclipsing Toko Tuki, on the brink of reality, was a character that manifested out of fear, madness, and hate. Uka Buka.

Ki stuck with smashing and bashing other people for his family, his team, which seemed to be more Uka's style. Since Uka was with him most of the time now, Ki became used to appeasing the spirits' desires. They did have similarities. Even though Ki didn't like feeding his dark side, he enjoyed having a floating companion. Whatever its traits were, he felt closer to Mother Earth with Uka around.

The worm engraved staff he found in the mountains lost its power to luminate. The lumination of Tuki's blessing. Even though Tuki did not wisp around him like Uka Buka did, he still cherished the artifact of love and kindness and yearned for it too to materialize. Although that yearning for something he could not have only built upon Ki's fear, Ki's fear fed Uka Buka with more power.

To keep his mind away from the insanity of the situation, he did copious amounts of research on how bad the system of planet rehabilitation really was and began a plan of action: He watched government policies and debates, focused on corporate movements and their polluting mannerisms, and finally, nuzzled in tight with thick blooded warriors that would also march on the path of environmental righteousness.

How did he get so lucky? The whole rugby association now, Mermaids, Stingrays, and Grunion, ladies, kids, and men, combined together to make a beneficial environmental impact. Ki was just a lead advisor, but Baggans, Safa Scott and a handful of Mermaids ran the show.

They found events to support, politicians to protest and habitats to clean. They were a group of Zero Waste Heros, and even as good as that sounded, Ki still wanted to morph them into something more dangerous and threatening to the unconscious, insensible, delusionary republic of consumerism.

The team, the Grunion, were ecstatic they won the last match of the season, making them the California State Champions. They stood around drinking pints of beer while cheersing their previous opponents. Everyone either had some tape around their limbs, bruised eyebrows or lacerated cheeks.

Baggans, one of the bigger and more brotherly players of the Grunion, jumped on a chair and started to sing their team's song.

"Me, Me, Me, Meeee." Everyone turned to him, some cleared their throats, and the party was silent for the moment.

"Weeeee are the Grunion you hate or love us, we come in Harmony!"

Beer sloshed from Baggan's cup as he jigged back and forth with the song. The rest of the Grunion sang along, and Ki and their big Korean prop Jason Su, stood below the rain of beer. Having fun catching what they could in their own pints.

"We swim in the ocean, we fuck on the sand, we play some fine rugby!"

Ki felt a rough hand on his shoulder. His Captain, the South African, moved close to Ki's ear as Ki leaned back and sang along with Baggans to hear Safa's news.

"The transport is ready to fly Z." Ki nodded, pulled his phone out of his pocket to check the time and continued Baggan's lyrics.

"One thing you'll notice our drinkings ferocious, with speed and agility. So grab your beers and five of your mates, it's off to the boat race for me. Heyhey!!" The whole bar, both teams, fans, and patrons alike, cheered their faces off. The rumble of the crowd and feeling of warmth and security rose amongst these broad shouldered merry men. As the boat race, or team vs team chug off was getting underway, Ki gathered the goon squad for a little sideline arrangement.

As they went outside through the back gate of the bar, Baggans began singing another song, "Today is Saturday! Saturday's a rugby day!"

Today was Saturday, April 22nd 2020, which was the Earth Day Festival. A lot was going on and the group was taking it step by step. First, they needed to win the Championship match. Done. Now they needed to get to the Earth Day Festival in the alloted window of time befor–.

"Hey Wino, was it Soul Majestic that played first or King Zero?" Ki opened the sliding door of the tinted windowed sprinter van and six of them fell in. Kavika Pines and Adam Vander were the pilot and co-pilot, looking back at the boys to make sure no one's stolen pint would topple over in their advance. Mokes, the Hawaiian Stoner, lit his joint up as he settled into his seat. Sheriff Worden signed Mokes to put out his smokes by drilling his fingers into his palm. Mokes took another hit and motioned he didn't know what finger drilling meant.

"Put it out you little pothead. We will be there in 3 minutes." The Sheriff ordered while reaching over, grabbing the joint, and snubbing it out gently into the calluses of his palm.

Ki grew up going to this festival, he knew there would be families, his mother, city officials, and live broadcasters tapping the concert. This was important, very important. Earth Day was birthed in their little town of Ellipsis after a massive 1970s oil spill in their coastal waters. Ellipsis had the history to give reverbication to their group's voice. This was a very important day.

Ironically, the band named King Zero was letting Ki and his group of Environmentalists up on stage after their set, thanks to Stoney Mokes' association.

Wino finished shuffling through his phone and answered, "King Zero is first up."

Pines turned around from the front passenger seat, "You guys gotta jump out in t minus ten seconds."

"Once we get out, Mokes and Stretch, find the Mermaid squad, the rest of you with me backstage." Wino rubbed away the sweat from his glasses and took a deep breath. He was a heavy set nerd that ran as much as he could out on the pitch, but definitely walked when there was a whistle. To make up for his lack of physical fitness, he was quick and with it mentally. All people were useful to a rugby organization, especially one like theirs.

The van door slid open and they poured out quickly, "We'll see ya back at the pub." Ki high fived Pines and twisted Vander's nipple, hard, then ran off snickering towards the reggae music.

Ki swung around the crowds of people; feather crowned flamingo girls, shirtless hippies, parents with little flower children, locals, friends, and merchants, to make it backstage by a large shady patch under a fig tree. There were thirteen of them, six Grunion, six Mermaids, the Woman's rugby association, and one little youth rugby Stingray named Tommy Perez, Tommy Boi for short.

There was also another group of girls that called themselves the Mermaids that Ki wanted to get the attention of. They were at the festival somewhere as well, probably selling merch or swimming around in their expensive mermaid fishtails. They were an organized group that taught little kids the consequences of pollution, cleaned up trash on the coastline, advocated no plastic bags in grocery stores, and fought to ban plastic straws, all things Ki wanted to also boost in awareness.

The rugby girls congratulated the Grunion for winning the Championship and thanked the boys for coming out to support. Ki wiggled his toes in his Converse and stretched his back by rolling his shoulders. Girls who fought for the planet turned him on. Girls who also battled on the green fields of Valhalla put him in a tornado of emotions.

His melancholy thoughts came in a poetic storm.

Mermaid Sonnet
Thy coral in thine hair doth sing…

Ki's focus suddenly split as Mayor Force pulled Sheriff Worden off to the side of the party. Her face was inches from his.

It looked as if she wasn't happy they were there, her eyes frequently rolling from the thirteen rugby members and back to the Sheriff. The Sheriff on the other hand always had a jolly attitude. You could see that he was in a good mood if you knew him. He was a big ginger Irish lad, sweet as a mint and funny as a porcupine, that was until things got serious. Then bear sized porcupine spikes would spring out to cast a menacing shadow over its prey of trouble makers and rookies.

"Sheriff Worden, I understand you and your group mean well but this lecture was not scheduled. Earth Day is about the planet, not team sports and the little activist roles you play. I mean this all in the most productive way possible, and I hold your integrity to the highest degree, but there are still three missing persons under investigation from last year and you are playing, Save The Planet with these hippie beer drinking hooligans! I have the Board of Education, the Keefer family, and the Nature Conservation Organization up my ass right now. What the hell happened to these missing people?"

"Mayor Force, these Hooligans, are well connected throughout the town. And a non-profit that helps clean up this City is a god-damn Pagan blessing. These lads are nothing but gentlemanly, Mayor, and the Women are truly a bunch of hot-blooded angels." Sheriff Worden announced the last part a little louder, probably trying to get some sexy time points with the Mermaids of beautiful athletic builds.

Stretch, a lengthy blonde with a, I'm the man in charge image, crushed a beer can behind his back and slipped it in his back pocket as King Zero waved them up. Sheriff Worden eyed the Mayor hu-morously, apologizing with his eyes but laughing with a slight smirk at the unfortunate timing of occurrences.

Euphoric Jessie Vazquez was the first to go on stage; she hugged King Zero's singer and took the mic. "Heyyy, King Zero everyone!" The rest of the twelve followed her on stage. By the dance of the surrounding trees there was a sweet breeze in the air. The elements were happy to celebrate at least one day of gratitude for their Mother. The grand Fig tree shading the crowd creaked in recognition.

"We, us…" Jessie moved her hand, acknowledging the people at her side and the people out in the park listening. "We honor Mother Earth today by happily thudding our feet onto her soil and enjoying her globe of acoustics with the vocals of King Zero and the Souls of Majestic. Today is the celebration of our planet! So we wanted to get you ready for making today the start of an Earth Year!" A rush of whispers passed through the crowd; most gave words of encourage-ment, and others were simply curious.

"This organization of people," again Jessie swept her hand in an integral circle like it was part of a Hawaiian dance. "Has one grand focus of helping the planet in many different ways. Let me present our Stewards! Sheriff Worden will help keep the peace! Which is always needed to establish a sanctuary for growth." Her hand moved from the Sheriff and gestured over to Mokes the Hawaiian and Nick Sage the Chilean scrum half. "Waste management and gardening." Jessie moved over to Safa the South African and Honey, a heavy tittied Asian prop,

"The Webmasters casting our web out in cyberspace to help identify our presence on social media. Jaclynn Poxer and Doctor Katie Neilsly conducting Environmental Statistics and Marketing for zero wasteful procedures and materials."

Jessie tried to pinpoint Amy with her open palm, taking a moment in her search because Sly Amy was much smaller than the other rugby girls.

"Amy Callaway, a Surveyor Surveying our Ecosystem and Animal biodiversity shifts. Tawa Pawni, helping develop the most efficient ways for agricultural growth and compost/soil escalation."

Jessie had little 13 year old Tommy Perez by the shoulder now. His bare feet muddy by the off paths around the park. Wino stood behind him, his glasses in the middle of the bridge of his stout nose.

"Our social delegate and his apprentice and youth mediator. And finally, I and the rest of our Association will be in charge of Enforcing these radical adjustments. We aren't talking about regulating wasteful products. We want an end to wasteful products. Our ambition is to create pods of people like us around the nation to help quit the comfortable outlet of using One Use plastic throw away items.

"Whoever is in charge of this mass polluting capitalistic scheme is doing it for money and money alone. Money doesn't heal the planet, it only aids a defining evil towards ruining our planet. We are having a major problem ENFORCING Environmental changes in society. Making you comfortable also makes them money. Anthropocentric Human Supremacy is what keeps the planet square instead of the voluptuous sphere she should be!" The crowd was wide eyed, their jaws hanging, minds lackadaisical in their psychedelic haze, previously thinking Earth Day was a free day to do drugs and chill.

The Mayor's eyes blazed as she stood right in front of the stage looking up at Jessie and Sheriff Worden.

"This is the year we hold hands with our Planet, join forces and beat back those narcissistic no gooders. Our new non-profit, Earth Enforcement Association, is simple. We, the E.E.A., live our regular lives as a close-knit circle of friends and associates that can be there to quickly help others with quality numbers and a strong work ethic. The base of our strategy is for any group that puts on a zero-waste, environmentally friendly event or party, we will help cater, design, organize, and secure for free. Anyone who wants to plant trees, grow mushrooms, or create compost piles, we will also be there to help. If any anthropocentric person thinks they are better than the dirt that they stand on, we will be there to advise a different path." Jessie's slight twist on the word, advise, was unnoticeable to anyone that didn't know her.

Ki was beginning to feel comfortable, he was glad King Zero warmed up the stage. It had good withstanding energy as far as he was concerned. He looked over at the Mayor and all the spectating faces and realized now was a great time to give them a break. Jessie thankfully thought the same. "Viva La Earth, Blessid Earthlings!"

Two of the Mermaids, Doctor Katie Neilsly with a blue green mermaid strap covering her tits and a gregarious Honey cracking relevant Earthling jokes like they were eggs, lightened the mood and went over how to keep in contact with E.E.A. The girls pointed over to their Earth Day booth that had rugby merchandise and new Earth Enforcement Association shirts with one large image of Planet Earth, or one of all seven of our continents in the hands of a Mermaid.

Some people showed conviction on what was said. They stood up a little straighter, their eyes steadied a little finer, and the E.E.A. booth became a whirlwind of human interaction. All in all Ki was proud of his new crew. The statement was out and their conscience was clear for whatever may come next.

Smasher & Basher

The fan was cocked to full throttle. Baggans sat on the edge of his bed looking at the litter of Hawaiian shirts, wide brimmed hats and sunglasses that covered his floor. He sat there to sit, no worries, no thoughts, just sitting. After a moment as that first spark of the day settled in, he wondered. Clutter isn't bad for the environment is it?

He made some eggs and some of Ki's weird morning wake-me-up mushroom tea, then sat down at his desk. As his computer was turning on he tweaked a Cancer Relief Rugby ball on its stand so the brand, Samurai, faced him and the pink ribbon faced the door.

While organizing his things he muttered his song, "If you're on the pitch, We're gonna hit ya. Better start to clench, because we're gonna hit ya." He sang over and over, eventually making a repeat of just, "Ohhh, We're Gonna Hit Ya."

Baggans finished up his Carbon Credit Allowance investment plan and his company's financial mumbo-jumbo, left his house, the Shire, and went out for a late lunch. He started his own business selling Carbon Credit Allowance Stocks, a system that takes money from big polluting companies and gives it to environmental growth non-profit associations. The more big corporations pollute, the more money goes to helping the environment.

Ki had asked Bags for the short of it once, and Baggans gave him the longer, bolder answer.

"Carbon Credit Allowances, let's see. California's legal mandate is to reduce statewide emissions to 40% below 1990's emission levels by the year 2030. The declining supply of CCAs will create higher costs for industries emitting GHGs. To help with this process, I look for investors to invest in CCA stock. The more that stock goes up the harder it is for these big corporations to buy the Allowances, there-fore restricting their rate of production and pollution. The high price of CCAs are the key to emission reductions for the Cap and Trade program.

"The Cap-and-Trade program imposes a compliance obligation of facilities that emit at least 25,000 metric tons of covered carbon dioxide equivalent per year, otherwise known as covered entities. Covered entities represent approximately 85% of the total California emissions, based on emissions per unit of production, so as not to penalize increasing production or reward decreasing production. Because the Cap Adjustment Factor ratchets down the free allowances given out each year, Covered entities must either continuously decrease their emissions per unit of production or purchase an increasing number of CCAs.

"Emission reduction potential in most industrial sectors, such as cement, mining, metals, refining, etc. are limited as abatement costs and are dramatically higher than current CCA levels. Therefore, for economic reasons, covered entities should continue to buy CCAs until CCAs are projected to be a multiple of current prices. The penalty for non compliance is set at 4x the amount of the actual obligation. To date, compliance has been almost 100%.

"Increasing demand and declining supply are expected to drive CCA prices higher. Later, increasing your bond price.

"Targeted industries and covered entities include transportation, electricity generators, commercial and residential energy, and the industrial sector: Refineries, oil & gas, cement plants, food processors. These entities are targeted as they are assessed as representing 80 - 85% of the total Greenhouse Gas emissions produced in California."

Baggans was righteously smart on the inside, he just appears to be a doltish oaf because it's good for his drinking.

Everything in their town was really only a ten to twenty minute bike ride, and on this particular day an avid Honker Doddle was honking his horn at a really really slow elderly Asian man trying to cross the street on a red. Baggans jumped off his bike, leaving it in front of the Honker McHonkinton and helped the fella to the curb. As he returned to his bike, the honks persisted, but Bag's face kept pleasant, collected and unfrazzled.

A few minutes later he made it to Eureka! A restaurant slash fine drinking establishment Baggans loved. He ordered two pints from the nice brunette bartender with her hair tied back in an upward style 70's ponytail.

"Food sugar?"

"Beer's just fine. Thanks Miss… Ahh, look who the cat dragged in out of the pond, ol'Fishy!" Baggans raised his pint in front of a delighted smile.

"Heyo Bags! Mer." Fish and Baggans Mer'd, the club's secret handshake, only it was done with an index finger and thumb pinch then twist.

"Oy Bags, thanks for the pint." Fish twinked and happily took a seat at the bar next to Baggans. Fish had a little tic around his right eye. It wasn't really a twitch, and it wasn't really a wink, so his friends called it a twink.

"Two more please Miss, whenever you'd be getting the chance… Ahh Fish, you ready to get a run in with the boys?" Baggans' first pint was finished within a few seconds of his question.

"A little fun in the summer day sun. Beers with the boys after too I reckon?"

"Aye, Thursday's a drinking day…" Baggans pointed at the pint that Fish thought he finished. "I'd say over the head on that one bud." Fish grimaced and turned his glass over his head and waited for the last droplets of beer to pour into his strangely black hair. Fish was one of those guys with a defined farmer's tan and tattoos in all the places you couldn't see.

"Zero waste la de da'de da." Fish sang, grabbing his second while air cheersing the barkeep and cling cheersing Baggans.

"Ah yes, on that note. Z has a plan for us tonight."

"Hm," Fish inched a little closer and whispered. "Another midnight Graffiti sesh?" Fish then went from whispers to a wisp of purs, and Baggans could barely hear him. "Plastic Bags Are for Losers?"

Baggans responded in a normal tone, "Um, I don't think so lil Fishy, he said somethin-" Baggans stopped, and his eyes fiercely blazed at an occurrence outside of their bar.

Fish, now attuned with the outside, did recall the sound of a plastic water bottle hitting pavers. Baggans got up and headed outside. Fish gave him thirty seconds before following, not to interrupt the man's flow.

With rugby you learned to trust in your brother's ability to handle situations as well as being their support through thick and thicker. Thin they could handle on their own.

Once Fish got outside, he saw that Baggans had a tall young white guy with loose baggy clothes by the shirt collar, hilariously telling him not to pollute in his soft tone.

"Listen to me. You littered. And not only-" The guy swung at him, and by his terrified reaction, it seemed like he broke his hand on Baggans hard head. Baggans slapped the tall wanna-be wangster littering douche with his big gorilla hand and the guy hung dazed and teary eyed.

"Now listen up. You littered, and not only that, you were littering plastic, a material that will never biograde and which alters natural habitats."

"Someone will throw it in the recycling!" The tall guy was now shocked and wide eyed at the reason Baggans was berating him.

"No bro, Americans generate more than 250 million tons of solid waste every year. 90 million tons of that waste was either recycled or composted, and Natural Geographic just came out with the fact that 91 percent of plastic doesn't even get reused or repurposed! You, are part of that problem!"

Looking around at the spectators for help the baggy clothed guy spat out at Baggans, "No one gives a fuck faggot!"

Baggans locked back his hand and swung again, this time using his shoulder for a little more power. He laughed a disassociated ha, while he backed away from the fallen polluter. He was in shock at the dude's ignorance and pissed at his unkindly attempt to explain himself. The guy spat up at Baggans and a millisecond after, Fish jolted forward and knocked him out with a heel stomp.

"Awe Fish, come on man…" Baggans voice was filled with sorrow.

Fish pulled at Baggans to leave with him. "You smash, I bash." He preached matter of factly.

"Let's go Bags, I already paid the barkeep."

Eyes still on the injured man they just confronted, Fish bent over, picked up the empty plastic water bottle and tucked it into his waistband. All of the spectating eyes were on them as they meandered off. Whether you hate us or love us, we come in harmony.

***

Once they were at Fish's pickup truck, Baggans lifted his bike into the bed. Fish came up and casually bumped his forearm to Baggans' forearm.

"Basher," said Fish assertively with a twink.

"And Smasher," breathed Baggans gloomily.

Baggans weighed in at 220 pounds and Fish 170. They metaphorically resembled a slow and powerful Ape and wily Baboon duo on the pitch as well as off. Fish was a guy that looked menacing and was menacing to all that weren't his friends. His extreme actions on strangers were because of his undying loyalty to his buddies. Baggans loved Fish for this but hated how radical he became in certain situations.

Fish could tell that Baggans wasn't happy about the beat down, so he spent the time driving them to rugby training reminding Baggans why they do what they do.

The year is 2020 and Trump is in presidential office.

Fish rolled his neck around in preparation for the conversation.

"Trump just took us out of the Paris Climate Agreement. A group of leaders and nations around the world whose goal is averting catastrophic climate change. Adopted by 200 other countries and not by ours.

"Him and his Chief of Justice continue to limit wildlife conservation and weaken environmental requirements and regulations for projects that open up land for oil and gas refineries. Weakening limitations on carbon dioxide emissions from power plants and continue to drive coal as our main energy source, a fossil fuel that could destroy the world's atmosphere single handedly if we continue using it." Fish twinked, his knuckles ran white around the steering wheel. People were being pushed slowly towards a future of extreme retaliation. If you knew what leaders and corporations were doing to the planet, the natural reaction was to be as pissed as a Revolutionary.

He wasn't sure if this lecture would help Baggans, but it was good venting for himself. A reminder that most people didn't deserve this heavenly orb of existence. Fish was always a believer in underworlds and golden worlds. Demons and Saints thrown into both. Good souls stuck in the shadow of the Underworld and Evil souls clawing at the towers of Eden.

"Their plot my dear Baggans is only allowed because the shield and sword are obsolete. Their excuse is to keep everyone living an easy comfortable life, no matter what we do to the land we stand on. As long as we are soft and happy with everything we could ask for right at our fingertips. The people need their nuclear, destructive, expensive energy to live without hardship."

Baggans meekly interrupted, "Bro, we just knocked out a worthless small fry polluter. There are probably a billion more just like him and they will keep coming. That was stupid and ineffective."

Fish now heard the rubber from his stick shift squeak as his hand tightened around the knob. "Yeah, true… Ki really opened up our eyes. That smooth talking bastard. Now we need to adjust our priorities and check our emotions… At least the Police Force is short on staff or we might be in trouble."

"The ignorance was always there, Fishy. We were just too busy pounding beers and bashing heads together to notice."

"No wonder they didn't want us up on that Earth Day stage…"

Baggans punched Fish in the arm and reassured him. "Let's go play rugby, maybe it'll help ease some of that anger, eh Fishy?"

Fish twinked once again and shifted down to park.

Bingo Night

In the year of falling cliff bums, Ki yearned to create some sort of decisive path. Either making a long term plan of listening, talking, debating, and advocating; things that seemed to Ki to be a steady way of playing himself safe, or dive into the depths of rebellion and E.E.A vigilantism. There was no real danger in situations where a heated chit-chat could lead to someone spilling their tea, but living with boiling blood and righteousness tickling your spine, that was more interesting to Ki.

Within historical fluidity regarding good and evil, evil morphs reality into something so absurd that goodie goods are blinded by it, disoriented by their sheer dumbfuck narcissistic agendas. Fooled by the flash bang of idiothood. Causing the good to continue to do good while evil continued to do fucked up shit. Evil must be dealt with by evil, dumbfucks versus dumbfucks. And the good live on.

Fight for every inch of Mycelium weaving over Earth's surface. Grab evil and choke it with the fucking chemical waste that evil shits out every second. Burn all the money that makes evil powerful and see how they slither back into the waste of their creation. Into all the meaningless crap that helps everyone be shittier shits.

If the plastic bag didn't exist, we would instead have imperishable, sustainable bowls and baskets that you simply grab, use, set aside, grab, use, set aside. How many plastic or even paper bags would we save if we just used one reusable holder? 365 a year? 3,650 every 10 years. That's a big impact through just one person.

The creators of wasteful products are the evil that hemorrhages the planet. Day after day expelling poison into the globe for one reason, wealth.

Ki crumpled up his newspaper and Trump disintegrated into black and white wrinkles. The sole idiot of idiots that deteriorates forests and oceans for his oil extractions, reversed regulations of power plants shooting out carbon dioxide emissions, stopped rules against methane emissions from landfills, relieved corporations on spending money towards reducing their carbon dioxide emissions, and most recently, written in the crumpled up newspaper, withdrawing the United States out of the Paris Climate Agreement, a world organization dedicated to saving the environment.

Deep inside Ki, he didn't want to do what was socially correct, he didn't want to debate for decades and slowly inch towards environmental compromises. Good needed teeth. Ki wanted to go for the throat of fallacious power driven honchos. Ki wanted to be bad, he wanted to be righteous, he wanted to be an evil that evil saw as evil. A desecrater of evil.

Ki finished his homemade morning brew with valerian root, cinnamon, reishi and lion mane mushrooms, a relaxing agent for restless times. No coffee or drug could match a healthy desire to fulfill a known destiny.

His eyes were wide and maddened while he worked that day. The wooden shaft of the hammer creaked as he swung full behind the head swings onto the chisel. With his spasmodic rage, the hammer would miss every now and then and blunt his hand. The feeling at this point was almost welcomed.

Uka Buka grinned over Ki's shoulder as he worked, giving him a companion while he was alone.

***

That Thursday night, April 27th, was heated with rampant hearts and restless livers. Like Aussie Cam Madden and Lunch Lady Su, Ki wore his sky blue Grunion t-shirt and formed his tokens into a quaint semi-circle around his Bingo sheet. The Mermaids beer sponsor was a wooden bar on the outskirts of town and was a perfect gathering spot for a loud and rambunctious group to do their rollicking routine.

A girl with a full arm sleeve of tattoos and a smashed-in nose called out BINGO! She kissed Baggans' cheek and ran up to collect her reward. Everyone, including Ki, was smiling. They were enjoying the present dual-sided comradery that resonated within their town's rugby association. Comradery in a brutal yet elegant sport, and camaraderie in a brutal yet elaborate cause for environmental change.

There were a couple more Bingo games before the bar had to close. The Golden Roster, Thomas, the rugby knuckle cracker and supplier of their fancy transport sprinter vans, won the last game of Bingo. Before accepting his reward, he pounded two beers at once, stacking them into a marvelous waterfall construct and leaving a face of awe and dismay on the bartender behind him.

"Who's driving the Roster's van to the club house?" Baggans asked the group. When everyone giggled instead of volunteering, Sheriff Worden spoke up.

"I'll drive the bunch of yas." The Peace Officer seemed to dedicate himself to the rugby club as much as he did to the Sheriff's Department. He was loyal, noble, smart, and tenacious, and because of men like him, Ki always had two plans during these secret operation meetings. One plan was for the good people that were just too good, and one plan was for the troubled, the people that really had an issue with the society they lived in and would do bad things for good effects.

The bump bump in the party van raised spirits and woke people up out of their beer commas. Tinted windows secured the club like atmosphere for transport to the Club House, which was also known as the Fish Tank, in the rich part of town where Fish lived. Fish always had other rugby nomads and foreign players stay at the Club House, like the Aussie brothers for instance. There were several rooms, an ocean view, and a cozy family sized basement. The Club House kept the team tight, and when they were tight, they were strong.

Music thudded against all the walls in the Club House. The E.E.A, or otherwise known as the Grunion and Mermaids, spread throughout the house. The backyard, kitchen, and large living room were for the partiers, and the comfy den was for the philosophers and sleepers.

Baggans was asleep in a recliner while six other diehard environmentalists lounged on the three different couches. They rolled joints, scrolled through their cell phones on whatever eco-friendly event briefings were up and coming, or moved their tongues toward productive discussions.

One of the Mermaids was giving examples to Wino about things that offset Greenhouse gases. Doctor Kate Neilsly, the Geologist and usual medic on the scene, had three long cleat scratches up her thigh that definitely would turn into year-long scars. She brushed her short hair over her right ear and continued, never loosening a smile on her cute but stern and focused face.

"Sustainable forest management, destruction of high global warming potential gasses-" Ki liked her, she reminded him of his high school sweetheart Lexi, except for being a beast physically and a super mysterious superstar.

Ki finished his joint, popped it into his mouth and continued listening to bits and pieces of another Mermaid's environmental theories. The beer mixed with the weed was giving him choppy little mind swells.

"Planting more trees in populated areas- We'u Bop -will create a sky filter that captures and stores methane from- Shine! -animal manure or mine…" Jaclynn Poxer was an environmental scientist working her own angles in breaking the system. Changing the technological age to the zero age. Poxer also had Tourette's syndrome, and her moans and bleeps made everyone around her find her irresistible. Her friends would literally sweat at holding back the urge to pick her up and hug her like an adorable, sporadically cursing puppy.

"A zero waste storefront that incorporates student outreach field trips. This would help our youth discover the negative effects of -mmph- industry molds early on. The children could then, and only then, teach their parents. We-" Poxer squeezed her eyes shut and whistled like a tweety bird. "-Start at ground zero with age zero." Her shoulder curled to her chin and then instantly released, relieving her to keep stretching normally on the rug. Poxer's tics usually made her body tense up in an involuntary position or created an abrupt randomized vocalization. Most of the time when she was in the spotlight they would occur simultaneously.

Her curling blonde hair was tied back in a ponytail, revealing defined shoulders and hilly little muscles and veins bulging from her neck.

Baggans woke up for the end of Poxer's digest and grumbled, "Zero!"

The congenial watery eyes on Poxer shifted over to the entertainment of Baggans' revival. Zero has been Ki's nickname his entire life, but the Rugby team started calling him Zero on their own accord, and he always felt a little awkward around Poxer because she was so obsessed with the zero revolution. He frequently wondered if she was also obsessed with him just based on his nickname. Even though Poxer's numerous girlfriends reminded him she was just a badass lesbian biatch. She believed in zero bullshit and zero waste, and it really did seem like she was moving closer to a more legitimate resolution than Ki's plans of anarchy and chaos.

Wino, taking the role as the event scanner for tonight, went over to Baggans and blew a haze of smoke around him, settling him back into his recliner. The big prop retreated back to the couch and spread a leg over the armrest.

"So there are three main events going on this weekend. The big one is Trump's Environmentalist advocating for more offshore oil drilling this Saturda-"

Mokes cut in with his index finger embedded in the turtle tattoo on his neck. "That mofo is loaded with kabuki. That would be an easy one for us to protest."

Ki looked over at his island brother from another mother and Uka Buka triggered somewhat of a storm in his head. It was unlike Mokes to be so… outspoken.

Wino stretched out his jaw and continued, "This other event is pretty interesting as well. Tomorrow afternoon the Coastal Chumash Indians are displaying an ancient art of medicine collecting in recent wildfire burn areas. Rangers will be there along with a diplomat from the Governor's office. It seems there is a decision to be made on either cutting down the burnt forest or harvesting the grounds and cultivating the land so the trees can regrow properly. They are the true stewards of the forest and know when and how to burn forest foliage and trees so the fires don't get out of hand like they have been."

"I've heard of this before but have seen nothing on the news. How did you find out?" Ki was intent on his curiosity.

"Tawa told me in passing."

"Ah, yeah Tawa. Is she a Mermaid?"

Jaclynn Poxer, A.K.A Pinky Boxer responded from the den rug, her legs split as she stretched from one leg to the other.

"Tawa is a Coastal Chumash that hangs-" Poxer let out a moan tic that sounded like sex.

"-Around us because of the support we give to the biosphere, not rugby. But, I wish she'd join us. Mhmm." She lapped up the air while making a conscious sound of pleasurable fulfillment, then went back to her smirking meditative stretches.

"How many of us are available for this tomorrow?" Wino asked.

Bingo Night

As Safa, the Grunion Captain from South Africa, was talking about how he could possibly shoot up the mountain as soon as he was done with work, soft rhythmic tunes of music from upstairs drifted closer and closer. Good ol' Safa was always trying to be there for his mates even if it was way out of his way. He had short dark salt and pepper hair and a thin webster type body, but held a heavy metal background that made him a slim lovable badass.

The music reached the basement door and Boom! Came the melancholy Spanish angelic voice, Biig Piig, Perdida.

Fish came through with his boombox on his shoulder and serenely walked down the few steps singing with Biig Piig, "I just want to lay here… smoke my spliff, drink my wine. I think I just want to lay here… until my hurtings done."

The plastic water bottle they picked up early outside of Eureka hit the side of Fish's head and there was only one person in the direction it came, Baggans. Fish turned down the beats so they could continue their chit chat and he walked over to where Baggans was reclined with his eyes closed.

Doctor Neilsly started disclosing her Friday afternoon routine and the possibilities of making modifications in order to make it.

"What are we making?" Fish asked while he was poking Baggans in the chest and whispering, "Rally Bags, Rally."

Baggans backhanded him in the balls, just getting the tip of his fingers into contact. Fish dove for the reclined bear man, but Mokes grabbed Fish midair and sat him down.

"Just listen for a second," Mokes directed Fish with a smile and then passed the marijuana stick to him, his face pained and contorted.

Bchind the action, Uka Buka pulled out of the den shadows and was laughing in deep, entire face bobbing bellows. The ball flick got him gleefully bobbing, but the whole back and forth of physicality drew out an enormous, "Uka, BUKA!" Followed with more deep laughing bellows.

Ki looked around at each of his den mates, and no one moved a muscle at Uka Buka's guffaw. So he reverberated the events going on Friday and Saturday, and the room completed its acclimation of its new arrival. When Ki was about to ask Wino for the third event, Fish hastily tried to respond first, however only a burp of smoke came out.

"I'll go, I don't have to work tomorrow."

Then Baggans' deep voice tiptoed in, "I'll go too, it'll be a long lunch is all, no problemo."

"Zero, I'm guessing you are going too. No work tomorrow. Maybe we will pick up the slack on Sunday?" Fish was actually Ki's boss. He hired Ki into his Stone Masonry business pretty much right when Ki joined the Grunion. Fish usually hired all rugby players that needed work. Especially the foreigners.

"So it'll be the three of us. I'll talk with Lacy tomorrow morning for more information. She runs the feed store where I get ZooZa's food, and she is Coastal Chumash. The rest of you can organize protest signs and Ocean Relief banners for Saturday's debacle at the Reagan Center. The more people the better, so give everyone a heads up… What's the third event Wino?" Trevor was his real name, Wino however fit him perfectly, his suave intelligent demeanor and full voluptuous body.

"There is a Pollution Awareness Day Sunday. I believe volunteers are walking the beach to pick up trash and talk about how there is 270,000 tons of plastic in the ocean and how 8 million pieces of plastic find their way into the ocean every single day." Wino finished by pressing his spectacles hard up against his face with his index finger.

Safa was looking down at his phone, "I found something. William Barf is having a book signing for his new book release about Donold Dump. Dumping old Attorney General."

"Isn't his name William Barr?" Doctor Neilsly noted, always needing the correct information.

"Bingo." Safa replied with a too clever smirk.

"Where's it at?" Ki had his feet up on the table and slouched on one of the couches next to Safa. He was loosening up now, they had plans set and held wispy medicine in his lungs. His blue Grunion t-shirt revealed a ripped lower stomach above his green Volcom sweatpants.

"The Nixon Library in L.A"

Miwok Tribal Stewards

The grace of the place was serine. Every tree branch seemed to be a necessary limb in summoning the surrounding magic.

Ki lifted his chin above the one perfect limb of a tree that mimicked a pullup bar. His eyes were wet from the beauty of the transcending oak with many tentacle-like branches abreast sun rays shooting through the corner of its canopy leaves.

Letting go, the dirt around Ki's boots puffed out in a nova cloud of dust. No one ever came treading through this part of the park. It was so relieving to have an open part of the town with no one around. He soaked in the canopy above him and meditated on its energy. His mind racing through their roots, under the city, up the foothills, and into the mountains. He wanted to understand the old traditions of the native people but also knew the nipples of nature only truly nurtured the long bloodline of stewards. People that followed their ancestral religion as kin to nature. Trees as their brothers, flowers as their sisters, the sun as a father, and the moon as their grandmother, or whatever anthropomorphic identity they cherished.

Ki desperately wanted to be a part of this tribe. To practice traditions of loving what is blatantly alive in front of us. He wanted to build his totem and breathe Paganism, being Earth's templar knight, or maybe in a Pagan eye, a Rainbow Warrior.

Ki got a vibration in his pants and really started to believe the Natural Gods were calling to him, accepting him. Then another buzz came and he realized it was a text message from his phone.

Baggans, We pick you up in 30. Ki had to get going in order to make his pickup arrangement and have enough time to get a couple conversations in with the tribe members before they began their ceremonies and exhibited their knowledge in controlled wilderness burns.

The sprint back was always a chase to catch up with ZooZa.

Ki's doggy always kept a solid dozen paces ahead while they raced through the forest preserve by the sea cliffs. The dirt paths surrounded by overgrown brush benevolently reminded him of a grand exploration of evolving deja vu or a forbidden garden that shrouded itself from the consumptionous grasp of mankind. He would welcome friends to the piece of magical preserve he has found, just as long as they found gratitude for its being. Ki was sure most would. He touched under his left breast and felt refilled with hope and content.

The winding of the trail took them to an outlet on the main walking path by a wicked looking tree split by lightning. The main path led back to the entrance, then to the street, and finally to his mother's humble little green domed abode.

Baggans picked him up shortly after and they headed off to the top of the mountain range and into the national wilderness. Baggans' Cadillac Deville floated over the highway, bouncing through dips like a boat rocking over ocean swells. At first the drive was quiet, almost along an eerie roll. As if this drive was a transition point, an unconscious rift.

Something was changing in the cosmos that made the boys sit and eat it up.

Baggans lit up one of his Black & Milds and Fish lit up an old half joint he had to lick a hundred times to get the wrap just right. Ki sat in the middle of the backseat very very comfortable; the wind, the speed, the security of having two brutes in the front taking in their moment of chill. It was all a nice break of peace.

"Oy Z? What did Lacy have to say about.." Fish searched his mind for what they were doing, or how to explain it, "about whatever we are doing out here. How are we going to help the Native Tribe become the… ahhh, Stewards of the Forest again eh?"

"She said there will be other spectators in the forest as well, mostly Chumash, coastal and reservation alike. She told me the keen thing to do was just to watch and be another important witness of how the Natives walk amongst the forest compared to the leaf-stomping white man." Ki took a pause and watched the sea meet the land ten miles away and a couple thousand feet down. He inhaled. He exhaled. Warm wind blew in, over and about his face.

Fish's straggly dark hair blew around his little blue and green earth earring, and Baggans peered over his right shoulder to check on what Ki was doing. His hair was clean cut, front greased back and over, with buzzed sides and thick manly stumble for his beard.

"Lacy also told me the coastal and reservation natives do not particularly get along. One hundred and fifty inland tribe members near the Chumash Casino receive money from the government, while the thousand other Chumash tribe members don't. Some of them even have more tribal DNA than the reservation casino Chumash tribe members. With us just being there could neutralize certain situations. We are to keep the peace and focus on watching this guy, Dr. Don Hankins, a Plains Miwok fire expert.

"I also got some info from my mom Leia. Being a state ranger she told me about the Cultural Fire Practitioners here to revitalize cultural burning practices. In previous years they'd be shot or arrested for arson. The reality is that the old native way is much better than the modern prescribed control burns. Their ancestral bloodline concentrates on wildlife habitat improvement and fire hazard reduction burning, which will maximize biodiversity in the forest. Our forests now are in danger of uncontrolled wildfires that can be easily ignited with even a lightning strike into a dense population of old overgrown trees, burning up the roots and charring the soil of the forest's ecosystem. Leia said, one of the most diverse land ecosystems in the world was right here in California.

"Take a right here Bags… So these tribal native fires will allow the plants and trees to grow back quickly, more diversified and more resilient. The ecosystem then will be gifted with more native plants and wildlife, helping the creation of various fungi and floras regarding medicine, which also increases the richness of pollinators and plant-to-pollinator interactions in the ecosystem. That's what Lacy said," Ki giggled at his, that's what she said briefing.

"Her cousin's friend's tribe, the Ojibwe Culture, harvests blueberries, and the blueberry bushes love a nice fire cleanse every other season. We will see what Doctor Hanky is up to, but that is the gist of the tribal versus government pyrodiversity clash."

"You're not doing one of your weird poems right now are you? You better not, I'm driving." Baggans uttered lightly.

"Well Bags, lucky for you I think we've arrived." Fish jested.

Baggans pulled up to one of the only places to park, and unlucky for them, it was the closest spot to the conference. Fish got out of the Caddy and rubbed his stomach in a manner of hunger.

A small acre of land had been burnt with a charred stump for its centerpiece. The land was booming with mushrooms and crazy looking plants that were unrecognizable to the rugby boys. About twenty people were there and everyone kind of looked similar, but there were subtle identifiable differences based off of what Lacey, the Feed store lady told him. One of the groups of people were the reservation Chumash, distinguishable by their long hair, nice jackets, and fancy boots. The coastal Chumash were dressed a tad more casually, a few with short hair, and half seemed to have tattoos on their chins and necks. Then there was Dr. Hankins, a Miwok tribal member, three government officials, three firefighter chiefs, and a couple environmentalists by their earth tone clothes.

The boys were in the right place. They decided to split up so they didn't look like hooligans waiting for a fire show. They would possibly receive more information if divided anyways.

Ki, of course, meandered straight towards Dr. Hankins, and Baggans and Fish tripped over each other going the same way towards the Coastal Chumash pod.

"Go talk with those guys Bags." Fish pointed to the snobby, arrogant faces huddled together around a patch of fresh looking Rishi mushrooms.

"Nope, they don't want to talk to me."

"Well, give me a couple minutes with these guys then, eh bud." Fish twinked. You always knew Fishy was serious if there was a Twink.

Baggans drifted back towards his Cadillac to clean off the dashboard. He timelessly swiped the dash and left little clean streaks. He pinched at an old parking stub and then slid the non-sticky side of an old sticker off the dash ledge to fall in his palm. As he was reorganizing the shells and driftwood, a girl's voice spooked him to the point of honking the Cadillac horn with his elbow. Baggans looked up at the girl, then out the passenger window to wave out his apologies and that everything was alright. The looks outside were savagely stern, but luckily both Ki and Fish diverted their serious attention.

Ki helped nudge Doctor Hankins into meeting with the politicians and firefighters, and Fish showed off his totem tattoo. Relieved, Baggans sat back in the cold yet supremely comfortable Deville leather seat of his Cadillac and looked up at the girl with green and gold bands holding her long dark braid. She had high cheekbones, green and gold irises, plump lips and eyebrows kinked in a way that showed a humble intelligence with stubborn humor. Her shirt pocket had a trippy melting rainbow flower logo and her skin was bronze with no tattoos. Tawa Pawni was in her element.

"Hi, sorry to startle you. I'm Tawa. I know you three are with the Earth Enforcers Association. Is that why you came?" The question was pleasant coming from her tongue, she meant no disdain, she was only curious.

"Yeah, our friend Wino told us that you told him about the importance of today being a good example of expert land stewardship." Baggans waited to see how she ate his response, then continued when she still held a questioning stare.

"See over there next to the guy examining a mushroom, the Japanese guy with the swirl thing in his buzz cut, that's Ki, and he kinda started the Earth Enforcers Association." Bags thought of Ki's dulling humor, his lessening smile, his torn muscles and too often seen white knuckles. His speeches, talks and jokes, basically everything Ki did was for the environment.

"All his time is dedicated to helping the planet. We came here because we want to support the tribal way of forest preservation and intention for biodiversity. Advocate for your cultural burns and support you because we believe you guys always had it right; the belief in what surrounds us, instead of the common imaginative holy human stuff."

The girl Tawa looked happily amused and a little surprised, "What surrounds us?" She was enjoying playing with him, opening him up with a cute smile and as few words as possible.

Baggans lifted his hand to feel the breeze. His Hawaiian style shirt was undone to the belly button button. His flip flops flopped out in an angle and his shorts were high up on his thick thighs, it was the Baggans way.

"The wind, the heat from the sun, the water from a spring, the song of a bird." Baggans surprised himself with his instinctive response. Z's Poems finally got stuck in my head, he thought. The girl's natural presence opened Baggans up, freeing his mind to the simplest terms of living.

Tawa nodded, then pointed to the man who held the mushroom and was showing a display of eight different jars of soil.

"We call it cultural burns not only because it's been a part of our culture but because we are cultivating the land, birthing a Phoenix to revive the space in which we live. Right now Dr. Hankins is showing how quickly diverse things grow from nutritious soil after a cultural or controlled burn, however that's not the big picture. This land needs stewards who really take care of it regularly, not just watch over it as your rangers do." She looked at Baggans, waited, and finally decided to go more in-depth.

"When these forests grow over the summers with vegetation and foliage from broken branches or brush, they leave kindling, which can be the spark of massive fires that deal catastrophic damage. If you go another notch higher, trees absorb the carbon dioxide from your nuclear plants, millions of transportation devices, cattle, corporation mumbo jumbos. Our trees then absorb these Greenhouse gases, these atmospheric killers, and then when they burn…" Tawa was fired up.

Baggans had to look around to see if the others were watching their conversation. He felt like everyone should hear what she was telling him.

"All that stored carbon our magical guardian trees of life have gathered, becoming bigger and giving us good clean air, now goes right back into the atmosphere where the GHGs get stuck and heat up Earth, creating more unbalance, more fires and more depletion of the Ozone. Indubality a destructive cycle.

"Someone needs to start guarding the guardians. If not the indigenous people then someone else, but SOMETHING has to happen."

Tawa wiped at her forehead and lowered her voice back to the melancholy tune of which she started.

"That is what Dr. Hankins is really getting at over there, and we are pretty sure the state officials are beginning to get the picture. However, the illustration is nowhere close to as clear as it needs to be."

Ki walked over to Fish, who stood near the coastal Chumash. They watched the officials and Doctor Hankins as the three environmentalists asked their questions involving the experimental charred acre.

"You guys should come to this festival we are having tonight. It'll be good for you. All of you." Tawa smiled and gave Baggans the directions.

After the questions and the main event began to conclude, the boys walked up smiling and interested in what Baggans got himself into.

"Hello Tawa." Ki said respectfully.

She nodded her greeting, "I was telling your friend Baggans about the stewarding agreement we are trying to uphold."

"Agreement with who?" Fish asked smiling, while stretching his back in a crouched position.

"Agreement with Earth," Tawa swept her hand in a semi-circle across her midsection…

After a thoughtful pause, she then marked Doctor Hankins with her gold, green eyes.

"My Uncle probably drilled everyone with ecological diversity, propagation for medicinal plants, improved soil quality, improved grazing for horses and cattle, and risk reduction policies of catastrophic wildfires?" Tawa's questioning smile was directed at Ki.

"Yes, along with cracking a couple jokes about what the reservation Chumash are wearing. You must be proud of your Uncle. He does seem to be taking care of our Mother."

Tawa nodded with pride, then reverted to what the future held. "I was also telling dear Baggans that there is an Element Festival happening further into the mountain. It'd be great if you guys could come?" Another question of hers that was filled with cuteness. The funny smile, lifted shoulders and open arms really sold the invitation.

Fish had both hands on his midsection now. "If there's food, we are there baby."

Elemental Festival

Uka Buka floated in the backseat with his head out the window, eyes wide, mouth wet with slobber, tongue dangling out. Just a floating mask. A gargoylic spirit of humanization. Ki blinked twice to clear the fog out of his ears while they drove deeper into the mountains.

Fish was looking back at Ki. "Yo Z what do you have to eat man, I'm starving."

"Let's go straight to the Festival, they'll have good food there."

"Ya, but we have to wait till nightfall to sneak in, which is like another hour away."

Ki rummaged through his backpack and found a couple oranges and an avocado. He rolled them over Fish's left shoulder and they fell right into his lap.

"That will hold you over. Listen Fish, Baggans you too…" Ki looked back at Uka Buka. The tiki face returned his gaze, tongue swirling in helix rotations. Within seconds, Uka Buka unexpectedly blitzed forward with a loud grumbled chant, where all the letters formed into one splurged grunt, 'UKA BUKA!' And the tiki spirit went straight into Ki.

"Whoa dude, you alright, maybe you should take one of these oranges." Fish lobbed an orange over his shoulder for Ki to catch. Ki realized he jerked hard as Uka Buka charged into him, and he saw Fish's eyes looking at him warily in the rearview mirror.

"Ya, thanks… I probably do need an immunity boost." He began peeling and wondering about these tiki spirits. Can Uka Buka control me from the inside? Ki didn't feel any different. He wondered if Uka just spirited through him. Where was Toko Tuki? Tuki was tattooed on his skin and embedded in his heart. Uka wasn't even a ghastly essence; he just seemed like a solid chunk of hardwood that spontaneously did as it pleased. No transparencies, no magical wisps of air trailing Uka's comings and goings, just a piece of floating bark.

Ki accepted Uka Buka's presence at this point, especially journeying back so close to where he had first found him. Uka Buka made himself more prominent around the Mountain. If Ki hadn't felt so uncontrollably destructive when Uka was around, he'd probably cherish the time spent with the spirit companion.

Ki needed a distraction from Uka Buka and now was not the time for it to be weirdly charging into him.

Ki's distraction of course, was his madness. "So let's consider food. Most of the food we eat is fucking Bull Cocky boys. Let's start with the hamburgers, beef. The massive cattle bins, cattle ranches, or whatever it's called when cows are side to side most of their lives until they head over to the slaughterhouse." Baggans and Fish's faces were twisted and uncomfortable, yet nodding in acknowledging another Ki lesson.

Ki went on. "Well that bull shit inhumane raising isn't even the half of it. The abundance of cattle grazing murders the ozone. Cows have four stomachs, and inside one of those stomachs is fermenting grass or whatever they feed them. All day that stomach ferments and all day that cow burps, creating methane gas. The reason there is an overpopulation of cows is that there is an overpopulation of beef-eating fucks that can't eat one vegetarian dinner to save their life!"

They were driving on backroads, and there were cattle everywhere, but they had acres of room. The grazing here was beneficial to the environment. It's when corporations create a cow Hell. That's when the knife should spear directly into the greedy executive's brain that thought of the demonic idea. But of course, it's necessary; again, we need to look after our lazy ass population and feed the fat fucks that leave no beneficial mark on this planet in the first place.

"So fuck any place that burns through fifty cows a day. FUCK THAT... Then there's fucking Palm Oil. You boys still listening?" Fish and Baggans nodded and continued nodding, and looked at each other nodding, and then snickered.

"You da mentor man. I'm just as pissed off at big corporations rapping the planet as the next green bean, but I don't know shit... Actually the more I learn the more pissed I get... and the more not hungry I become..." Fish took a bite of the orange and the juice sprayed out in front of him.

As if the squirt reminded Ki of something he reverberated with conversation, he continued. "Most food, especially snacks and junk is made with Palm Oil. The Palm Oil Industry, mostly in Indonesia, intentionally burns their forest for veggie oil profits. As we just heard from Doctor Hankins, a tree on fire releases all the CO2 that tree has been storing over its entire life. So not only are these guys wacking their forest off, they are wacking the ozone too. The locals are just doing as they are told and trying to survive, but the higher ups… those are the wicked ones…"

Ki paused and studied the backside of his friend's heads. "Guys, seriously… Thank you. There are so many people that either don't get it or don't fucking want to, and that is exactly why I'm fucking pissed off all the time and this damn Uka Buka is frea-"

Baggans only moved his eyes towards Fish, and Fish scratched at his dome. "Uka Buka, like the little guardian guy in Crash Bandi-coot?"

The buzzed head, squinty eyed, scared browed Ki couldn't seem delusional in front of his top believers, his Smasher and Basher. He wondered if his mentality was eating at his appearance, or was his rough appearance just a part of his mentality? Both were frightening, but maybe not so frightening for fellow Ruggers.

Luckily, he did know of Bandicoot's guardian, Aku Aku. "Ya, I can't get past a boss and it's driving me nuts." Ki sat back and took a breath. He had to take a chill pill. The trees bled together as one blur. That's what the Uka Buka was, a forest elemental. The wooden petri-fied face, the leafy hair, and deep horizontal lenticels slashed random-ly across his face like thousand year scars.

Fish triumphantly noted to Ki, "Well hit me up next time, because I am a badass boss killa brah!"

"Looks like this is the place." Baggans pulled over and parked in high reeds on the side of the road behind a wide oak tree. Fish's hand was playing in the reeds outside his window, reminding Ki of when he did acid and parked in fogged over high reeds, feeling the truck's engine purr like a warm stalking beast, feeling the ecstasy of life through the mist and the grass. The balance of temperatures between the cold air and the warm motor.

"Hey, we should do some mushrooms or something. It is a festi-val…"

Fish looked around at his mate's faces, but they only held stares and empty shrugs. "Alright, weed will suffice. Bags you sure this is it? I didn't see a sign, any vehicles, nothing."

Baggans was cutting open the avocado and peering up at the twilight sky. "This is where Tawa said to go lil Fishy." He handed Fish a big slice of avocado on his knife.

"Why don't you roll us all a joint for inside, then we will find our way in.

***

It was dark when they tiptoed through the heavy brush on the steep hillside right under the noses of the gate vendors. When the three husky mid-twenty year old males made it into the parking lot, they stood up straight. They walked towards the music that bumped in the valley under the hill they were on. Their eyes wandered the treetops where a rainbowocracy of laser lights rhythmically swayed through their leafy canopies.

A group of people gathered around a pitch black large cylindrical shape pointed to the stars, and a girl called out to Fish, "Hey, you want to look at Jupiter, it's really magical." Her voice was sweet, loving, and as genuine as a freshly birthed soul.

Fish turned to Ki and Baggans, "I'm going to hang with the Jups for a while. Where in this fairyland do I find you guys again?" Fish's eye twinked harder than usual, closing longer and with more grit, then opening with sparks twinkling.

"The fire realm," Baggans said while tossing Fish a bic lighter with an Astronaut cover.

Beyond the telescope was a lit-up pathway that meandered down a long, steep hill into the valley of music and lights. The hearts of Baggans' and Ki's picked up speed and their eyes widened, trying to soak in as much of this elemental fun fest as possible.

Once down in the valley, the layout and abundance of art decorating the forest surprised them. They anticipated an arena of dancing Native Americans and pow-wow chants, surrounded by engulfed totems holding immense historical power. Yet this festival seemed like it was put on for all woodland spirits, open hearts, and free wills; people that love one another just as much as they love the planet. Integral Compassion. Brilliance in the rainbowocracy of elemental nobility. This was where the walking spirits worshiped the flowing elementals.

As they strolled along the paths and split alleyways, they found fountains of water recycling over smooth intricate rocks of earth. Swooshes of air spinning, dancing, rippling over beautiful hanging tapestries that created comfy enclaves open to all campers. There were open tents with multitudes of pillows and blankets sprawled out and awaiting a relaxing soul. Tree branches were used as frames into other elemental realms. While lights were used as portals into different areas. Some places under the forests were dark with hidden rooted treasures, and some places were lit up as bright as day for a gauntlet of pleasures. One of these places was… the Fire Realm.

By this time, without drugs or elixirs, Ki and Baggans felt full of energy, full of lucid ecstasy. It was like Ki's dreamland, an orgy of good people in between nature's lips. The two broad shouldered fellows stood in awe in front of the Fire Realm, where an old, completely open firetruck embellished craned nymph swings on either end of itself. Jetting high above the top patio was a flamethrower that blew out flames whenever the fire gods fixed for more heat. The gut of the truck had an open bar with stools along the side, distinguishable as a fire bar.

Baggans lipped, WOW, and Ki slowly turned him around. The sound coming from that main stage was so euphonious. Their shoulders dropped and swagged as their feet slid their bodies into the crowd. Flags and banners were scattered around the stage grounds as group locators for friends to find friends or shy hearts to find a zone that fit their frequency.

Under the wavering skull and crossbones, Ki and Baggans resided. They danced, watched the fire dancers, hugged each other's shoulders, smoked one of Fish's joints and grounded themselves into the earth under the stars, basking in the simple bliss of being alive. The flag over head swung back and forth, tattered and worn, sun grayed and frayed.

When Random Rab's set was finished, they laughed around the rainbow-lit jugglers and meandered once more to the Fire Realm, even more in reverence after the connection between music and place.

"I have to take a piss before going in there." Baggans ran off, and Ki stayed and wandered over to the Waste Zone.

There was compost for organic material and a recycling bin that held clean plastic bottles and containers. Ki swiped his nose at the site. The waste bin only held wrappers, face masks, and a couple apple cores. Ki pulled the apple cores out and put them into the compost. It was nice to see an empty waste bin, an organized recycling and a full compost bin. Ki breathed, relieved of the gratified land, then suddenly jumped as the fire bar spit out flames, roaring into the air.

"I'm back," Baggans pranced up to Ki's side, "Did you have to go?"

"I already went."

"Where, When?"

"Now, in my pants." Baggans looked down at Ki's beige pants, and Ki punched him in the shoulder laughing. "I don't have to go. I must need some more water." Ki pointed to the fire bar and moved Baggans in that direction. The place where fire ignites the blood and water soothes the body.

They grabbed a couple stools on the end and sat in front of hot water dispensers and intricate bowls of tea bags. "Ah, we need cups," Baggan's thick forearms lay defeated on the bar top while Ki produced his metal cup from his belt.

"We will share," They both smiled, drank, and talked of their previous journeys, searching for a time that came close to anything like this, an Elemental Fun Fest.

The tea mellowed them out even more than the marijuana, and they jumped down from the fire bar and drifted into low drooping tree limbs where lights secured a path through a darkened gate of a shrouded patch of greenery. Once they passed under the limbs, the energy completely changed from plasma jets roaring out of decorated cylinders to tiki torches lining a dirt pathway. At the end of it was a grand Willow tree sheltering a half dome of metal poles triangulated together, covered in tapestries and trinkets. The smell of gasoline faded into a flowery incense that could pull any nomadic nose into stability and hermithood.

Ki remembered the Willow tree that resided out of his fourth grade classroom. That tree helped him choose a poetic path instead of a life of deserted exile, a life of blood for blood. Maybe he'd thank this tree for the endowment of the last.

The upbeat music faded from the main Fire Realm area to melodic eastern brass tones with an angelic voice humming in Mongolian. The Willow tree hid the band from the stars. Benches lined the perimeter with more cozy pillows and blankets that covered the ground where people stretched and talked.

Hanging between the colorful multi designed tapestries on the dome poles were highways of fairy lights and a beautiful dream web at the dome's inner apex. Potions and vials were lined up on little wooden shelves, coupled with potted succulents and herbs. At the very far end, directly across from the entryway, were four people; two of them seemed like they represented the King and Queen of the Willow grounds. The King blew his saxophone in a way that set the relaxing mood as well as expressed his feelings. The Queen sang gently in her ancient Steppe dialect. A lean faced Hawaiian guy situated himself close by. He was tall, had long dark hair, and wore a tank top, which revealed ripped muscles that fit his intense, strict face; an odd face to see in a place like this. And finally, Tawa. She stood next to the lean Hawaiian and turned to look across the open Willow space, waving Ki and Baggans over to them.

The gold rimmed rainbow lenses of Tawa's circular steampunk glasses reflected the Willow encapsulating Ki and Baggans as they walked up. Tawa introduced them, "Colin, this is Baggans of the Shire, and Ki of Midworld. Baggans, Ki, this is Colin Richardson, the compost cultivator and mycelium expeditor. Angela, the ear of philosophy and weaver of elemental realms, and finally Lowrey, a mushroom farmer in the medicine lands of the Cali, Oregon border."

They nodded their hellos and Colin put his saxophone down to his side. Colin's blonde hair was receding, his chin was strong, and his eyes were bright blue.

"So we have a hobbit on vacation and a Japanese gunslinger that matches Lowrey's angry chin." The girls laughed, but the guys stood around trying to gauge Colin's character.

"Guys it's okay, we are all brothers here. Especially if you two are devoted to the planet's wellbeing. Tawa told me you came to the Cultural Burn site in search of a way to help. Well, I have just the thing for you…" Colin stood up and put his hands on the guest's shoulders.

"Let's venture to the Water Realm; I feel too much heat here. Let us cool down with aquatic chillwaggery."

They traveled as a party of six for a while, then Tawa pulled in two more of her girlfriends and Lowrey went off to the edge of the Water Realm to chat amongst a larger group.

Bubbly wet sounds cushioned the rest of the group's heads as if a mermaid cuddled you into her bosom and swam you to her underwater cabin. There were at least a dozen fish tanks varying in size outside and in front of the centralized tipis, and two girls and a guy were the only other occupants in the area. One of the girls had her hair in twirly buns and was juggling a purple, blue, and green ball while conversing with the healthy looking dude with moccasins and a frayed sleeve cotton T with twine lace ties in his V cut.

Ki's eyes drifted from the hypnotic fountain of juggling balls to the colorfully lit up trees behind them. Terror softened within his bones as the sudden reverence of seeing Uka Buka came over him. It was amazing to see such a spirit camouflage itself amongst an array of colors as well as its natural habitat. A spirit watching life go by. Watching with a chilling flat stare, wooden planked face interspersed within the tree's foliage, colors wavering against its ridgelines. Amazing how he, a regular human, could even see a spirit, an actual natural spirit from Mother Earth. Uka Buka might have been terrifying, but the whole conception of him was truly beautiful. Ki couldn't help but revere… him. He had been wondering where Uka got off to when he couldn't see him. Was it possible Uka was usually concealed somewhere, somehow, just watching. More frightening thoughts made his eyes unglued from the mask in the tree and drifted back to his present situation.

Colin sat crossing his legs in the corner of one of the open tipis filled with heaps of pillows and ground blankets. Angela went for tea with the girls and Ki and Baggans sat with Colin.

Colin's blue eyes watched Ki's green. "I know who you are, Ki. You are the guy that got into fist fights at school because someone put their banana peel in your idolized recycling bins."

"I sensed encroaching darkness within them. So fuck 'em. Also I never swung, it probably just seemed like I did by the exaggerated way they reacted to my challenge."

"Exactly. Exactly why I respected you; however, I'm sure we still see things very differently."

Ki gave a questioning eyebrow raise, and Colin continued. "I believe we should set good examples by doing the best we can do individually. I live off the land, I try to incorporate sustainable living and gardening into schools and youth programs. I work with the soil, I grow my own food, I don't buy into any consumer materials, I have a good life. I set an example that I hope others will follow, I do my part to help the planet without bothering others. You.." Colin chuckled and glanced between Ki and Baggans.

"You shove climate change down people's throats, you're chaotic, like an environment thug, instead of peaceful protest your mind goes straight to destruction and violence. Instead of being patient, you try to swim upstream. You don't believe in people. Instead of a green thumb, you are cursed with red, the color of fire and blood."

Baggans looked over at Ki, and unexpectedly saw that he was calm and content. Ki nodded, his palms upright on his knees, "Yeah, that fits my description… In order to battle wickedness, good needs mean warriors of their own. Otherwise, evil powers will walk all over the world, stomp us into the ground, and use us to fuel their machines that pump out more and more harmful emissions every day. I will not sit in my self-righteous wallow and watch the planet literally burn. I'd rather burn those fucks to the ground first. Maybe once they are stopped, all their consumer fuck lemmings, all those fat lard people that have zero worth, zero thought, zero compassion, will die with them. If I go to Hell for the better good, then so be it."

"Well Ki, it sounds like a long and hateful road. I mean, you and yours could help Angela with advising her clients in zero waste lifestyles. I hear Jaclynn Poxer is very involved as well, a Mermaid rugby player attached to the Earth Enforcers Association, as well as opening up her own zero waste refill store, that is impressive. Hopefully, she will join us in inviting field trips to our farms and her new sustainable store so the kids can soak in the correct way to grow and preserve at an early age. They could possibly teach their parents the right path. We are progressin-"

"Not fast enough. Listen, I don't know how I'm going to make the world a better place, but I do know that I want to be more of a force to be reckoned with instead of a fly buzzing in an elephant's ear. I want to be a tsunami that washes this filth off our globe. Politicians are getting worse and more corrupt. Small changes in the 90s and early 2000s are being undone or reversed. The darkness is eclipsing our Mother."

Tawa and her friends came back and sat next to them. They lounged and giggled, stretched out and tinkered with their toys and trinkets.

"Okay, well." Colin smiled at the girls and turned to focus back on Ki.

"Enjoying life for what it is and what we have is always an open road… I have something for you and yours that'll better suit you than I. Our town's waste and landfill organization is run by an old mobster family, the Zendolini's. The 'Zen' Waste Industries has the largest contract in the city, and every year they can renegotiate more of our city's money because no competitor can stand against them. Zen Waste Industries owns this city, and there is much more to manage and distribute than they care to do.

"The fastest way to solve Ellipsis' waste problems is to create a sister organization with the Zendolini's. I already have a non-profit that collects compost from some schools and a few restaurants. We and ours use that to propagate our local gardens with enriched soil, reducing methane emissions from landfills and creating a sustainable, reusable system. If we had the town backing us under the brotherly arm of Zen Waste Industries we could compost the whole town.

"You might have a more direct compromise or compelling arrangement than I had for Mr. Zendolini… You have the E.E.A and rugby team that could be good influencers for the Zens to join with us. If you at least try to help us I'll give you a snidbit of information that could… entertain you and yours. It has something to do with officials voting on the Oil Rig removal operations two Tuesdays from now, and they won't be voting in ordinance. Can. You. Believe. It?" For the first time the ambiance was still. It revolved like hush'quilty, pursing lips of silence.

Ki slowly put his words together, "This isn't some movie we are pretending to be the protagonists in. You want, what I want, or as you put it, You and yours want what I and mine want. I'll talk to the Zendolinis."

Tawa put her hand out. Again, in the reflection of her rainbow steampunk glasses, there lay two coconut milk chocolates shaped like mushrooms lying on a note. Ki saw that the note had a name, address, and time written on it. Her fingers were inches from his chest. Her fragrance blossomed in Baggans' dome. His stomach tying knot after knot...

The juggling girl with twirly buns uncovered her Hydraulophone tuned at a very low pitch and jangled her fingers over the holes pouring out water, falling at extended depths for louder sounding drips drops and plops. The beat was slow, almost sad… and very dark.

"Lastly, come to one of my gigs, unwind and enjoy yourself. A little R & R. The location is a great top notch hotel. We play by the pool and live El Grande." Colin giggled and twirled a blue light stick around his index finger, then whimsically another spinny time elapsing light manifested, trickery rotating amongst his appendages.

Ki was wondering about R & R. He always thought of it as rugby and rocks, but in this case, it must have been to rest and relax… There was no time for that.

"Enjoy Tawa's chocolate mushrooms. They'll increase the connection between you and the elements." Colin winked.

"I wish Tawa could have told me that." Baggans said blushing, finally seeming like the work was over and the fun was about to begin.

Ki popped the mushroom up in the air and it fell into his shark snap and he gobbled it up.

Baggans tossed his in the air and it landed right on his wide red tongue. He peered at it looking down from his wide and previously broken smashdom of a nose. He was the Smasher to Fish's Basher. He pulled it in like a big Hawaiian frog. Haolle boii.

Ki lit up his joint and smoked casually, always tightly squinting when inhaling. "Thank You," he said as he patted Colin's shoulder and smiled, transforming the pat into a slight massaging rub on the back of his neck.

Ki picked himself up and took another drag off his joint. His back crunched and cracked as he stretched in a corkscrew manner. The stars overhead were bright twinkles winking at them in their good grace.

Ki easily made his way over to the largest fish tank to melt away. To try and slip his mind into the fluid ebbs and flows of a small ecosystem. It eased him, the smoke eased him as well.

As he watched the fishes swim in and out of their cute little huts and reefs, a big eye glowed behind the glass of someone else watching the fishies on the other side. Ki discretely rose above the tank and found Fish shoveling a spoonful of fried rice into Baggans mouth.

Asagaio

The morning after the festival Ki made it to his moms. He lay exhausted on the couch with four differently spread pieces of toast. He munched with his eyes closed. A little rest and relaxation.

"Morning hun," His mom entered the room, seemingly amused at her son's exhaustion on a Saturday morning.

"Heyo Mom, I'm just taking a snooze. I have a rally I need to…" Ki gave up as if talking took just a little too much energy. "I have a rally at noon."

Being a mom, Leia knew how her son was feeling. The early morning held heat and later it would just get more hot. She was afraid when temperatures rose it would be Ki that burned too hot amongst the population. Leia stole the buttered jam toast and took a bite.

"Ki, why don't you lay still while I tell you a story." Her hair hung long and loose over her shoulder, the blue tint strip in her brunette hair took ten years off of her actual age. She soothed his chest with her palm, then gave him a couple pats and she began.

"There was a man in Japan who worked for the Kiza Club, which was more like a violent gang. A subdivision of Yakuza." Ki opened one hazy eye in surprise, then closed it again with his ears perked.

"They did horrible things, however, there were many platforms of operation, making some gang members worse than others. This man, your father, Asagaio, believed he could use the Kiza's strength in numbers to help the planet's wellbeing. He never refuted the drugs, money laundering, or gang brutality. He just wanted to use those soldiers to fight for something righteous and honorable… eventually. Asagaio had a group of guys he worked with and preached to. He spoke of the old Shinto beliefs of Natural Gods and Animist cultures. Everything, whether a leaf or a rock, was alive. Everything on the land or in the sea should be recognized and therefore cared for on some plain of consciousness.

"His crews were Kiza collectors. Trusted to go into shops to collect the Kiza tax for doing business in their area. One of those shops was a florist who made very little money, but Asagaio had a keen eye for the place. Whether it was the flowers and his deep love for natural things, or because I worked behind the counter that Summer…"

***

Asagaio slowly shifted from flower to flower, checking their stems and petals, even kneading the soil in search of a bulging root. His yellow eyes strayed off of four rows of potted sunflowers, gathering their sun from the afternoon rays shining through the wide ceiling windows overhead, and focused in on the girl tending the bouquets near the cash register. Less enthusiastically, he watched the door where three of his guys sat on their hunches rolling dice. His partner, Sokuru, leaned on the doorway, watching what passed by on the street.

The slow pace of examining each flower made the Earth seem to turn slower on her axis. Like it was a day that could last a lifetime. Where a meditative choice was crucial in the discovery of a blooming destiny.

The actual Florist was an old Japanese lady whose husband was close friends with Leia's father from World War Two. A friendship created in a P.O.W camp on the tail end of the war. Leia, being raised as a Californian lass, finished high school and wanted to explore the island of Japan, which shared currents with her ocean and memories of her recently deceased father. She made the trip over, found the old Florist, which led to the care of the flower shop with only one grand rule. Pay the man with golden eyes and flower tattoos circling his neck.

"Hi," Asagaio blushed, and the inked flowers ballooned as he took a big gulp. "Is there the ol' lady around?"

Leia smiled, set down the bouquet, and rounded the cashbox.

"I'm the old lady for today."

With the rainbow of colors and natural fragrances of the planet, formalities seemed like a joke. Everything was with ease. Leia never felt a tinge of danger or pressure. She might even deny the flower necked man his money as a way to play around and keep him there for a while longer.

"Your skin shows youth, it must be your surroundings ol' lady, cause you look wonderful. Have you, watching ol' western films lately?" They giggled at his serpentine way of speech and rough English dialect. Asagaio picked up her bouquet and held it unconsciously under his chin, creating a three dimensional center piece from his neck art. The image of his seemingly floating head in a sea of flowers gave her the chills.

"My name is Leia."

"My name, Asagaio," Their eyes locked into each other, with no worries or apprehensions. A moment later one of Asagaio's fellows entered and came up to his ear.

"Heya As…" The rest was said in their Japanese language, and while listening, Asagaio never stopped looking into Leia's green eyes.

His smile increased, "I have to go, may I take flower for the road?"

"Yes, Yes of course, do you want anything else?" Leia opened the cashbox, and quick as a goose, Asagaio's hand was on hers.

"No, just the flower Leia. Have nice day."

The next couple of weeks Leia dreamed of flowers shouldering Asagaio's head. They continued their long flowery flirtatious relationship in the nursery and Asagaio continued to wave off the money. Until the novelty of the situation piqued Leia's curiosity.

"Asagaio, what is your business here? Why don't you take the money that the Old Lady has set aside for you?"

"Because you are here, Leia," Asagaio's remark made Leia blush again for the fiftieth time this week. He loved her rosy cheeks as much as he loved Japanese Cherry Blossoms.

"Since you are new, first I need make sure these flowers are well taken care of. The money is to show faith to the Kiza, we have different fluidities than yours."

The pink in Leia's cheeks soaked out into a whitish sickly look. She remembered there being way too much blood in movies with the Yakuza. So much so that she couldn't watch the entire film. Kiza was just another sect of Yakuza. Ugly questions cycloned through her brain.

"Don't worry Leia, you are in no danger. You have done well with the nursery. And besides, we are different kind of Gyangu than you think." The air flushed with a whiff of lavender as the door sprang open with a new customer. Leia looked down at a rubberband she spun around and around her thumb.

"Let me show you. The nursery is closed Sunday. May I take you to my cherished spirit land then?" Asagaio's voice was sweet yet rugged like his throat had been burnt on the inside. Leia knew she'd be okay on this Sunday venture, but she was hesitant about going down this path with a Kiza member. Would she be okay on the next venture? Could she even deny him now?

"I'll go with you, but I have to be home before dark."

That Sunday Asagaio and Leia took a four hour drive out to Mount Fuji-san. The old lady's nursery was in Ena, Gifu on the fringe of Nagoya City. As they got closer to Fuji, the snow capped active volcanic mountain revealed itself and Leia started to see the signs of the Kami Spirits origination. The good and the evil spirits share interconnected energy with the universe and are camouflaged forces of nature within our planet.

"Our Kami Spirit's Shrine is surrounded by acres of Shibazakura flowers." The Shrine peaked out from under three bonsai looking maple trees with orange to red leaves. Mount Fuji rose behind the trees as a perfectly formed volcano with a snowy peak. Leia crouched and brushed her hand across the purple, pink, white, and blue Shibazakura flowers running as far as her eye could see, surrounding the base of the mountain. She felt her eyes swell.

Asagaio's light brown hair was beautifully tied in a topknot. His hair slightly blowing in the breeze as he spoke of the epic Volcano and the spirits that guard the land. He spoke until the sun set and added another blast of color as it fell behind the snowy mountain and brightened the flowery hues. His stone chiseled face held more shadows throughout its edging as the light fell and colors flourished.

***

"This was when-" Ki's eyes popped open as he interrupted, "That was when you two fell in love. Mom, why haven't you told me more about Asagaio before?" His hesitation was calculating. Calculating the times he's even talked about his father, let alone zero times ever seeing him.

"You never asked." She smiled in the heat of her outrageous answer.

"I'll tell you now, just listen." She was sharp now, mission ready, chest high and shoulders back. She sat how a guardian of the forest would sit. The ranger and steward of their holy lands.

"I'll fast forward. He brought me to the most beautiful places in

Japan for over a year. And mostly we went into Ise-Shima National Forest, where most likely, you were conceived under a waterfall."

Ki grimaced. His eyes were open now ready to soak in his legacy, but not quite ready for that illustration.

Leia laughed and then switched back to her stern and dilated storytelling.

"Throughout our first year together I soon fully understood your father and what drove him. He was a Kiza gang affiliate but his ambitions were for the land not himself, which soon became very dangerous for him and I. He believed he could use some of his gang members to do his bidding. If he said the right words in the right ears and calculated the correct job at the perfect spot, two things would get accomplished. One for Asagaio's secret agenda and one for Kiza's. But things never go as planned…"

Ki began a low growl as his mother pondered the past. "What went wrong? What was he doing to fight for the land and better his people? What Leia? I need to know."

"Ki, slow your roll Honey. You know how I don't like it when you push me." Ki fell back onto the couch and gave a cross-armed allowance for his mother to proceed.

"Your father believed the Kiza could be shifted into doing good deeds and helpful environmental actions, but every time he tried… things just got worse and worse. The gangsters thrived because of the aqueduct of blood that filled their wallets. Asagaio tried everything, from helping his crew's families to punishing fools unaware of their critical impact on nature and her kin. The punishment he dealt out was so severe that I believe it ultimately put a target on his back.

"Asagaio wanted to clean up the whalers in Taiji Bay. Guys that trapped dolphins, whales, and pretty much anything that was wet and had meat on it, were about to be on your father's hit list. Your father planned all drug deals and Kiza transactions there in Taiji Bay. Local pubs, restaurants, and anywhere Whalers tended to hang out. As soon as these transactions ended, he and his molded group of Kiza would have a couple drinks and Asagaio's hidden agenda would roll into effect. He told me a couple of sly, disrespectful remarks were all it took to get the salty harpooners ready to swing. In his eyes, the righteous act of knocking the teeth out of whale killing dolphin murderers was accepted in natural divinity and the Kami.

"His men, however, took it one step further. They hunted people just as easily as Whalers hunted whales. Regardless of what was done to initiate the fight, if anyone raised a hand to Kiza boss, Asagaio, it was the end for them. The brutality in the way the Whaler's killed whales was threefold in Asagaio's violence towards them. Asagaio was a good man, but I watched him transform. He began to believe that ending the Whalers was the only way for Japan to become a true global leader in environmental wellbeing. He couldn't protest to the Chiji or Governor because they wouldn't listen to a tatted-up brute. The easiest way to get what he wanted was through bloodshed.

"Then of course, the red river caught up to him. One of his top guys and closest friends, Sokuru didn't like what Asagaio was doing because it slowed down the money flow and began to create too many problems in the Bay. So Sokuru went to the Yakuza Elders."

Leia slowed the story down. Remembering her past with Asagaio was like wading against a heavy current, fighting back tears and focusing on each word to finish a sentence, struggling with the emotions that each word held. The remembrance of pain.

"Ichifuku Cafe was a beautiful dinner spot Asagaio and I used to go to. The owners were friendly, the scenery was exquisite, and it was close to the Ena's red bridge that crossed the Agi River." A tear made its way down Ki's mother's cheek, but her voice held no quiver.

"When Sokuru came in, I could feel it. The darkness. There was no mistaking it. Two salty ocean type men followed him. Not dressed in Whaler regs, but they were half suited up like Kiza. Like they joined forces. Whalers to Kiza. Your father turned to me and said, 'leave Japan now my love. Take this Key.'

As he was getting up he handed me a skeleton key… It was a small knife that had a long swooping edge and a sharp point on the last key tooth. The bottom of the key was twisted metal that formed somewhat of a smooth hilt for grip…

"The last time I looked into his dialed yellow green eyes, they shown with focus and fulfillment of nobility. Then he turned away, pulled his other knife out and flung it right into one of the Whaler's necks. He picked up a chair next to him and pushed proud yet slithering Sokuru through the window. After that more Kiza surrounded him with glistening blades and boot heels…"

Leia took a long deep look into Ki's eyes. There was only silence. It was the song of the gaze. In Asagaio's final departure, his eyes became what she remembered most. Leia stared at Ki, deciphering whether Asagaio's blood truly ran through him. Was his anger savage like his? Or refurbished like hers? Although hard to see through his squinty driven eye sockets, Ki's eyes held violent yellow green sun flares scrolling around his pupils like his father's.

"I ran. Cut a man across his face with the skeleton key to escape through the back alley. They were on my heels, so I leapt off the Ena bridge and let the current finally sweep me away. I took a plane back home to California as soon as possible and had you 6 months later. "

Ki hugged his mother and watched the muscles in his forearms spiral around to his wrists. He pulled back with his hands on Leia's shoulders and asked.

"Do you have the key?"

Leia tugged at her long blue striped hair, usually tied in a braid. She peered down at the carpet. Lost in her thoughts, her past.

"Mom, did you hold onto the father's knife?"

"Yes…" She said in a whisper. "Well… no."

Ki's face contorted, but his compassion for his mother softened his tightening jaw.

"Where Mom?"

"I buried it in Japan. But I kept it in a way. By naming you after your father's last word."

Rigrun

The Paseo Plaza was historically preserved in a two block cluster. Where ancient Spanish adobes hunkered down in dusty desert yards, Tatooin fashion. On this Saturday, late April, there were around four hundred people crammed in these blocks.

The Trump Environmentalist Representative slash Environmental Protection Agency's Chief of Administration and his colleagues stood on stage with their fingers up their bums, seeming like they didn't notice the banners and picket signs waving over angry faces. The representatives colored themselves up like the American flag because they believe in what America stands for. Go Capital-Consumeristic Patriotism!

Sitting in four chairs to the backside of the stage was the Offshore Oil Representatives and Ocean Energy Management staff. A name which was simply a decoy for oil corporations to seem more oceanic and green friendly.

No reason to worry everybody! We, the representatives of World Rape, follow a leader, a president even, embedded into a path of ruining anything that could help the planet! Enhancing everything that can harm the planet! More harm, more money. More money, more power. More power, more me!

A sign amongst the earth toned protesters read, 'If only \$Benjamins\$ were obtained by sustainability and developing ways that saved the environment, weak and shitty people would be poor while grateful loving people would be rich!'

This particular sign eventually pressed itself into the face of a pro-ocean oil drilling politician. The man sauntered back like an Abercrombie and Fitch model, laughing off the sign slammed into his face. The other politicians and oil representatives standing with him all had their shades on and chins up, talking between themselves, talking most likely about the Paseo's savagery. Ohh and historically they were right. The Spanish enslaved and murdered thousands of native people in this area. Acting righteously against strangers, or otherwise known as, savages, because of their holy guidance. God's giveth power to thy who praise his word. A fable to migrate all men under one banner. Destruction for the good of the future.

The oil lobbyist peered around the rally packed block seeming to see nothing that was really there. To them it was all stupid pagan hippy dippy over-reactions and poor people trying to get attention. People on welfare didn't have anything better to do so, of course, they had to be here, just yelling to yell, because they were angry, because they were poor stupid angry fools.

The activists against extensive ocean platform drilling flexed below the day-built soapbox stage. Another sign close to the stage read, 'Benjamin Franklin studied meteorology and climate patterns!' The image on the poster was the iconic $100 bill Benji with sunglasses on and a lightning bolt scar on his forehead. Ki thought of their current president, a man who studied business economics, an art of lies, deceit and personal gain.

Behind the pressing mayhem, more activists filled the tight streets. They crawled onto tetor-tatoring fences, climbed metal gutters to roofs overlooking the Paseo, and engulfed parked cars. The energy of the zone was rebellious, destructive, and pissed the fuck off.

Ki strolled into the mass of people, taking his time to work through the crowd. He squeezed by a lifted truck with a Trump bumper sticker and a group of Surfrider Foundation Environmental-ists. One of their signs was an illustration of a surfer in a hazmat suit riding a wave of oil into a plastic ridden shore.

While looking up at the sign, Ki gripped his house keys kitty claw style and ran three of them along the side of the truck, making heavy indentations.

A short middle aged guy with dark shades grabbed Ki's left elbow, "Hey, wtf man!"

"Down with the system brother." In return Ki grabbed the Trump lover's trapezius muscle by his neck and squeezed as hard as he possibly could, and then pushed the man back in his contorted pain. Ki continued his sleek slithering through the crowd. Before he would have felt embarrassed for his destructive unraveling, but at this moment he liked it.

He wanted to hurt… everyone. All these bodies, all these people, even though most were eco-friendly, they still created a carbon footprint. The scene was over populated, just like their world. More and more people sucking the dick of Consumerism and shitting out what makes us strong and hard willed.

Uka Buka was propped up on Ki's shoulder now, almost like a badge, a reminder that Ki held on to something more special, more supernatural than these other people.

Sheriff Worden stood in the corner under an adobe roof able to see every bit of the event. His long red beard squared off at the end and his pale Irish skin glowed a little with his sweat. His hat tilted low above his red eye brows.

He laid people down in rugby just as he did idiots on the streets. Most stories he told were of letting people go and generally being a relaxed peace officer, but anyone who knew him knew he was a conscious ass motherfucker and was only relaxed because he practiced the justice system through 'his' ideals. If someone did criminal blurp t blurp, not wearing a seat belt or smoking the reefer, then fuck it, get out of here and don't do it again, but if it was damaging to life, damaging to the planet. You were fucked!

The static frequencies in the air changed and the Trump E.P.A Representative Scott Pruitt started speaking. Ki laughed when the first thing he brought up was the price of gasoline. Like that would unite everybody.

Ki continued to squeeze through the pillow of people, guided by the picket signs dancing above all the colorful heads of this nice California beach town. The signs clearly showed who all the environmental groups were. The Center for Biological Diversity had smaller signs; one was with a dead whale stuck on the front of a cargo ship and read, 'Drilling Deafens the Sea!'

Greenpeace had their symbol rotating in the wind and a smaller sign next to it read, 'Green turns to Black. This is really Wack!'

A dozen people away from Sheriff Worden was a table of Citizens for Responsible Oil and Gas, tucked under the brim of the Spanish adobe roofs. The Sheriff ran his eyes across the oil corporation goons more often than the rioting crowd. The City Council members held all reasonable strings that gave the block of historic Paseo any sort of order.

They held the calm air of political demeanor and understanding that kept the protesting from exploding anarchy.

Ki slowly continued forward, squeezing into the serpent canals of surfers, students and hippies, before it collapsed into a thick loud picketing wall. Five rows ahead of him was Scott Pruitt, the E.P.A Trump dog, beginning to smile and preach on how Offshore Oil Derricks create an exemplary and thriving ecosystem for sea life.

"Oklahoma is landlocked! Why the fuck are you telling us about OUR ocean!" The yell came from a group of people wearing mostly blue and green and just about 20 people away from Ki. Their signs were shaped as waves, fish and mermaids. The mermaids had chat bubbles saying, 'No More Pollutants, No More Oil' or, 'Stop Risking Sea Life For Diseased Life'.

Ki caught a glimpse of hands clamping Dr. Kate Neilsly's shoulders in appraisal of her shoutout. They did their homework. He watched Pruitt stutter and change the subject back to the high demand for oil. The Mermaids and Grunion continued throwing out logical suggestions contrary to his twisted rationalizations.

There was a hard smack on Ki's back that made him feel like putting his elbow straight into the smacker's nose, but then he relaxed and opened his arms for a hug. Kavika Pines and Adam Vander were Ki's old buddies from middle school. Even with their unbreakable bond, Ki's old girlfriend Lexi divided them for years, and their connections became less frequent. It was always a pleasure seeing the duo. They were usually up to something… devious.

Pines started it off, his hair still a little spikey. "Knew we'd find you here, Ki." Ki held both of their heads and nodded with happy watery eyes, then turned back to Pruitt's delirious verse.

"The backbone of this nation is through oil. The energy needed to run our industrial foundation, the temperatures in our homes, the transportation that brings your food!" Pruitt's tone was catty.

"What about the temperature of the PLANET!" A Grunion yelled.

Another person under the Greenpeace Banners roared, "Find another way to move your fat ass!"

Adam Vander tapped Ki on the shoulder and hinted to look down at his hands. There, Vander spun three smoke bombs around on his palms. "Cow-a-Bunga baby!" Vander popped all three and his eyes disappeared in the green smoke.

Ki stood there for a second, taking time to soak in what was happening and how it was happening. People coughing, moving, scattering, smoke billowing out of the block. Then he realized he had a covert opportunity to inflict the damage he so desperately wanted. A desire to feel something warm drip slowly down his face and puddle around his feet. He moved.

Forward through the five rows of people and he would be there, right next to the enemy. He moved through with no halting steps and no pushback allowances. The smoke only admitted glimpses of people's backpacks, shoulders, or heads through the green haze. Ki reached the flimsy metal gate and watched a picket sign that said, 'Not In Our Town Oiler!' go flying up onto the smoked out soupbox.

He grabbed a hold of the barrier gate's top bar and hopped right over where the smoke was thinner but still layered with a wispy cover. Then suddenly, he saw that pudgy little fucker, and Ki's next step forward turned red.

Zeppelin Blood Moon

Ki's forehead ran right into the Sheriff's red beard. A cozy halt to Ki's retributal advance.

The Sheriff pulled him in and whispered in his ear, "I think you've done enough Z. There's nothing left but trouble."

Ki was now looking up at Sheriff Worden, green smoke spiraling into one nostril and smoldering through his red beard. It was quite humbling to witness. Such a powerful citizen, yet still very close within the rugby brotherhood. Ki respected the man and was always happy to see him. However, today, the Sheriff put a stop to his knuckle buckles. The gears inside Ki's mind clicked and creaked, almost slipping into disarray. He needed to breathe.

"Thanks Whap.. Sheriff Worden. I needed a… a breath away from all that smoke." The Sheriff moved along, patrolling elsewhere, and Ki stood on the edge of the soapbox watching the smoke slowly linger out of the street between the old Spanish adobe buildings. Turning further he saw the block faced Uka Buka floating in the haze with a disapproving flat lined mouth.

Ki jumped down and went over to a nonchalant group of ruggers and old friends. The smoke slowly dispersed and the air cleared. They seemed to be exactly where he saw them last.

"Oy," Ki greeted, and they all greeted him back, then continued talking about the event. Fish made it over to Ki, along with Pines, Mokes and Jessie, a stern faced Latina Mermaid with a tight body. Jessie was also the Mermaid's Captain and one of the few founders of the girl's club.

Ki asked Pines, "Vander?" and Fish responded for him, "Vander who? I haven't seen Vander since Earth Day." Giving one of his twinks at the end to solidify his mischievous intention.

Ki directed another question toward Jessie, "Your watchers doing alright?"

During the Bingo late night meeting, Ki and the Mermaids planned on having a watch team log when staff came in and out of the local Coca Cola plant.

Jessie nodded and took a moment before responding. Her sharp latina sternness tightened her abs under her purple halter top. "Ya, I got confirmation that the night shift just arrived." Jessie's eyes burned through Ki's. "I still think stake-outs are a waste of our time. You're lucky those Mermaids can nerd out on their phones." She clenched her hand into a fist and abruptly decided to speak what was on her mind.

"You know what? Actually. You're off somehow Z. You are never around anymore for our meetings and when you are you just bark orders and ask people to do stuff for you. You've only been a part of the club for one year. You're still a rookie in my eyes and you are pushing us in the wrong freaking direction. My Mermaids will "spy" on your plant, but after tonight we go back to following our own environmental enforcer's strategy. Do not call on us again!" Jessie rotated and walked off with her straightened back and chin exaggeratedly raised. Moments later most of her mermaids made their goodbyes and drifted off as well.

They stood in silence watching the crowds and people gather up and disperse in other areas. Ki let Jessie's words resonate. He knew why she blew up at him. His ideas were different and borderline dangerous. It was luck that he found this group of people, but he believed the moment to push for change was now, when society was on the brink of implosion.

With everything aligned how it was, this was the time he needed to use the people he had… his friends as tools… tools to get what he wanted. Ki made himself believe that this was what every good person wanted. This was what was best for the Earth. Sacrifices had to be made.

"Jessie is right, I've gone a little too hard too fast…" Ki paused, watching the strangers intersect around them. So many lives.

Him and his group could make a difference, a change worth living for. He was becoming so destructive this past year, just like the damn entities he was trying to fight against.

"Do any of you want to go with me to Nixon's Library tomorrow to see what this William Barr book signing thing is all about?" Books and the power of the written word sounded refreshing to Ki. Maybe being enclosed inside a library would settle him down a little.

Fish was the first to speak up, "Sunday's the lord's day brotha. I have to rest mang." He twinked.

Then Mokes excitedly announced, "We can take the van down there, it'll be chill. I need to make a pit stop at Venice beach anyway." Mokes was from the backside of Oahu, next to the Mokulua Islands, and Pines was from the Big Island. The two of them, island brothers, really enjoyed each other's company, so Pines agreed to come along as well.

The day's event was off and Pruitt was nowhere to be found. People rummaged around deciding what to do next for the weekend, and finally their group concluded a departure with their secret hand kisses.

Ki meandered over towards the City Council table where Mermaid Kate Neilsly was chatting with a lady that had a Greenpeace badge on her breast. He looked through their anti-offshore oil platform pamphlets and brochures until he caught Kate's eye. She ended her chat and Ki went over to her.

"If you could tell Jessie that I'm sorry and to ditch tonight's idea."

"Ya, no problem." Kate pulled out her phone and slapped together a quick text, then slid her phone into her back pocket.

"Z, you still write your little poems?"

"I haven't in a while, why?"

"It shows. You seem more square, hard edged, forcing your way forward. Before you were more round and rolling with whatever happened, making the best out of a situation. Always positive and thinking about the Planet. That's why we all listened to you Z… The Planet just doesn't need a reduction of pollution, it needs love, it needs kindness, it needs people like us to see its majestic beauty.

"If you're not doing anything tonight there is a poetry slam at the downtown Roasting Company. At the very least come down and have some tea with a close friend. I'd like to listen to you again." Kate softly clasped her hand with his.

His butterflies made him rub at his chest and he nodded.

"Okay."

He wondered why all the girls saw a change in him. Was it just girl gossip fluttering around town? Did his boys feel the same way? Or was it Uka Buka's more frequent presence? He had been showing up more often, thirsty for disaster, waiting for something to break. Ki walked away from the Paseo thinking about Dr. Neilsly.

***

Vagina grace'd with a dance upon thy gates of heaven.
The oath to die for her, hath unfolds the periodic nobility.
Doth venture down thy volcanic dwelling of tear eleven,
Simply to flex your grasp amongst tranquility.

Bosom, thy tenderness and care of a rainbotic unicorn,
Galloping into the bouquet of blossoming plunder.
Adorn to stealing the hearts of pure and puffy clouds in storm.
Shedding water and giving life to our kin down under.

Cradled in the earth thy lady intertwines her security of roots,
Guarding from theft of her flower to never mourn.
Divinely gifting soil to recognize that that flower means only love.
You love, they love, all love will be blown through the angelic horn.

The duty of thy flower challenger resides by duty of love,
Doth thy love duty or is she merlily a shove.

Ki set down his pen on the miniature-sized notepad, which was quite perfect for his fourteen line sonnets. He turned around to stretch his back on the creaky old chair that partnered up with his dusty one seater table. His whole room was a grip of dust and ZooZa hair. Being a zero waste freak he held the curse of a thousand containers, jars and vials all about the kitchen and cluttered in his room.

He had all of his adventuring treasures he's collected over the years. They lined the walls and corners of his bedroom and bathroom. His old chests, his clothes, his notes, colorful tapestries, plants, clubs, paddles, balls, ZooZa toys, sticks and staves… They all belonged and they all made him feel comfortable and introvertly safe. He looked down at lil Z and she gave him a bark and scratched at his darkly patterned area rug, removing the film of crumbs and hair for a clean spot to lay down.

Ki's pen tip rested perfectly under the word love. He missed his old girlfriend Lexi and the feeling she gave him in living a comfortable slow life. Work, Chill, Love. He could have gone far with just that.

He sat there, now remembering what she last told him, and twisted his mouth in regretful scorn. Ki, there is too much hate in your heart. You hate way too much, and all I've ever asked of you is to love. Why can't you just belong? Accept your life and everyone else's. Accept the time we have to live and how we live it. Believe that love will triumph over all wrongdoings eventually. But mostly just enjoy this wonderful gift of life we were given. I am breaking up with you. I need to live my life without hate and I know it will take you time to shift between the balance of peace and chaos.

She was right, he thought. Ki still needed to see that balance for himself, and in order to do that he needed to dial one side back a couple of notches. Either chaos or peace. If he took a break from one the other would grow stronger, but at least he'd figure out what he wanted his balance to be. At least he'd know too much chaos was bad or too much peace was not enough.

The pen rolled off the notepad and he tore the sonnet page free. Ki folded it into a neat little square. On top of the paper square he wrote, To Neilsly. The pen hovered after the y. He wanted to write more but instead concluded with a wispy heart. He got butterflies again while he tucked the note into his wallet and then picked up his magical mountain worm engraved walking staff and laid down on his bed.

He closed his eyes and moved his hands along the engravings, trying to feel its energy. Was it Uka Buka's staff of reckoning or was it Toko Tuki's staff of enlightenment? A stick that could charge a battery and bring light. Able to bring a bit of happiness in a blight had to be an artifact of Toko Tuki's love. Although Uka Buka stayed with him, accompanying him into hate and madness. Because he held onto the staff he also held onto this illusion, this madness?

A buzz fluttered under the blanket and Ki pulled up a recent message from Jessie.

"Hey Ki, sorry about earlier. Didn't mean to blow you up in front of your boys. My girls are back and said the plant was quiet when they left. No guards. Night."

Another buzz vibrated his phone. It was a message from an unknown number.

"Tick for Tok. Please talk to Zendolinis."

Ki got up and walked outside. He stretched as a clock would. For that matter, he thought as a clock would and muttered as a clock would.

"Tick for Tok, Tick for Tok…" He grabbed his wallet and pulled out the note Tawa had given him the night of the Elemental Festival.

Scott Pruitt, 22307 Dansfield Airstrip, Midnight.

He knew of the strip. It was right under his favorite backpacking mountain and deep, deep in the bush away from town. Uka Buka Mountain.

"It's about time we go back." Ki whispered to himself. He half wanted to bring Uka and the worm engraved staff back to where he found them. He also half wanted to be closer to the mountain so he could feel the immense power of Uka Buka again, dark as it was, the mere essence of its spirit hovel made Ki's heart flutter and race. The worm engraved staff waited to be brought along, for it was the enchanted item that relinquished its magical secrets.

Ki grabbed his darkest clothes, a beanie, the staff and finally made a tweet tweet whistle to grab Zoo Za'mara's attention. "Time for a ride girl, let's go."

On the way to the airstrip, he stopped at the downtown Roasting Company and saw some Mermaids and Kate Neilsly sitting under a glowing full moon. They were drinking tea and hanging around a cozy table with pillows all around their seats. Ki sighed, scratched his temple and did his regular thumb to nose scruff, which he usually did when he felt decisive about doing things his way.

Ki's sonnet to Kate squeezed right through her jeep window and fluttered to her seat, right where her perfect little butt went… He finished daydreaming about what tonight could have been… then bounced out to the airstrip only an hour away.

While weaving on a windy road about five miles away from the airstrip, a shadow rolled across the land. ZooZa popped up on the passenger side door and peered out the open window. The temperature was definitely warm enough for a t-shirt at night; however, with the wind and the cascading swell of this deep valley enclave, there was a weird brisk chill coming down from the mountain.

During most of their ziggy-zaggy ride a full moon hung over Ki's destination. A lunar pin of sorts. The luminescent sister sphere of Earth hung alone in a clear sky. He drove on a little further and then around a long bend clustered with tall oaks. The tint of red started to fill the half paved road and ZooZa gave a little whimper and sat back down on the passenger seat.

Ki moved his head out the open window and looked up again. The shape of a blimp's tail end was now silhouetted across an unforgiving blood moon. A taunting, dark red, planet Mars looking moon that held the sky in a petrifying seis.

Ki thought of what people a couple hundred years ago would have done when they saw a lunar eclipse. The Earth blocking the Sun from the Moon. He remembered the Demon Moon chapter in Stephen King's novel The Wizard and The Glass. He shivered with chilling tendrils along his spine and rolled into the dirt driveway of the airstrip area, headlights turned down to low dims.

The parking was vast so he parked on the end furthest away from the strip and away from any obstructions that blocked the sky. Ki watched the blood moon with lil Z and felt like he was really enjoying the gift of life at the moment. There was so much to think about with a blood moon overhead. However, the longer he stared, the more Uka Buka made its presence known.

"Uka. Buka." The plank face murmured. Ki shifted through his center console, grabbing the little things he needed to roll a joint. He wasn't exactly sure what he'd do next at the airstrip so might as well sit, ponder, and watch the night sky with Za.

He reached behind the passenger seat and grabbed a blue frisbee for his rolling tray. Za sparked up like they were headed off to play catch, but Ki patted her on the head and reassured her that this was just a boring ol' recon mission with a dangerous looking moon overhead.

As he started rolling his joint, Uka Buka drifted in and out of the nearby forest. A hovering plank marked with ancient tiki tribal earlobes, squinty eyes and blocky teeth. Uka looked as wicked as ever as the lunar eclipse bled its color across the land. The Earth spirit tiki head stayed away from Ki's truck, on the fridge of his imagination, but still very present, bouncing with blood moon mana.

Ki stepped outside with Za, put the joint to his lips and searched the sky for that Zeppelin he saw before. Must be a private party of high douchery standing… Ki lit his joint and inhaled a glob of smoke. He blew it out towards Uka Buka.

Why a Zeppelin? There were only about 30 on the planet, he thought. It seemed like a dark cultist operation to take a blimp up during a lunar eclipse. He didn't put it past the Trump administration or whoever was running the plans to harm Mother Earth. It actually finally made more sense. Doing stupid shit, diverting planet rehabil-itation, striving for more overpopulation with Pro-Life campaigns, doing this… dark secret sacrificial ritual crap. They must be fucking possessed by some crazy demon. A demon who was now revealing themself through the blood moon, maybe showing themself through Uka Buka too. Ki had so many questions. He spat in frustration because he knew his questions would never be answered.

The aura of Uka Buka was red, just like the moon. Fucking imag-ining this crap, he thought, while rolling his eyes and taking another hit of his joint and pinning the blimp, now showing itself again far off to the East, high over a mountain of trees.

Za was sniffing around where Uka Buka hovered and developed a couple growling barks in the direction of Uka Buka. Ki shifted around his truck and headed over in that direction through the high grass. He had to back up his girl.

Suddenly, Uka raged, vibrating spasmodically, dark colors flashing around him like blasts of chaotic energy.

"MoOOOO00ooNNnn." Then Uka Buka rushed straight for Ki, knocking him over like the feel of a hard gust of wind.

"Holy shit, maybe I'm not imagining things." ZooZa galloped over to Ki and continued peering back in the direction of Uka Buka's streak East, in the direction of the blood moon.

Time was strange those next two and a half hours. It was slow and he thought it could have been because of his indica ganja, but fast because of all the things racing through Ki's mind. Why the fuck were seemingly evil people going up in a blimp during a blood moon? It all seemed irrefutably evil. Ki rubbed his jawline with his index finger in perplexity.

When the Zeppelin began floating back to the airstrip, Ki rifled through the litany of possible decisions he'd have to make on what he'd do when the Zeppelin arrived. Trying to decide on at least a handful that would be informative and not too radical.

The rugged hexagonal sides and sharp edged contour made it seem more like a metal airship than a big elongated balloon. That's what made it a Zeppelin and not a blimp. The moon was wickedly whole again, shining its white light down on the land. The Zeppelin's shadow came across the parking lot and it slowly began to descend for landing.

It was 3:11 a.m Sunday morning when the Zeppelin touched

down. The first to pour out of the Zeppelin and start transporting luggage outside were the workers, or in this case, servants, who held a frightened demeanor on their alien faces, looking like they were third-world country refugees. They were finely dressed in mostly gold and white tuxedos. Although dressed for a ball, some were less put together than others, almost as if they witnessed something very strange onboard. Their movements weren't tired late night stumbles or happy 'works almost over' jots. Their walks were preoccupied with solemn thoughts and grave memories that they simply wanted to escape. Their tears showed in their crooked strides, periodically looking over their shoulders.

As the moon cast its dullest shine, Men, mostly caucasian, some Indian, some Asian, wobbly and haphazardly, came down the Zeppelin ramp. Some were helped by their servants and some continued their conversations with each other like important business was strictly the basis of the skyhigh blood orb party Shabanza.

A guy with graying hair and a bald monk front walked on the heels of a slow stumbly fat fellow. The graying monk then quickly veered off to the side to take a racehorse piss. Afterward, he flicked both hands at his sides as if to flick the piss from his fingers, then casually walked to his Mercedes Benz, license plate EPruittA.

He opened the door, sat in his driver seat and gave a long sigh of relief. The car air was thick and encapsulating. Odious air elements of farts and bad breath already trapped inside.

Duct tape went over his mouth and pulled him back against his headrest. The tape slipped from the panic of its victim with snarling snot pouring out of its top edge. Ki slammed the butt of his six inch, Crocodile Dundee knife at E.P.A Chief Pruitt's temple, somewhat elegantly as to not shake the vehicle too much, then gracefully shifted it to Pruitt's adams apple as his arms tried to wrestle at the tape now tightened around the headrest and the center of Pruitt's mouth.

Pruitt's murmuring quieted and Ki whispered in his right ear.

"Do not move or say anything until I tell you to, you understand?" Ki's voice was soft like the Reaper's hot breath.

"I do not wish to hurt you, I just need a little information." Through Ki's adrenaline he realized Pruitt never answered his first question.

"Answer, now." His voice was still steady and calm. However, his eyes kept swaying from the back of Pruitt's head to the six vehicles still left in the driveway.

"I do not wish to hurt you, I just need a little information. Do you understand?"

There was a pause, then Pruitt released a yelp. Ki covered his mouth with his left hand and bashed the butt of his knife at Pruitt's temple and cheek three more times. He actually did want to hurt him, that wasn't the problem though. Getting caught might turn into a cluster fuck. Ki watched outside and behind the Benz where the Zeppelin was. He was fully pumped with bad boy adrenaline, yet scared he was doing the wrong thing, but righteously pumped he was doing the right thing.

There was a group of people standing four cars down from Pruitt's, and two people now walked down the ramp. No one heard. Good.

Ki could not let Pruitt yelp for help again. These secret fellows, most likely rich, most likely powerful, all seemed weak as they shivered in the summer night breeze. Ki gritted his teeth at how their meeting during a blood moon was probably a conference to elevate ventures on everything Ki hated.

He used his right knife hand to scrape another piece of duct tape loose, ripped it off the roll with his teeth, then slapped it over the existing duct tape on Pruitt's mouth. As Pruitt was still dazed, he didn't struggle with the tape. Ki wrapped more rotations of duct tape around his head and the headrest, then around his arms and the backseat. Ki searched Pruitt's pockets and tossed his wallet and his phone onto Pruitt's lap.

"Give me the password." Now the phone was in Ki's left hand and in front of Pruitt's face. His knife was still in his right, with the tip of the blade in Pruitt's right nostril.

Pruitt slowly put up a shaky hand and dialed 1666.

Ki shook his head in acknowledging what he previously suspected. Pruitt was a part of some demonic cult of butthole sniffers.

Ki checked back outside around the Zeppelin and blinked at seeing Uka Buka floating there right next to him. Two backseat drivers from Hell.

He accepted that no one was coming because at this point he didn't give a fuck if they came or not. They manufactured a way of life that made wasting shit a normal thing. Made living so easy for everyone that they in turn became so weak minded they gave in easily to the dark power. Creating an intricate culture of freedom reversal. If commoners believe they have everything in a material sense then freedom would seem at its highest. Harmonious Freedom Bells ringing in the wind. Even if a good person wanted to change a hysterical problem cultivated by government hands they would have to wade through the unlimited pleasures and unlimited comforts that procrastinate rebellion to a later date. Life was too good… for them. But all around, in places these slaves of freedom could not see, immense and vulnerable ecosystems of natural life decay to ruin. A burned world for the benefit of us, narcissistic century beings of waste, hateful to the brink of fated calamity.

After the International Energy Agency reported that all companies needed to stop investments in new oil and gas developments to reach our world goal of achieving net-zero carbon emissions by 2050, oil and gas companies defied the call to reason and spent more than $80 million in lobbying alone. Republicans or simply politicians in power got paid massive amounts of money to shut out Green energy campaigns and promote more oil and gas infrastructure.

Politicians like Senator Joe Manchin, who literally decided that they would rather destroy the planet and make a little extra cash from the bowels of its destruction than let renewable energy action take place. A nation of waste and gluttony just because of these fucking mother fuckers, these fuCKS right fucking here.

No wonder his password was 1666. No wonder his stench was a sour encapsulation of fucking shit.

Ki gave Pruitt a hard bash in the right temple again, and Uka Buka gave a rumble sound of delight, "Uka Uka." Ki was currently glad Uka Buka was floating next to him now. Like an Indigenous being stripped of their land and finally getting a small fraction of reckoning. Now he could show Uka Buka what he was really about and how much he really cared about the planet.

Life Has Value by Chill Bump, played very quietly on Ki's phone. He wasn't sure how it clicked on though. He sensed the mountain had something to do with it.

Ki caught Pruitt peering to his right looking for help from his outside politicians. Ki gave him another big slam into the temple.

"Uka Uka." Uka Buka growled looking dead ahead at Pruitt, bobbing his little face planked body up and down in the air.

Ki watched over his right shoulder for Uka Buka's approving stare.

Pruitt's head rocked back and forth like he was concussed, dazed in pain and confusion.

"What did you talk about on the Zeppelin? Who makes all these fucking decisions about promoting environmental destruction?"

Ki's voice wasn't soft anymore and it wasn't quiet. It had a devilish, hateful wisp to it. The sound of pure rage. He couldn't see Pruitt's face, but based off of the massive blows to his dome, he realized he may have gone a little further than he intended.

The passenger door handle clicked. Uka Buka bellowed a roar and watched the men hungrily. There were four tuxedo suited dip-shits standing around the Benz, obviously aware that there was a big problem. They all had something annoying about their appearance. One had his pants pulled up too high. One had rosy cheeks put on with heavy makeup. One's fake hair was falling off. One was very muscular and he plainly was thinking about how cool his arm looked pounding on the Benz window instead of the danger Pruitt was in.

They circled the car and yelled their little voices out, calling for their servants, calling for help. They were scared, and with that fear Ki wanted to escalate their feeling of fright. His mind began to slip away and the blood moon floated in its place.

Ki kept coming back to why these guys made the horrible decisions they did. He gritted his teeth until his jaw cracked with the clamped pressure. His Crocodile Dundee knife glistened from the moonlight to the East and then slid across Pruitt's throat to the West. Blood spilled onto both of his hands.

"Uka Bukaa!" Uka Buka blobbled with laughter, his tongue sticking way out. Tongue looking bewilderingly like real flesh and flobber. Ki watched the other white suited idiots grab their faces in horror, blinking away or pounding at the windows. He looked around at each of them while washing his hands in Pruitt's blood. They all thought they were the center of the universe. They all thought they were the heroes, of what kind, Ki could not figure.

He quickly unlocked his door and shoved it open into the muscular guy that was pounding at his window. Ki briskly got out of the Benz and swung a heavy kick at the chin of the fallen muscle man laying in the dirt. He rotated on to the others. This was easier than killing a fly on the wall, because these beings actually deserved every bit of horror Ki could muster.

There were still a dozen people there. All standing around the

Benz now. Servants, a couple pilots, and the dirty white power boots of the Blood Moon Cultist that love to rape the planet for everything she had. Stripping her for her oil and resources, harming the ozone with nuclear emissions and greenhouse gasses just to make money. Just to make them fat with money… for what? Why do they go to these lengths to make money? For what reason, other than to horde it away. What good have they done… Ki pulled his bloody hand down his face and pinned his stare on the closest douchebag. The man he stared at looked like he was the owner of a fast food franchise. He had very rosy chubby cheeks, white hair, and flat dull eyes.

Ki pointed his knife and marched directly at him. At that moment a lot of things happened. There was the yelling and screaming, which kind of drowned itself out in the moment, and the pilots and servants ran aside, definitely in terror and not willing to risk their lives for their evil bosses. Nevertheless, a Blood Moon Cultist security guard charged at Ki thinking he'd outmatch him, and at that same moment gun shots fired off. ZooZa's far off barks from inside Ki's truck muffled in between shots. And finally, Uka Buka, bigger than ever, encapsulated the sky above the arena where Ki moved his knife through the pinnacle of waste, laughed its chuckle that bubbled out of its planked aboriginal tiki face.

While Uka Buka chuckled overhead, Ki watched four surviving white suited weirdos, politicians, Blood Moon Cultists, and Illuminati, who fucking knew, run for a van that some of their servants already occupied. The red taillights of a black truck and another van sped away, and moments later the last van spun their tires and high tailed out of the airstrip lot. Ki stuttered away as well, towards ZooZa, away from the fallen men.

Pot bellied chubby cheeks was the one to empty his clip out at Ki, right as the security guard lunged for him. The body shield was a lucid memory of a dance immersed in a storm of laser fire. Ki had never been shot at before and at this point he didn't really know if he was alive or dead. He passed his hands over his body looking for holes or wet spots of blood. He checked his feet, his butt, his balls, his ears, nothing. The miracle of 17 bullets missing him had to be more than luck. He didn't believe in miracles, especially miracles that had him in the spotlight.

Most of the bullets that were on point hit Ki's meat shield, and obviously all the other bullets must have just zoomed by, missed in

Mr. Chubby Cheek's frantic panic of getting Ki away from him. That all still seemed outlandish. Was he that scary looking? War painted blood clawed down his face, scary enough that the guy flipped away 17 bullets to the wind?

He looked up where Uka Buka was hovering. The tiki face was in the process of joyously shrinking and happily fading away amongst the voids between the stars. The white of the moon illuminated the two gold-white and hemorrhaging red suited men lying dead in the dirt. Uka Buka seemed content with its night and ready for rest. Was it Uka Buka, his spirit guardian, that had saved him?

Ki smiled at the dead, but quick as a rabbit snare clamp felt ashamed to go see Za. He felt sick, almost to the point of petrification. He had to move though, but so much had happened. Death. Live's stolen by his rage. He shook the sorrowful feeling away and thought of Vikings. He settled ZooZa and then raced to work.

First Ki went through the pockets of Mr. Cheeks. He covered his gross stabbed cheek and bulging eyes with an abandoned jacket and then grabbed his gun and his wallet. He went to the security guy to do the same, carefully trying not to touch a wet bullet hole, and grabbed his wallet too. He took off his own shirt and tried whipping away as much blood off his hands as possible. The gas can in the bed of Ki's truck would come in clutch tonight.

He cut Pruitt's body loose and pulled him out of the Benz, laying him on top of the other two. He then dragged a heavy log over and placed it to the side of their bodies. Ki's eyes were focused and set for survival. He didn't know what he was doing but he knew he didn't have any time to do it. He wanted any possible evidence burned. Going with his instincts and with the flow was his best course of action.

He revved up the Bens, turned it around and gently touched the front bumper to the log, slowly pushing the bodies closer to the airstrip and away from the brush. Once far enough away that the flames wouldn't jump to the dry brush, he revved the Mercedes Benz up high enough to drive it over the log and the bodies, making a loud crunch and squasshh sound.

Ki took off all of his clothes and threw them in with his other kindling, soaking the crime scene with gasoline to burn the evidence. He pulled $1900 bucks from the dead guy's wallets and noted their owner's names for later research. He threw the wallets in the blazing fire and then looked down at Pruitt's phone. It was a heavy smart-phone with a dense cover and he knew the password.

Pruitt's calendar app popped up in his search for upcoming events. There was nothing that stood out but an address in late October. He decided to hide the phone and Chubby Cheek's gun in a bush on the way home. All precautions were necessary, a GPS tracking would ruin him. The current time was 4:43 A.M and light from the eastern sunrise glossed over the cirrostratus clouds running the length of the sky.

It's been a full hour and a half and no police, no cavalry, nothing. He was going to take the mountain ridge roads back to avoid any oncoming emergency vehicles.

The controlled fire warmed his naked body under the foreboding moon. Just like the olden days… When a Blood Moon actually meant, stay the fuck inside.

Sunshine Sunday

The echo of Mokes' motorcycle owned the tunnel. During his next wide turn he extended his knee out to be inches away from the asphalt. Letting off the gas, he coasted with his humming engine down the next block and then bumped up a driveway and petered by four storage lots cooking in the Sun on a Sunday morning. The fifth lot was at the end of the yard with a squat palm tree casting its shade over the gate. Mokes put his foot down, pulled his black-leafed helmet off, and inhaled a large spindle of air. The slip of his lighter and joint came out simultaneously during the slow three steps over to the metal gate. The lock clicked loose and Mokes opened her wide.

The yard was visible through the gate. It was a homey storage yard of metalwork, rocks, and one dark blue Astro Van. His butthole always puckered while he walked through the comfy and secluded grounds and into his van. It was like riding on a water balloon and Mokes felt like anything was possible with a solid team and a van.

He put his joint in between his plump philo-islander lips.

Gentle, he told himself. Relax. Time is on your side.

Mokes expelled three puffs of white swirly clouds. His left hand encapsulated the joint while the right spun the padlock around his index finger. In his early teens, he began to realize time was a tool for preparation, and preparation led to fewer mistakes. He was known as a calm quiet surfer kid. People always wondered where he was and why he was always late. Mokes' game was to pause and reflect.

He paused. He reflected. Mokes smoked.

Waiting, eating up air like it was an objective moment of time. His fingers wove together hanging before his groin. Shoulders slouched and chin prominently, positivity, thoughtful. A patient pose was his Era of Being. So he waited and meditated on zero mistakes while ironically billowing out clouds of mystical smoke.

***

In this town there was the mountain district, hill district, level district, and beach district. Ki's mom's house was located on the hill slash beach district, an ocean overlook, a residential community sharing a cliff with the town's lighthouse.

Mokes turned down his music and analyzed Leia's jungle house for a minute. He watched the vines wrap around the gutters and extend onto the roof, with plants just as tall and doubling the height of the surrounding neighboring fences.

Mokes walked up to Ki's half of the house and heard the shower going. Calm snot rockets shot under sparklets of water.

"Yo Ik" Ki backwards. A nickname only Mokes had for Ki. "I'm outside braddah. Vans here and ready ey."

Mokes was already moving back towards his van to roll another joint.

Ki responded nicely, almost lovingly in a respectful camaraderie sense, though a tired voice came from under that rainy sound of water. "Be right there Mokes."

Mokes gently plopped onto the van's passenger seat, turned on the Sunday morning radio and relaxed for the weekend news. As he waited he folded up his rugby mermaid bandana to tie around his head. The way he folded the blue green bandana made it look like the ocean fusing with a forest canopy.

The radio finished its slow morning reggae beat and the rapid contrasting voice of the news reporter slipped on with an energy of urgency and great importance.

"Three bodies were found at a small airstrip early this morning. The bodies were under a vehicle in a gruesome attempt of a Blood Moon bonfire next to an unregistered Zeppelin. The identities of the deceased are John Lapel, Drake Darlibouski, and Scott Pruitt. Examined to be gathered for a Zeppelin meeting after Pruitt's stance on preserving offshore oil refineries in the El Paseo Ronald Reagan center.

"Many angry protesters were there Saturday to meet Pruitt's environmental deregulation regime and now further investigation is being conducted on footage of suspicious suspects at the rally. The Mayor wants our citizens to be aware of any barbaric tale of who did this and report to authorities as soon as possible wit…"

Mokes slowly turned down the volume dial as Ki walked out of his side gate. Ki was suspect number one for Mokes. He's always yammering on about that midnight stakeout stuff. Could I get in trouble for affiliation? Do I want to continue with such a disastrous force? Mokes' pledge was to stop big money and weak politicians from ruining the islands of Hawaii. So… whose side was he on? This was a time that defined who Mokes was, but there was no time to ponder in his smoky cloud filled brain.

"What up Mokey? Howa bud?"

Mokes' mouth hung a little open in trying to decide what to do. Time. He needed time. This was a big monkey wrench thrown into his spokes. He turned up the volume dial and watched Ki's eyes as Ki stood with his forearms resting on the driver-side window.

"Witnesses said the assailant was tall and marked in warpaint or blood across his face. The act seemed too strange and brutal to be orchestrated preemptively; something went wrong, and the assailant got very angry very quickly. Colleagues of Pruitt tried to run over to help him but he was trapped in his vehicle with the assailant. Lapel and Darlibouski were.."

Ki's nose wrinkled a tinge but his jawline never clenched, and his steady gaze drifted from the radio to Mokes. He looked dead into Mokes' eyes.

"Sounds like somebody is just as mad at these lying dumbfuck politicians as we are. Good riddance." Ki's eyes flared with steady heat, he was focused, dialed in, excited about having an extra morning dump of adrenaline in him. Mokes figured he could be just juiced on having an example made out of a bad politician that fucked around with the planet too much, but Mokes knew, those eyes held a renewed strength and happy ferocity, a blood-drunk spring to his lips as he grinned.

"Let's leave it alone for now." Mokes absorbed some of the blood moon adrenaline exuding from Ki. He lit his joint, motioned Ki to drive the van, and gave him one last piece of advice.

"And next time this comes up, whip that wicked smirk off your face. It shows a reckoning… Let's go pick up Wino."

***

Wino, A.K.A Dance Party, A.K.A Trevor a wine sommelier, was very tall with thick legs, a little belly and rounding shoulders. Having a young shaven face yet an old mind, he used the rugby club as his outsourcing for wine distribution and social awakening. He loved the club, he loved girls and he loved being a part of the resistance.

Wino blabbered as he gorged on Dorito chips. "Says here, Scott Pruitt wanted to run for Attorney General so he could be in charge of the Justice Department. Looks like deregulating environmentally friendly bills was his main campaign. He was even one of those that lobbied to withdraw from the Paris Climate Agreement. The gathering of the world's best nations to fix this plunge towards world catastrophe.

"We are drastically exploiting our natural resources and all Pruitt cared about was his derp-tee-derp families and their coal mining. Forcing century old jobs back into the market. He really came from another world. Nearly every country on the planet made a commitment to reducing fossil fuel polluting emissions except for the douchebags in power of our country. Contradicting decades of research by scientific institutions, including his own agency, the Environmental Protection Agency. President Dumbfuck and him just mocked climate science. Whoever burned this guy did us a favor." Wino continued munching on his chips and scrolling through his cell phone.

Mokes turned back from looking at Wino and faced forward, eyes directed out the window but watched Ki in his peripherals. It looked or felt like a shadow hung over him. Mokes' sister taught him the best way to see someone's aura was through the corner of your eye. Ki radiated something like Venom's breath. It was a bright sunny day but he resided in the shade.

They pulled off the Imperial Highway and towards the Nixon Library.

"Ten minutes till we see Nixon's Library and the book openings."

Mokes thought about who they were during the two hour drive. He pondered the fact that they all put so much energy into hating the bad guy and fixing problems that seemed impossible to fix. The stress and sadness, the weight of anger that ate Mokes up day after day, but something had to be done. Just like in the sport of rugby, Mokes liked to be in the thick of the fight, and that required a sacrifice.

He knew there was another way to live; a lot of his influencers lived in the Buddhist fashion. The wave rider flow stat. They lived self-sustainable lives and kept out of the business of others. They were happy, content, and kept away from judging people, only loving their own.

Vigilantism was unlawful in Human Law, however, completely lawful in Natural Law. Divine Law he cast into the latrines. Natural Law came from reasoning with intrinsic values based on the evolution of human development. The Sun gave us life, not God, and nature nurtured us, not religion. Divine Law was created from weak men seeking power, only by using the words of the 'Gods' to give them strength. Now, for these diviners to build vast armies, they tell women they don't have a choice in having a baby. Clearly a divine scheme to make more dumb dumb soldiers for their religion, in an already dumb dumb ridden world, equaling out to dumb dumb-topia. Fuck Divine Law, and fuck people.

Mokes cringed again, disappointed at his frustration, his hate. He needed to get away from all this. He just wanted to live in a little cove and catch waves with a little nani. He peered over at Ki again with his peripherals. He always liked how Ki looked. The scars on his eyebrows, the stubble on his chin, his short buzz haircut with patterns shaved around his ears. Alas, that wasn't enough to risk a confined spot behind prison bars. As soon as Mokes got the chance, he was going to call the authorities on Ki. His mind swam in Poseidon's torrents with the thought. Was that because it was, deep-down, the right thing to do?

Wino directed his research towards Nixon and his old regime…

"So Nixon actually established the National Protection Agency, which was responsible for enforcing the Environmental Protection Act, which he also put into effect, just like the Clean Air and Clean Water Acts in 1970." He removed his spectacles and whipped the bottom of his eyes. He was smiling and pleasantly continued.

"And, he signed the Endangered Species Act in 1973. Which protected endangered species from extinction based on an increase in city development and economic growth implications that looked over the concern and consequences we'd have on our wildlife. The last republican president that actually gave a snuff about the environment.

"The war on drugs however renewed more segregation than ever before. Causing selective discrimination in our communities and putting my good brothers behind bars for a lifetime… Exactly for what you guys are doing right now." Wino's black hand tightened around his phone. Mokes slowly took his joint out of his mouth.

"Blah, Blah, Nixon was there for the space race.. Yes, the end of the Vietnam War... and the Water Gate. That scandalous busy bee. He had a good start with his environmental foundation, but if trees were black it would probably be another story."

Instead of speaking like a normal person, Ki recited a poem.

"Populace hath inadequate concern.
Where thee walketh fer blocks to see nay flower, only urns.
King Concrete holdeth ground where vines yearn.
True color ready for the burn.

At the great Pendulum of forgotten logic,
Books teeter on their crowded shelves.
A Presidential Sneak alluring to society's dusty gothic,
Swimming through the halls of Watergate on elephants dressed as elves.

Respect falters against a man that sentences another,
For smoking the reefer and being a brother.
A dead scallywag hath a monument center of presidential knowledge created;
All praise thy sneak that destroyed black families, imprisoned and segregated.

And now I say to you my dear brothers,
Shall we charge into the spider's den with each other?"

Pines rose up from the back seat, his hair fundled up like mid timber pine trees in disarray. His eyes were heavy with a hangover that would poop out a migraine from the mere thought of the word.

"Is Ki sonneting about old politics now? That's right up your alley, eh Mokes?"

Mokes looked in the rear-view mirror at Pines. The aura of brown and yellow rotated around him, like a bruise or a guy that needed to use the restroom.

"Yep." Mokes cherished his Hawaiian Social Action poets, which was another reason he really liked Ki. Yet, he was still torn, working next to a fresh cut murderer… poet.

Ki turned the van into the Nixon Library parking lot and they all got out to stretch and discuss. Mokes helped Pines by pointing out the restrooms and medicating his head with another joint, while Ki and Wino talked over more details about the book signing and library layout.

They all decided to leave Pines out of their group for a couple reasons. If three ruffian looking Hawaiian hooligans and a very large black nerd walked into a white republican book signing, Nixon would haunt the house. Even without Pines there, they'd have way too much attention on them. This was an informative mission, nothing more.

As they reached the grand entrance of the museum, Ki spat right on the glossy marble floor and opened the swinging door. Mokes was watching the faces of a dozen men standing at the entrance. It was hard to tell if they were retired police commissioners, business men, or politicians, but they all had that full douchebag whiteman look to them and none of them blinked at Ki's disrespecting spittle. Cowards. Wino did an exaggerated step around the glob of spit and entered.

The library was both a museum and a federally operated establishment of national archives, containing many presidential papers, monuments, historical images and artifacts. There were heroic photos and documents all over the central hall of the museum. Outside the back doors were where a hundred or so people were gathered around for William Barr's book reading and signing event.

Wino stopped and read a plack that said there were 45 million pages of official white house records from the Nixon administration vaulted away in the library. At the end of the plack it thanked Nixon's daughter for the 25 million dollars to build this memorial of Nixon. Wino found himself alone and began a quick jog to catch up with the guys.

The back courtyard was a 40,000 square foot area with a large elongated pond in the center of it. The event was at the head of the pond in a large open field of freshly cut presidential grass.

Ki and Mokes went into the dense crowd of people to get a closer ear at what William Barr was reading.

'Blah, blah, blah, I told him so, I told him there was no evidence of election fraud. I told, I told, I did, I did.' That was the gist of the former Attorney General William Barr's segment reading of his book. Everyone loved William Barr now, like he was some kind of hero for telling Trump that his paranoia on miss cast votes was bull shit.

While Barr read on, a reading of around thirty minutes it seemed. Ki looked around and watched the people that were there. As if he was a lone bird surrounded by tarantulas. It wasn't their intelligence or strength that gave them an air of intimidation, it was their money and narcissistic agendas. He continued looking but as Barr kept reading, Ki's senses focused more on his hearing than his sight. Barr's writing was truthful about Trump's presidential term and he bashed the hell out of him. Ki also mauled over that the whole book was just a political trick to make himself appear great. Another opportunity for money and fame.

Ki remembered listening to what Barr spewed out two years before, on how mail in ballots were dangerous and how it opened the floodgates to voter fraud. This guy had everyone wrapped around his finger, jumping Trump's ship right as it began to sink. Another liar and shithead. Ki scowled and curled his lip in disgust.

Everyone began clapping hysterically. As it died down, his hype man, possibly the publisher, opened up for a Q&A dialog, and within an instant a voice closer to the pond asked Barr a most provocative question. The voice was young and filled with earthly power, yet humble with a ting of disrespectful heat at the tail.

"Mr. Barr, if you were the Judge, Jury, and Executioner for Trump and his revolt on the Capitol building, what would you sentence him with?"

Barr grumbled and gobbled his fat throat for a moment and rose his chin high in fake nobility. "I wouldn't sentence a man for something he did not do. He pushed for a protest but the people created a riot of violence, not him."

"So the radio host of Uganda shouldn't be prosecuted for inciting mass genocide on the Hutu people?"

"Excuse me, I am going to have to ask you to leave. That question has no relevance."

They couldn't see the girl but could hear in her voice that she was being thrown out by security.

"Why, because they were African? And Trump raised an army of ignorant white southerners!" The pause seemed like a hand was preventing her speech. Ki saw a path that would directly intersect with the security and the voice. Meanwhile, Barr asked for another question and a chipper French guy asked about Barr's future as an author.

At a hands length away, Ki shoulder charged the security guard right under his shoulder blade and he instantly released the girl. Ki grabbed Tawa and hustled her out to seem like he was helping. The shoulder charged security guard raced to catch up with Ki, but oblivious to others he didn't see Wino as he cut him off with his big body, creating a gap for their escape.

Tawa yelled out right before they left, "Why are you protecting a man that is obviously insane with narcissism and greed. Willing to hurt anyth-,"

"I rather that than the country's greatest threat! The democratic party pushing their progressive Environmental welfare agenda. I'd rather vote for Trump again than a hippie free loading Democrat!" Barr's crowd around him cheered and pillowed the ex-attorney general. They loved the drama and they loved the hate.

Ki got Tawa into the museum and around a couple bends and turns. They hid in a nook under a piece of the Berlin Wall. The elementary artistic graffiti face above guarded them as they took cover.

Ki put his hat on Tawa's head, took off his flannel and traded it with her black leather jacket. It was a tight fit but they at least looked like different people. Tawa had a white scarf in the pocket of her jeans and she wrapped it around Ki so he looked like a grunge tennis player.

"Baggans mentioned you'd be here. Colin wanted to know about the Zendolini's."

"You couldn't call?"

"I thought this would be more exciting. Definitely more your style right?" Tawa's voice was fun and exhilarated. She already seemed like a friend and a good addition to the crew.

Ki texted Mokes to meet Tawa by the car. Ki had one more thing he wanted to do.

No one looked at him twice when he went back outside to the event. Ki picked up the book, One Damn Thing After Another, Memoirs of an Attorney General, twisted it around, opened it up and started reading the last chapter. When he was four people away from getting it signed, Ki read the last page.

Then Uka Buka appeared, swaggering behind Barr and looking directly down on his head. As Ki approached the table with the former Attorney General and his pen, Uka Buka acted like he was eating Barr's hair, every three blocky teeth ghost gobbles looking back at Ki, as if Uka was inclining Ki to eat his hair as well.

Barr repeated himself, "Hey Mister, who would you like me to sign the book too?"

Ki looked down at Barr a little stupefied. The darkness of last night soaking into his bones.

"To My Dear Mom Abigal Julius Bones." Barr took the book with a raised eyebrow and opened it up to the cover page.

"Oh, could you sign the last page please."

Barr turned to the last page and finished signing, making the name Bones look wickedly cool in cursive.

As his pen shifted towards the final ink stroke Ki plucked a gray hair from the top of his head, put it over the freshly written signature and slapped the book closed.

"Heyyy what the -" Barr was flabbergasted and quite dismayed to the point of not knowing what to do after such a pluck. He stood up.

"Aye Sir, well thank you kindly. My dying mum will be greatly appreciative of your gift." Ki said very loudly so everyone around could hear. A couple people even gave an 'Awhh' of empathy towards Barr.

Ki turned and went straight for the van.

When outside, Toko Tuki blasted by Ki's head and spiraled up and around Tawa, finishing with a great Tuki yelp of gratitude. Tuki's colorful bird feathers waved passionately through the air and its colorfully painted wooden faced smile grew with its accelerating speed. Ki was immensely surprised, and paired with his surprise came a flash of joy. His friendly idol Toko Tuki finally came to life! If only for a moment, it felt as if a rainbow was crossing over a lonely hill. Ki was about to stroll up to the group spouting his displeasure with those political businessmen, but altered and strolled up with a grin and a nose flick with his thumb.

"Aye Aye, good to see everybody is accounted for, eh?"

Tawa and Mokes had to wrap up an important conversation it seemed. Even for their first time meeting each other they already seemed to have something deeply in common. One was from the Hawaiian Islands of Oahu, and the other from the Coastal tribes of the Chumash Californian natives, both peoples taken over by floods of transformative settlers.

Tawa spoke first, "Hi Ki, have you visited our trash friend yet?"

"It's still the weekend Tawa, I was planning on visiting him Monday.." Ki responded, and Tawa looked at him for more. "...Tomorrow…" He finished, wanting to ease her tense face.

"Okay good, because I want to go with you. I'm happy to be connected with a fellowship of people that actually do something, and I want to help."

Mokes' eyes lingered on Ki. What was Ik intending to do with the Zendolini's? Tawa had no idea about Ki's Blood Moon history. Would she be okay with a Planet Redemption Murder? If she was, I'd be. Wait, would I be? Just because of a nani? Mokes shook his thoughts out of his head.

"You know Tawa, there are bigger problems than just a waste organization holding up local composting facilities," Ki said.

"Well I say, aim small, miss small. If we can't fix what's going on in our small town first then how are we going to fix the entire country?"

Tawa took off Ki's flannel and her boobs bounced in her tight white shirt.

Mokes' eyes fluttered like he was about to fall asleep, his shoulders slumped and his tongue rolled out of his mouth, lapping it back in within an instant.

Ki quickly took off Tawa's scarf and jacket, remembering he must have looked so silly asking for Barr's signature. He caught a glimpse of Uka Buka flying around in their van, then vanished in a blink of his eye. So much blood. Ki put his palm to his forehead then snapped it back to see if there was blood on his palm.

"What are you talking about? Are you okay?" Tawa said, half worried, half intrigued.

Ki must have voiced his delusions. "So much blood rushing to my head. It's been a long weekend. Mokes, can you drive please."

"Ya, no problem. It is my whip, you know whey." Mokes knew Ki had something to do with those murders last night. This was dangerous. He wanted to keep Ki away from Tawa now.

He spoke up, "Ik, I could go with Tawa to handle the Zendolini guys tomorrow. It seems like you need some rest."

"Sure, sure, are you okay with that Tawa?" Ki fluttered and gazed at his future seat sitting shotgun in the van.

Tawa looked Mokes up and down and rolled her wooden ring around her finger for a moment.

"Ahhh. You made a deal with Colin. You remember that deal?" She intently watched Ki to see if he would get the hint. Watching to see if he even remembered Colin's deal. Pruitt's whereabouts for a little muscle at Zendolini's. Tawa was feeling pretty frothie after yelling at Barr, maybe she could harness that froth for tomorrow's meeting. Ki did have a long weekend… maybe his head wouldn't be in the right place.

"Ah okay fine. Alright I'm good with that." She surrendered, a hint of pity in her eyes as she watched Ki quietly yearning to sit in the passenger seat and zombie out.

"Well great, I'll give you my number Mokes and we can meet tomorrow around noon."

***

Once they got back to Ki's house, Mokes helped Ki to his door. He seemed feverish, slow, sick, and fatigued.

"Get some rest Ik."

"Thanks Mokes… You think you could roll me one of your little joints before you go?"

"Yeah, no problem Ik, I'll roll it up and bring it in braddah."

Mokes went back to the van with crazy dubstep beats shaking all the windows. He ground the ganja up and rolled a fat joint.

"Yo, Hey DanceParty!" Mokes waved his arm at Wino, DanceParty was tapping away at his phone in the back seat, as if his fingers were little feet dancing on the screen.

"I'm just dropping this off and I'll be back in a second!"

"What!?" Wino was in his full grove and honestly didn't give a fuck.

Mokes put up the joint and pointed at it then to Ki's house. Wino gave him a thumbs up.

Mokes jumped out of the Van and went over to Ki's pickup truck. He wanted a moment to diagnose what was visible. Maybe he'd find a concert ticket or Taco Bell receipt from last night. Any proof that would lead him further away from being a murderer. He opened the passenger door and sat inside looking around for a minute or two. He just looked around with his eyes. No dipping and diving with his hands scrambling all over the place.

Sunglasses and animal bones were on the dashboard. An Amulet of a Totem filled with weird faces was hanging from his mirror. Stickers ran all over, on the sides of the center console, under the steering…

Mokes scratched at his stubble on his defined, rigid chin.

A finger length of scabbed red marked the underside of the steering wheel. Blood.

Mokes got out of the pickup and went for that fat joint as if to smoke her. He stopped. He was always the guy that held his patience. He waited, he thought, and he tried to make the right move. He tried to make a decision right then. This was the time to turn him in. He had the proof.

He also remembered who they were really fighting against, these hidden demons, these scum that fuck up everything, the big money politicians that run his islands now, ruining them with big lights, fancy hotels and exploitation of his culture. Only a small portion of Hawaiians still have their ancestral land solely because scheming Haoles move in and kick the natives out more and more every year. Strangers with filthy money, money created by manipulating the environment.

Ki was just trying to fight that, not just drawing on a piece of cardboard and bobbing it up and down in the air. Mokes felt ashamed of himself for the nights when he was so pleased at doing just that, but really, what did protesting accomplish? A sign to tickle big corporations, who laughed at how helpless the low socio-economic class really was.

Mokes felt his anger boiling, and felt closer to Ki than ever.

"Hey you going to do something with that joint or what Mokes? Let's smoke it! What the hell?" Wino yelled. His big black body filled the window as he peeked out.

"Come on, get your head out of your ass you backline little bitch!" Wino drawled. Smirking a little from his snag at the backline players of rugby.

Mokes smirked too, "Be right there!" He made his decision for now, and went inside Ki's apartment and delivered the joint.

Za Bark

*Will there ever again be a leadership of Philosophers who speak of
bettering humanity?
Or hath a jester taken thy throne, thus making Lords out of the tendrils of dark and fluidic things.
Demons slain amongst these fields of tar, splattering the sticky black
with their chicken neck strokes of jerky mobility.
Grown titans growling with horns and teeth, abandoning thoughts of
wings.*

*Why can't thy mind rest on sunny greeted blossoms,
Or honey treated fruits not processed, not unknown.
Doth rather portray a grander allocation than the Can'ts of Gotham.
With Hope a thoughtful Queen could have a gentler touch than pre-
viously shown.*

*Songs of love for each other brought a driven population,
Alas, more bodies cometh collision of wasteful zeros.
Thou future songs sung of enjoying insemination,
Conduct a fine component of truer heroes.*

*The world needs philosopher Kings not fuck heads.
But what do I know, I'm just drinking rum to mend the deads.*

Ki took a long swig of his rum bottle, creating a swaggering
motion like he held a wavering cutlass before setting it down. He
flicked his pen over his sonnet and it clinked against the wall. The
dial on his speaker was set on one notch before full volume, as Tool,
a band of rhythmic guitar and drum instrumentalists jammed forth,
blocking out the morning sounds of construction workers jackham-

"

mering across the street.

Ki decided to take Monday off. He usually felt like he worked eight days a week, and never getting sick or having any desire for a vacation. Being on the grind felt best to him, but today was a day to lay back and rest.

With sunshine blasting against the front shades of Ki's house, a few middle slits slapped open, and golden green eyes peered out, squinting in bitter light. There lay across the street three men. One was actually lounging by a bush looking at his phone. Another finished pounding a petite water bottle and threw it in the street gutter as if his scattered waste showed how hard he was working. And finally the last of the three, jackhammering with one hand and watching his phone with the other.

Ki retreated back to his den and nodded to the beautiful melodies coming from his speaker, every now and then interrupted, of course, by an abrasive cough or yelp of laughter.

The jackhammer sound Ki was used to. Him and Fish worked to finish the job. Every time. Everyday. They worked efficiently, rhythmically and with respect for the land and neighbors around. Yes, they too were loud, but… not like these guys, they were wringing up his brain like it was a wet towel.

Busying oneself was Ki's motive now. Zoo Za'mara needed a walk and maybe these guys would spark up and get to work in an hour. If they all got to work Ki would have no problems. He had already murdered three men. He didn't need to murder three more.

As he walked outside of his door, Za took a long glance at the guys working across the street. She pursed her lips as if to let out a bark, but she held it in and they commenced on their little hour walk around the neighborhood.

Morons, wasteful shits, littering the planet. Ki concentrated on anything other than the flash of madness he's been leaning towards recently. He thought of Toko Tuki swirling around Tawa, a grand lady of righteousness. He smiled at that, then smiled at the other dog walker crossing paths with him, then smiled at the way Zoo Za'Mara waddled off to smell a bush. When Toko Tuki spun into existence yesterday, he noticed it was during a semi happy gathering, while Uka liked to play around gatherings of anger and hate.

Ki turned the last corner before his house and was slapped in the face with heat. The Sun rested on his cheeks the block before the turn, but the three men were what really flushed them out. Now all three simply chatted away, all drinking their petite little water bottles with four more empty plastic water bottles scattered around their work area. Ki decided to call Fish and escape the collapsing hole of pure rage.

As he walked to his door the three men stared at him, watched him like he was weak and alone. Za barked. She normally only barked at figures in the dark, or sporadic randos, sometimes birds. In this case, her emotions linked with Ki's, and those stares cracked a couple eggs. Ki winked at Za and they went inside.

When he called Fish, Fish told him that he was gathering materials for a new job and he'd see him tomorrow, 'get some rest ol buddy ol pal,' he teased.

Ki tapped his foot, cooked up some breakfast, and began to think of Uka Buka. He began to think of his wink to Za and the balance between good and evil. The way to create balance was to vanquish the evil, rip it out of the ground, root by root. His vision became darker, his thought process narrowed, and the day's future became absolutely black.

"What a nice Monday eh Za." Za looked at Ki from his bed, curious at the day of lounging and doing nothing.

He listened to more laughter and now a heightened volume of shitty club music. He dared himself not to look out the slits of his window shades, but he did so anyway within an instant. There they were again, an hour and a half after Za's walk… not doing jack shit. More plastic petite water bottles littered the ground, scattered everywhere. One of guys even looked directly at his window.

Ki slapped his sneakers on and headed for the front door. "Come on Uka, it's time for another little chat."

Ki made it across the street with their full attention now. He slowed his pace and really soaked in the moment. It was a hateful moment, but filled with so much beauty at the same time. So much feeling was captured in moments like these. It was like a ball of energy with lightning tentacles attached to every part of the universe. Pumping, absorbing, exuding. Xing for Christ's sake.

Now across the street and standing nearer to the three monday mayhem boys, all beauty was lost. There was a disgusting taste in Ki's mouth. His thumb powered on his handheld speaker and slowly raised the volume, not quite to max level yet.

"What the fuck you looking at? Punk!" Ki yelled, trying to look at every single eyeball. All three stepped in closer. One, the Dj of the shitty nightclub music, jerked his arm up as if to punch, but the center guy, the one previously on the jackhammer, put his arm across his chest. The third guy rounded behind Ki to get perfectly in his blind spot.

"What the fuck? We goin fuck you and your little dog up essay! Coming over here like that."

That was usually enough for Ki to make the first move, but he wanted to explain to them why he crossed the street before they went unconscious.

"There are less wasteful ways to drink your fucking water than littering and wasting all these fucking little plastic water bottles, AND, bumping shitty fucking music… Here's some real music for you!" Ki thumbed the volume to max, and Korn, Reclaim My Place, Thwapped on.

"Do you not have any fucking -" Clock!

The center guy's eye flickered to the guy behind Ki. The plan was to counter the blindside but he was way too late and got clocked in the back of the head. With his forward momentum, he pushed the DJ laborer and their leader, jackhammer boy, away to give him a little space to recover.

Uka Buka must have shielded Ki's head on that blindside punch. He felt fine, great in fact, ready to sink his knuckles into this group of… worse than shits. Shit or manure could fertilize the land and be used for growth; this group was the opposite.

As Ki grabbed the swinging fist of the DJ, he was clocked again in the back of the head, only maddening his rage more and quickening his movements. He couldn't lose, not to these scum. The jackhammer guy did a front kick that pushed Ki off to the curbside. He had a fair shot now. All three of them were in front. Korn's instrumental entered a melody that pumped all the body's blood into areas you wanted it, power generating over his shoulders, down his forearms and into his fist.

The three acted like the fight was over, like Ki would back away after a couple love taps; but now he knew their strength and the only hard hitter was the foreman jackhammer guy.

Ki walked back up to them, analyzing who to crash on first. He liked the jackhammer guy the most, so he'll take him last. They ran their mouths, but Ki held his speaker right up to his own ear. He decided on the guy dressed in white sweats of all things, the fuck that swung twice on the back of his head.

"UKA BUKA!" Uka Buka confirmed the thrilling experience.

Mr. White Pants landed another fist into Ki's left eye socket, but Ki moved through the hit, wrapped his left fist in his teal blue work shirt so he couldn't get away and then full lean back headbutted him, crushing the guy's nose. Smushed it, broke it, and blood spattered all over Ki's and the other guy's face. Ki then did a long wide swing right, that smashed the hard metal speaker into the guy's left ear.

The adrenaline bubbled, it showed itself through the drool and spittle on Ki's trembling angry lips. The other two amigos at this point were scared. They already tried their kicks and punches, which had little to no effect. They continued to back away as Ki advanced. The beat of the drum 'Thwacked' on!

The worst one of the three, his puffy cheeks, tattoos circling his neck, nice buzz cut, his poor, poor choice in music, was a couple feet further away than the jackhammer guy. Ki really wanted to get his licks in on this wasteful piece of shit. Based on what Ki saw today, this guy probably fucked the Earth up every day. Just wasting shit, just fucking around not doing anything but wasting shit!!

Ki threw the speaker at his head and charged. As the supervisor beat at Ki's right side, Ki grasped the Dj's ear to pull him down just enough to get five hard, pummeling gorilla hits in. Leaving him to fucking cry in the dirt.

Ki turned to the supervisor, who really wasn't super anything. He was just the only one that actually did something all day. The guy put his hand out, signaling Ki to stop fighting.

"Fuck you and you're fucking fucks. Ya fuck!" And when Ki turned around half the block was there watching the whole thing go down. The local versus three baby blue shirted construction guys. The spectators were close, looking as if they would have jumped in to break it up if it went on a little longer. A couple of kids had their phones out, and a dad asked if Ki was alright. An older couple just looked around the yard in amazement, and one other older dude had his phone up to his ear, probably calling the police or the property owner.

Ki bent down and picked up his speaker with blood all over it. He powered it off and went home.

"Pick. Up. Your recycling before you leave. That's really all I wanted." Ki said through gritted teeth. He wanted to seem like he was on the right side of things in the eyes of his neighbors. I wonder how much they saw… If they saw Uka, go Buka.

One of the spectating kids slapped his phone away as Ki walked past, scratching his head and starting to feel uneasy about what he'd done. Uka Buka appeared again, directly in front of Ki as he made it into his driveway. When Uka Buka first appeared to him, the hardened tiki plank face looked scary and mean, now Uka made Ki feel as if he'd absorbed those traits himself.

***

The cops showed up and Ki went through the whole story. One officer was talking to Ki, a couple other officers were speaking with the construction guys, and one cop was with the neighbors getting a witness report.

Ki and his officer talked around the bed of his pickup truck. After about thirty minutes of everyone's discussions, a girl cop walked over to where Ki and Officer Whitney were.

"Where is your speakerbox?" The jacked and pretty girl officer grunted at Ki.

Officer Whitney, a Hispanic cop who seemed to always carry a smirk with him, and Officer Timely, looked at where Ki nudged their attention. Casually hidden under his toolbox and behind a couple rocks, Officer Whitney grabbed the bloody speakerbox with his latex glove.

"You never mentioned this in your story."

"I regretted using it, but at the time it was just… there, ready to be used."

Officer Timely's dirty blonde hair was pulled back tight and the veins in her forehead bulged in her frustration, "No wonder two of those guys need medical attention. We are going to have to take you in buddy."

"Whoa, whoa, whoa. They still haven't picked up their recycling. Are you kidding me? That's why all this happened, and they still just fucking left it." Ki's surprise calmly startled the officers, but as his fury gained more momentum, his voice got louder and louder.

"Pick up your… garbage!" Two of the Amigos gave murderous eyes in Ki's direction. The one with white pants and blood splattered all over his face was in handcuffs while a medical team swabbed at his broken nose and smashed ear. The Dj was being watched by a couple EMTs, holding his head between his knees on the curb, and the jackhammer supervisor was glaring at Ki and logging the scene in his memory.

"Officer Whitney, can you follow me inside my house real quick? I just want to make sure my dog will be okay while I'm gone."

Ki went back inside, patted Za on the head and poured her a big bowl of dog food. "What a fucking week eh Za?"

ZooZa looked up at him with big watery eyes and hovered her little paw up in the air as a solemn gesture to not leave. Ki's heart wrenched, creaking and twisting in his chest. He felt stupid. He felt he had lost. He felt like what he did was a waste of time.

Next time it'll be for something. Next time I will make a difference.

Zendolini Waste Industries

The Palo Santo fragrance cleansed the air of the Zendolini Waste Management office. It cut through heavy vibrations like tension or anxiety and ate up most misconceptions on how this office was presumed to smell.

Tawa walked into the greeting hall with a gray button-up shirt, no collar, eastern style, and sleeves rolled up past the elbows. Mokes stood adjacently a step behind her with a clean white T imprinted with a small logo of a sun rising over teal mountain peaks. They both had dark tan skin, longer more dreaded hair than other normal folk, but their clothes and shoes were clean, crisp and uniquely business-like.

Tawa strode up to the young white girl behind the receptionist counter. This Monday afternoon the girl was racing around her little area, almost looking like a cartoon about to huck a bundle of files in the air while spinning herself up in the telephone cord. The mass of cubical units behind her also seemed very busy, but the workers were still pleasant.

Mokes cut in before Tawa could get a word.

"Hi, I was wondering if you could set me up with an appointment to see Mr. Zendolini, I have a very intriguing proposition for him."

The receptionist threw back her blonde hair with her right hand, then put her index finger up and gave her gum one slow ponderous chew while staring at Mokes face. "Sure, let me check in with him. If you could please." She motioned to the seating area.

After a few minutes she slurred, "Zendolini will be ready to see you in thirty minutes, may I ask who you are?"

"Jordan Mokalua and Tawa Pawin."

"With the City's Composting Foundation." Tawa quickly added in.

While waiting they both went outside to Mokes' van to hang

with Pines. Pines, or otherwise known as Kavika Pinederuso, with the Pineapple hairdo in Grade School, was sitting in the driver seat smoking a joint and scrolling through his phone.

These days someone could be perfectly content anywhere, as long as they had service and weren't needed elsewhere. Pines looked up when Tawa knocked on the front windshield and strolled over to his door. Mokes stayed at the passenger side window, not wanting to get too comfortable and also be able to watch Tawa's mannerisms from afar. She was what all of his friends idolized in a woman. She was smart, tough, independent, a party animal with a conservative respectful edge, and golly gee she was damn hot, or beautiful, it was hard to decipher. The way a girl walked, or the way her eyes looked at you must have been the moment when you were able to choose between, Hot - red rocket go Boing! Or Beautiful - where your heart strings pulled tight and your gut fluttered. Right at this moment, it was hot.

While watching his phone Kavika Pines sprung up with surprise and started coughing uncontrollably. He leaned over so Tawa could look at his phone as well.

Tawa's eyes looked confused as her mouth looked amused. "Ki went ham on those construction guys! That guy is a little troublemaker…" Her eyes synced up with her mouth and Mokes finally caught what she was saying.

Pines' eyes were swelling up. To Tawa it might have seemed like he was worried about his friend, but Mokes knew Pines was desperately trying to hide a smile. Pines was always proud of his old friend's decisions on when to throw down. Pines really looked up to Ki.

Pines dialed at his phone and called Ki's mom, Leia. They talked for a couple minutes and then he hung up.

"She said he was charged with assault and battery and has one month in jail before parole."

Mokes was watching Tawa bite her lip in excitement. He studied what turned her on, and this definitely made her giddy like a schoolgirl.

Mokes went inside the van and leaned on the armrest.

"Tawa could you go inside and be ready for Mr. Zendolini if he so happens to be ready early. I have a few things to talk to Pines about, privately."

Tawa tweaked her mouth to make an amused dimple in one cheek.

"Sure thing, Boss." As Tawa walked off sarcastically, she fiddled with her long, black, dreaded braid that hung over her shoulder. The two boys watched her hip thrusts go side to side for a moment.

"Pines I need you to…" Mokes' way of life was to always take it slow and do the right thing. This decision wore on Mokes and used up a lot of energy just thinking about it, breaking his slow-roll, cool stroll lifestyle.

If anyone would understand, it's Pines, One of Ki's oldest friends.

"Pines I found blood on Ik's steering wheel a couple days ago. It was the day after…" Mokes began speaking out of the side of his mouth in a low whisper.

"The day after that Oil Rep was killed."

Pines dropped the roach and clapped out the ember on his shorts, "Oh shit."

"Ya… So the fact that he is in jail could lead to more investigations or searching through his belongings."

"Oh fuck, oh shit oh shit." Pines was sitting up straight as an arrow now and obviously in distress.

"It's okay Pines, you might still have time to go over to his house and clean that shit. Get some bleach and a rag and scrub the inside of his truck, leave a window halfway down and get the hell out of there. I have to stay here to deal with this Zendolini man."

"Okay Mokes, I gotta go… So… Get!" Mokes smiled and jumped out of his Astro Van. Pines raced off as Tawa put her head out the door, "Mr. Zendolini is ready, get your step on Boi!"

Everyone was always telling me to hurry now. Damn Rapidos. Mokes thought of this as he walked inside and caught the scent of Palo Santo again. The receptionist led Tawa and Mokes to Mr. Zendolini's door.

Inside the office was a pillowy soft green carpet. A color Mokes remembered from a movie he couldn't exactly pin. He just remembered the film being super gangster and things not going to plan.

"Mr. Zendolini? Sir, Mr. Mokulua and Ms. Pawin are here now."

Mokes was impressed by the receptionist's greeting. It was very comforting to be introduced so well.

A jolly cigarette ridden voice on the other side of the door told them to come in.

Tawa walked in and slapped her folder on Mr. Zendolini's desk. The folder had an eclipsing web that filled the cover. A web of the perceived Compost City Development Timeline.

"We are here to expand your business and save the planet." Tawa directed, absolutely serious and stern.

Mr. Zendolini laughed and pursed his lips at the girl. He took his time, which Mokes really admired. "Relax, I got time to hear you out. I am a reasonable man." He found his reading glasses and slowly looked over the folder.

Tawa spoke in a slow rhythm as Mr. Zendolini opened the folder to the first page. She gave a narrative on the process and procedure: Picking up food waste as compost for a handful of new gardens, curating the town's soil, using anaerobic digestion to help produce biogas and natural energy for heating and electricity. Important pickup and drop-off zones are attached to a dozen standby contracts with schools, restaurants, farms, and gardens.

Then Mokes spoke on how Zen Industries could expand and be a model industry for other waste organizations around the country. It wasn't too far-fetched from what Zen Waste Industries has already been doing, plus the Senate was working on a proposal for a state-wide mandatory organic waste collection bill. This was the perfect time to push for a compost relief plan.

"Money and respect, all made by one constructive decision." Tawa said with a smile and a wink. The wink, she wasn't even ready for. One of those body glitches that you just have to see through in a particular moment.

"Hmm. Sounds like it's missing something. How does Zen Industries profit again?" Mr. Zendolini moved his lips around as he thought it over.

"It would be $40 for any pickup less than 500 pounds a month commercial. Residential clients stay exactly the same because we are just picking up their green bins as usual, but instead of restricting organic food scraps, we advise for its disposal in the normal gardening bins. Later once the gardens in which we are dumping the compost are abundant, profitable and self-sufficient, we could work in a percentage for Zen Industries from the new food productivity."

"Hmm, so do what we are doing already, but with a few additional commercial stops?"

"Yes, we might even be able to find interns or someone that'll do the driving for a cheaper rate, like a volunteer." Tawa had a calming voice. It had a native feel to it as if she were reeling in a fish. She definitely believed in sustainability and benefiting the land with a determined organization. She knew Colin, her, and other city environmentalists could do it themselves, however, the Zendolini's held the largest contract in the city for waste pickup. There was no other choice but to go through Zen Industries.

"I understand the importance of the Green Movement, especially during our climate change crisis… I'm just one of those people that… doesn' like too much attention."

"Then split the city's waste contract with us so we can do it."

Mr. Zendolini gave out a massive laugh and gently swooped his reading glasses off and onto the Tawa's folder. "Too big of a risk, you could turn into a major competitor of mine in later years…"

Tawa replied, "If you're a waste company you are in the best position for waste management. Later down the road we could possibly create Zen Gardens with all this fine compost. Maybe more funding for environmental pioneering. Industrial exports of food systems that tend to waste loads of food in their transports are a major problem. Your industry could bring local regenerative agriculture and food systems in direct connection to the community instead of outsourcing. But first we need to start with assembling the community into our cause. The waste and compost is our cause in order to improve the effects on a better community towards non-wasteful traditions."

There was a pause in the room, and then the phone rang.

RING! RinG!

Mokes jolted from the abrupt sound and Tawa giggled at him. He lifted his chin and tugged his shirt tightly downward, giving back a cool grin.

"Sure, just tell him I'm almost done with my meeting. Five more minutes." For the first time meeting Mr. Zendolini, he looked stricken and tired. He peered down sadly while tapping his finger on a little purple gushy pad. The pad had the same application of a stress ball but flattened to the desk. Mokes had never seen anything like it and he couldn't keep his eyes from coming back to it from then on.

"Are you two associated with that new environmental group… the E.E.O?"

"The Environmental Enforcement Association, EEA." Mokes slipped that in quickly to be clear but not falter with Zendolini's thought process.

Mr. Zendolini shot out of his slump and thought for a moment.

"We can give this… Compost Aid, a try. Zen Industry Compost Aid. There are a few requirements however."

Mr. Zendolini dialed a number on his corded phone. "Send him in Roxy, Thank You." He hung up and looked back to Mokes and Tawa. "My son Brock will be in charge of this operation. You will contact him for equipment, trucks, transportation, destinations, your interns or volunteers, the works. Then, I'll need a weekly financial summary on what you used or spent money on and what you'll need for the upcoming week, every week. I also want to know how my son is doing. Maybe you could write that part in code… His code name will be Rock, instead of Brock."

Mokes and Tawa looked at each other, however, for very different reasons. Tawa thought Mr. Zendolini was losing his mind right in front of her, and felt silly just being in the same room. Mokes looked at Tawa because of Mr. Zendolini's son's name, Brock. With a name like that, you got to be some kind of hard case. Then his stare froze past Tawa's shoulder as the office door opened behind her.

Brock… Zendolini.

Brock had a fresh scrape on his wide bronze-age looking nose, a faded tint of a shiner under his eye and a hand wrapped in medical tape. He came in with curiosity riding his blonde vaulted eyebrows and was pleasantly pleased with a pair of his peers standing before his father.

Tawa nodded, and Mokes took his moment of thought. Eyes focused in the vicinity of current actions, but his spirit and mind were off having another tea party at the back of the room. He needed his body to go with the flow. Mr. Zendolini cracked his neck as he leaned back to watch his son enter the room.

"Yo." The refreshed moment of a simple two letter greeting was very similar to the moment when he first walked in. It felt like another wrench was thrown into the plan and everybody knew it. Everybody knew Brock was the Wrench, including Brock. But Brock liked it.

"What's going on PopaZ?" His white shirt collar was popped up on one side and his pin striped vest rested unbuttoned.

"It's a new business plan that I wanted to run by you…" Mr. Zendolini told Brock about their compost idea and how the partnership would run along smoothly.

"You would run the books Brock, the customer contracts, and the drivers. They will help with customer relations, compost delivery and placement."

Brock stared at Mokes. His face contorted in thought. Both Mokes and Brock were in their own heads. A dance of thoughtful spirits. The pack of Zendolinis' really did live true to their name. Father Zendolini explained the compost aid very intelligently and calmly and Brock listened in the same manner; however, something was dark about their Zen, something malevolent and limp, like a dark purple bruised aura clashed with a green aura of peace, or maybe it was a green aura of money clashing with a purple aura of dreams.

"We will keep in contact with Tawnia and … Moke." Mr. Zendolini confidently established.

"Tawa and Mokulua. Yes, we will keep in contact." A funny tinge ran down Mokes' spine as Mr. Zendolini raised an eyebrow. Strong arming an already established strong arm. Was Mokes ready for that? Was he in any position for power exertion? He felt like Mr. Zendolini opened up for weakness when he got Tawa's name wrong. He had to set things straight, especially right off the bat. Even so, he did admire the Zendolini's for some reason, hopefully that showed through his eyes. Eyes were telling.

Tawa's stormy green eyes fizzled at Brock's lightning rod green eyes, which brought a chill with the hint of jacked dilation to his pupils. Their tempest eyes both locked together as she stepped by him. Mokes smiled at Mr. Zendolini and closed the door behind them. A lasting tingling sensation ran down his spine. He reminded himself that Mr. Zendolini wasn't a mob boss, but how the hell would he know, he certainly acted like a mob boss.

Brock swung around to the front of his dad's desk and slid a chair over to plop down on, rolling his back and shoulders into it until he found the optimum position. "Alright PZ, Popa-ru-ni. What's happening?"

"Don't get formal with me today Brock. You need to start taking something seriously and you can start with me." There was a pause. The silence between a father and son was for the son to absorb his mistakes and the father to gain back his patience.

"There are many different kinds of people in this world. A fighter is of the most important kind. I am proud of you for that."

Again Mr. Zendolini gave a pause after his slow speech, and Brock nodded in affirmation. Then Mr. Zendolini sped up as he moved into the business end, "But I get the feeling that you are fighting for the wrong reasons. I want you to take this new job under your wing and fight to make it work. It's a good cause for good people.

"Take Ta-wa's and Mokes' business plan over to Chiki Charlie and go over it together. Until you get her up and running steadily, I'll be taking away your cash flow."

Brock's eyes never wavered, he only pushed his right hand's knuckles into his chest, audibly cracking a few. "But, they are hippy's PZ. You really think it's a good enough idea to risk our assets on?"

Mr. Zendolini laughed, stood up and walked over to the window to watch the gray cloudy sky hang low, engulfing the city.

"Son- " He turned and looked at his son. Mr. Zendolini's big sturdy chest and wide shoulders gave him the happy Kingpin look, however, with gray friendly barbered hair and a chiseled face.

"There is another matter regarding this Environmental Enforcement Association." He seemed to chew the title like a tough piece of meat.

"Mr. Scott Pruitt was murdered a few days ago and I believe the EEA was involved somehow. Pruitt had extremely important information about us and the Zen Industries on his cell phone. One of those mutts knows where that phone is. Find that damn phone Brock, or at least find out who's calling the shots over there. And if you have to play their Hippy Dippy game, then play it." His voice puttered out softly, like his hope for the future was already lost.

"No problem Popa Z." Brock rubbed the bottom of his boot on the green carpet. He knew the importance by his father's tone. Everything was on the line now.

"What is this…" He inhaled through his nose. "Smell called again? I need some for my bathroom."

Mr. Zendolini conducted a gentle huff of a laugh and went back to his desk. "It's Palo Santo. Burn this stick, little by little." He tossed Brock a couple sticks and Brock caught them both with one giant hand.

As Brock opened the door to leave, Mr. Zendolini gave him one more piece of advice. "And Brock, stop busting skulls and use your own, eh?" He gave a slow point to his own dome and winked.

"No problem Popa Z." And Brock closed the door behind him.

Pines' Panic

The engine of Moke's van hit its maximum RPMs as it thundered up the hill. Kavika Pines pushed out of the door and ran over to Ki's truck. He whispered to himself that he needed to hurry.

Pines was one of Ki's best friends starting from middle school. His loyalty, heart, and love for his friends were his greatest traits, but in some instances where his greatest traits ballooned amidst the occasion, the worst of his other traits ballooned with them.

With a clouded mind Pines walked back to the passenger side of Moke's van to block the view from any peeping toms. The problem he now faced was himself. He was high, he was forgetful, and he was in the process of doing something direly important for his best friend.

"Fuck," Pines whispered, while he searched for a rag around the van.

"Bleach, bleach.." Deciding to slow his pace, he walked around the side yard to get into Leia's house through an unlocked door. He scrubbed Za between the ears as he went in. She was so excited that she pee'd all over the floor.

"Ahh noo ZooZaaa." Pines grabbed the bleach under the kitchen cabinet and a fist full of rags. He swooped up the piss on the tile, quickly grabbed Ki's keys off the wall and went over to his truck.

Ki's Keys, Pines giggled in his stoney buzz.

He started to feel better, he had what he needed, he was making jokes, his buzz increased. This was fun. He felt like a ninja on a secret mission.

Passenger side. Gotta stay concealed.

As soon as he opened the door he spotted the blood under the dashboard and froze. Scary thoughts and frightening outcomes raced through his mind again. My friend killed someone… Could they still be friends? Could he still smoke with Ki and feel safe? What if he got caught cleaning up his mess?

Pines looked around the neighborhood and was forced to wave at an old lady walking her dog. She shook her head and continued her walk, pulling her bulldog along as its curious nose wanted nothing more than to sniff Pines and the truck.

"Fuck…" Pines whispered. Then his mind shifted again. The smell of the truck, the stickers on the dash. This was his old buddy's truck. Pines was with him the first day Ki could drive. He felt the warmth pour back into his blood. Ki is a fucking badass. Standing his ground. Doing right for the Planet. Those guys probably had this coming, those damn narcissistic ocean killers. They are the murderers.

Pines now switched himself into a more serious mode. He whipped off the blood and cleaned the steering wheel and dash. His head was deep under the driver's seat looking for any more bloody footprints.

"Shit, I should probably vacuum this baby out.." And as he rose up from under the seat, he saw a police car slowly roll up in front of the house. "Fuck…"

"Hello there Officer, how go-goes it?" Pines choked out as the tall white male officer stepped onto the sidewalk in front of Leia's place.

"What's going on here?" The words came out as a bark, like he already knew exactly what was happening.

"Oh, I was just looking for a dog leash, my buddy's dog, ZooZa, needs a walk." Pines smiled a little at his wittiness, but the officer was already looking down over him and at the passenger side door.

"Smells like bleach!" He looked inside and saw the rags and bottle of bleach.

"Awh, I tipped it over when I was looking for the leash and I was just trying to soak it up." Pines' mouth hung open wondering if he should give more reasoning.

"Why is bleach… nevermind." The officer called in some codes over his radio. Then closed Ki's truck door and turned Pines around.

"You're being arrested as a suspect for accessory to murder. You have the right to remain silent. Anything you say can and will be used against you in a court of law. You have the right to have an attorney present during questioning."

The cold steel of the cuffs clapped closed as Kavika Pines' eyelids did the same.

"Fuck…"

"Fuck…"

Fish & Baggans

Monday after work, Fish grabbed a seat at Tozymoto's restaurant and ordered two pints of beer at the bar. The bartender told him he could only have one at a time.

Baggans entered the restaurant on queue and Fish pointed at the new lumbering customer coming his way. The bartender turned around to pour the pints.

"How's the business Bags?"

"CCA's are going to pop, just gotta keep on grindinggg." Baggans expressed with a big smile and gulped half his pint down in one swig. He wasn't trying to prove anything or be anyone special, he just loved beer.

"What are these CCA's again?" Fish twinked.

"Big Corporations need to buy Carbon Credit Allowances to pay into how much they pollute. If I get big CCA investors that means big corporations spend more money. Hopefully, deterring them from polluting. Those Credits then go to non-profits and acres of land that help grow trees and defend the environment. Creating a balance between growth and decay."

While explaining they both kind of had a swinging eye on the tele in the corner of the bar, it was silent but the subtitle rotator read in red.

Scott Pruitt killed at a local airfield. Secret Societies under investigation.

"Ohh, secret society, whoaaa." Fish exclaimed and then looked back at his beer.

Baggans' eyes squinted a little longer at the news, then he asked, "How's the stone biz going?"

"Ohh it's a little rocky, but things will level out!" They both laughed, then asked for two more pints, four carne asada tacos and four cauliflower tacos.

Baggans' phone started buzzing on the bar. It read Mokulua, with an image of a great cloud of smoke concealing everything but long eyelashes.

Baggans clicked on the speakerphone button, "Yoyo Mokes."

"Hey Braddah, have you heard from Pinesy?"

"Naw, I never talk with Pines brah." It was funny to see a husky gorilla in a suit throwing beers back and talking like he had his weekend board shorts on. A proper business man with his Shire swagger.

"I lent him my van to go check on Ik. It's been over an hour and I'm stuck without my ride." There was a moment of silence. Mokes was hinting at something but was waiting for Baggans to figure it out. Baggans figured it out, but he didn't want to involve himself, hence the silence.

Fish, however, needed to know where Ki was.

Fish leaned closer to the phone on the bar top and lightly said, "Alright, we will cruise over to Ki's and see what's going on. Then we will call you back."

"Alrighty, thanks cheches." Mokes fluttered, and a girl's voice perked up in the background.

Right before Fish was going to hang up, Baggans calmly asked,

"Mokes, where are you at anyways?"

"I'm with Tawa at Zen Industries. I thought Pines would be back quickly to grab us after our interview with Zendolini but…" Baggans cheeks darkened. He grabbed his beer and sat back. Fish knew what Baggans looked like when he was in deep thought, and he most likely knew the focal point of where that brainstorming came from.

"Alrighty, we will hit you up in a minute. Peace." Fish hung up the phone and asked the bartender for their tacos to go.

After walking two blocks through the lower downtown plazas they reached Baggans' Cadillac, and Fish asked Baggans, "Want me to drive?"

Baggans threw Fish the keys and they got in. Fish loved driving the old Cadillac Deville with his arm out the window and his chin held up high.

If the car floated, he floated. The Cadillac was a masterpiece of ingenuity.

When they reached Leia's there were two police cars and a tow truck loading up Ki's pickup truck. Mokes' van was in the driveway, which made the scene look way sketchier. It looked like it had pounds of weed and whirlwinds of sand inside. Fish slowed down and adjusted to park, Baggans finally spoke up.

"Dude keep going we gotta get out of here."

"I'm going to grab Mokes Van." As Fish started to pull over and park, Baggan's eyes widened so big that they made Fish laugh out loud. Baggans wanted to say something, but he knew the Police could read lips, so he kept his mouth shut and tried to hum the words like a ventriloquist.

"Dude. What the Fuck."

Fish got out and walked over to Mokes' van. The three police officers watched him, but never budged to stop him.

As Fish backed out of the driveway, he looked out the passenger window to Baggans and gave him the 'guess there's no problems' sign. Baggans gave back the 'guess not' look.

Fish turned up the radio and went straight to Zen Industries, no phone calls needed. The town was small enough that Mokes could wait five minutes. After all, he was bringing his Astro Van back. At a stoplight, Fish turned around to get a better idea of what he was driving. There were a couple wetsuits, a surfboard, a rugby ball, coffee mugs, pillows, blankets, and a heap of clothes. He's never spent any time in Mokes Van. The two of them were always together but for some reason always apart. They never talked about anything interesting and they never slapped each other's butt out on the pitch. It was as if their souls didn't want to link up, like their charges ricocheted off of each other. Mokes wasn't a bad guy and Fish thought he liked him, but there was this barrier.

"Hmph."

The smell in the air changed and Fish knew he was getting close to Zen Industries. It was a whole city block of landfill and Solid Waste Collection Vehicles everywhere. The main office building was on a separate block and away from clashing and grinding noises. Most of all it had hundreds of tall plants and trees surrounding the Italian looking Villa, as if you were entering a Zen Giardino in the middle of mountains of garbage.

Mokes waved Fish over to park next to six large Plumeria plants and a metropolis of interweaving vines on the eight foot high driveway wall. Tawa was on the phone with a big smile on her face. Her body language was calm and subtle, but she paced and bubbled over with nonsensical laughter. The juxtaposition of being that happy in a place of this stature made it seem like these two did some cool shit today.

"Oy!!!" Fish said when driving up. "You guys have a good meeting?"

Mokes strolled up to the van window, "Oh yeah, a step closer to reducing the amount of leaky methane emissions from landfills! And…" Mokes thumbed over to a smiling Tawa pacing in front of the Plumeria trees.

"Ohhh yeah, you guys had a good meeting. First of all I didn't even know Islanders could say words with r, g's, and C's. You are really coming along ol' Mokie boi." Mokes slid open the van's side door and waited for Tawa to finish up her call.

As Mokes was explaining what happened over at Ki's pad, Fish interrupted him and asked, "Who the fuck is that?"

Mokes saw the well dressed mass of meat exit the front door. "Zendolini's son, Brock." Mokes' voice sounded as if it had to go around a wall. It was deep and guttural, like his nuts were dropping more and more at Brock's every heavy booted step.

Brock's eyes gleamed in those bright green spherical windows and pinpointed pupils. His eye lids looked woken with no sign of ever making them droopy in the past. He strolled around like a prized fighter. His scars on his face and arms, the wrap around his fist, and clothes like his closet was worth a million bucks. Brock had no sluggish steps coming toward the van. It was like Fish and Mokes had to keep their focus on him as he was walking up, like Brock was already speaking to them with his movement in his jaunt over.

Fish watched and wondered, what is this guy's vice? Fish always looked for a weakness in people he just met. It was part of the whole sizing the guy up thing, and of course, it made him feel better. It's the, 'Fuck them. I'm the best,' mentality. At least till Fish got to know them, then they would usually become best friends. The tougher the stranger was to get to know, the more grand their relationship would be later. That's what happened between him and Baggans.

The first time they met, Fish was bouncing at a sold-out music club, and Baggans wanted to come in with all of his friends. Baggans tried to muscle his way in and Fish muscled back. Then, after a few slow and almost cuddly gut punches and pillowed body hits, a girl from inside said something about rambunctious rugby freaks. Fish understood Baggans then, joined the rugby club, and that was all it took, a few moments of understanding that created a platform for respect.

Now it's this Brock bro. Fish put on a small smirk as Brock made it to the van. After working through his social issues with meeting strangers for the first time, Fish could at least try to consciously show more tolerance and acceptance.

"Yo. What's your next move?" Brock was very serious and very lazy with his greeting.

Fish scrubbed at his stubble on his jawline and watched Tawa finishing up her phone call by the Plumaria's. Tawa's ecstatic smile shifted to a wily grin. She knew they just took one step forward, but there were a dozen more obstacles to get over before anything actually got the change they wanted.

Mokes put his arm up on the backseat and relaxed in the shade of his van. "Next move is to go to these major compost accumulation zones and set up times for compost pick-ups. We are headed to one of the middle schools now. We already have multiple farms and gardens that will take the compost, and those are going to be our main compost drop off zones."

"You need a logo. If you had a logo on your van you wouldn't look so unbefitting. Maybe squeeze some Zen'sation in." Brock was quick with his words like his father, and he gave Mokes an easy smile. Tawa saw the mild nature of the new business partner and hopped off her phone.

She mouthed Fish a, 'Hi Fish', which looked way more sensual than she probably meant. Her sweaty collarbone gleamed in the sun over her gray button-up. She went over to the van's sliding door where Brock and Mokes were talking.

Mokes responded, "We already have a logo. It's a silhouette of an earthworm holding up a mushroom flag."

"I get it, worms speed up the process of compost decomposition and really healthy soil produces good mushrooms. The thing I would change instead of the mushroom flag, is a Z flag. It could stand for Zendolini Industries, or Zero Waste, or Zero emissions. All things the EEA is striving for… right?"

After watching the twisting faces of Mokes and Tawa, Brock became even more serious than he was before.

"Look, let's just make this clear. This is how we can help each other. First, the Zendolini contract with the city is the main reason your composting dreams will come to life. The Zendolini's have the permits, vehicles, employees, finance expenditures to get it done. So this only works if the Zendolini industry takes the credit for this operation. Remember that. It's a simple formula. You help save the planet, Zendolini gets the credit. And maybe I could meet this EEA chief soon to really know what you're about." The silence was a weight on everyone's tongues.

"Okay, see y'all later. I'll be in touch." Brock turned and walked over to his white, lifted F350 truck and drove off.

"He really holds your attention." Tawa breathed in a trance. Then she snapped back to reality.

"I need to head over to the compound and start organizing this new business with Colin."

Mokes looked at Fish, then back to Tawa, "Alright we can drop you off, we have some team stuff to figure out."

Jail Birds

A shadow captured, stuck in a run,
Unwavering in solitude and created by one.
Jilted rotations of the Moon and Sun.
One bulb for all bars to block the light of none.

Thou bars doth a song if the Warden praise,
Else loney tinges and twangs drum as misfortuned beats.
Sing in the halls with the caged beasts in concrete shade.
For music doth not swing in cells amongst tapered feet.

Ponder the crime in the chimes of time.
Wherest doth thou crime tend in poisoning dirt?
Wherest doth man frequent while dumping loads of calamity?
My crime at least is buried deep in the earth, barred from hurt…

"Chains on the rightful living unlock an instrument of haste,
To weigh the wrongful dead away from heaven and chain them in
place."

Ki had no pencil or paper this early in the jail bird stage. He ran through his poems over and over in his head to refine them and pass the dungonous time. The righteous feeling restlessly shot excitement through him, and his first gut reaction was that being in here was for a good reason. Had he gone mad? He has done wrong but felt right. What side will he choose? Do wrong for the right reasons, or do nothing to do no wrong. Ahhh, he thought to himself, there is greater flaw in the latter. Deep in his gut he felt doing nothing was the greatest waste of life or time, and waste is definitely in the realm of wrongness. Therefore, he was right. At least for the time being. There are always other ways to ponder on the subject of right and wrong, but for now Ki enjoyed his temporary conclusion.

"There is no sound I'd rather hear than a woman's voice or my cuffs clink," Ki rhymed to his cell neighbor, falling in a single file behind him. Ki motioned breaking an invisible bond around his wrists.

"Ahh, you have the prison blues. The funny thing about that is, we ain't in prison, we in county jail where most of us will be released in a few months or less. So enjoy your stay and don't bring us down with your droopy eyed bullshit." The older heavy set latino man responded with his annoyance rolling through his voice.

Ki walked the rest of the way to the mess hall in silence. The old man was right, everyone had their troubles and so far his weren't that bad. It would take a much longer time to reflect his sorrow on the basis of the Earth's suffering. Ki didn't care if he lived or died or spent all of his time in solitude, as long as he did it on a planet that was treated with respect. Respect for the Earth should be written law, and if it already was, it was just an ink smudge. A verse written without teeth like the mythologies of Greece. Another Fantasy.

It was early morning. The first meal was in the mess hall, where all tormented souls drooled in their hunger. Ki arrived in his cell right after dinner was served last night, so he was wolfishly hungry for whatever they threw at him. He got his tray of oatmeal, bread and an apple and sat down in the mess. He recognized some locals and passed respectful nodes. The Asian guys recognized Ki's slightly tilted eyes and watched him as the white peckerwoods watched him like the arrogant jail birds they were. Ki could pass as an Asian guy or a white guy. He stayed alone, however. He would rather be with a philosophical gang than any other. Any green leafy bandana boys in here? Any tree hugging hippies that want to play chess and talk of environmental vigilantism?

He stayed alone all day and no one spoke with him until night fell and his heart burst with both pleasant surprise and throbbing pity.

In the mess hall, the last meal before bed. Ki hunched over his meal and ate at a quick and steady pace. When he was finished, he looked up at the ceiling. He longed for a book. A book was the key to a great escape from a boring hole filled with discomforting darkness. A book was also a great excuse not to mingle with doudou brains. He decided to look up and think rather than have his chin tucked in on his chest looking down like a depressed and scared dweeb.

He was a proud local boy that not only could handle his shit, but he also itched for something to handle, a little Uka Buka action. He always wanted the challenge of facing evil dead in its eyes, and then giving it the ol' head butt so there would be a higher percentage to taste blood on his lips. Fight with your head not your fists, that's what his mother always told him, however she probably met for him to use his brains rather than his skull.

The guys that Ki chose to sit next to were three lads of different color. They were all caucasian but their skin tone was way different. One pale cowboy looking dude had blonde blonde hair, leaving it naturally short. One of the other two sitting across from him had red skin with longer black metal band hair. His skin seemed permanently sunburnt or perhaps he was always blushing or anxious. The other guy, obviously a fisherman, had a dark brown tan and short light brown hair, almost sun bleached.

Ki waited to digest his food with his arms crossed over his chest. He thought of how Shakespeare would hang in a place like this. Based on many of his stories about tribulation and tragedy, he guessed Shakespeare might even be the king of the lockdown. He had imagination, he was entertaining, he would rap words of wisdom all day every day. He would bring that remembrance of old and lasting flames back to the inmate's longing hearts. He would show hope through incarceration. He would reveal beauty to the iron bars that cast still shadows.

Ki's attention turned to the guy's conversation two arms lengths away from him.

"I'm the billy that get, gets the shit. I get it. It's called black gold so it is. It be ruining the underwater forestations. They be eating kelp forest up so they do. They have this endless hunger and clone themselves too. I'd say we should fish em' up good and ready, but there's restrictions see. There's an annual lottery on who gets to fish em' up."

"For a minute there," the lengthy cowboy with the whitish blonde hair spoke. His index finger up while resting his elbow on the table. "I thought you were speaking of 'black gold'! My black gold is coal, not those spiky balls with Aristotle's asshole for a mouth."

"Ahhh, haha, see you do know. You know of these beasts. Your right they should call it purple gold, because most of them darn thing-a-wigges are that purple urple, i'll tell you what."

The fisherman was definitely from the west coast but talked like a crackhead from the south. Stuttering and blabbering like he should be fishing shrimp not urchin.

The chubby guy with fiery skin crunched his apple and said, "I thought black gold was something both of yous don't have, because ye sitting here with me behind bars, that's why." He glanced over his right and left shoulder. He thought himself funny, the way his mouth was permanently tweaked up in a smirk and his eyes quickly met everyone else's with hope to capture their glee from his humor. He was a young Englishman, and Ki guessed he was probably studying abroad and got into some American College trouble. An English metalhead's favorite pastime.

"Well, we don't get many red coats over in Wyoming, but we have plenty of turkey shakers like yourself. Young kids, never seen a box in their life. Stuck in the mines and loading up coal. We do all the damn work, just to have our 'black gold' go straight to the big corporation fellas. Making billions off of that dirty stocking stuffer. People need energy, yes sir. I'm not sure if people really need the uni crap. Delicacy as it is." The blonde cowboy scrunched his nose in distaste.

The red skin kid from England got up and headed for the kitchen. Ki slid in a little closer next to the crackhead fisherman and across from the cowboy.

"Hey, I'd like to know more about the coal industry… Burning that shit pisses me off. Seriously damaging our atmosphere, just for the excuse of supplying energy to everyone. Well everyone has it too damn easy already. It's time for a little struggle and natural selection if you know what I mean!" Ki felt his heart beating, his forearm ached, and his neck pulsed with the blood shooting through his veins.

"Whoa brother. Let's start with our names and what you're in here for." The cowboy's eyes were fully attentive now on Ki. He seemed intrigued but cautious.

"My name is Ki. I got into a scrap with some Mexi'Cants right outside my house. I'm in here with an assault with a deadly weapon charge. My speakerbox."

"Seems like your rage could be the deadliest weapon of all eh? Well, that's not too bad. I'm actually in town for renewable energy reasons. I've seen what coal does, not just to the planet, but to my people. They are digging up death. They need to just leave it be… but they never will. They will run this world into obliteration just to have their fucking night-light on and feel secure while they are alive. The world gets skinnier while we get fatter. My name is Rummy. I don't drink it, but i'll play it…"

Both Ki and Rummy looked over at the leatherneck fisherman. He was biting his nails and humming something. "My name is Hank. Ahh, I probably did too many drugs, Aye."

After that Ki and Rummy had their heads together for a little bit, until he saw a beautiful yet terrifying scene. One of his oldest dearest friends in an orange jumpsuit was looking around for a spot to eat. Ki realized he must have been hard to see, being hunched over and so engrossed in Rummy's information about Wyoming and the Coal industry.

"My eyes," Ki said. His eyes were actually watering a tad. Brother Pines what did you get yourself into?

***

Kavika Pines had a sharp face with a Leonidus style beard, accompanied by his Greek olive skin and spikey hair. His eyes said he was shy but fierce, quiet but loyal, without fault. So far in Ki and Pine's long relationship, Pine's eyes have never lied. He was a true friend and companion. Ki only really knew this with certainty because they'd already both been through multiple situations where two paths were available. One path was deceit and cowardice and the other was trust and bravery.

Ki pinched the upper bridge of his nose to try and lessen his emotions. He was glad to see a friendly face and overwhelmed with love for his devoted friend, yet he could also feel things changing in his life. Things were getting worse and stretching further and further away from the gentle life of blissful sheep barred in a grassy prairie.

The cinematic wisdom of how an imprisoned populace would react to hugging another inmate with tears of joy, would obviously lead to very few advantages. Instinctively, Ki knew that playing Pine's arrival with indifference and cool postures was the best way for them to proceed.

The mess hall began to thin out as inmates drifted to the recreational yard for their last glimpse of a sunset sky, leaving straight backed Ki an easy target for Pines to spot. He rose from his dining table and walked over to the four very different caucasian fellows, one being hardened Ki, looking more and more Asian as his eyes kept squinting in focus and determination.

"Oy mate!" Pines said with a happy smile, yet worried eyes.

If Ki played it cool then Pines would play it cool. That's how a comradery bond worked.

"Pines. Brother. Sit." Ki still smiled, but his voice was stern. He nodded to the open spot on the bench next to him. Pines walked around and sat next to Ki, wrapping his arm around his shoulder and giving a good squeeze.

"You have some talking to do, Pines." Ki said while he wrapped his arm around Pines' neck and squeezed him back.

"You, inmate. Go pick up your food tray. Mommy's not here to pick up after you." A large Mexican guard billowed out to Pines.

"Aye," Pines got up and went over to clean up his tray. Ki told Rummy, the Wyomingite Cowboy, that they should chat more about coal tomorrow. Then he too got up and walked out to the yard with Pines, catching up with what went wrong and future plans on how to handle their time behind bars.

The Chess Tables

The yard was actually three yards put together on one outdoor block. There was an area to exercise your body, with weights and half of a basketball court. The meat heads and sporty types resided there, and adjacent to them was the yard of thinking minds, where half a dozen chess boards were set up with bleachers and benches around the area for chats and discussions under the shade of the high jail walls. The third portion of the yard was the wasteland, almost like a track but only defined with scarred brown grass from the heavy foot traffic. It was another chat area, always in the sun and available for walking rotations.

Ki and his new crew sat at a bench that resided behind two chess tables. Ki and Pines sat to either side of Rummy. The crackhead fisherman played chess against a wispy white haired old man that seemed dreary, yet slightly interested to have an unexpected challenge. The man's shoulders were thick, especially for how old he was. Other groups filled the chess tables and benches chatting away, talking about life.

"Coal is a very inexpensive source of energy that creates electricity and produces heat. There is about two hundred years of coal left to dig and use as energy just in North America alone, however, if not fully cleaned then the sulfur and nitrogen particles left on the coal get caught up in clouds and water vapors, which later create Acid Rain that harms acid sensitive organisms and could also strip nutrients from tree foliage."

Ki caught his breath and then continued. "This destroys their leaves and leaves them less able to absorb sunlight through their greenery. The greenery, or otherwise known as chloroplast of green leaf pigments, captures the sunlight and begins creating chlorophyll that uses carbon dioxide and water to produce life-sustaining carbohydrates and sugars to generate growth. When burning coal, heavy CO2 emissions are released and get trapped in Earth's atmosphere. Then the Carbon Dioxide sits there, trapping in the Earth's heat from the Sun, creating radical climate changes that scar the shit out of our planet. The dry equator, the melting of ice caps, and developing conjuration of storms. That's most of what I know about coal. I like it, don't get me wrong. It's a cool old plant fossil fuel that hardened over time to create a nice substance for energy, but people rely on it too much."

Rummy nodded to Ki's explanation while looking down at his crossed fingers. Pines watched the chess game, totally content within the shade and a little dissociated from Ki and Rummy. Too many times he has heard Ki's environmental ramblings.

Rummy picked up his head and spoke, leaning back against the yard wall. "They are trying to Gasify coal, which, I think, is then able to steal the carbon dioxide from the coal, creating a purified form of energy with very little pollution. They also found a way to absorb the sulfur and nitrogen particles with a limestone paste. Anyways, I'm not sure how much these cleaning techniques are being implemented now, especially since the Republicans have been deregulating a grip of environmental procedures. So in addition to that I'm really sour about how we mine it. The whole male side of my family has died from the black lung disease. Too much silica dust inhaled from the mines.

"My brother died from it last year, and since then I've been finished with coal. I've been on a search for a nice woman to carry on my lineage. I thought I'd find a nice activist hippy girl in California that was like-minded…" Rummy took a deep breath, grabbing a quick glance at the chess board.

"Rook to C7, Hank what are you…" Rummy let his words fade to the white haired old man trapping Hank's King with his Bishop.

"Check Mate." The old man said with a grin.

"Anyway, the girl, the girl. Oh yes, the girl I found was beautiful and perfect. We seemed to be on the same page, but when it came down to the reality of actually having a baby… she wanted an abortion. Well, that's why I'm here." Rummy shifted out wide and propped his forearms on his knees.

"I went with her to the clinic to get it aborted, even though I pleaded to keep it, my legacy on the line and all. Anyways, I waited there for four hours, and this bible thumper guy dressed in slacks and a white shirt was spitting out blasphemy towards the clinic, preaching about how we were murdering children and sinning against the divinity. I watched him those last two hours, boiling. Getting more and more infuriated by his idiocy. The guy had absolutely no idea. Y'all Californians be wylin I thought. Anyways, I watched, and as soon as I saw a droplet of spittle fly through the air and hit a saddened girl on the cheek while she walked out of the clinic, I broke, and well anyways, I kicked his leg in and broke his kneecap." When Rummy finished he looked up again from his interwoven fingers and noticed fishermen Hank, Pines and Ki watching and listening to his story.

"Anyways, I believe I got off course."

Ki took a break from the conversation and watched six guys play basketball, shirts versus skins. One of the skins, a tall, muscular black guy, dunked hard on a shorter, scrunched-up face Asian dude. Ki could barely make out what he was yelling in triumph.

"Straight from the underground Boii. You've never seen darker punishment, cause im from the deepest depths of the streets!"

Everyone was back together talking about chess strategy, along with two other black guys in their mid-thirties wanting to play against the old man with wispy white hair. Hank the fishermen walked off to the track and everyone formed comfortably in their new positions. Pines started chatting with the black guy who wasn't playing chess at the moment, and Ki caught his name before he started questioning Rummy again, Charles E. Smith.

"There aren't just miners right? There is heavy machinery digging craters of coal that can also easily load it straight onto the train cars?"

Rummy held his pensive thoughts while turning from the chess board to Ki. "Yeah, loading up one hundred tons of coal per car. I mean we're talking loads and loads of that shit. Miners have to rely on conveyor belts that pull little carts full of coal up hundreds of feet from the underground. Anyways, it's a steady system they have."

"It's a system I intend to break. Whether through the conveyor belt, the train deliveries or power plants burning it. If bills and regulations won't work, then something has to change." Ki tilted his head toward the early afternoon sun and embraced the sun with all of its light. He felt good. Even though completely overwhelmed and stressed with the ignorant destruction of their planet, he absorbed a new sense of hope. They were in jail, previously thought of as an arena of hate and depression, but now sitting amongst friends and thinking minds in such a place, he felt that not everyone was wasted space.

"What I'd do for some lead and a piece of paper." Ki breathed.

It was the new chess player's turn, but he stopped, pulled out a pencil and a pocket notepad, and tore one sheet out. He then wrapped the sheet around the pencil and gave it to Ki.

"Here, have this."

"Ah wow, thanks man. What was your name?"

"The name is Andre Richie and this is a trade not a gift." His voice boomed softly with the most suave confidence Ki's seen in years. This guy is the boss of all the boss's.

"Aright," Ki said excitedly. "How can I be of service?"

Andre Richie chuckled, "I hope you really needed that pencil and paper."

***

It wasn't that Ki direly needed the paper and pencil. It was the creation of fate and making new alliances with a team of cool jail birds. It was having a little fun in a place where fun did not exist. It was a bloody life worth living.

Ki walked over to the basketball court and stood on the sideline. He watched for a good five minutes before taking off his shirt. The guys with their shirts on were winning so they'd play next round, king of the court style. While he waited he joined up with two other guys waiting to play. One was the tall black guy that was a dunking machine and the other was a lengthy black guy with a calm and collected scholarly face paired with spectacles.

The game ended and the Kings of the Court did their trash talking and victory waltzing around the new team. A white guy that wore his orange jail cap backwards spun the ball on his finger in front of the guy with glasses, Spec.

"Can you see it Spec? Come on, get it No Eyes. Come on fool." The white guy taunted, but Spec had no response. He bent his knees in a light defensive squat and was ready to play ball.

The first play, the backwards hat guy took the ball to the paint, charging his shoulder into the ribs of Spec. One of his teammates called out, "Peter", obviously wanting the ball for a free three-point opportunity, but Peter drove past the dunk master for an easy layup.

Ki could see why Peter was threatening, he was muscular, tatted, and head shaven in a gang affiliated fashion. The others worried about a guy like that; he was the King of the Court, he was tough, mean, and had enough idiot homeboys around him to feel unstoppable. Ki had a couple tattoos too though, scattered in random spots on his back, flowers, vines, and trees praising the colossus sun, a graying ink splatter on the top of his spine.

For the Sun Gods… Ki rotated his right shoulder and drifted a little away from the guy he was supposed to be defending. That guy yelled for Peter to pass the ball again, but Peter pretty much made the same move, which Ki was ready for. As Peter used his arm to aggressively spin around Spec, Ki made it to him with a shoulder charge. Peter fell off his path to the basket and hit the court with a backwards somersault. The crowd 'owh'd' and 'awh'd' and the chest bumping began as soon as Peter sprung up.

Ki wasn't good at basketball. If he had the ball he'd find a way to pass it as soon as he could. He never was confident in bouncing it or playing keep away, and he'd be lucky if he lobbed it up just right to make it in the hole. He was really a rugby player, so he knew how to hit with his body and he knew tricks on how to play dirty. This Peter guy was his mark and he deserved every bit of dirt.

Earlier, Andre Richie gave out the mission as a humorous ploy to see how Ki would react to such an outlandish request. However, he did say that this Peter guy has been bullying everyone on the court, and that Spec, Chris Junior, was Andre's nephew.

"You looking to get your ass beat, fool?" Peter tried pushing at Ki's neck while also trying not to gather the guards' attention. His voice was low and dangerous.

"I'm going to finish you boy." He growled.

Ki was going to talk back, he did have things stored up to say, however, nothing came out. He just soaked in the sunrays and enjoyed the spectators gathering around to see what will happen next. It was also interesting to him Uka Buka didn't pop out to see what all the commotion was about.

"Our ball," Ki noted. "You dropped it like a bitch." Ki looked back at his teammates. The dunk master was smiling back at him and little Chris Junior was still very focused, probably more so now that the game had a little danger added to it and that there were still 10 points to be scored. First one to 11 wins.

Peter thudded the ball into Ki's stomach and got as close as he could on defense. Ki swung an elbow around, Dennis Rodman style, and was met with a fist in his gut, knocking the wind out of him. Ki off-loaded the ball to the dunk master so he and Chris Junior could have a play. Peter then grinded his heel on Ki's toes center court and Ki pushed him off. The blocky skin headed twit's eyes were crazed with fury, and he started to look more like the menace of society he imagined this place would have.

Chris Junior hit a jump shot and the ball was back at center court with Ki. His opponent was again, nudging his face inches away from his own. He did a pump fake, meanwhile swinging his head around to hit Peter in the chin. He bounced the ball around him and got a pass off to Dunker before he was grabbed from behind and dunked, himself, into the asphalt.

Pines rushed in as the other skinheads rushed from the other side of the court to go against him. There was a thirty second brawl before the guards broke it up.

Ki smiled, blood covering all of his teeth, and yelled over at Peter. "Now that's Yard Basketball!"

Peter just watched him. Quiet now. Never letting his gaze off Ki as the guards separated the two groups.

The next morning, Pines and Ki went over to the benches by the chess tables. The area provided a nice nook of cover to watch over the yard. They sat behind the table where the older white haired man sat in his usual spot, playing against another graying fellow.

"Never realized how enjoyable a gulp of fresh air could be." Pines unhinged his jaw and gently inhaled the slight breeze. Ki watched his friend do this, staying quiet to give Pines the peace of air he deserved.

Ki was worried about investigators finding blood or any other evidence of the Zeppelin Murder. Not only would it get him in major trouble and put a halt to his radical environmental revolution, but Pines...

Of course things had to be harder than they needed to be.

"Sorry Pines. I wish you didn't get involved in all this bullshit." Ki shouldered his buddy and he smiled back at him. Loyal without fault.

He told Pines yesterday morning what really happened on the night of the blood moon. The night of the Republican environmental representative's murder. The night of the Zeppelin. Pines responded by punching Ki in the shoulder and calling him a dumb ass mother fucker.

All yesterday morning Pines was pissed at him, but then he rushed into Ki's rescue during the basketball game showdown and they were instantly back to loyal comrades, fully understanding one another once again. Except one thing that hid in the shadows of Ki's mind. The one thing he knew he had to keep secret. Uka Buka.

The floating wood plank spirit hadn't shown itself the entire time Ki's been locked up. Maybe there was too much cement around the jail. Too confining and not enough nature. Uka Buka usually popped up when Ki was angry about something. Enraged about people's environmental ignorance. When he first encountered Uka Buka, Ki was alone with ZooZa in the mountains. Immersed in nature and immersed in his boiling emotions and thoughts. Those bums on the shore cliffs pissed him off, but Skinhead Peter pissed him off too. Why didn't Uka Buka come then? Maybe because Peter was just a bully and he wasn't harming the environment?

It's probably better for the environment that they were all locked up and unable to heedlessly cause waste. Uka Buka was a soldier of Mother Earth, a figment of Ki's imagination. A very bold figment that Ki couldn't control. He needed to puzzle that out later. The time he had in solitude has given a little bit of his sanity back. Clarity will come. At least there was a balance to Uka Buka's darkness. At least Toko Tuki showed him light. Something Ki could use more of while incarcerated.

Week two of being in jail and Ki thought it was time for something to happen regarding the case. Thus far the only outside news he got was from his mother Leia. She visited Ki one day and then Pines a day later, cringing at the fact that Ki not only somehow got his best friend in jail, but also broke his own nose while locked up, making it jagged and bent to shit.

After that basketball yard brawl, Ki's face transformed a little. It wasn't only his broken nose; he also lost his tooth to the right of his two front teeth, which made him look more like a hockey player than a rugby guy.

All in all, Leia laughed it off, loving both of them and showing faith that this was just a dark cloud passing over, and later, they would enjoy beers while taking in the sunshine.

She told Ki she was taking care of ZooZa and there was no bad news thus far. No good news either, but as the old saying goes, "no news is good news," her eyes twinkled with exalted cleverness.

"I think we are going to have to make a push Pines. The time is now. No one is doing shit in this world and I think… Well I believe we are the ones that need to do it bro."

Pines looked into Ki's eyes. He knew what he meant, yet he also knew about Ki's recent temper from the last three months. Pines was deeply worried about their fate, but he understood the sacrifice for the benevolence of the planet. He nodded.

Other guys started drifting in around them now. They gave the two friends space and had no means of interrupting, they just felt more comfortable and safe around them. Ki and Pines stood up to the bullies. A heavy expression of respect made time in jail kind of pleasant. Life slowed down and philosophy picked up.

Rummy sat talking with a couple new tenants on the bench next to Ki, and Andre Richie took the loser's chair and began setting up his pieces to play against the rampant chess playing old man. Andre put the queen up to his nose and gently inhaled, giggling afterward to the old man's slight huff of a laugh through his grin.

Ki took out his little palm sized notepad and pencil. Since that day he faced off with Peter, Andre gave Ki any amount of paper he desired, however just a couple days after the event Leia gave him a small jail allowance and he used it to buy a notepad and a few more pencils.

"So… We must think and plan for the greatest effect. You know me, Pines. I'm not the smartest weasel out of the bunch, we have to concentrate and reflect as much as possible. Let's start with an area we wish to change." Ki pointed the end of his pencil at Pines.

"Our town." Pines said excitedly, noticeably enjoying this time strategizing with his best friend.

"Ah, well I believe the Mermaids and Grunion are taking care of our little town. Plus we want to make a loud statement, something that's never been done before, something that makes our risks worth it. Hmm, maybe let's begin with that. What we want to change. Let us make a list of the worst pollutants of our time and who is in charge of them." Ki licked the tip of his pencil and jostled his body a bit while smiling, feeling like a scholar and… revolutionist.

Pines scooted in a little closer, "There's the over abundance of plastic and failed attempts at recycling." Pines is a manager at a smoothie shop and has worked hard at replacing plastic straws with paper ones.

Eventually, most of his customers demanded the plastic straw back because the paper straw would fall apart too easily. Now customers can choose between a paper and plastic straw, a small victory but nothing that will make a difference.

"Yes, of course. So… plastic. Let's make it simple for we are simple men." Ki winked at Pines and looked up to see a few others giggling.

"Who makes plastic? At least in America?"

Someone spouted out before Pines could open his mouth. "I used to work for ExxonMobil. They produce a shit ton of plastic. Being the kings of sucking oil. Plastic making was an easy transition into a sister business. They pull in 2 million barrels of crude oil a day." The information came from a balding latino man who was watching the chess match.

"Yes, another big polluter as well, oil. The largest accidental spill was in the Persian Gulf, spilling 210 million gallons, in Florida. The BP's deepwater horizon oil spill lost 130 million gallons. The spill right here in our channel, sparking the creation of Earth Day, was when a refinery spewed 3 million gallons right on our shores. Probably over a billion gallons of oil spilled into our oceans already, destroying aquatic ecosystems everywhere." Ki felt his jaw locking up and his mind getting hot. He took a subtle, deep breath.

"ExxonMobile is definitely going on this list, however, I believe their plastics are more structural and made to last for one purpose, not tossed in the trash after a moment's use. Someone like Coca Cola is responsible for that. I read that Coca Cola is the largest plastic polluter today. Producing 3 million tons of plastic every year, which is like 200,000 plastic bottles a minute."

"Yeah, Coke goes well with plastic polluters. I was thinking of another pollutant I was surprised by when watching this documentary. Cows." Ki could hear Pines' stomach rumble as he said cows. The man had a heavy appetite but always retained his six pack.

"Cattle are responsible for 40 percent of America's greenhouse gasses. Methane gets emitted into the atmosphere simply by passing gas. Their methane burps and farts have 80 percent more heating power than carbon dioxide. And I wonder why we have so much cattle? Because there are over a billion fat fucks gobbling down fast food hamburgers every day. We are turning our little slice of heaven into an overpopulated dump of hell." Pines bitterly released. Ki was proud of how much his best friend picked up over the years.

"A primary reason I don't eat meat. Very good Pines. I'm putting down cattle, Conventional Agriculture, and the overpopulation of the human race. The synthetic fertilizers, chemical pesticides and growing of the same crop year after year degrades the soil and releases carbon into the atmosphere. Who would be ultimately responsible for this? Mcdonalds? Or the Honky Tonks growing our food?"

The voice from the old chess player with wispy white hair came as a shock to everyone, he rarely spoke about anything other than chess.

"I migrated here from Brazil and we exported tons of beef to Burger King. I was a lumberjack and they moved us to cut down areas of the rainforest to make room for cattle ranches. Cleared enough space to raise enough cattle for low-cost hamburgers. I hated chopping down so much life." His voice cracked and he exchanged his knight with Andre's pawn.

"Another addition. Deforestation. Destroying the primary tool that pulls greenhouse gasses out of our ozone. Thanks George. Okay, I'm putting Burger King and Cattle Ranchers down as incentives for ecological destruction."

Pines chirped up, seeming the most uppity Ki has seen in years.

"Should we talk about renewable resources and repurposing biomass other than wood?"

"Nope, sorry little Pines. I know trees are in your last name, but this is a discussion on destruction; let the hippies produce sustainable alternatives."

"Then what about pills, doctor prescriptions and vaccines and shit. Don't Pharmaceutical Companies pretty much pay the F.D.A to allow them to sell us whatever they want?"

"Ah, well this is true but I.. really don't..." Ki rubbed at the back of his neck while he tried to get the words out. "..care if, you know..." Ki wanted Pines to read his mind at that moment, giving him a constipated look like, you know I'm an Asshole, but let's not let all of our friends know I don't care if people get fucked up by aggresively influenced, optional, chemical 'immunizations'.

"I do agree the FDA and Pharmaceutical Companies need to be turned upside down and let all their bribes to approve their drugs and chemicals fall away from that system. You can do anything with money these days, everyone is being bought out, and nothing is safe… but that's kinda what we are going for Pines, to make people feel so unsafe that an inevitable rebellion starts or some kind of political hero gets enough of a boost to change this country." Everyone around was grunting out air blurbs like they had something to say on this matter but were hesitant in warping the conversation.

"What's the FDA again?" A Mexican guy in the back asked.

Andre Richie responded from the chess table. "It's our national Food and Drug Administration that regulates bad shit going into our foods and drugs. But, like Ki was saying, big Ag and Pharmaceutical companies are now funding the Administration, opening an unrestricted gateway for letting cheap and harmful stuff through to the mass pollution."

Andre Richie's taller, more defined brother, Charles E. Smith, interrupted to change the subject. It seemed like whatever he was thinking had been brewing in his mind for a while, and he had an easy opportunity to cut in after his brother.

"Bless'd be, regarding injustices, we are sitting in the creation of what is truly truly the catalyst of many of our problems. Our grand and white led judicial system. That is something that needs to be destroyed and rebuilt anew!" He was sitting back against the wall pushing back his nail callus' and speaking with a swagger that made you want to dance.

Charles continued to himself, "Even the brothers involved in the Senate don't always make the 'right' decisions."

"What is the 'right' decision, brotha? Cultural vastness and ideal freedoms make right and wrong more… difficult to solidify? What's funny about what y'all are saying is y'all ready to do more wrong to make things right." Andre Richie said, chuckling while moving his bishop to the center four squares of the chess board. He had moved his queen in a precarious location while he was talking about the abundance of culture and ideological freedoms. Old George took the bait.

"Check Mate."

Old man George Awhh'ed at the finishing maneuver.

Charles E. Smith mused his chin with his index finger and thumb. "I knew you were going to say that."

Andre Richie chuckled again, "If you're so clairvoyant my dear brotha, why not test your skill on this board of advanced tactical squabble."

"I'd rather be in a pit with ol' Peter the Pan man over there."

"I'll play you." Ki spoke up. He wanted to break up the familiarity and Jail bird tweets. Too much talk, too much attention. Plus everyone wanted to get a word in now.

Ki liked Jail. There was very little waste, no over abundance, no nonsensical plastic to be used for less than a second and thrown into a landfill. There was a lot of time to think, write, and meditate. Even chess had grown on him.

Pines took Ki's bench spot and eagerly watched as the players set their pieces in their designated squares. Spec, or Chris Junior, walked back and forth silently rhyming to himself and doing his thing, however it felt like he was the group's Lookout and first line of defense, though they didn't need it. The area around the chess boards was a beacon of diversity, a place where beings could be.

Ki noticed a French looking guard a small distance away from the tables chatting nonchalantly to a Spaniard with short dreadlock hair. It reminded Ki of a rugby team, a mismatched worldly bunch of brothers and sisters. Ki felt a warm chill hanging onto his spine, like a pillow serpent wrapping its smooth cradle of sly strength around his bones. He hasn't felt that body buzz, that security and warmth since the Elemental Festival, the place of Fish Tanks, Fire Jets and Shroomizoic realms.

Spectacles glanced over to Andre and gave him a nod of assurance.

"Welcome," Andre told Ki, and gently thumbed a border pawn forward.

The other guys broke off into discussions of injustices and victimizations. Pines was mostly intent on the chess game. Listening more to the wooden flat bottoms of the pieces sliding on the marble table of checkered battlements than the yammering criminals.

It was a many headed argument made by men that have obviously done something society saw as wrong. Would their families see as they do? Pine's father died when he was seven and his mother became a revenant traveling musician after his death. They moved from school to school until Pines resisted the school transfers more as he got older.

Because of the mega bond between Pines, Ki and Adam Vander while in Junior High School, Vander's mother offered to house Pines his freshman year of High School so Pines could have a settling family structure. A structure of loving one another no matter what kind of blood was inside or outside their hands.

Leia acted as another mother to Pines as well. She was proud of him for staying next to her son. Following him into the depths of a dungeon to keep her son company.

Ki watched the chess game unfold and pondered a life that may mean dying for his family, his brothers from another and his people. Emotions swelled. Good emotions, ones that made him proud and happy. He began to think that those emotions were worth holding onto. That at least seemed right to him.

"Ah, you have a very aggressive play style… That was foretelling by the way you spoke of revolution Ki."

Ki looked up from the board and at Andre Richie, his cheeks were a chub cheer and awhub sincere. Ki looked back down and he Castled his King and Rook, a solid defensive move.

Andre continued warmly, "I've played many chess matches and what impresses me most about the game is its variability. Almost every game has been different, only 32 pieces and the fate of a kingdom, or queendom rather, falls on the fluidity of the people around her. Every Chess game will have its own tale. Knights can act as honor guards, bishops can be radical suicidals, or Queens can become heroes." Andre replaced Ki's knight with his Queen.

"I've always wanted to write a novel based on my chess matches. The story begins with the first pawn advancement of my first match and ends when my King has finally fallen."

"Sounds boring," Ki broke his honest jab by giving a smile with his tongue sticking out of his new tooth gap.

"Ah yes, perhaps. But you, or my opponent, are what makes the story interesting. This game for instance," Andre sat back and opened up his palms to the board.

"You're attacking relentlessly, sacrificing your pieces, which seem to be all directed at my King. In my novel you would be a great but angry Lord with many devoted assassins willing to die for your cause. You do all those neat tricks like switching your knight with your rook, but in the end no one's left… Check." Andre air clicked an imaginary time clock.

Ki had two pawns, two knights, his King and his Queen. The only way to prevent his King from capture was to sacrifice his Queen. With his pawns and knights far off in enemy grounds, no one will be there to avenge her. He felt time clicking away on the invisible clock. He felt the raw emotion of wasting a good piece. Ki tipped his King onto his side in surrender.

"I only ever really wanted it to be me. It only needs to be me." Ki looked at Andre with humble sincerity. He knew he probably sounded like a crazy person to Andre. His quest had a lifetime of sadness tattooed throughout its parchment. He couldn't expect anyone else, or even a jail bird wizard like Andre to know how deep his rabbit hole meanders down.

Alas, to not sound so poetically insane in front of his good friend Pines, Ki quickened his facial features, turned alive again and called for a rematch. "Let's play another round, this time I'll raise the ol'Dragon Banner and send in my toxicologists." Ki rose a couple inches off his chair and let out a bubbly splurt slurt fart.

Fentawhap

The next day was very cloudy. The heavy mist in the yard hid three of the yard's walls when standing at one. Ki and Pines kept to themselves and went over what they would eat when out of jail. The conversation lasted all day. Pines went back to spam and rice many times over, and Ki wanted endless hot bean and cheese burritos on top of pizza. They giggled and felt at ease on this day, the exterior eyes were softened by the mist and it felt like they had a break to relax.

As twilight colored the sky, they strode into the mess hall for dinner. The hall was a brisk contrast to the mist in the yard. It was a clear square where everything was visible. They followed the herd with cheesy burritos and spam slowly slipping out their reality.

Ki embraced the visibility of the room and used the ink blot of the sun on his back like the power orb that it was really meant to be.

Last night Ki played around with words in honor of the sun. Words the sun might even use if it had a voice to share. Words that Ki desperately needed right now. Before the darkness of his setting completely ingurgitated his soul. Not knowing what was happening with the Pruitt case wore on him.

Once he finished the sun sonnet, in his lightened and gay manner, he discovered another use of the sun's radiant rays. To shed some light on Peter through the pirouette of brightly words. Ki liked giving his enemies a little piece of him, one last attempt of peace, or one last push that shoved them over the edge. Ki didn't care either way, he just wanted to test out the psychology of the matter. He gingerly remembered giving fourth grader Frank a poem that expressed his feelings and a little sense of truth. Even though Frank kicked Ki in the nuts he turned out to be an alright person later on.

Ki rehearsed the poem while waiting in the food line. Pines' broad back was nice to bounce his words off of.

"Sun.
Son, let me show you the light.
The Darth of fire bringeth no color,
And cast into its shade of cooling sight,
The blind balance of lawless right.

As we worship the floating sphere of heat,
Could we grasp its lessons of being?
Ultimately so pow'rful it best keepith out of range of our fleets.
Able to heal if absorbed, and torment if un'free'ing.

Taketh my energy, my solar flare,
Which giveth growth and possibilities of life we could share.
Taketh the warmth and blasting glare,
Rotating revolutions for you to bare.

Sun giveth my son life.
Thanketh the Lord of Patience and brilliant light."

Ki picked up his food and headed over to where Pines was sitting, right between Rummy, Andre Richie, his nephew Chris Junior, and Charles E. Smith.

After Ki sat down, Pines spoke to him in a half whisper with a spoon full of mush hovering in front of him, awaiting entry for consumption.

"Some regal spread eh?"

Ki huffed, and he noticed Peter staring at them two tables down. His thoughts returned to the sun and its power and glory. He inhaled a deep breath and sat up straight. Fire, Burn… It wasn't exactly his subconscious that said that. The inner voice felt ancient, totemic. Uka Buka was coming back.

Ki tried waiting for Peter to leave the Mess Hall first. Pines and him speaking solemnly with their table mates about their past lives. Andre and Charles were Sports Broadcasters for Strictly Sports Productions, Old Man George was a retired Carpenter from Brazil, and Andre Richie's nephew, Chris Junior, was a semi-professional hockey player. Then there was Peter, obviously a dumb shit hate bucket that probably jerked off too much in his mother's basement.

"Alright here we go boys." As soon as Ki got up, Peter and his posse came over looking like they were about to leave too. The huddle was a notch of confusion and disillusion for the guards. Ki left any intention of spinning rhythmic words for this dodo brian. He wanted to rip one of his ears off instead.

"Hey fucking cunt, I'm going to kill your ass." Peter was a head taller than Ki, but the Sun triumphed in all heights. Peter was a scary mofo, but Ki had the blessing of inner light and felt darkness empowering his fists.

His salty swagger between goodness and badness made his mind swim. As Ki was about to say something back, he saw Old Man George slipping between Peter's backup goons, and within an instant, George pulled Peter's pants down to his ankles.

Ki gave Peter a hard push and watched him fall. "We have bigger fish to fry then you, you little whiny ass bitch!"

The crowd stirred to an aggressive face-off, waiting to see what happened when Peter rose.

"No wonder they call you fools, Peckerwoods." Charles E. Smith jestered. The laughter spiked a testosterone filled row as everyone started pushing and bumping chests. It took Pines two to three glances to notice the entire Mess Hall surrounding the skinheads. The Correctional Officers broke up the mobbing bunch in a jiffy and Ki heard a familiar voice behind him.

"Mr. Pines and Mr. La'dori. Roll it up for release." Fentawhap the massive red headed Sheriff that was a part of the Grunion Rugby team, had the slightest smirk on his face. No one in the Mess Hall would know that smirk except for Ki.

As the group dispersed, Ki nodded gratefully to Sheriff Worden, A.K.A Fentawhap.

After they retrieved their belongings, the Sheriff nudged them to follow. "Over here, I need to talk to you in private." The two of them walked over to Fentawhap's patrol vehicle. The breeze felt intensely amazing. The freedom to look up and see stars empowered Ki, he felt fucking great. Pines let them go with pleasure and stretched while scrolling through his phone.

"Well, no hard evidence. Probably thanks to Kavika for 'accidentally' spilling that bleach all over your cab."

"Oh, Pines was just looking after lil Z. What do you mean no hard evidence? Everyone saw me smash my speaker on that worker's head."

Sheriff Worden got real close and growled his words into Ki's mouth, "I matched your tires with the treads leading away from the bonfire of bodies and gasoline. I know what happened Ki. Now you and your friend are out of jail. Probably dodged twenty years in federal prison. The least you can do right fucking now is be honest with me." His voice was low and steady, his teeth and tongue freshly brushed by the smell of it.

Ki took a second, he hated lying and Fentawhap was somewhat of a brother to him. "Exact match eh?"

"Yes. That was enough to incriminate you Ki, and charge Pines with accessory to murder! How the fuck did you go to that extent?" Fentawhap made a slight motion of slitting someone's throat, however, it was done at his waist to stay ambiguous.

Ki felt bamboozled about his situation. "What about the Officer that arrested Pines? He was there when Pines was using bleach to clean up my truck."

"Pines did well. No blood was found, and when I did the tire tread investigation and found a match, I slid it under the rug."

"How did they initially think I was attached to Pruitt?"

"The anonymous witness identified a gold Toyota from the Zeppelin crime scene. Then Officer Whitney was saying how he pulled out a bloody speaker box from the bed of a gold Toyota the next day." Sheriff Worden studied Ki and hardened his tone.

"I need to know you're alright to be out in society. To be close to our friends. I need to know you're not a twisted fuck." Again, his voice was very low and hot.

"I was just pushing him for more information. Searching for who pulls the strings in these destructive environmental decisions. And we were getting somewhere, somewhere fucking dark. Then his friends came over and he did exactly what I told him not to. The guy was bottom of the barrel Fenta, and I think he worshiped the devil."

"Listen to me Ki… I… I understand." He was still close. His kevlar vest was bumping Ki's chest ever so often, and Ki was pinned between him and the patrol car. He smiled and leaned in even closer to see if Ki would lean in or away. Fentawhap smoothly leaned back and laughed.

"Oh Z, your face is so fucked up. It looks like you are always right about to sneeze with your smushed nose and squinty eyes. And that missing tooth!" Sheriff Worden weezed out the last of his laughing bellows and tried to straighten up.

With a relaxed face he continued, "There was something very serious that happened during the Zeppelin Blood Moon night…"

Ki watched his eyes. They were honest eyes, but darkness lay behind them. Grit. And at that moment, laughter.

"Z, let's go over here. Man, your face is hilarious. I think it's the tooth. Just try and keep your mouth closed for a second, yeah?"

Sheriff Worden moved them under a tree trunk shadow and took a deep breath.

Worden produced a note and handed it to Ki. "A certain somebody," he tilted his eyes to the note, "is looking for a secret informative data chip. This chip was inside Mr. Scott Pruitt's cell phone. Since his phone is gone, somewhere…" Fentawhap slowed down for that part, obviously hinting that he knew Ki took it.

"The local mob is in an outrage." Fentawhap shuffled his voice down to a whisper. "I overheard them outside the Precinct talking about Pruitt's cell phone and needing it for its classified information… Something about resolving their sins…

"Anyways, we will worry about this later, but you need to know that Zeppelin ride was ridiculously covert. We can't find one…" Ever so slowly Ki was opening his mouth and revealing his teeth. Sheriff Worden's laughter stole all literary consciousness right out of him. He tried recovering with squinted eyes and controlled breaths while motioning Ki to close his mouth.

Straining not to smile, Worden continued, "We can't find one person that was there that night. Our witnesses were anonymous. Even my superiors say it might as well have been a ghost ship sailing amongst the blood moon. Mr. Pruitt was also the only identified death. The other two, based on dental records, had altered their identities in our database. So we can't talk to their families or check on what they were doing or see where they came from. Pruitt's wife is all Xanaxed out and as much help as a goddamn stranger.

"Based on the mob losing their cool over a dead man's phone, I'm betting that phone has some juicy shit on it, bad juicy shit. Bloody, Moony shit mixed in with all that ghostly business. I'd stay far away from -" Fentawhap gestured at the note he recently handed Ki, "unless you want a beheading." There was a moment's pause. Ki looked up from the Sheriff and then at the stars as Sheriff Worden scanned their surroundings.

"Thank you Connor, Thank you for everything… but mostly thank you for being opened minded and truly caring about real fucking justice. That comes from the gut. It's hard to trust your feelings, but that's what sets us apart. This is a big mystery that can uncover a lot about why our world leaders are so fucked up, I think." He looked down at Worden's note, it read, Zendolini.

That's Zendolini Waste Management, why in the hell would they want Pruitt's phone? They're the mob? Ki's thoughts were hoodwinked at this new information.

Curiosity still tingling through Ki's brows, he cracked the knuckles of his right hand with just the clench of his fist. "I'll investigate this further."

"Ahhh, Ki, no you don't. I see that look. I'll see to these boys eh. You, my friend, need to keep a low profile. This is my case. If you want to help, bring me Pruitt's phone. I'll see you soon. The end of the year banquet is coming up. You should be there… and by the way, you still need to go to court for the speaker-bashing assault, alright?"

"Yeah for sure, I am very sorry about that too."

The Sheriff shook his head and began walking away with a smile.

"What about a ride?"

"See you guys later. LATER Pines!"

EDEN

Dave Baggans loosely hung the phone to his ear while dangling the microphone part anywhere that wasn't his mouth. He gave a quiet giggle at Fish, barely managing to juggle a reddish bamboo printed scarf, a Lagunitas bottle of beer, and a green apple. The humor came from the manner he had to toss and catch the twisting slow falling scarf.

"Yes, yes, the CCA stocks are bulletproof, government operated, more and more people for consumerism, which means more reason for companies to pollute and get their product out."

He grasped the phone a hair more tightly and listened with intent eyes. "Yes, the more a corporation produces waste and is intent on their traditional wasteful systems, the more money they spend on Carbon Credit Allowances, which later fund Environmental Beneficial Policies. Yes, Yes Mrs. Willshire, Yes I will tell her. Okay. Okay talk to you soon."

Baggans stood up from his chair and was just barely fast enough to catch the shook up Lagunitas bottle Fish threw at him. He looked down at it, "Ahh, I'll take the apple."

"Ahh, what about the scarf?" As Fish was flossing in between his butt cheeks with it.

"You take the scarf bud. Let's get going, Tawa's counting on us to make an appearance at Eden." He popped the beer bottle cap and a volcano of fuzz went straight to his mouth as he guzzled it down.

Within five seconds Fish folded up the reddish Bamboo leafed scarf and tied it over his brow. He might have looked a little like Rambo but without all the muscle. Fish was just Fish, a bag of skin and bones, a fish ready to swim upstream at a moment's notice. His body was regular, his thoughts were grand and happy, and his heart descended from the Sun's own grace. Baggan's heart shown just the same. These two guys were ready to unleash righteousness for the Planet, and if that meant getting a little rough around the edges, then say la ve.

Fish had a tank top, bamboo leaf bandana and a little slice cut into his nose from stone chips flying and hitting him in the face. Baggans was fully suited in his business clothes, but they were loose and flashy. Bags always looked good and comfortable in slacks and a button up. Something about his heavy size made whatever he was wearing seem appropriate.

They jumped into the Cadillac Deville and drove out of midtown to the Garden of Eden.

***

"We have the Fisheries, over fifty contributing restaurants, one High School, two Junior Highs, and two Elementary Schools all dumping their Biomass here at Eden Gardens. If we had a hold of three other composting slash farming locations; one mountain side, one east side of town, and one ocean side, that would be ideal." Colin leaned a bit on the shovel as he talked. He was turning the compost with his intern before the Zendolini group showed up. His blonde and balding head was slick with sweat.

Tawa moved in a tad closer to speak, "Other than the 1383 Bill of Statewide Mandatory Organic Waste Collection coming into effect. I also had an idea to incentivize the community towards composting instead of throwing their compostable waste in with landfill garbage and recycling. Lunch Lady Su's uncle owns a gas station on the main strip. If we could give residential compost points towards gasoline, cutting their cost down on transportation, they could be motivated to compost more." The main strip Tawa spoke of divided the quaint town of Ellipsis in two, making Eden a central downtown location.

Colin nodded his head and turned around to watch his intern rotate a pile of organic matter. Brock slid in as if sympathetic for once.

"Our trucks use biogas through our Anaerobic Digestion process. Giving out gas coupons and using biofuel could be advertised as a strong incentive to join the cause."

Tawa, Colin and a Mermaid named Honey, a quick, split the lines and hit the gaps kind of rugby player, were all there staring at Brock in surprise. One of the first moments Brock seemed to be on their side, interrupted with Fish sneaking up and covertly trying not to distract the group. Baggans was off seen talking with the intern, now taking a big chug of water from his metal canister.

Brock looked back at them and his tone changed from sympathetic to harsh. "The two trucks we are already providing for the extra compost pickups puts our vehicles to the limit. That means no backup vehicles for Zen Industries. If you guys are planning three more locations, you'll have to show some revenue at Eden first. Think of this as a test pilot…" Brock did a consciously calming exhale.

"We are trying to help, just don't take advantage of our generosity."

The testosterone heated the afternoon gathering as if the sun flushed in disappointment. The comic, the geek, the Honey of ages revealed her offerings with glee. "I'll drive my truck and do some pickups."

"The Zendolini's have garbage packers Honey, one truck can get to… maybe 700 homes which is about 7 tons of biowaste. Even with your new Toyota Tundra, it would only allow you to carry a ton and a half, which is about 160 homes. Even then, you wouldn't have a packer, so there would be a gigantic pile of green waste and bio scraps strapped to the back of your truck." Colin had his mouth open to give Honey more examples of why her idea wouldn't work, but Tawa gave him a hard thumb poke in the ribs.

"Well shit, you guys need to lighten up a little bit and just go do it. Once things get momentum more people will join in on composting. It seems easy enough, just throw your biowaste in your green waste bin…"

Honey thumped her foot down to solidify her statement.

"Hmm, maybe we will need larger bins if households are doubling up like that."

One of Brock's two associations, Tony Two Fingers, boasted a low bubbling laugh with his thumbs tucked into his waistband. The other, Charlie Do Little, stood there quietly, spinning the center part of his ring on his index finger. Around public ears, the two of them, of course, went by Tony and Charlie, but Colin extensively did his research on the Zendolinis, and he knew a bit of who they were, even if it was just the smallest bit.

For instance Charlie Do Little was Mr. Zendolini's right hand man. It didn't seem like he acquired his name from being lazy either. He seemed more like a thug who moved very little and didn't say too much, but when it came down to the nitty gritty, he'd create a lot of pain.

Colin had always told Tawa everything, so Tawa watched as Tony rubbed the back of his head. She expected to see mutilated digits, but his hand seemed to actually be a regular Italian sausage mitt. The only irregularity would be the three large golden rings on his right hand, index, middle, and thumb. Tawa suddenly puffed up, and decided she'd follow through with more detective investigative practices later on in life. Two gold rings on two neighboring fingers.

"Why not leave the biowaste in the landfills, it decomposes, right?" Tony didn't say that as a question, he just spoke guido.

"Yes, the organic compounds do biodegrade but our Earth wouldn't reap any benefits from it. Enriching the soil is much more progressive. Plus, left unkept in landfills, it'll create methane gas, which has 85 percent more global heating potential than CO2." Colin answered, loving to dish out information, especially to the legendary Zen Mafioso boys.

"Major nono," Tawa added, now hoping Tony Two Fingers would just stick those golden rings where the sun don't shine.

"Hmph, I got a lot of questions. Lots of scientific, ahh, probabilities going on that I don't quite know about yet." Tony rolled back on his heels with his arms crossed and only his two thumbs popping up from his forearms.

Brock whispered in Tony's ear, and after an indecisive moment of twirls and shuffles about where to go, he walked back to their black executive Zen Industry's truck.

Tawa was very impressed that these types of men still existed, she thought all the wiseguys died in the 90s.

Charlie, easily the tallest of the three mobsters and standing to Brock's right, was an older gentleman with short graying hair and a godfather style look in his eye.

"Let me guess. We drop the loads right where Sally Young Mud is shoveling the Yuk?"

Colin nodded and Tawa stepped forward as if knowing what was about to happen.

Charlie spoke up before she broke a twig.

"That's all we need to know, the pickup and the drop-off spot. Take it or leave it. Don't bug us with the rest. Every two weeks we get four truck loads for our Anaerobic Digested Biofuel. And every month you pay us the transportation fee for all loads that are dropped off into your farms… Have a nice day."

Tawa shook with impatient nerves, "How much is that going to be?"

"We will see at the end of the month." Charlie put his hand on Brock's shoulder and they walked away.

Fish stepped into where Brock was standing as if triumphant in having the last stand. "We need a dump truck for our own waste management business."

"They have the city contract Fish. We can't do anything without their consent." Tawa responded like a Fairy's whip.

"Maybe we could advocate composting for fuel. The more composting a residence does, the more biogas points they could acquire. Fossil Fuel Gasoline is at an all time high. And maybe the Zendolini's could be in the market for a renewable source of vehicle fuel."

Tawa bludgeoned a smile at Fish and forced herself to relax her shoulders, looking at Colin for a Fish debriefing.

Colin acknowledged the look and spoke gently.

"There is the Renewable Fuel Standard Act that requires gasoline manufacturers to mix biofuels with commercial gasoline. So ten percent biofuel is already in our everyday commercial fuel. Supposedly any amount higher than ten percent biofuel cycling through our vehicles will be… defective…" Once Colin caught momentum in divulging information, he'd preach and teach all day long.

***

Baggans picked up a pair of gloves and slapped them across his left hand. "Heya Tommy Boi. How was your season bud?" Colin's intern was no other than little 13 year old Tommy Perez, an 8 man for the Stingray Youth Rugby Team.

Tommy took a break and drank some water.

"It was alright. We lost most of our games, and coach is struggling with finding a position for me." Disheartened, he chugged more water.

"Ah that's ridiculous you're right where you belong, 8 man is the forward's captain bud. That's a great position."

"Coach tells me I need more weight and muscle. So I was thinking I'd join the gym this summe-"

Baggans interrupted, "I've seen you Tommy…" Baggans rolled his eyes in annoyance with the youth coach.

"Listen, strength isn't measured by how big your arm is, strength is doing what's right, no matter what. Do what's best for your family and what you believe in. Rather than going to a gym, be there for your mates. Be a kid and run around. Your Coach thinks he's some kind of professional trainer for the All Blacks or something wicked…" Baggans scrubbed his head, wondering if he was being a good mentor. Tommy Boi did look significantly more cheered up, and he picked up his shovel with a little more vigor.

"See, look at ol'Fishy over there Tommy. That is one of the best number 7s I've ever played with. You know why?"

Brock and his guys were getting in their truck to leave while Fish stood there listening to Colin with his mouth open.

"Because he's smart?" They both started laughing hysterically. Tommy even fell to his knees in the compost, sobbing, then got up and seriously answered Bags question.

"Because he's there for every tackle, he's there for offensive support, and he's there for his mates."

Baggans shook his finger at Tommy, "Fucking exactly Tommy. See you got a good head on your shoulders too. A perfect 8… Sooo you thinking about joining the Grunion when you graduate?"

The Banquet

"**I** love titties!"

"I love TitTies!"

"I love fucking Titties!"

"Ohhh, drink! Down in one. Down in one." The roar of the Grunion echoed throughout the brewery's backside alley. There were thirty rugby affiliates and twenty-two friends, family, and fans, of whom were really only Mermaids or girlfriends of a Grunion player. The server girls dashed around the long table with blushing rosy cheeks, replacing dozens of pitchers at a time. The owner of the bar stood to the side with a grand smile, talking with Baggans and Fish about the present Banquet's costs and provisions as well as next year's sponsorship.

"I'll always sponsor you boys. I sponsored a track team years ago, but they damn sure didn't drink as much as you guys."

"See, even rocket scientists make miscalculations every now and then!" Baggans yelled back, slightly bouncing side to side in his excitement. This setting, the rugby team, the brotherhood, he loved it with all the blood circulating through his heart.

"We just won the Southern Californian State Championship Pete! Let's make it a $10,000 sponsor instead of $5,000?" They looked into each other's eyes.

The group of Grunion burst out in another roar. "Why are we waiting! We could be masterbating! So drink Mother Fucker, drink Mother Fucker, Drink!" The unfortunate lad that broke the most recent Player of the Last Match rule was struggling getting the last of his beer down his throat. His smooth chin and blazed eyes of exhilaration showed that he was one of the young rookies of the bunch. Being young or a rookie didn't mean you were hazed more in rugby, just meant you had to get used to following the rules made by the gentlemen who play a hooligans game.

The rookie finished and yelled out, "I love titties!" Then another spouted, "I love Titties!" Was heard at the far end of the long table. A phrase you had to say after you finished your beer. Merman's rule. Merman being the Player of the Match, and being there are matches year round, the rules always change.

Fish and Baggans reverted their attention back to poor Pete. Pete was a retired rocket scientist who loved beer, so he created this brewery. He usually had the entire backside of his brewery devoted to the rugby team and continued business with the regulars in the front, but of course today was different, today even the regulars trickled into the back to witness the celebration. A Championship win and the end of the Grunion season. The Banquet.

"This…" Pete was already a little bit tipsy as usual, so he meandered through his vocabulary before finding home. "You… boys, are fucking great. I love you guys. I'll do $7,500 with an additional keg for every home game next year!" Pete rocked back and forth, the drunken, jolly rock that just made everybody want to sing for him! He downed the last sip of his beer and cheered, "I love TITTIES!"

The Grunion responded harmoniously with Baggans and Fish at its lead.

"For He's a Jolly Good Fellow, For He's a Jolly Good Fellow, For He's a Jolly Good Felloww! Which nobody Can Deny! No One Can Deny!"

The clash of beer glasses and the rumble of dancing on top of the tables created a chaotic vibration of excellence that made the server girls send out the busboys for pitcher refills and broken glass clean ups. It was like carnival entertainment right there at your local brewery. And once the singing started, songs would roll on throughout the night.

Fish twinked, stuttered and moved through the singing crowd of fans and Grunion. With a sloosh of beer he successfully unlatched the back alley gate and bear hugged Ki's head.

"Welcome back Brother! You're one ugly son of a gun now, eh?" Fish kissed him twice on the forehead and went in to hug dear Pines behind him.

Ki walked in, administering their secret Grunion handshakes for every player he passed. He hugged Mokes, kissed Jason Su, was handed a pint from Wino, and locked eyes with Sheriff Worden, who was cracking jokes around the center of the long table with a couple star players. Some of the best rugby players Ki has ever seen, in fact.

While Worden's eyes were still locked onto Ki's, the Sheriff downed a full beer within a second and yelled sternly, "I Love Titties!" The humor of the entire situation broke a slight smile on his lips.

Ki responded by downing the full pint Wino had handed him, and yelled in defiant competitive glee. "I Love Titties!"

Then within moments, six more sporadic boasts of "I Love Titties" shot out throughout the team. The last being Baggans. They cheered and laughed and refilled their pints.

***

Ki was in the corner with seven of the Grunion superiors. He absolutely loved his rugby team. He looked down the long table at all of his mates and knew no one had an ounce of hate in them, maybe a tablespoon of hate, but all in all they were happy and loving. They were lucky enough to let out their aggression on the pitch, allowing a surreal confidence and ease in the real world. The best thing that Ki adored about the Grunion Rugby Club was how they left zero waste in all their event wakes and during all their games. Without even trying. Every year, the club provided each player with a cup, and beyond that, the players simply followed the basic guidelines. For example, one of many set rules was, once you finished your beer you had to tilt your cup over your head to show that none went to waste.

Another unconscious no waste tradition was the team always drank from kegs that were reused, and they always played with the same rugby balls year after year. Really the only wasted material was athletic tape for injury prevention, but Ki let that slide. He didn't know any other association with this amount of people that wasted so little. His eyes watered, then he straightened up quickly, looking back at Pines telling the story of Peter the Skin Head and Ki's altercations in jail.

"When I saw them, Peter had his trousers down to his ankles with Z standing directly over him with one missing tooth." Sheriff Worden spouted his perception of the story while walking into the Grunion elder's circle with a pitcher of beer in either hand.

"Sounds like another one of your Fentanyl cases eh, Sheriff Fentawhap?" Stank Dick, the Captain of the Club jokingly asked, a little hesitant in how the Sheriff would react.

"That's right Stank, always standing over unconscious bodies or folks with missing teeth, either on the pitch or out on the job." The group laughed and settled in.

The Grunion's South African Coach chimed in, always preparing for next season and trying to motivate and guide everyone to their top potential. "You be playing for us next season then?" He said in a brisk South African accent.

As Sheriff Worden and Coach joined heads on strategy for next season, Ki found a moment to ask about how their environmental subdivision was going.

"Well, we sort of have a contract with the Zendolinis." Baggans put in, kind of looking away and uncomfortable about bringing it up. Worden gave a quick concerned glance at Ki and went back to his conversation with Coach.

"Tawa and Colin are taking a big step forward in creating compost collection centers and biowaste hauling but… but the Zendolini boys are…" Baggans thought for a moment, "Come on Bags spit it out." Mr. Lunch Lady Su expressed while munching on some cheese quesadilla. He had a cooker's apron on and his arms bulged out of his shirt, a fine Prop Tight Head, Number 3, who always cooked for the team no matter in what setting.

"Mafiosos." The group got quiet. Stretch, a tall blonde that played Lock, number 4, slowly sipped his margarita after including his input. Lunch Lady Su pointed at him with his elbow. "Buffalo Stretchy boi."

"Oh, well I guess I'm not buying you guys drinks at Lucky's."

He jiggled his head like they do in Bali and switched to his left hand to down the margarita. Everyone stared in anticipation and then he yelled, "I Love Titties!" Baggans finished his "I Love Titties," and Fish, of course, followed, "I Love Titties!" Even though he was about forty pounds lighter, he always tried to keep up with the big boys, which was why he always blacked out during an outing.

Twilight softened the sky and the clouds wisped by in a purple haze. Fish went out to search for more pitchers and Baggans continued the Grunion summertime environmental agenda. "Aside from the composting, now that it's summer, the team could start doing trash pickups along the coast most Saturdays and work with the Mermaids on sequestering carbons and gardening Sundays."

Ki nodded, "Nice. Make sure to check the Summerland Cliffs too, there's polluters that hang there and tons of trash-," he stopped because he noticed Sheriff Worden giving Ki another look, but this time it was a suggestive glare, connecting the dots as he tinkered through the flush of alcohol in his investigative mind.

Ki looked down and pretended to fix his missing tooth.

The cheers of 'Titties' and 'Merman' paraded the team right out of the brewery and down Ellipsis' windy lamp lit streets, all the way to their night time pub, Unluckies.

***

The hard stomp and bustle of momentarily courageous youths walking from bar to bar passed through Pines' marijuana haze as the smoke twisted through the sidewalk air. Fish stood with him and twinked at the sight of a group of night-ready Mermaids laughing their scales off while heading into the late night rugby bar.

"One hell of a night, eh Pines?" Fish said with a smile that cut his face in two.

"I'm certainly feeling good." Pines responded with his gaze set in the cosmos. A lot was happening to him recently and secrets were a struggle when surrounded by close friends. Pines could easily feel resentment with Ki, so Ki decided to leave Pines alone for the night.

Kate Neilsly nodded at the bouncer of Unluckies and he stepped aside with a grin as Kate and three of her teammates sauntered in. The head bouncer was also a member of the Rugby Association board. A retired old brute who still managed to keep the boys safe late at night as the Vice President of the Grunion.

Kate wore a black mini skirt with a blue green scale halter-top and her other Mermaids wore hot summer get-ups. Jacklyn Poxer sauntered in wearing blue green scale tights that her butt ate right up. So, instantly after they walked in, a line was created outside of Unluckies. Most of the locals called the bar Luckies for short because it only took one outing to discover the bar's sarcastic humor.

The Mermaids continued past the main bar, through the dance floor, through the alley of bathroom dandelions and straight to the back where there was a super open space with heat lamps and star visibility above. It was more of a lounge with a balcony overhead and a tiki bar in the corner by the back door. The girls had the confident fighter strut along with their thick muscular thighs and calves that almost made them seem like they were a part of an Olympic team.

The three dazzling beauties swiftly spun up conversations with the Grunion, and Kate Neilsly stepped between Ki's legs after he sat on a

185

stole with his index finger hooked through a steaming mug.

"Tea!?" Kate exclaimed. Honestly taken back by Ki's choice of fluid intake.

"Aye, a gentler buzz on me mind, body, and soul."

Kate turned to the bartender and asked for four shots of tequila. She eyed Ki if he wanted to join. His eyelashes fluttered in a relaxed no.

"I love your look Ki." She remarked while dreamily looking at his mouth, longing to be kissing his missing toothed smile.

Ki gave her what she wanted and smiled. "I love your mermaid top."

She blushed down and passed a hand over where her tits were getting hard.

"I missed you at the Speak Easy Ki… Was it because you were getting yourself in trouble again?"

"I-"

"Jessie told me. I know what you are up to." Kate turned again and took a moment to collect the shots, pass them around to her girls, bump their butts together, and throw them down the hatch. Her eyes glazed and she nuzzled her upper thick thigh closer to Ki's crouch. Her black skirt lifted just enough to see tan skin and a string of white cloth.

"I like a man that fights for what he believes in." The bartender passed her a steaming mug and she set it down next to Ki's.

"Cheers to the destruction of the machine. Where catastrophe is the only means toward a better world…" Kate Neilsly's face turned in, acknowledging new arrivals before her eyes pulled away from Ki. It was obvious she didn't want to depart from their moment of attraction, but the materialization of an explosive energy challenged her stubborn lust.

Cheering and shouting were effects Baggans had on younger players when he entered a bar late at night. Tawa Pawni trailed behind him with her usual steampunk rainbow shades and long flowing black hair taken out of its dreaded braid. Compared with Tawa, Colin's fashion style was bland and boring, yet his cool unperturbed existence reversed the effect of his boring clothes. He was just a normal guy on the outside, but on the inside he was as colorful as Tawa's lenses.

Behind the rainbow children came two tough guys. One of the

bruisers had cauliflower ears and a scar on the back of his head, while the other guy was taller than most in the room and dressed very well, seemingly walking with the confidence of a powerful CEO of a company.

Ki didn't know what Jessie told Kate, but it probably wasn't anything about the Blood Moon night. It couldn't be.

He pulled her in by her hips and whispered in her ear, "I have zero time for waste babe-a-tini and you are everything but. You are the unseen world I want to explore."

***

Baggans meandered over to off-duty Sheriff Worden, Fentawhap for tonight, and introduced the Zendolini to him. Ki had the group in his peripherals, though his hands grasped something he'd been wanting for a long time. A hot lady, check. A lady that had enough clairvoyance to know Ki's beliefs may be the only way to actually get some environmental productivity done. Double check, with a Mermaid on top. He glanced at the bucket of cherries behind the bar.

People could be holistic in ideals and beliefs or simply reside in a life of chaos, where destruction comes easy to them. The mind's integrity wilts to patient thought provoking agenda's and sloppily retracts to primitive and instinctual ways. Ways of destruction and ruin. Ways in which you can see a change and feel the action that a being deeply desires.

Neilsly has a doctorate and makes plans for conservative, environmentally beneficial affairs; the fact that she is turned on by Ki's savage decisions must only be because her primitive state was loosening up tonight. People were complex. Light and Shadow were not separate entities, they are one in the same but different based on their surroundings. Blending together as juxtaposition just as preservation and ruin relied on one another to create one another.

The night drew on and became more like a dream. The walls seemed fuzzy, the people a blur, and yet there was a frequency to everything, like invisible lightning bolts were ricocheting off every surface. For Ki, the bundle of friends collapsed in on one another made the storm worth being in.

A plume of smoke came in with Pines and Fish as they walked through the backdoor and joined Tawa's collective. The group seemed a little louder and on edge. Their voices raised periodically and their smiles only wrinkled as a nervous habit. One would think a

Sheriff, an Environmentalist, and a Waste Industry Overseer would be able to accomplish some beneficial productivity even with cocktails frequenting their lips.

Uka Buka flew rotations around Tawa and the fresh bruises of Brock Zendolini. Ki knew Brock from his high school days when he won Lexi away from him, and he knew of his mysterious connection with Pruitt and his phone. Now however, was not the time to investigate, and he was very happy to see the Grunion doing their normal new guy harmless shit-talking routine. A few others were not happy with this, however; by the way Tawa's hands were on her hips she had expected the Grunion to be drooling over a big guy like Brock, but Brock himself wasn't taking the team's quirky sense of humor lightly, which only motivated the Grunion to stir the pot more and more. Seeing how far they could push the newcomer. Brock had the marks of a tough guy, but if he hadn't gotten the marks through the means of athletics, then to the Grunion, he was just a punk-ass brat. His other friend with the scar on the back of his head was pushed out of the circle at this point.

Kate was moving her lips and tongue as if talking was a form of foreplay. She wanted Ki to come with her into her next hot yoga class. Over her, Uka Buka dashed about the room as happy as a newborn clam. Uka would have fit great on the wall behind the tiki bar, although the multi-dimensional real contour of the cartoony wooden face was mostly frightening. There to stir the tepid emotions of others.

He grabbed a black dahlia flower on the end of the bar and held it up between Kate and himself. "Kate, would you be my shadow for tonight, pull outta here and take a spill?"

Kate looked mischievous, an eyebrow crooked, lips partially pursed.

"Only if you give me a rhyme of what you're thinking of doing?" A great pleasurable smile elevated her ears as she waited.

Ki looked at where Pines and the deliberating group were, then at the back door, then up at the stars, and finally back at Kate.

"Aye me Lady, here is your rhyme… We dive to a squat, like in a scrum, but with me as your lickity lock, holding you fine," Ki winked and turned her around to show the funny drunkards stumble while he poetically planned their night.

"With their shoe laces tied, they can only collide, unlucky they can't follow your skirt tailed grace. A flow towards the back, i'll give the bouncer a smack, and we're out of the watering hole they call a groovy place. Once beyond the darkened streets, I'll lay you down and rub your feet, giving your imagination time to warm up the sheets, before finally we fall asleeps."

Kate leaned her head back on Ki's shoulder and smacked her lips. "Ahh, that sounds nice. Let's say our goodbyes then, Shadow Master."

Kate went over to her Mermaids, and Ki went to spikey haired Pines and company. "Aye, we headed out." Ki's hand was on Pines' shoulder, but he looked into his other rugby mate's eyes. They did their secret hand shake and Ki nodded a polite goodbye to Tawa and finally let go of Pines' shoulder, "I'll see you tomorrow bro."

"Wait a minute." The relaxed monotone of Brock almost made Ki smile. A possible altercation. He hoped for outlandishly rude comments, anything to give him an excuse to make Uka Buka proud.

No, no Uka right now. Damn Sheriff is standing a foot away. His troubled thoughts made Uka Buka spin around the bar like a tasmanian devil.

"You are Zero and that's your buddy Kavika Pines. You ran that hippy rodeo in High School. This little group makes a lot of sense now. So far we have talked about murder, the environment and recruiting me and mine for rugby-"

Lunch Lady Su belted out his loud laugh, "You know you want to."

Brock continued, keeping his focus on Ki, "But no one told me you, the lil' cunt that stole my girlfriend, was here and affiliated."

A black dahlia reflected back on the rainbow lens of Tawa's cool shades, her face stoic and hardened. Kate held the burgundy flower up to Ki's nose and tugged at his arm.

"Time to smell your shadow's feet, you hunk." Kate shook with surprise as she saw the serious faces around them.

"See you later, Zero. I might join the team for a spell afterall, if it gets me a chance at ya."

Uka Buka bobbed over Brock's shoulder looking at Ki, almost tilting its planked head to the side like a dog would do at their owner's curious behavior. Ki was bewildered, that was one hundred percent true. There were so many different streams of fate he could swim down. The sun gods told him to lock his knuckles in Brock's shirt and give him a shove, Uka Buka would have loved that. Shove, fight, curse, condemn Brock's sorry ass into the dirt of the rugby pitch.

What kind of stream of fate did he want? He looked at Sheriff Worden and decided he'd float for tonight. The rugby guys will most likely take care of Brock. They didn't like outsiders talking shit to their mates. Only they got to do that.

"Join the team Brock and we'll see how long you last. Cya guys later."

Ki smiled and walked away with Kate.

Later, while walking home through the dark streets of Ellipsis, he felt good about the night and his interaction with Brock; after all, that young Zendolini was the biggest environmental tool out of the entire crew and would be a great intimidation piece out on the pitch. Ki was also free, out of jail, and minutes closer to snuggling up with his year long crush. And with regards to his passion, his destiny, he was a day away from getting to work… True, blue, no one knows you, destruction.

Brock's Pizzeria

Ki left the bar Unluckies and the group swaggered in uncertainty. One of their leaders, insulted by a Zendolini, and now arguments were steadily fluxing into the conversation. The vibe was off, and Tawa looked ready to depart, giving Brock Zendolini an idea.

"Let's head over to Saul's Pizzeria. I can get us three large pizzas on the house." When he saw that the team was on the fence he added, "and there's kegs of beer."

"We're in," Fish said as he finished his beer. "I love Titties!"

Stretch entered the Pizzeria with his arms around two girls, followed by Tawa, Fish, Baggans, Lunch Lady Su, Pines, Brock, and finally, his scarheaded buddy. Everyone else stayed at Unluckies or went home. The Pizzeria was a dive bar with class. It had dim lights, a handful of drunkards, and a couple groups of gangster wise guys covering two booths in the corner. After they grabbed their beers and sat down at a large booth waiting for their pizza, Pines had something on his mind that he wanted to ask Brock.

"I overheard you talking with Sheriff Worden about a dead man's cell phone?"

Brock grabbed his vest with two hands and let his shoulders droop with the weight. "Oh Kavika, let's not be subtle. I know you and your little E.E.A band of mischiefs were ready to sabotage Pruitt's environmental schemes of pushing oil and regulating the E.P.A. I'm actually starting to think you guys killed his ass. Ah, before you get your panties in a bunch, I think that mother fucker also deserved a big ol' dick up his ass too, but his phone had some confidential numbers on it that would help us improve our waste industry. So now that we are on the topic of me helping yous, what the fuck happened to that dead guy's phone we call Representative Scott Pruitt?"

The guzzling sound of Stretch finishing his pint turned Brocks' attention toward him. As Stretch opened his mouth, Brock quickly interrupted.

"Do, Not, say that stupid shit in my pub, bub."

Continuing his non-abashed smile, Stretch quietly said, "I love titties."

Brock's cheeks darkened and big hands curled into fists. The laughter that came from tall blonde Stretch and his two cute new girl-friends cut into the surrounding mafiosos' conversations. The Pizzeria turned in on their booth. Flood lamps dimmed and chairs creaked.

Baggans picked up his glass and took three large swallows. As his glass tipped over his head, Brock's butt hovered over his seat. The satisfaction from getting the chance to dig into Ki's best friend Pines was all but lost, and his face was full of regret for bringing these ram-bunctious ruggers to his Pizzeria.

In Baggans' ambiguous but fully aware manner, he cheerfully yelled, "I LOVE TITTIES!"

The riot of sprung bodies tipped over every bottle and can on the table, and Baggans' blood splattered the red wall like tiny pepperoni slices. Tawa was faster in retaliation than any of the boys, and slashed Brock across his chin and nose with her nails. He responded with a slap across her face, and then she gave him two more swipes on his forehead.

She smirked and yelled over the fumbling drunks rushing to get to their feet.

"You slapper. Thought you'd be more rock than paper."

"I'd say you are more scissors by the way you fight girl!" All around them the Pizzeria brawl fully commenced. Brock's many rings were what cut Baggans' upper lip, so Pines, a six year jujitsu trainee, focused on completely restraining the heavy hitter. Meanwhile, the other rugby boys slowly funneled out of the booth one by one, com-pletely laying out the jump suit, clean shaven wise guys that attacked them like the dumb low timing criminals they were.

After a minute of scuffle, Charlie Do Little pressed a knife to Fish's throat and called out, "Fermare!"

Fish twinked and slipped out a calm, "Fuck You," to Charlie, only antagonizing the darkened man to press the blade further into his skin.

"Get!" He released Fish. Tawa spat on Brock's pants. Big Lunch Lady Su dropped a metal pizza tray on the ground and walked away cautiously from two Zendolini garbage truck drivers, one of them rubbing his fist in pain. Stretch stepped over a knocked-out chubby guy and helped the two girls out of the booth. Pines released blood-ied Brock and grabbed Fish as they went for the front door.

When most of the E.E.A was safe and huddled by the door, Baggans finally got up off Brock's friend with the cauliflower ears and scar on the back of his head. The dude was glaring up at him madly with bloody teeth and a swollen shut eye. Baggans wanted more but knew he was in no position to keep fighting. Other guys, Zendolini workers or random late night drunkards, stood around trying to look tough for their friends or chicks that still resided in shock. For a loud and rambunctious Saturday night downtown, the five minutes inside this Pizzeria were as silent as a slumber party. Dozens of people breathing heavily and one guy snoring under a table.

Breaking the stillness of the room, Baggans walked past Charlie toward the front door. He threw a sudden right hook that clipped Do Little in his left cheek, staggering the suited up boss back to another red leathered booth.

"That knife was a bad… bad fucking idea." Baggans growled. The couple guys that were going to try and defend their boss, instead blocked Baggans path to the door. He shoved them out of the way and the Grunion left, back to Unluckies to tell the others of their unlucky exploits.

Disaster Master

Birds tweeted and garden metal chimed. Peace tickled Ki's toes as sunlight shone through his window. A moment of love was worth everything he's lived for. Fear was a joke, and hate all but vanquished. Yet, the merge of mind and reality soaked in, and Ki reminded himself that what he truly loved was being threatened, and that threat needed a slap of retribution, even if it was just a speckle of due fate, at least it was something. All because of love… He laughed to himself at the strange equilibrium of love and hate. They seemed to breed in each other's existence. Love is never simple; the element transforms, it spikes in moments and smoothes out in others; however, with love comes the fear of losing it, breeding a hate for whatever may threaten.

What of the monks that practice love only and love for all beings. They live lives that have exiled hatred. But to exile hatred, one must exile themselves. Because emotional elements blow like the wind. A transcendence. It is everywhere and can take many forms. Envy, Greed, Fear, Lust, Wrath, Fuck Brains, are all kin to their mother of hatred. A sore of emotions that seem wasteful and inefficient. Hate continues to melt in anguish and over time, ferments into evil.

Ki slipped out of bed with Kate, grabbed his phone and keys and went for a drive. A moment of space and thought was something he was looking forward to. Little ZooZa curled up next to him on the passenger seat, totally content with her master's decisions.

ZooZa wasn't the only totally comfortable, unknowingly obedient mutt around. Half of the world was so easy to live in these days. The privileged could pretty much go anywhere they wanted, and if they didn't want to stray too far from home there were events, concerts, and parties a block away and accessible every single day of the year. The 21st century even had endless creative ways of entertainment through games and virtual reality, creating an easy escape for poorer societies.

If someone were to choose to become a witch they could throw on google, order some books off amazon and join a Diviners Guild on their PlayStation. Boom, you're a fucking witch, bitch. Evolution made it easy to live, easy to be. We've made it easy to be selfish bastards and live comfy cozy lives. Being in Jail was even easy. Slippery Ki was out in a couple weeks after bloodying three lives. Ki squeezed the steering wheel as he wove in and out of forest roads. Do not give in to the dog's life. Do not obey, do not slow down, however tempting that may be.

The road became thin and ridden with little lumps, bumps, and asphalt patchwork. The last house into this wilderness vanished after Ki turned down another path surrounded by old oaks, and his speed slowed to a lurch down the trail. He didn't worry about anyone coming ahead of him or behind him; it was early enough on a Saturday morning for most to be asleep. Regardless, on this road he would just seem like a hiker looking for a trail up the mountain. He was lucky to live so close to a National Forest, one his Mother stewarded for over twelve years.

Uka Buka awoke when they came nearer to its mountainous hovel, bouncing in the air and serenely watching out the window into the dense forest as Ki's truck wove along the road.

At the top of the mountain was where Ki first encountered Uka Buka. The floating head scared the shit out of him, and it still did just in a different way. Uka was like a salivation, a thirst for blood, or perhaps, as far as illusionary tiki faces go, simply a yearning for change.

The canopy of the trees turned a brighter lime-colored green, and Ki rolled down his windows to try and hear the flow of the nearby creek. Uka flew out of the passenger window, and lil Z sniffed the air behind him, slightly closing her eyes with the blissful fragrance of the wonderful outdoors.

Water shushing land was heard a dozen tire rotations ahead and around another bend. As Ki crawled around the turn there was Uka, bouncing off the side of the road above shrubbery and two twisted, gnarled trees. While little ZooZa padded about sniffing around the edge of the creek, Ki walked over to Uka Buka, bent down and picked up Scott Pruitt's broken cell phone and Mr. Chubby Cheek's empty pistol. Uka Buka continued to float, slightly bouncing, completely stoic and unrevealing in what it wanted next, just a floating tiki plank spirit, blending in with its environment and embodying an essence of nature.

"What does this mean?" Ki held up the broken cell phone while questioning Uka. Uka flew inches forward and then just as quickly retracted back, like it acknowledged the phone's presence.

"Uka BuKa." It said in a mischievous manner that definitely warranted some stamp of importance to Pruitt's phone.

"What are you?"

"Uka Buka!"

Ki tossed his body back towards his truck and shook his head in expecting that Uka Buka would say anything other than Uka Buka. He whistled, watched ZooZa jump into his truck and headed out.

Shadow Tactics

The two sabotagers rested on their bellies, peering out of a bush at the nearest Coca Cola factory to their home. They had a plan and it all had to begin now, right as one of the strongest recorded El Nino's was hitting the Pacific Coastline. Their cover being the loud clatter of the rain, the cozy feeling of wanting to be hunkered inside, and the cold air prodding the weak with sickness and disillusionment. It was hard to witness a couple vigilantes if they were obscured by the gray lines of El Nino rainfall.

Pines and Ki were drenched with water and wet with excitement. They lay there waiting for the last Coca Cola truck to go home. It has already been two to three hours, and not being able to entertain themselves with phones, they rummaged through the mud to find things to pass the time. Ki slowly and ritually stuck twigs in the soft soil in front of him. Once the twigs were sturdy enough and stuck up in defiance of their factorial enemy, he'd try and secure a flat stone on top of the twigs.

"Aye Sally, the twigs be our audience tonight."

Earlier that day Pines and Ki went over the plan and code names. Ki came up with Kira, and Kavika Pinederosa was given the name Sally in a roundabout way.

Pines gave Ki an irking look at his new name.

"Sally I need to know you're in on this, you don't have to do this whatsoever. It's risky brother."

"That's Shadow Brother to you.. K-, Kira. I want to do something more, and this is it. Being a Shadow Brother means I'll always have your back. I'm in, so don't fucking question it again."

Even with Pines' pointy beard and fierce tan cheekbones, he always carried an air of sweetness, like his kind heart pumped an endless river of kindness through his skin, radiating that empathic light that showed through his eyes.

The white Coca Cola pickup truck still sat there in the rain.

"Alright, maybe that's just a parked company car sentinel. Let's try and open those doors and see if anyone is really there. The Mermaids said the coast was clear at this time and on this day of the week. We should be good."

Pines nodded his head. His black beanie tilted at an angle, covering one side of his head more than the other.

Ki tapped his twig stilted stone and whispered, "Uka Buka," as if the words casted a ward spell.

They picked up their three gasoline canisters and ran up to the factory. Halfway there, Pines crouched and raised his paintball gun up to his eye, then took fire on the cameras fifteen feet up on the corner of the roof overhang. After about ten paintballs, Ki ran for the door with his backpack strapped to his chest. He paused. Nothing was heard but rain and the swooshing of cars on the nearby highway.

Ki didn't know much about company security systems today, but he was happy not to hear any alarms. He pulled out his pick lock set as Pines ran in behind him. The tension pick bent in its stress at the lower part of the keyhole and the specialized ribs of the other pick gently clicked the lock's pins up. Multiple resets happened until Ki became anxious and impetuously rumbled the pick in the lock, then suddenly they heard a click, and the tension was released.

"Get ready Sally," Ki whispered. He turned the knob and the machine sound clashed with the rain at their backs.

A flash of unexpected light hit Ki in the face. His eyes weren't exactly blinded by the flood light, but the surprise left him in a blur. Eyes fuzzy with a fresh spike of fear and adrenaline. Fuzzy with Uka Buka swirling about like a tornado. Ki meant for Uka Buka to keep watch this round, not morph into a delirious monstrosity obscuring his sight.

As he looked down and away from the light, a barrel slid out between his legs. The paintball clip littered the flashlight-holding security guard, and the light danced around the room, fostered by the man's discomfort.

Ki pulled his rope out of his backpack as he ran over to the guard holding his groin area and tied him up. Words were being spewed from his mouth but nothing of importance. The Shadow Brothers quickly developed a makeshift gag of duct tape and a rag, then Kira pulled Sally back to the door.

"Ki!.. I mean Kira. There's nothing to fucking burn in this cement shit block." Pine's voice was shockingly calm, clear, and direct. He just messed up one of their main rules for code names. Don't say real names. Pines' less enthusiastic sound after recovering with the name Kira showed his disappointment, but he still stayed calm.

Ki instantly discovered his new name Ki-ra was the worst code name choice. "Call me Zero, Sally." He looked around, still wondering what to do next.

"The security guard could have called someone when the camera was blotted out, or while listening to the lock being picked. We need to get out of here."

The floating plank of wood with vines and leaves draped around its face, bobbed around a big office with large windows. A sleek, dark reflection of a desk and a wealth of paperwork littered on top of it was seen on the big TV screen mounted on the office wall.

"Burn the desk. Burn all their paperwork. Maybe it will jump over to the machines. I'll move this guard outside and away from any harm. Then maybe we can bash the more delicate looking pieces of machinery and throw some of the sand outside into the fuel and oil inputs."

Sally Pines gave a large smile, either because of the great ideas of sabotage or because Ki wanted to preserve someone's life. Pines' usual spiked hair was matted down now. Somewhere in the chaos he lost his beanie. Ki looked around near the entrance and found it right where Pines was shooting under his legs. Most likely tinkered off by his crotch.

Outside Ki knelt down to tie the security guard up to the company truck's wheel rim. After finishing his constrictor knot, he got a glimpse of a raging fire inside and hurried towards the flames with a bucket half full of sand. As Pines ran around bashing the portions of the machine that could be broken, Ki went to the head of the serpent and dumped his sand into the machine's fueling center.

Am I going to have to learn about machines to destroy machines? Ki pondered the irony and felt drier by the second. His clothes were only semi-damp now because the office fire was consuming the whole corner of the building.

Uka Buka eerily watched the flames. It was rare to see Uka Buka from behind, and in this case, being heavily silhouetted by the bright light in front of him, Ki had never seen Uka Buka so darkened.

"Alright let's get out of here!" Now Sally Pines' voice was broken and quivering with excitement. They ran up to their first hideout under the bush and paused for a moment, looking back at what they did.

It was about a two-mile hike back through the foothills near the coastline to get to their car. The little desert landscape was decently covered with little trees and brush, but it wouldn't help much when looking for cover if a helicopter was overhead. Still, the brush was just fine from the view of the main roads and highway.

"You go on and get the truck, I need to wait here and watch what happens."

"What!? No, Ki we gotta get out of here."

"Sally…" Ki drawled, trying to get Pines to start using the code names by the powerful down thrust of his brow and elongation of his name.

"We need to know how fast they respond, or if they respond at all. We have walkie-talkies, let me know when you get back to the truck, then you can pick me up quick on the highway."

The sky had clouds ambiguously cast about. Stretched out, majestic, eerie clouds making the world seem a smaller globe than it really was.

Above the sea and over the islands to the far West arched our waning crescent moon. An elongated cloud just passed her by and the dark side of the moon was clearly shaped. The tail end of the cloud looked like the Zeppelin on Pruitt's fateful night. The light side of the crescent showed him the reflection of the sun, the burly beast that always seemed to be waiting, watching, and making sure everything was going to be alright. Night was almost day, and their escape was right around the corner. Ki felt like his dreams were unfurling into reality. Just need to destroy the infrastructure of the last 100 years. No more machines, no more problems.

He lowered his head so he could watch the Coca Cola factory through the stilted twigs and braced stone. He was going to need all the help he could get, and at that moment, totems and natural divinity seemed the most reliable source.

***

Ki and Pines sat at their local breakfast joint. They were freshly showered and everything was tidied up and hidden away from their first job. Gas canisters, bolt cutters and all. Conveniently for them, a friend of theirs rented a cargo container next to the beach so they could easily come and go, store and unstore as they liked. This was a major benefit growing up in the same town their entire life and keeping strong connections with friends and acquaintances.

The warmth and buzz from the coffee made Ki relax as Pines read the paper. A major element of the printed word, the torn binding and the smell of parchment had always brought a relaxation to his reading. Cozy little word portals opening gateways to news reports and fairy tales. Scrolls to the past, present and future.

Ki watched Pines with betrothed eyes. Across the front of his shirt was a basic image of a wave then a … and a basic image of a mountain. This was the most commonly used symbol of their town Ellipsis, which made Ki feel even more at home.

"Man Pines, you are pretty quick on the trigger if you know what I mean. You can keep a level head in shakey situations."

It took a moment for Pines to respond, and when he did his eyes slowly brimmed over the newspaper.

"I think we have to do better than that Ki."

"Yes Yes, I know. There are so many fucking walkers on green and blue you can't get away with the simplest factory disassembly…" Ki drank his coffee and leaned back, more.

Pines could see Ki's moment of agitation and pushed the jar of sugar over to him, still focused on the innards of the black and whites.

"Thanks Sally," Ki joked with a grin. Pines closed his eyes in a regretful remembrance of the name.

Ki's coffee buzz left him in a chatty mood.

"I don't like trying to help the planet by using fire. It's too wild and unforgiving. Too much environmental harm can come from it. We needith honor the sun and all her fiery fury… but not like that. The other element we could use as a nice backhand and a strong show of force is water. The element that thirsts for aquatic redemption from product producing tyrants filling up our ocean with 8 million tons of plastic every year. Air can join in as well, she's being choked up by relentless greenhouse gas emissions. Our land being stripped clean of her resources to hamper the same shit bag human beings that shit all over shit. See, we don't need fire; there are other ways.

I'm not quite sure how to use the elements of air and land against its foe, but we will think of something… I've always wanted to derail a coal train, like the Monkey Wrench Gang. That instance was kinda like using the machine against itself." Ki merrily mused over the idea.

Ki held his finger to his lips as if to soften his continued whispers to the splayed open cover of the Ellipsis Newspress. He went on talking to himself about simply deciphering Earth's elements and the intricate design matchups with core emotions.

Pines put the paper down on the mahogany table top and turned it around so Ki could read it.

It Read, A Piece of Harmony with Pruitt at Peace. Then under the title, What the Administer of the Environmental Protection Agency Deregulated With The President of the United States.

Pines decided Ki's yammerings in a crowded cafe was enough and nodded to the door. They got up and left the joint, only to enter into another joint that was pulled out of Pines' front shirt pocket with the Ellipsis Mountain logo on it. Ki's face was engulfed in the paper.

After pulling Zooza out of Ki's truck, they walked a little and reached a dry brown lawn with a couple benches and watched the world pass by. Pines and Ki stood. One blowing smoke out of his mouth and one steaming smoke out of his ears.

"Says here, 240 billion plastic beverage bottles are used yearly, half of which is for single-use purposes, and a quarter of that may be recycled. Estimated that 10 million tons is dumped into the ocean each year… Hitting the beverage bottle producer was really a good start. Their companies use crude oil for-" Pines gestured for Ki to turn to the next page.

"Check out that list Ki." Pines broke into a quiet whisper, "You already did a huge service to the world by deleting such a gnarly environmental foe. This Pruitt. The mother fucker could be an alien based off of what he's done. A massive Cunt Alien. I don't even want to try and think about his, or their, reasoning behind this shit. It's fucking crazy. I guess money, maybe power. Maybe receiving a smile and pat on the cheek from other white cunts that also like to rape Mother Earth for all she's worth. And what's even wilder is that it's not just him, or a few of the privileged elite, it's half this country. They voted, they support and reverberate the hate that they hear. We might have to use fire Ki. Apollo looks after his little sister Gaia, and right now humans are her number one enemy."

Ki started to read off the list of environmental deregulations that

Pruitt and President Trump passed through legislation.

"They removed protection agencies from more than half the nation's wetlands. Withdrew the legal justification for restricting mercury emissions from power plants. Argued that the Obama Administration misinterpreted its obligation under the Clean Air Act to reduce carbon pollution. They worked to open up more land for oil and gas leasing by limiting wildlife protections and weakening environmental requirements for projects. Justifying it by saying environmental agencies were overstepping their legal authority.

"Oh, we've heard this one before; removing the United States from the Paris Climate Agreement, an international plan to avert catastrophic climate change, adopted by nearly 200 countries. Right, they're creating the Keystone XL pipeline that would ruin all habitat in its path, potentially leaking out toxic rivers of oil which could easily pollute fresh water resources in the area… Here's a new one I haven't heard of, burning the tar sands in Eastern Utah's Uinta Basin, which alone will increase the Earth's temperature by a minimum of 2 degrees celsius." Ki's voice became a heavy monoton. Dialog that was packed with heat. A still volcano holding back an eruption.

He steadily read on, desperately wanting to know the environmental damage done but also trying to work through it before his mind exploded.

"Weakened gas standards and fuel economy for regular cars and trucks. Revoked California's ability to set stricter tailpipe emission standards. Canceled a requirement for oil and gas companies to report methane emissions and made it so certain facilities could produce polluting chemicals known as volatile organic compounds." Ki took a puff of Pines marijuana joint for relief and then continued.

"Withdrew a Clinton-era rule designed to limit toxic emissions from major industrial polluters. Amended rules that govern how refineries monitor pollution in surrounding communities. Relaxed air pollution regulations for a handful of power plants that burn waste, coal and electricity."

***

"Withdrew climate guidance directing federal agencies to include greenhouse gas emissions in environment reviews." Tawa Pawin took a deep breath and read a wee bit faster.

"Repealed a requirement that State and Regional authorities track tailpipe emissions from vehicles on federal highways. Changed rules that allow States and the EPA to take longer to develop and approve plans aimed at cutting methane emissions from existing landfills. Most of the proposed policy that would have strengthened pollution standards for offshore oil and gas operations and required them to use improved pollution controls. Amended Obama-era emissions standards for clay ceramics manufacturers. Relaxed some Obama-era requirements for companies to monitor and repair leaks at oil and gas facilities, including exempting certain low-production wells… These leaks are a significant source of methane emissions. Proposed revisions to standards for carbon dioxide emissions from new, modified and reconstructed coal power plants, eliminating Obama-era restrictions that, in effect, required them to capture and store carbon dioxide emissions." Brock had a finger up, like a gentleman waiting to interrupt. Tawa gave him a glare of cold ice, telling of only one thing, listen or die. He put his hand down, accepting the fate of the hour.

Tawa continued, "Again, this is what the Trump Administration and his EPA imposter of an Administrator, Scott Pruitt, attempted or mostly completed while in power.

"They lifted an Obama-era freeze on new coal leases on public lands. Finalized a plan to allow oil and gas development in the Arctic National Wildlife Refuge in Alaska. A move that overturned six decades, six decades of protection for the largest remaining stretch of wilderness in the United States!

"They opened more than 18 million acres of land for drilling in the National Petroleum Reserve in Alaska, an abundance of land previously owned by the public on the Arctic Ocean. And adding to this outrageous intrusion, the Obama Administration had designated about half of the reserve as a conservation area. Then, it says here Trump's Admin-losers withdrew proposed restrictions on mining in Bristol Bay, Alaska, despite concerns over environmental impacts on salmon habitat, including a prominent fishery, resulting in significant degradation of the aquatic ecosystem. Then after that, the scum also lifted a Clinton-era ban on logging and road construction in Tongass National Forest, Alaska, one of the largest intact temperate rain forests in the world. Scarring the land and ripping out trees, macro-ecosystems…"

Tawa sputtered like she was going to say more but the President's actions had already said enough.

She continued after a quickened eye at Brock to see if he was still listening. "Approved construction of the Dakota Access pipeline, less than a mile from the Standing Rock Sioux Reservation. Rescinded water pollution regulations for fracking on federal and Indian lands. Withdrew a requirement that Gulf oil rig owners need proof they can cover the costs of removing rigs once they stop producing. Moved the permitting process for certain projects that cross international borders, such as oil pipelines, to the office of the President from the State Department, exempting the EPA from environmental review.

"Changed how the Federal Energy Regulatory Commission considers the indirect effects of greenhouse gas emissions in environmental reviews of pipelines. Revoked an Obama-era executive order designed to preserve ocean, coastal, and Great Lake waters in favor of a policy focused on energy production and economic growth. Loosened offshore drilling safety regulations implemented by Obama after following the 2010 Deepwater Horizon explosion and oil spill, including reduced testing requirements for blowout prevention systems, which seems to be pure reckless idiocy.

"Proposed opening most of America's coastal waters to offshore oil and gas drilling. Proposed easing the approval process for oil and gas drilling in national forests by curbing the power of the Forest Service to review and approve leases. Approved the use of seismic air guns for gas and oil exploration in the Atlantic Ocean; the Obama administration had denied permits for such surveys, which can effortlessly kill marine life, deafen whales and disrupt fisheries."

Brock started to drift, "LISTEN UP YOU FOOL, FUCKING LISTEN TO THIS! THEY! ARE CHANGING THE PLANET. THREATENING OUR MOTHER! NOW IS THE TIME TO HEAR THE FACTS AND KNOW THE TRUE ENEMY OF THE EEA, especially for the son of a Waste Stewarding Association. Refuse, Reduce, Reuse, Represe, Recycle. Oh, but that's the old way; now it's deRegulate, Reverse, Revoke, Rollback, Retire. Just based off of what I know about this shit, they are cuddling up with industrialized lobbyists to sell products that strip our planet down to nothing!"

The defined beautiful beast of a young man went over and took a seat behind his desk, placed his now lightly scared chin in his hand and used his other hand to wave, continue. Tawa directed her green frost nova eyes back down at the overly wrinkled-up Newspaper.

"They weakened the National Environmental Policy Act, one of the country's most significant environmental laws, in order to expedite the approval of public infrastructure projects, such as roads, pipelines and telecommunications networks. The new rules shorten the time frame for completing environmental studies, limiting the types of projects subject to review, and no longer requiring federal agencies to account for a project's cumulative effects on the environment, such as climate change. Revoked Obama-era flood standards for federal infrastructure projects that required the government to account for sea level rise and other climate change effects. Pretty much saying they don't believe the science and climate change is a hoax.

"Overturned an Obama-era guidance that ended U.S. government financing for new coal plants overseas. Revoked an Obama executive order promoting climate resilience in the northern Bering Sea region of Alaska, which withdrew local waters because of oil and gas leasing and established a tribal advisory council to consult on local environmental issues. Restricted most Interior Department environmental studies to one year in length and a maximum of 150 pages, citing a need to reduce paperwork. That one is funny. For the trees, they said.

"Withdrew Obama-era policies designed to maintain or, ideally, improve natural resources affected by federal projects. Why the fuck would they do that? End environmental impact reviews of natural gas export projects at the Department of Energy. And how did they get away with all of this!?

"They fucked with the animals too. They rolled back a roughly 40-year-old interpretation of a policy aimed at protecting migratory birds. The rule imposed fines and other penalties on companies who accidentally kill birds through their actions, including oil spills and toxic pesticide applications.

"They cut vital habitat for the Northern Spotted Owl by more than three million acres in Washington state, Oregon and Northern California. Opening up the land to timber harvesting. Changed the way the Endangered Species Act is applied, making it more difficult to protect wildlife from long-term threats posed by climate change. Relaxed environmental protections for salmon and smelt in California's Central Valley in order to free up water for farmers. Removed the Gray Wolf and the Yellowstone Grizzly from the endangered species list... Overturned a ban on the hunting of predators in Alaskan wildlife refuge. Reversed an Obama-era rule that barred using bait, such as grease-soaked doughnuts, to lure and kill grizzly bears, among other sport hunting practices that many people consider extreme, and I'd say cowardly as all hell. Proposed revising limits on the number of endangered marine mammals and sea turtles that can be unintentionally killed or injured with sword-fishing nets on the West Coast! Opened nine million acres of Western land to oil and gas drilling by weakening habitat protections for the sage grouse, a bird imperil.

"Scaled back pollution protections for certain wetlands that were regulated under the Clean Water Act by the Obama administration. Revoked a rule that prevented coal companies from dumping mining debris into local streams… So they revoked this rule because they want to pollute the local water? What the fuck." Tawa's face wrinkled in pain as she glared at the Newspaper. Her face was so contorted with angry astonishment that it seemed the paper would go up in flames.

She closed her eyes in pained frustration and went on. Reading slower now as if to protect herself from these flat out mind-blowing environmental sins.

"Weakened a rule that aimed to limit toxic discharge from power plants into public waterways. Ah, okay they do want to screw around with local water. How is this fucking allowed? The Trump Administration extended the lifespan of unlined holding ponds for coal ash waste from power plants, which allows the ash waste to spill onto our Earth because they lack a protective underlay. And they allowed certain unlined coal ash holding areas to continue operating, even though they were previously deemed unsafe.

"Withdrew a proposed rule requiring groundwater protections for certain uranium mines. Recently, the administration's Nuclear Fuel Working Group proposed opening up 1,500 acres outside the Grand Canyon for nuclear production.

"Limited funding of environmental and community development projects through corporate settlements of federal lawsuits. Repealed an Obama-era regulation that would have nearly doubled the number of light bulbs subject to energy-efficiency standards. Changed the process for how the government sets energy efficiency standards for appliances and other equipment. Withdrew proposed Obama-era efficiency standards for residential furnaces and commercial water heaters that were designed to reduce energy use. Changed a 25-year-old policy to allow coastal replenishment projects to use sand from protected ecosystems. The former head of EPA Scott Pruitt stopped payments to the Green Climate Fund, a United Nations program to help poorer countries reduce carbon emissions. Reversed restrictions on the sale of plastic water bottles in national parks designed to cut down on litter. They reversed that, despite a park service report that the effort worked and no one died of thirst."

Brock heard pressure in Tawa's jaw, and her chin looked stressed, like she was gritting her teeth hard.

"Here are some other deregulations they tried for but were pushed back by lawsuits and reversals for their stupidity: Tried to repeal the Clean Power Plan. Tried stopping the regulation of greenhouse gasses from aircraft. Tried loosening the fishing restrictions intended to reduce bycatch of Atlantic Bluefin Tuna. They delayed a compliance deadline for new national ozone pollution standards. They delayed the implementation of a rule regulating the certification and training of pesticide applications, and finally, they tried ending bathroom water efficiency standards because Trump feels he needs to Flush the Toilet 15 times to wash down his fucking SHIT!"

"That's horrible Tawa. I hope your idea isn't to group me up with those weirdos just because of our fight last weekend…" Brock said with a grace of innocence.

"My 'idea' is to show you that bettering the environment is more important than ever right now. I thought you were calling me into the Zendolini office for an operational termination… Why did you call me in here?" Her confusion grew as her words fell through her teeth. Her stance, once tight and upright as a board, relaxed, and her feet slightly slid to either side, giving her a more casual grounding.

Brock chuckled in his fist. "I invited you here to give you good news, Tawa. Mr. Zendolini must have read that same paper this morning. Based on the community garden reports and the steady increase in organic waste pickup results, he wants to expand our resources to an open lot next to the beach. It'd be a great spot for another compost revolving garden." Brock smiled, cracking the scabs of two long scratch marks under his right eye and across his cheek.

Tawa blushed and twisted her body closer to the office desk. "Ah, well… Thanks, that's… great news. Do you mean the gated lot next to the Ellipsis Cemetery?"

Her appreciative acknowledgment of this newly found recognition was silent and thoughtful. Brock finished his giggling, sat up a little straighter, and made to welcome Tawa more wholeheartedly while practicing his duty as an up and coming businessman.

"This isn't some trick Tawa. That fight last weekend was just a late night bar brawl, we all are used to that. Not used to losing, but used to the yammer. I haven't met anyone like you and Colin. You're dedicated to helping others when there's nothing but dirt, struggle and garbage waiting for you at the other side…

"Honestly, my father told me to focus on what the EEA wants to accomplish and to help as much as we can. Something is different about him, like he is trying to get me ready for something, something I haven't foreseen. I can feel it. This time it's not about money or prospering as a business." Brock seemed to have divulged almost too much empathy and sentimental information, making Tawa stir uneasily. Brock switched his attitude to his congenial Brockish.

"You guys have softened him. All this urgency to save a planet that will easily outlast us for another million years. Don't you hippies believe in, let be, be." His right shoulder rolled forward in his usual way when waiting for her reaction. An antagonized reaction.

"Because it's fun to fight. Especially against ones that need a real good beating. You heard what I read, all of that," she pointed her thumb behind her, "bullshit. They are next up for a beat down." Tawa grabbed her jacket.

Brock shrugged off her frustration, "For this new compost lot by the cemetery, we wanted to use Ki as the Garden's head boy. Do you want to go out for a coffee in the Nino and clear up the compost integration operations?"

Tawa definitely wasn't taking any bullshit today. "No… send an email."

Charlie Do Little

The Sheriff's station was a stone's throw away from the recycling center where Mokes worked. He was the material recovery supervisor and Sheriff Worden was the Sheriff. An unlikely duo, however, they still went out to get lunch together every now and then.

This day, now deep in the month of June, they got back from lunch and the Zendolini goonies were there waiting in the parking lot.

"Heya there Sheriff. We wanted to ask yous a couple more questions about the… case." Tony Two Fingers was squinting as if it were bright outside, or he just could have been thinking too hard. The clouds did cast a mellow gray rainy atmosphere.

"Alright come inside, we will sign you in."

"Okay Sheriff, we will be there in a second." Sheriff Worden stood there watching both Tony and Charlie curl in to question Mokes. He didn't like it, but he had to take a shit so he tried to hurry them along.

"Leave him alone ya? You got questions for me then come on in."

"Alright Sheriff, we coming, just one moment with the kid." Charlie spoke. And with his cool charm and slow speech Charlie usually got what he wanted. Sheriff Worden went inside reluctantly.

"You want to make a buck kid?"

Mokes was no kid, but he always struggled with having money, he turned toward the two black long coated thugs, acknowledging the next phase of the conversation.

"We are looking for something," Charlie looked around to see if anyone was in earshot, then nudged Tony to finish what he started to say.

Tony unexpectedly put on the spot, spoke slowly, one word and then another, speaking like a train gaining gradual momentum.

"One… of our clients. Lost… a cell phone. With very important information." There was a long moment of silence.

"Now we are going to need to hear you speak." Charlie growled with his gurgling raspy voice.

"How much we talking?"

Charlie stood up a little straighter from his lean into Mokes. "I'll give you $1000 if you find it."

"I've heard about this phone you guys are looking for and I think I have a pretty good idea where it is. I'll find it for you for $20,000." Mokes had his left arm across his chest, holding his right elbow up that extended to his right hand, bracing his chin.

Charlie responded by stepping forward and leaning into Mokes again.

"15,000"

"25,000"

Tony jetted forward, grabbed Mokes by his collar and thudded him against his van. "You scheming little shit." Two fingers on either hand were still wrapped into Mokes shirt. Charlie put a calming hand on Tony's shoulder.

"We will do it for $20,000 kid, if we understand each other clearly. You don't mess around with us, and we won't mess around with yous."

Charlie punched his Beretta barrel into Moke's belly button. "Ca'pesh?"

Mokes pushed Tony's hands off of him. His eyes bulged at the pistol threat right in front of the Sheriff's station. Right after the Sheriff himself was just outside.

"Yeah, I understand."

Blood Sonnet

The rain thundered down on Sheriff Worden's squad truck. He fiddled with his pen while lounging in the cozy darkness of the inner cab. Across the street and adjacent from the tall Eucalyptus trees was Ki's and his Mother's house. No one would see his truck if they were pulling into Ki's house. Only if they were leaving would they have to drive by his squad truck. So he comfortably sat there waiting for a sign, waiting for Ki.

Their little beach town Ellipsis seemed in a world of its own this past year. The Police Department had been under an intensive two year investigation for misconduct, money laundering and fraud. Old officers were being sued and questioned and young officers were relocating to more affordable locations for buying homes. Mayor Patricia Force was on the brink of definancing the police force, and the Sheriff and his handful of Deputies were doing everything they could not to have Ellipsis slip away… or slip into another's control.

Around the same time the Ellipsis Protection Services went under audits and investigations, the City also signed a 300 million dollar, 15 year contract with Zendolini Industries. Thus in contrast to the Police Department, hardly hanging onto what little employees they had left, the Zendolini's have been building an army of workers.

Zen Industries ran the trash pickups, construction zones, recycling centers, street cleaning, and disposal of anything unwanted. Because of these standard, pretty much mindless jobs, the Zendolini block, the Dolini Pits, have tons of raggedy low income workers waiting for their chance to get into the waste organization. Praise of the Zendolinis littered the Ellipsis' streets. Drug addicts, criminals, and the clinically insane flourished their love for the Zendolinis because they gave them all a chance at working real jobs. Undying loyalty for the Zen Industry was brimming out of the Pits. Sheriff Worden knew a bit of the inside scope, but he had to go deeper.

Once you've been in with the Zendolinis long enough or perhaps have shown your strong devotion, they will set you up with an optional promotion into the familia mafioso. Sheriff Worden hadn't found any proof of the Zendolinis committing crimes, but it was in his gut; he knew just by the fucking look of them, the way they walked, talked, and ate. The Earth Enforcers Association was his closest chance in discovering the truth.

Their little rugby club had the Zendolinis on edge this summer, being attached to so many of the Zendolini webs, he knew one of them would lead to the truth. It was just a matter of time.

Worden wanted to talk with his teammate, his brother from another, his friend Ki. The Zendolini guys were getting desperate and now after banquet night, they knew Ki was suspect number one. Not to mention how horribly pissed off they were after losing that fight at their local pizzeria.

Charlie used to try and spit orders at him almost every other day; 'Where's Pruitt's phone? Do a sweep of the Airfield and the surrounding forest. Check every sign pushing activist for minor offenses the day of the Oil Rig Rally and see if the suspects have any leads on Pruitt's killer. Give us highway camera access. What goes on in the EEA?'

Mayor Force thought the Zendolinis were doing the City a favor. She wanted to get the most out of her 15 year contract and she probably wanted to hire them as private investigators now that they were showing such an interest in a leading politician's death. It seemed like Force was upside down. Maybe it was time for an abjuration of normal traditions in society and flow into a revitalized nobility, a World Oath. An oath that upheld the sustainability of nature. Or maybe Mayor Force was right side up about the Zendolinis… Maybe whoever was in command of the town's waste was the ideal leader for this place. Criminal or saint.

Worden's gut feeling kept clenching at their name… The Zens must have become bolder in using another source for information because he hadn't seen them around for more than a week. On the other side of things, the restless EEA has been pretty gregarious. Tawa Pawin and her friends were also powerful activists that pushed for the green movement and were pushing Mr. Zendolini in doing more compost work. He must be keeping her close for a reason…

Mr. Pruitt, Administer of the Environmental Protection Agency, was inarguably enemy number one for all Environmentalists, a true demonic dumb dick, Triple D. Based on how the Zendolini wise guys spoke about him though, they were happy the fuck was underground, but that didn't change how fucking important his cell phone was. To an outside eye it was very fucking important to them. To them all the activists were suspects, but why did Zendolini care about an anti-environmental man's cell phone? What secrets were intertwined? Maybe the Zendolinis were covertly big green activists and just wanted what Tawa and the EEA wanted. Maybe Pruitt's cell phone was an aid to environmental peace…

Sheriff Worden tucked his pen into his shirt pocket and pulled his black beanie over his ginger red short mohawk hair. He knew those Zendolini guys were bad. They looked like the stereotypical wise guys. Suited Gentlemen on the outside, brutal bangers on the inside. The Sheriff just knew it was his job to read people. By the whites of their eyes, those boys were dangerous. I should be staking out the Zendolini's, not Ki's Mother's house. He thought.

Right before he was about to take off to the Zendolini's, Moke's rugged old van pulled around the corner. Another place where if you were coming up to Leia's driveway, you couldn't see around that hidden corner. Mokes jumped out and ran through the rain and into the overgrown jungle of Leia's backyard.

***

Mokes had a grizzly new attitude. Baggans and Fish were giving him shit for squeezing in with Tawa so quickly, and he didn't receive the Back of the Year award during the end of the year banquet, an honored MVP for the quick and more tactical guys on the rugby pitch. He felt alone. Everyone had their primaries yet he was always left on the side. Mokes also wanted to be finished with his low paying recycling job. The mentality of always trying to do the right thing and to help others was weighing him down. Too much work and too little reward.

He sauntered by a half dozen large plumeria trees and then sidestepped by the rose bushes, finally getting enough room to walk regularly by the vegetable garden with walls of tomatoes, squashes teetering over the edge and sprouts and green vines leading to whatever else. Birds of Paradise and huge Hibiscus Iris Elephant Ear leaves hung over his head, making him feel like an Egyptian Prince having his serfs shelter him from the rain. He laughed at his thoughts after passing the Egyptian Star Clusters.

Leia always walked Ki's friends through her jungle and tried to explain each plant to them. Mokes must have known the Star Clusters were coming up because his mind went straight to Egyptian historical culture while looking at the Elephant Ears. He stood there deciphering how his mind could intuitively solve problems without even a second's concentration on the matter. There had to be some kind of science to it. Maybe he connected the sounds of Leia's dozen wind chimes with internal mind melodies.

His shoulder brushed against a tortuga wind chime, and he slapped another sun chime with his index finger. The Garden Jungle sang. He took a moment's pause to listen to the patter of elemental rain on the abundance of green life. The sound and the feel of the organic water, felt like it was cooling off his brain. He needed that. He also really needed a joint, however what he was doing was already high in intensity. Mokes finished his walk through Leia's jungle after passing several bright orange Canna Lilies that surrounded the path to the back door. Leia's house was always unlocked, and he opened the door slightly and yelled inside,

"Hello? Leia, Ki. Are you here? I was wondering if I could borrow something?"

Mokes went in after he heard no response, took off his shoes, and slid on the wooden floorboards to Ik's room. He knew exactly where to check first. Ik's cluttered closet had most of what he owned thrown inside, regardless of its importance. The closet ranged from $10,000 checks to Top Ramen seasoning packets.

He shuffled through, finding two broken phones and a half smoked joint. One phone had a faded outrigger paddlers sticker on the back, which was definitely Ki's, and the other phone was naked, more likely Pruitt's. He pocketed it, put the joint in his mouth and slid out the backdoor.

The sudden flash of light blinded Mokes, surprising him into dropping the joint on the wet tile. He bent down to pick it up while covering his eyes, but as he went to get up, the Sheriff was hovering over him with his flashlight pointed down on him like an abduction ray. He tried to move back and stand up out of his crotch, but the Sheriff blocked his rise with his knee.

"Fentawhap, what's up bro? What are you doing here man?"

Mokes accepted his position for the time being. With police, he tended to surrender.

"Answer me within three seconds or I'm taking you in. Why were you inside Leia's house?"

Mokes locked his jaw and had just enough time to put on his serious face and throw out an answer.

"I needed to use the toilet. I literally just got here and I was just leaving. Give me a break bro."

Sheriff Fentawhap gloomed over him, his head directly over Mokes, his crotch in his face, almost slapping him with his billy stick. The light beam moved to the side and Mokes saw that Fentawhap's face was crinkled in red rage. The freckles didn't make it anymore forgiving.

"I'm sorry Sheriff, I really needed to take a shit. I was on my way to this new girl's house and felt the runs coming."

"What girl?" Sheriff Worden thought of Tawa, anyone but Tawa. Mokes didn't deserve a girl like that.

"A new hottie from Tinder bro. Damn, let me get up at least." Sheriff Worden moved back and offered his long handled flashlight to help him up.

"I was driving by and saw your van. Why didn't you park in the driveway?" Interrogating came naturally to him, questioning his friends didn't. This was hard for Connor Worden, which pissed him off more because Mokes put him in this situation.

"I didn't want to make a big deal about it."

"Well it's definitely suspicious Mokes. Get to your date. I'm going let Ki know about your little shit problem. See you later, bro." Fentawhap, Sheriff Worden, never really liked the backline for one grand reason, he was the frontline. The frontline smashed while the agile backline got to score all the points and set up their cute little plays.

"Hey Mokes." Mokes turned around and was slapped by a limp Canna Lily.

"What did the Zendolini boys ask you last week after we had lunch?"

"Oh, they were just shit talking the Transit Center I work at and were telling me to come work for them."

"Will you? Will you work for them?" Sheriff Worden's mind swam with the possibilities of having an inside man.

"Ah, maybe. Their hourly is way better than mine right now, but

I won't be able to grab lunch with you if I switch, so it's a toss-up." Mokes put his hands out like a justice scale and snickered.

Sheriff Worden blushed and walked Mokes out of Leia's garden. He made it back to his squad truck and wished he had a multi-use Umbrella Shotgun. It would be so surprisingly fantastic and it would totally make him feel like a sly secret agent.

The rain dumped onto the quaint neighborhood streets. It dumped on him, his wide muscular body catching a downpour of raindrops. It felt good, even great, like the rainy night was some epicly climactic moment, but having a shotgun umbrella, two forms of security right out in the open, that would be epic. He shivered with the possibilities.

He turned on the truck heater and watched Mokes' tail lights trail down the road. The cop in him wanted to desperately follow his ass, to see where he was really headed to. The Grunion in him said to leave him to his strange and give the guy a break. Grunion were so close, so taking an emergency number 2 at your teammate's house when they weren't home wasn't completely out of the ordinary.

Sheriff Worden made it down the road where Moke's was waiting at the streetlight to take a left. He gave Mokes and the inside of his van one last look over as he passed by his passenger window. While turning right towards downtown he watched Moke's van veer left. The tail light shape, the size of his van's rump and the seven faded stickers on his rear window.

Mokes, he's an alright blok, but now it was time to investigate the late night Zendolini operations.

The drive down to the Pits took a little longer than usual. It was pouring rain in a town that was used to a couple sprinkles every year. Gully's were backing up, rockslides were toppling over retaining walls, driveways were pooling from faulty drainage, and people were happily laid back inside because nature brought them an excuse to slack off.

Hunker down, it's wet outside. A cozy night where the air was warm and the streets were mostly empty. A great time to think and drive…

The wheels of Sheriff Worden's patrol truck rolled slowly to a stop. There was the faint yet pungent smell of garbage that made the Sheriff clear his nostrils with air. Again, being his detective self, he parked his truck in an inconspicuous location. This area was filled with lower socio-economic people's vehicles. They'd pack small homes that rarely had driveways to begin with, so most vehicles trickled down here to the Dolini Pits.

The Sheriff turned his lights off and rotated to his back seat to grab his green rain poncho. The massive 25 by 50 foot entryway to the waste consolidation zone was right there in his passenger side window with a 150,000 pound bulldozer in front of him.

Damn machines just like this one were wrecking this planet, the Sheriff thought. Digging up mountains, clearing out forests, mining out resources. He wouldn't be surprised if they sent machines to harvest the moon's cheese soon.

This particular machine was alright since it's for shifting through landfills and ran on some biofuel. The Sheriff remembered Colin talking about the positives of green energy anaerobic digesters. However, he said it could be more harmful to the atmosphere. The combustion of this gas in reusable energy created Nitrous Oxide, which had 200 times the heating storage capacity of Carbon Dioxide.

Colin's ultimate sustainable remedy was about waste diversion, like composting and refusing plastics. He said it's about sequestering the carbons out of the atmosphere. He said the problem lies with refrigerated vehicles transporting farmed vegetables and meats into cities. Cities should have their own local source of food, community gardens, urban farms, and toros and boars as pets. Instead they waste their gas on transporting produce in and waste out. Taking a lead in pollution with 30 percent of greenhouse gas emissions just from the transport industries in our nation. Anaerobic digestion seemed great; however, there were better ways to focus your biowaste.

Here he was, slowly rolling his F-250 super duty down streets just to look at shit. What a hypocrite. It's not bad enough leaking CO2 emissions into the air, but the constant necessity for gasoline was teeth grinding.

The Sheriff always daydreamed of the Wild West days. Where a good horse was all you needed. A Sheriff's badge, his horse, and his six-shooters. Clean air and clean justice. People didn't need fucking gasoline, making their lives even softer. He always wanted the gasoline prices to skyrocket so people wouldn't drive everywhere for any reason. That's a simple way to help save the Earth, right? He wanted to slap the sillies out of people who complained about high gas prices all the time.

He nodded his head to a new beat. Use Fossil Fuel? Then Slap a

Fool. Those million year old plants are aged like fine wine. Skyrocket that dinosauric decomposition! It should be $500 per gallon of gas. But the gasoline companies won't have it. We can't get a climate bill passed through our Congress because a quarter of our Congress is funded by fossil fuel companies. The money goes into raping the planet and human beings love that shit.

Sheriff Worden spit and instantly regretted that he was still in his truck. He hustled his poncho on and headed out. The bulldozer was across from a large block of construction material stores. Adjacent to the landfill was a building hidden by tall trees and long hanging Amazonian vines. The Zendolini corporate building took up half of the block, and posted up like a Sicilian Syndicate's mansion.

By its appearance, the building was pure business in the middle with white Greecian plaster, tinted doorways and windows, and a grand green intricately carved out sign that read Zen Industries. On either side of the brazen rainforest entryway was the mansion. Still one whole uniform of a building, the attitude of the halves were very different. The balconies and tall plants and trees encapsulated its secret homie mansion vibes. Sheriff Worden checked it out from Google Satellite and it had a quartyard and pool behind it all as well.

There were two lights on at the Northern wing, possibly one room with two windows, but it was difficult to see because the humongous Kapok Tree paired with two King Palms and two Dat Palms around it. A tall spiked black fence went around the entire estate.

The Sheriff found a little cover in the wooden Venetian pergola entry archway. He pushed back his hood and tried to see through the plump leaves of the Kapok. In the Northern quarters of the mansion, the sun-colored light just shone in Mozaic fragments, so he shuffled around, looking elsewhere. The gate was locked. The mansion was hidden by a jungle, and the doors and windows were tinted. There was nothing.

Dispatch called through his radio for an emergency code 451. He asked a couple of questions and told the dispatch about his location. A deputy was close by and said he'd check it out first. The Sheriff waited and watched the rain.

"Slap a fool if ya'll taking fossil jewels. I'll be cruel, riding my mule, checking on things, at the Dolini Springs." He looked around in the direction of the bulldozer. He was impressed by how well he could hide his truck. He was a ghost, a shadow amongst the fold.

The rain droplets pelted down with the same tempo, but there was a staticy noise added to it. He checked his radio again and made sure all channels were off. The sound was definitely still there. He turned around and there, under the Zen Industry sign and above the tinted out doorway was a dark figure spitting out red ink, Hitmen and Murders, the ink read.

He pulled his flashlight out of his belt and flicked it on. Instantly, he gave out a yelp for his mistake and pressed the flashlight into his poncho to hide the beam. He then moved quickly to the side of the pergola. The spray painting hooded figure turned around to see what the flash was, possibly thinking it was a bit of lightning from afar and went back to finishing his lettering.

Sheriff Worden knew he had to be secret if he wanted to follow the vandal. He was locked out and there was nothing he could do otherwise, except scare him away. Maybe if he stayed a ghost, he could catch him by surprise.

Then woefully a flood light beamed across the yard from the balcony where the two lights had been on, and a deep Italian bellow roared out. Nothing he could make out through the rain and enraged Italian curses, but the Zendolini guard definitely spooked the figure into jumping from the fourth ladder rung down and sprinted south-ward. The ladder toppled over and the red paint graffiti lettering above the tinted door stitched to his mind.

Hitmen and Murders skipping on the Dead.
Loving to bury their marks in the filthy grounds of Zen,
Eliminating sprouting truths again and again.
Handling The One Order's Waste by incinerators to darkening Dens.

Thou the Mob doth God's genuine cycle.
Creativity is a bust, only a crust of dust.
Evolution is a must, hath thou killer of lust.
Buff up your Priest so thine can waste your children's trust.

Organic things expire quicker than chemically plugged slags,
Fertilized, well, materialized, by men of hate.
Only remedy being Naturalization pulverizing accumulation of wise hags.
Burying the damaged robotics that run into late.

Our land needs death, this is true.
But this time the death should be you.

The vandilizer bolted off to the side of the building where the community office was. The mansion entry was really just for looks. The door was probably always locked. The sign, Use The Door on Pyrenees Rd, was probably glued on the tinted black door.

The Sheriff peeled his eyes from the poem in red paint and focused his eye on the figure of movement who quickly slipped under the black spiked gate and into a parking lot. The smash of a car hood echoed down the narrow street of Pyrenees as the Sheriff began to skid around the corner. The vandal hopped over a white plastered ivy wall and was out of sight.

Following the runaway's smash path, the Sheriff pointed his boots on their tips to look over the wall and got a good look at the vandalizer. A shine came from his ear and a glistening scar showed above his eye under that darkening hood. He sat on a blacked out bicycle cruiser, forearms resting on the handlebars and looking back, looking right at the Sheriff's ginger head over the wall. He waved and then took off down the main street towards the beach. Missing tooth in that smile? Everyone knows Ki loved his sonnets. Even the Zendolinis...

"Ah, Sheriff?"

The Sheriff hopped down from the trunk of the Honda Accord and walked nonchalantly over to Tony Two Fingers, all while being drenched by the warm El Nino rain. Tony placed the black umbrella between the two of them, two of his fingers curling around the bottom of the handle.

"Yes..." The Sheriff answered unpleasantly. Not sure if he was more irked by the vandal or by Tony and the Mansion of Secrets.

"Looks like you chased off our defacer..."

Tony just stared back at him, no response would be coming out of those plump red lips with that stare.

"Any idea why they wrote Hitmen and Murders on your wall?"

"Why were you outside our gate?"

"I'm asking the fuckin-"

The Sheriff was interrupted by his dispatch calling him in for backup on Leviosa Boulevard.

"Immediate response, code 1019 over and out."

"I'll check in tomorrow." The Sheriff moved to go back to his truck.

"Sheriff. Take this. We have plenty in the office." Tony looked benevolent for once, generous, and the more water that rained down his plump cheeks and heavy skull, the more fear in his eyes revealed itself.

The Sheriff took the umbrella without a word, folded it up and gave Tony a nod. He jogged back to his truck, grabbing a quick photo of the poem sprayed in red, and set off to Leviosa Blvd. It was a 1019 squeeze, meaning someone did a crime and was trapped with no escape.

As Worden drove at high speeds, only taking ten minutes to get to the next town over, he unlatched his shotgun from the backseat, dug out the duct tape in his little toolbox, and placed both next to the umbrella on the passenger seat.

He screeched to a stop by the Deputy's pursuit vehicle.

"Deputy. What's the cinch?" He asked through his window while standing outside his truck and organizing his things on the driver's seat.

The Deputy never took his eyes off the three story Victorian building. It was run down, rotted out and paint chips littered the building's perimeter.

"Sir, we have Officer Timely and Officer Whitney out back watching for escapees. We believe the suspect inside is a Fentynal dealer and she just pistol whipped three transients with a Desert Eagle, sending two of them to emergency care. I saw her alleged BMW pulling off the interstate when I was on my way to the scene. I followed her here and watched her run into this house with a hostage."

It was pouring rain during the hot summer night. El Nino season was here. Sheriff Worden clicked up his umbrella and pumped his shotgun. Within three clicks his dream came true. He closed his eyes, taking in the moment.

"It's time to get weird Deputy Stokely. Hold this." Deputy Stokely took the umbrella shotgun and studied the weapon with the Victorian building in the background. The glasses of young ripped Deputy Stokely fogged up.

"What do you mean, weird Sheriff? What's your plan?"

"Plan is… The element of surprise… and abnormality." The Sheriff thought back to his new Environmental Oath idea. Breaking the traditional ways of life that have led to an Era of Earthly Destruction.

"Sheriff, you're… what the hell are you doing with your clothes?"

"Abnormality Deputy Stokely. I'm going in. Alone. Watch my ass."

With his open umbrella, Sheriff Worden walked out nonchalantly to the bottom of the stairs. He knew the lady inside would be watching. They always watched. His happy trail that went down to his groin matched his mohawk haircut. His red mustache had Grunion Rugby Club and The Sheriff of this Mother Fucking town written all over it.

He yelled through the rain, using his nonthreatening Irish accent. "I'm unarmed and a little embarrassed. I'm going to come in so we can talk this out. Right now it's your best option. Do I have your consent?"

The house was calm yet everything else was loud and vibrant. The rain, his heart thumping, the feel of the fat shotgun handle in his wet hand. For some reason though, it was the umbrella that made him feel safe amongst all the things that could go wrong.

"Alright I'm coming in." He looked back to acknowledge his pursuit with his Deputy and walked up the steps.

One. Two. Three. A reason to pee. Front door locked, let's bash it with me. Lady on the stairwell leveling her blunderbuster towards my weewee.

The uncomfortableness of knowing your dick could be blown off gave the Sheriff a spark of frightful dashing jitters and he spun and pointed the umbrella tip at the scary lady and moved left into the kitchen.

A loud, Pang! Ran through the house and a large hole made its way through the open umbrella. Sheriff Worden was pretty damn Irish, but not superstitious Irish. An open umbrella inside will not bring bad luck. Not today.

A new radical addict with crooked teeth attacked Worden with a kitchen knife and was met with the butt of his shotgun to the side of his head. The twist he made to hit the man put the open umbrella in the right spot again to conceal him from the maddened wench fentanyl dealer coming after him with her Desert Eagle .45. Another hole came loudly through the umbrella.

Backing into the living room, Worden was slammed in the shoulder with a baseball bat. He let off a warning shotgun blast at the kitchen entryway to keep the dealer scared and out of sight, then

Worden spun around as hard as he could, slapping the knuckles of the Red Sox player with the length of his umbrella shotgun. He blocked the next homerun swing, but when the bat and umbrella locked together Worden gave the Red Sox guy a solid red mohawk home coming headbutt.

The Sheriff's umbrella spokes broke after his last shot, which actually helped him move around the house more freely. He made it back to the stairs and ran up smoothly, yet desperately looking for the hostage. He came to the last door at the end of the hall and finally heard Deputy Stokely and Officer Timely rush in and stun gun the dealer holding the DE .45. Almost done.

Sheriff Worden angled his umbrella to the ceiling of the last room and gave it a shotgun blast, immediately back peddling to see what would happen next. Bullets from inside the room flew through the doorway at every height and width. Finally, after the flying metal ceasefire, he looked through one of the closest holes and saw another lady with long platinum blonde hair holding a teenage boy in front of her. Eyes bulging and her gun still pointed to the door. Her hand on the boy's chest. Her hand…

Sheriff Worden ripped the umbrella off his shotgun and poked the tip through one of the holes. Terrified, and probably coked up, she emptied the rest of her clip at the umbrella.

Busting down a holey door was a lot easier than a fully naked front door kick down, which left him with a sprained ankle at the very least.

With the shotgun casually held in his left hand, Sheriff Worden walked up, kicked the lady in the face and grabbed the boy.

"You guys clear down there?"

"Yes sir, everyone is contained and accounted for."

"Okay, I'm sending down a teenage boy, ready up." He pushed the boy towards the stairs and waited for recovery.

"Hostage recovered."

As Sheriff Worden, known to bring the Whap to the Fenta, turned around, he was surprised to have the blonde lady catch a cup full of his nuts. The grasp was warm, almost enjoyable at first, but she was just heating up. By the feel of it she seemed to have one finger curled around each nut sack and her thumb pressed to pop the balls. Her nails eventually dug in and latched on for dear life. This was her chance, his balls. She had his package hostage and all he could think of was, what's the safe word…

"Give. Me. That." Her voice was rough and her eye was slowly swelling up fat, but he could still see her beauty before the drugs and the downward spiral.

He slowly pointed the barrel of the shotgun at her face and she squeezed harder and harder, until finally, she broke. The grip loosened and she backed away crying.

Deputy Stokely came up and handed Sheriff Worden his uniform. "Mayor is outside Sheriff. She wants to talk to you."

"Than-" He coughed out his high pitched voice. "Thank you Deputy." He let out an astonished breath of relief before he started to dress up and prepare for the Mayor.

"Is this the suspect for the assaults earlier or the chick with the big plugger downstairs?"

"The Big Plugger Chick, Sheriff." Office Stokely pronounced.

The Sheriff rubbed out his balls through his pants and double checked if they were good. He nodded at the girl with tears running down her dirty face, showing his gratitude for not taking the ball squeezing too far.

"Stokely can you check to see if our friend Tony at Zen Industries has had any relation to this woma-"

"I can tell you that, you mutt. Tony is my ex-husband, that swag."

The Sheriff picked up her piece and understood. A Pietro Beretta, made in Italy, carried by wise guys, and a ex-wife with two fingers on one hand.

"What happened to your hand Miss?" Worden didn't know exactly what to call this beast of a human. She could have been pretty but witnessing her ravenous ways, her tough skin, her scowl, all of it made him want to invite her to the Mermaid rugby team. Catching and throwing the ball might be tough, buwt she'd be a great defensive lass. The nicknames that came with having two fingers on one hand would make her a very popular Mermaid as well. Two Fingered Ball Squeezer would be his fictitious name for her; alas, now professionalism was calling to him, and Miss Ball Squeezer would suffice.

A cackle rose and rose, as if the woman was gaining strength with every popping snicker. "My damn wedding ring wouldn't come off. Tony was a slug and I wanted out, so I cut my ring finger off and left it for his ass."

Worden watched her with a confused gaze. Still gathering his breath from the ballsack squeeze. Deputy Stokely rubbed at the back of his head continuously, amazed at the story the Sheriff was uncovering.

"I see your look. You're just a bunch of pussies. You try cutting just your ring finger off, damn pinky gets in your way." Her seriousness again broke and her mad cackling came back.

Sheriff Worden exchanged renowned looks with Deputy Stokely, then made his way down the stairs.

Outside there were three times as many vehicles then there were when he first arrived. News vans, a half dozen police cars and multiple blacked out suvs behind them. The Mayor stood at the base of the steps with her arms folded across her chest.

"Sheriff Worden! I need to speak with you pronto buster…" The Sheriff waved her to follow him to the passenger side of his truck so he could reorganize his gear and himself. Trucks were somewhat of a safe haven, a small mobile shelter. The Mayor positioned her umbrella to be a bit over the truck roof and open passenger door, making the truck safe haven even more comforting in the El Nino rain.

The Mayor was a middle aged latina lady with a little extra pounds on her, however her command was so definite that she was a true blue leader without question. She looked out for her people and knew what she wanted and how she wanted it done. If there was a mistake, then you'd hear about it. Well, the Sheriff always heard about it.

"Worden, what in the lord's name made you go into a crack house naked? Are you on drugs, Sheriff Worden?"

"No, of course not. I have a reputation to uphold. With the city and with my team."

"You think stripping your clothes off will help your reputation? Bless'd lord."

Sheriff Worden held his smile back. The rugby team would dub him a legend for tonight's exploits. Hell, even his family would be proud of him. He kept safe by stretching his neck.

Mayor Force paid attention to his arrogant stretch and scrunched up her face for debate, "Yes, your team. Your drinking buddies. How is that rash and impulsive non-profit EEA, hm? Earth ENFORCERS Association. A close knit group of friends that will 'threaten'! Anyone that doesn't believe how they do? Is that you as well Sheriff Worden? Because the rugby team pretty much seems like the EEA. And after your little frat party Streaking today! I am not happy with your-" The

Mayor went on about the Sheriff's failures, the chaos of Pruitt's case and more about the Grunion brutes. The Sheriff realized he was getting more and more turned on by the belittling, berating, be'ing-a-cunt-ing. The nut grab really was foreplay.

"And why are the Zendolinis calling me to check on you? What in Lord's name is going on with this town? Have you answered one question of mine yet?" The Mayor looked back towards the crack house, feeling flustered.

"Mayor, that new Earth Association isn't just Grunion, it has many outstanding citizens among them that are trying their best to create a positive change. One of the reasons I'm with the rugby team is so I can see what the city's innards are like, and what the underground is planning. Which leads me to the Zendolinis. Before I came here I was staking out Zen Industries and the Dolini Pits, because I was asking myself the same question you are asking me now. Why do the Zendolinis care so much about Pruitt's death? And what's with this this phone they are obsessed about? It all seems very incriminating. The freaking ex-wife of Zendolini's right hand man was one of the armed crack heads in that house. I mean… things are starting to piece together right?" He huffed and settled his breath.

"While I was at the Zendolinis tonight, someone wrote this on their wall." Sheriff Worden opened up his phone and showed the picture of Ki's blood Sonnet to the Mayor. She read, he continued.

"The Zendolini's are hiding something and I think someone in this town knows what. I just need to keep investigating, Mayor. This feels big."

The Mayor's shoulders dropped a tad and her voice softened. Her eyes now showed gratitude. That look in her eyes, or maybe the way she told you everything you did was wrong but then rewarded you in the end, made her command so powerful.

"Thank you for saving that boy and not killing anyone tonight. I… Your tactic was a little reckless, but your heart still seems to be in the right spot.

"Keep an eye on anyone in communications with Zen Industries. We cannot have an Industry of murders in my town. Especially one with the largest company contact in the city. Did you see who wrote this… Blood Sonnet?"

Thunder clapped for the first time that night and the rain started to dump. Almost too much for the Mayor's umbrella. Worden wondered if there were any umbrellas in the Sheriff's department storage.

"No Mayor, just a hooded figure that got away too quickly."

"Excuse us, Sheriff, Mayor. Could we get a quick case briefing soon? I feel like this street will flood with all this rain." The double poncho news reporter asked with excitement. Her umbrella had four large question marks around it, just like the Riddler's.

Worden and the Mayor looked at each other for a moment, and through Mayor Force's eyes all was decided.

She put her back to the reporter and spoke quietly to Sheriff Worden.

"Our town is on the brink of utter mayhem, I need you. Tonight you are the hero Sheriff. Yet, if you can, let's try and keep the zero clothing part quiet. We don't want anyone thinking we are," She moved up to his ear and lowered her voice to a whisper.

"Bat-shit crazy and totally suicidal."

Illuminati's World Eye

Six hours before the Blood Sonnet on Zendolini's wall.

Ki handed the Scott Pruitt's data chip to Safa Scott, the Captain of the Grunion, and an upper shelf nerd. The South African wore a spikey faced Metallica shirt and rotated the tiny chip from backside to frontside with his rubber tweezers. Wino stood behind him watching intently, his eyes magnified by his spectacles.

"Where's the cell phone, eh?"

"It's at home."

"Z, how'd you get this data chip out mate? Most phones don't even have a chip like this, and if they did, it would be terrible trouble getting it out."

"Honey helped me. But I didn't want to get her involved in what comes after pulling the chip. Which is reading the chip… You guys don't have to involve yourselves if you don't want the risk, but this data chip could tell us why the Zendolinis are so obsessed with Pruitt and his cell phone." The lie made Ki feel ashamed. He had to tell his friends that the data chip was from Charlie Do Little's cell phone. Because the entire E.E.A and Club disliked Charlie, hacking could proceed with little question. The lie was, Charlie thankfully had his hands covered in vinegar and olive oil at an Italian Deli and needed a washroom, so Ki simply picked up Charlie's phone sitting on top of the counter. If Ki told them the truth, that he swiped Pruitt's phone after committing a mass murder, well…

"Ah, if they take you in then I'll start worrying. In the meantime let's see what the Zendolinis are keeping secret. I've been craving a good crack." Safa, Stank Dick Scott giggled to himself and pushed the data chip into another chip holder and then slid that chip drive into his computer.

Green code and text instantly rained down his monitor.

"Ah well already, it's Covertis Security Company. They sell forty to sixty thousand dollar untraceable phones on the black market."

Wino coughed in amazement. "Wow, I want one." He drooled as he pushed his cell phone into his pocket and transitioned over to give one hundred percent focus to the situation.

Safa read through the code and dialed in a few keys for thirty minutes until finally his computer tower started to smoke. "Smoke, smoke!"

"Take the chip out!" As Wino was demanding he himself was doing. Wino grabbed the chip holder and blew on it. "It's okay."

"Ya, it just fried my motherboard, but i'm glad 'its' okay."

"Let's try a cell phone. We can put it in a bucket of ice, put a sheet of plastic down and run the data chip." Wino pushed up his glasses and started looking around the room for what he needed.

"Here, use my phone. It was a thousand dollars so we only have a forty percent chance it will fail." Ki offered his phone and continued to watch Wino create the cool down station.

"Hundred percent chance mate, but we will give it a try." Safa stripped Ki's cell phone, connected the data chip, placed the phone in the ice and turned her on. The screen went bright green, then purple, then blue, then black. They all waited, listening to the clicks and sizzles of the phone working out its new chip. The screen went white with a password tab in the middle of it.

"Password." Safa noted to Ki with a pompously postured straight back. Pleasantly happy with himself about getting to the password screen, Safa still managed an air of impracticality to assume Ki knew the secret hidden password of Zen Industries.

Ki's mind showed a blood moon with a laughing Uka Buka in the middle of it. He thought of that night and all of its horror.

"1666"

"Hmph," Four slow little clicks on the keyboard and a gut wrenching logo took up the entire screen.

"So, Ki had the Key to unlock pandora's box. Wow. The Eye of Providence, looking right at us. We've made it boys. Into the den of secrets and amongst the rays of the divine eye." Safa murmured, slowing munching on his cheese stick while staring at the eye within a pyramid, within the sun.

Ki waited for an outcry on discovering the Chip was Pruitt's, but there was none. Pruitt's name never popped up, but other names did and one of them was on a folder named Zendolini. The boys carried their squinting eyes and dropped jaws across the screen as Ki swiped through the information. All of them trying to read the smallest text through two long cracks on the phone screen.

"I need to check the temperature of my phone and get a closer look at this text." Ki picked his phone out of the ice and started reading with the screen inches from his face. Wino and Safa's stares were pained, like their big brother just took their favorite toy.

"We can't all read one little phone-"

"Dude, that was the One World Order symbol… The Illuminati. Why? I mean What-"

"Let me look it over first, and then I'll give it to you guys." Ki was going to say more but he couldn't help looking down at his phone and start reading.

Safa produced a usb android plug that was attached to another monitor. "Here, plug it in and we can read it on the big screen."

After three hours of reading very revealing completed criminal death contracts and execution briefing letters, the boy's eyes bulged at the fact that they had an Illuminati ledger filled with dangerous in-formation. It contained the dates, places, and victims of hits from the past fifteen years. It even had photos of the deceased, but Ki didn't want the guys to see those. The information was enough to spook the boys into, shit your pants jitters.

The Zendolini folder in particular was a list of every murder and elimination they completed. Based on how the briefing for each hit was worded, the Illuminati were the ones detailing the hits. Because it came from Pruitt's phone, he must have been the hit boss for the Ze-ndolinis. And now that Scott Pruitt was dead, the Zendolinis wanted to erase all proof of their crimes…

"The fucking Illuminati. Fucking silent assassins. I don't want anything more to do with that data chip. This is bad man. This. Is. Bad." Safa rubbed his balding head while pacing back and forth in his garage.

"You guys are going to have to skit-daddle. I mean I have kids boys. Shit, shit, shit!"

Wino got up and floated to the door like he was completely in his own head, in another galaxy, in trouble. His glasses were centimeters from falling off his wide nose.

"Illuminati are the ones mercing the progressive, worldcentric, environmental activists… Anyone with an innovative, revolutionary idea that could help save the planet…"

Wino opened the door to leave and Safa yelled, "Wait!"

"Wino, Zero, this is some serious shit. We cannot be blabbing about any of this to anyone! I mean fuck! I'd hate to meet an Illuminati assassin. I mean the Zendolini's are kinda scary but Illuminati. No one even knows they exist! We could already be dead for heaven's sake. Shit!" Safa kept his voice down but held full fervor behind each word. He pushed Wino out through the door.

"Go. Don't talk to anyone about this. This is serious Wino."

Safa turned to Ki, "Ik, Z, fuck sake. Ki. I'm grabbing my kids and wife and leaving town for a couple of weeks. I know you're going to do something Ki, fucking bullshit man. Just don't mention me, alright?"

Ki was in a daze maze of Safa words. Illuminati Assassins. Zendolinis Scared. Everything clicked. The Zendolinis were going apeshit over Pruitt's cell phone because the Illuminati were involved. The Illuminati were probably getting ready to merc some Zendolinis if they didn't show proof it wasn't them.

Ki was slapped out of it and Safa's new words broke through the haze. "Ki fuck! Leave my house at dark, I don't want anyone to see your ass okay? I don't exist either, alright?"

"Yes, yes sorry Safa. Of course you don't exist, you never helped me. It's a good idea to leave for a couple weeks. I don't know, they may be able to track my phone… I'll leave in the dead of night." With that Safa looked even more terrified. Scared into silence, he nodded his good luck to Ki and rushed out of the garage.

Thoughts wove into the misty maze of Ki's mind again as he stood there alone. Two hours went by, and he grabbed Safa's black cruiser bicycle, a black hoodie, and a backpack with 3 cans of red spray paint to throw inside.

Harmony

Why don't people cause more mayhem on busy holidays like the 4th of July? A fight for nature's independence could be a good fit for the day of separating from the parasitic dependency of humans. The 4th of July has the fragrance of boom powder, it's loud, hot, and chaotic. Tons of people, tons of traffic, tons of problems.

The wooden paddle 'thlooped' into the sea's swell as a moon silhouetted body twisted a reaching arm out to swiftly pull back against the water. The power of the stroke was seen through the rhythmic forward glide of the hull. A harmonious repeat. A song to the mermaids. A high five of gratitude to the salt of the Earth. This is your day, Little Ocean.

Ki was listening to the sound of the water swash against his outrigger canoe and showering rain droplets into the ocean. The sound was like the wind howling with platoons of spirit molecules singing amongst themselves in flow. Similar to the sound of a rumbling avalanche or a roaring fire.

Meditation within the elements turned them all into one. His heart pumped fiery water as he rode the waves. His face felt the brisk wind as he breathed out air. His eyes sought out the island ahead as his muscles tensed for strength. His soul burned with fury as the oil platform burned with fire behind him. He was angry, but the elements gave a better depiction of their fury. They didn't hold back for anything but themselves. They raged on.

Just a couple hours earlier, Ki was paddling out to an Oil Platform called Harmony. He climbed the steel structure of its pylons and found a half dozen gallons of gasoline by their warehouse. Harmony had been abandoned for over a year now. The oil well had been capped and the platform decommissioned by the West Coast Ocean Protection Act, an Act that permanently banned oil and gas drilling in Washington, Oregon and California waters; however, Trump and Pruitt, upheld by the secrets of the Illuminati, had further plans for these oil derricks. They kept trying to recommission the vampiric pipelines until they are lying in their graves.

Scott Pruitt being a perfect example.

When covertly scoping the place out, Ki found two men stationed on the platform to watch over it. Ki told them they could leave with their lives if they abandoned the platform. Droid and Will Bill were disgruntled at the fact they were being forced off their post, to the point of rebelling against Ki's pistol in their faces. Will Bill seemed like he knew no other life than guarding his isolated little wooden island, and Droid hated any random outsider. However, the resistance was tarnished by the Uka Buka in Ki's eyes. The deadly blocky plank headed mask finally made it to Ki's face. The pistol clicked as he pulled back the hammer, and rationality made its way home.

Once the rig operators made it down the billy pugh they jumped to their zodiac and ripped away in the storm towards the mainland.

Harmony was one of the largest Oil Platforms of the 23 out in the Pacific Outer Continental Shelf Region. It would cost 1.66 billion to completely disassemble and decommission them all. 1.666, Pruitt's password. Another bloody secret revealed, Ki assumed.

He did want to get rid of the rigs, but he really wanted to scare the bad guys wanting to use the rigs. He wanted to show the Illuminati that he was one step ahead of them. The Son of Sun, burning hot and shining bright with righteousness like every other radically righteous dumb fuck. What made him right? Who knew, but it fucking felt right.

Illuminati or not, anyone in power that wanted to fuck the planet in the most arrogant none, sensical, greed-ridden way was enemy number one to Ki.

Six years ago in 2015, there was an oil line rupture releasing 140,000 gallons of oil in a biodiverse stretch of the Pacific ocean coast line. A Pipeline that went from three Exxonmobil sea rigs to one inland refinery, Las Flores Canyon. This pipeline corroded and eventually split. Only a little time after the spill and destruction of ecosystems and oceanic life they started lobbying to get that Oil Refinery backup and running. The oil lobbyist and greedy fucks excuse for bringing the Refinery back was that it would generate taxes and give people more jobs. The fact was oil revenue made up 1.5 percent of the district's overall budget. They say it's for the people, yet when hundreds of local coastal businesses and thousands of fishermen protest against it, they completely ignore their concerns.

Now, as history has a tendency to karmatically repeat itself, just a month ago a 4500 gallon spill happened with a truck oil transport to Las Flores Canyon. Spilling over a groundwater basin that 200,000 people depend on for drinking water. It's for the people they say, not for the money. Mouth, Shit, Fucks.

His thoughts were in the flames.

A Deer silhouetted through the smoke,
Horns ominous quality, sharp and multuious, embracing a darkening
stench of piercing growth.
Herds of buffalo and grasshoppers guided with the path of flames
the Greyclouds invoked.
Kootenia Tribe, native to Northern Rockies useth red and orange
light to nurture the land.

Birthing fire as a phoenix that grows vegetation and medicine.
Smoldering roots tracing throughout the underground.
Hath the rightful vow in comparison.
Howling wind spirits gallivanting through smooth yet crackling
sound.

The red-match stewarding the land of the forgotten.
Burnith to bringth the Ceremony of a legendary nest.
The Alaskan Gwich'in tribe shadowing Caribou, entrusting what they
had brought'n.
Porcupine Quills woven as a sharp but embracing crest.

Red is one with Green
Creating the flower of Yellow Being

While putting most of his weight on the alma and iako outrigger side, Ki rotated around in his canoe and could barely make out the blinking red and blue lights of the coast guard and fire prevention vessels in the distance. He turned back to his island destination in front of him, peering into the globe's dark horizon. The rain hashed the waterscape and the swell of the storm rolled the surface of the sea.

Fleetingly, a solitary light popped out of the darkness. A light he had been expecting but from the opposite direction. The light mystically rolled across the sea and then would turn off for a minute or two, and then come back again in its rolling search.

Inhaling the power of the sea he felt as a Grunion. The ocean would be one of the best places for him to die. A great last elemental theurgy before descending into Earth's watery belly.

Ki paddled a little further to line up with the light's looming path. Uka Buka splashed in the swells and dove in and out of the water. Uka was like a happy dog riddled with anticipation to see its owner. Back and forth, back and forth, from canoe to boat, ecstatic about the future of possible human destruction; at least, that was what Ki believed.

He continued his paddle strokes, fully entertained by Uka Buka's excitement when he saw another figure stoic and static, colorful and proud, hovering over the water, seemingly guarding the island or simply watching the frantic being of its rival. The colors of Toko Tuki's feathers were dule and damp from the rain, but its aged, cracked wooden plank face held the strength of the sea, of the jungle, of who Ki wanted to be. He shook in the image and began watching Uka Buka with the same distaste as Tuki. Ki's grumpiness had reached full tilt as the mysterious boat saw him and approached with ease.

"Aye Aye," One man said.

"Ey, we'z been looking for you silly little chink." Four bullets followed, two in the bow of Ki's canoe and two in the stern. The gun was muffled with a silencer.

"Get the fuck in the boat before you get two in the head ya weezer."

Ki climbed aboard and the first person he saw was Mokes, then Charlie pushed him out of the way and clocked Ki right above the eye.

"Ohhh, I've been wanting to do that. Ya filthy muck."

Tony Two Fingers came up behind Charlie and bagged Ki's head, then the boat one eightied and took off.

They sat him down in a surprisingly comfortable spot and tied him up.

"Some environmentalist you are. Burning up an oil derrick. Oils going to spill all over our channel you cunt." Charlie yammered, more unsettled than he has been in years.

Ki lounged his arm on one of the spare buoy fenders and gave a small wiggle in the pile of loose cushions. "Oil well is capped. Derrick, pretty much abandoned, and a blowout preventer was -"

A steel toe boot hit him right above his belly button. His gulping gasps were from him trying to pull some kind of air back into his lungs.

"Slow the boat down Bobby." Charlie's voice came back down to his usual calming melody. His knees cracked as he bent down to Ki's ear.

"Don't get comfortable. You have a stupid fucking name, ya chink, and im bloody pissed out my ears after chasing you and that data chip down." Charlie's smooth whisper made Ki's struggle to inhale sound even more pathetic.

Charlie checked Ki's pockets while he gasped for air. He laughed at the pistol in his waistband and threw it overboard.

"Come on suck it in. Suck it in. I'll give you a moment before I do it again… I want Pruitt's data chip. We know you have it. Your little buddy Mokalua told us, and because of that little graffiti poem you did on Mr. Zen's estate, we know you fucking read through the data chip and all our 'classified' information. You know we are not the guys to be fucked around with."

"Hey Charlie, it's Mr. Z; he wants to talk with you." Tony chewed, sounding as if he was eating a pastrami sandwich.

Charlie and Tony went over to the wheel cabin and Mokes slid in to take their place.

"Ah, Ik you really got yourself in a coconut now whey. I honestly…" Mokes paused with his chin to the air, gathering thoughts before continuing.

"I'm sorry Ik but the deal was too good. They offered me land in Hawaii and an executive position at one of their Zendolini Waste Industry centers if I told them who took the phone. I can help my home so much more with that in my pocket. Support my local social action poets in the fight against the influx of migrating Haoles pushing the natives out, a clean waste management business, and freshen up my island's water man. It's been my dream braddah."

"You betrayed me. For something we could have done togethe -"

"Naw man, you have lost your mind bro. Seriously, what'd you expect will happen after killing people. And pulling your friends into all of it. You've lost it man. I don't agree with your extremism, and THAT is why I turned against you. Because you'd just pull the whole team down with you. You betrayed us."

Ki's face contorted under his black bagged veil. The truth hurt.

Mokes spoke up again, "I mean look, you fucking burt down an oil derrick. Doesn't that go against what you believe in."

"Mokes, the people that build oil derricks are causing way more ruin than me burning one down. It's all hidden agendas. They make it look nice and neat, but it's really destroying the environment in a soft and non-conspicuous way. My way is Ugly, but it only harms them, not the environment. You know this…"

Charlie came back.

"Alright we coming up to the dock. Mr. Z wants to talk with you before I mess you up too bad ya chink. So think about your situation and make the right choice. You can be respectable to Mr. Zendolini, give us the data chip and live on doing whatever weird greenpeace shit you do, or you can make it hard on us, and well, then we will make it hard on yous before burying you under 100 tons of rotting waste. Ca'pesh?"

Tony giggled in, "Hey, that'd be pretty ironic. An Environmental zero gets buried under what he spent his life fighting against. I like that. I hope your friends cry for your loss too." He made the 'Waa Waa' sound as the boat bumped to the docks.

"Here we are, at Charon's bridge to the afterlife. You better make the right decision boy, or he'll psychopomp your ass to hell."

***

The car ride was pretty quiet; however, in his blind peril, an eerie feeling washed over him as they moved through the transportation stages. He always saw Uka Buka, heard Uka Buka, maybe felt a gust from Uka as it rushed past him, but right at this moment, in his blind awakeness, the feeling of the floating tiki spirit was repulsive. He, of course, has heard Uka Buka say Uka Buka, but now, with his other senses dialed up, he could hear every slobbering, slurping little spittle juice out of him. Every slurp seeming like a credit toward death.

Ki didn't know exactly what Uka Buka was doing, but it felt like its eyes were bulging, its face was morphing between all the elemental textures, and its energy was pure Uka Buka madness. Leaves and flowers embedded into his face felt endangered of heating up from all the raw emotions shifting over its spirit; excitement, lunacy, eagerness, calm cold insanity, rage, hysteria, joyful arousal of pain. The monster was out and immeasurably drooling over the Zendolini Stronghold.

As they walked Ki into the unknown building he blindly recognized that they passed at least four guards and went through three doors. He stuttered down an extended fleet of stairs and sat down in yet another comfortable seat.

The bag was lifted, and there was Mr. Zendolini, who was as big as King Pin himself but with a much friendlier face than the Marvel villain. Uka Buka looked around the room and over Mr. Z's shoulder as he eyed Ki up and down for a couple minutes before speaking.

"Looks like Charlie gave you a true blue shiner." Mr. Z handed Ki a glass of water and Ki drank it without hesitation, hands still tied together.

"I just want you to really listen to me first, Ki. Then we both will talk about what is to happen next."

A loud pop went off outside and then another. They must have taken him to the heart of Ellipsis. Close to downtown near the shore was usually where an abundance of fireworks went off. Uka Buka rolled its black white eyes in euphoria.

"So, first, I want to explain my business, my real ambition, and my true intentions." Mr. Zendolini sat on a dark green couch across Ki's chair. The room seemed like it was an old man cave, with dusty bottles of wine, a flat-screen TV, posters of bikini models, and a round green velvet poker table. Outside the room were two silhouettes of men seen through the frost designed glass window of the door.

"When I began Zen Industries I was young and determined, but I started on a clean slate. After a couple years I received an ambiguous letter asking if I wanted to join a certain… society, the Illuminatis… They actually never gave me their name, but they gave me half their sigil, which instilled some interest to follow through with them." Mr. Z was calm yet focused like he wanted to live every moment of every second. Just being alive made him comfortable.

"Then these certain somebodies said I needed to take care of certain things, to gain loyalty and put in my dues. These things started off very small, smashing windows, telling people what to do… telling people what not to do. It was small time scare tactics, but the reward was great, mostly somebody somewhere dropping off loads of cash at my doorstep. So I gained a little more interest in these secret somebodies, because at this point I definitely knew they were, some - body." Mr. Zendolini stared at Ki as if trying to decipher whether or not Ki really understood or not.

"My small jobs turned into bigger jobs. The bigger the job, the more the money, see. However now these jobs required breaking legs, beating people up on the list, and finally conducting contracts and doing what I did best, taking out the trash.

"So I got a crew to do my dirty work while I focused on increasing my business… Until my son Brock turned 10. At this point I had a representative that I went through, who, funny enough, turned out to be the Environmental Representative of the Trump Administration. I did not like this man, Mr. Scott Pruitt, even 20 years ago he was a piece of shit. He was a Senator working against the rights of women having abortions and escalating the rights of criminal Christian White males. The Zendolinis were in a very bad situation and I wanted my son to have a clean slate just as I did when I started my business. I did not want Brock to grow up in this…"

Mr. Zendolini raised both of his hands to display where they were. "A house of secrets with a Mafioso mentality."

Dull faced and bored to death, Uka Buka was caught up in ferris wheel rotations during Mr. Zendolini's story.

"Now, Brock being 10 and coming of age I then tried backing out of this contract with Pruitt. No more killing, no more hiding, nothing. No letters, no money, just leave us out of it. So he, that little wiggling piece of merda, just kept the jobs coming, saying each time it'd be the last one and that I just needed to finish certain jobs to get out. Until finally, I was fed up and said Fuck your Illuminati pow- er-tripping shit, I'm out, and if you push me further, I'll sic my boys on your little Illuminati ass.

"Well, that's when I received a manilla folder that had every letter of mine, every tape recording of our calls, incriminating pictures, all the blackmail to take me down. On top of that, Mr. Pruitt put a hit on my family if I ever tried backing out of the Illuminati again." Mr. Zendolini took a deep breath and a sip of his wine, sinking back a little further on his couch.

"Until you killed the mother burdener… At first I was happy. My ball and chain finally broken and my enemy defeated. But then I received another ambiguous letter saying they wanted Scott Pruitt's phone, 2 million dollars and a letter of confession and reasoning behind mercing him." He rubbed his hands over his head in annoyance and took another sip of wine.

"Your little friend Tawa and our wily islander Mokes came to me the next day with the Compost idea. In our meeting I eventually found out they were associated with your new rugby group the Earth Enforcers, created just a month earlier. So I thought, with a name like that, it was bluntly obvious that someone there had something to do with the shitbag Administrator of the Environmental Protection Agency's death.

"Knowing I was close to the culprit and that I had to proceed into my own internal investigations with Mokes and the EEA, I sent the pyramid eye, the Illuminati, the cash, and told them I was close to catching Pruitt's real murderer and that I'd get his phone back to them as fast as possible."

Mr. Zendolini chuckled and sat forward.

"Which leaves me to you, Ki. You see my dilemma and you see we aren't just Hitmen and Murderers like you said in your sonnet graffitied on the front of my building." His smile turned to a darkened, annoyed teeth grinding.

"So where's that datachip Ki?" Uka Buka leaned in on Ki as Mr. Zendolini did.

Then with a rush of unexpected wind Toko Tuki flew in from behind Ki and started barking at Uka Buka. They bobbed around the poker table lights, transitioned into various argumentative heights, and rotated circles above Mr. Zendolini's shadows and Ki's mind. Ki tried to hold Mr. Zendolini's eye contact while Uka and Tuki yelled their names at each other. He started to like Mr. Zendolini, especially after sitting down and listening to him. Maybe his charm was why he was such a good villain.

Mr. Zendolini saw the uncertainty in Ki, however.

"You know the stakes, talk to me. Tell me where it is, and everything will go back to normal."

"I don't want normal. I want fucks with power to eat shit."

Mr. Zendolini grabbed Ki's arm and turned his skin in an Indian burn fashion. His tone was heated but was still level and relaxed. "Do you know what power is boy? Power is death. You are on that path if you don't fucking wake up!"

"Power is the ability to save life! If I give you that data chip, I'll need you to sign a contract to enhance the town's gardens and use your workforce to help Dr. Hankins and the Moki tribe steward the forest to help preserve life. Tell the Mayor it's your new design to better the Environment and cut down on wildfires."

"You're in no place to bargain."

"You said you want to do better. You've been wanting to do better, for your son Brock. Show him the right way."

"All I want is the damn chip kid, you have no idea. We don't have time for this!" Again, Mr. Zendolini had a calm serenity, but the menace flashed through his eyes, and simultaneously, Uka Buka smashed against the wall, causing a painting of a great ship to fall.

Mr. Zendolini was startled and headed for the door to check with the guards outside. Uka Buka looked larger, towering over Toko Tuki. Anger and hatred fueled Uka Buka. Enough for his force to break through the spirit realm and into Mr. Zendolini's den.

Ki had an idea. Uka had been pissing him off and making him hate more and more, but what if he shared love and kindness, then Tuko Tuki would blow up with power. With Toko Tuki around, love was around. Love, companionship, security. Maybe that's what Ki needed to get out of this mess.

"Okay Mr. Zendolini. Okay, I'll tell you where the data chip is, but first let me talk to my friend Mokes. Please Sir."

Mr. Zendolini went for the door and told one of his guys to go for Mokes and Brock. As the door opened a rhythmic noise of a flaring showering firework was heard.

Eyes closed, Ki meditated on what was next. He concentrated on love. He imagined a long grassy plain with yellow flowers weaving around scattered trees and rolling hills. He remembered the good times he experienced with Mokes, true times.

The sound of the den door closed and Ki opened his eyes. Mokes drifted around the poker table and Brock and Mr. Zendolini talked in anxious whispers by the door.

"Mokes come here Brother." Ki waved him in with his tied hands, like an entrancing spell.

Once Mokes started making his way closer, Ki began his experiment with angelic focus.

"Brother Mokes, I see you bro. I knew you were with the Zendolini's. Sheriff Worden told me you were at my house, and I saw that

Pruitt's cell phone was gone. You were right, I was the bad guy in this story, and maybe that's why I didn't try and stop you. I respect you Mokes and just want you to carry on in a path of righteousness and love. Forget about me and the phone, just hold true to the team and honor them."

Toko Tuki spun up to the ceiling as Mokes' back straightened from his repentant slouch. He was confused by Ki's change of heart, but Toko Tuki felt its loving power, growing bigger and bigger in its endearment.

"I'm sorry Ik."

The den door opened again and two tall well suited men walked in with Charlie. Through the frosted door window behind them, the hall looked packed with the silhouettes of many men.

The first tall man spoke with an unusually low voice.

"This is him?" He eyed Mr. Zendolini like he was a teenybopper punk. Ki felt closer to death than ever before at this moment, but at least there was some peace with Tuki around and Mokes forgiven. The ultimate power of love was on their side.

"Did you kill Mr. Pruitt?"

Ki nodded. Yes.

The man pulled out a beretta and pressed it into Ki's forehead. "We don't require his data chip, you Ki La'dori are required to die however." Ki smiled back with loving eyes, and at that moment, Toko Tuki rushed into the tall black man's chest, and Uka Buka followed, taking the fight inside an Illuminati. His index finger released the trigger and his hand squeezed the hilt. The gun slightly jostled in his hand as he readjusted his grip. His associate stepped forward in his hesitation.

A large quake shook the room and everyone looked past the walls and ceiling. "What the fuck was that?" Charlie said, while pulling out his piece and posting up next to the door.

"I had my friends follow me here. That quake was probably the Sheriff knocking on your door." They all looked at him in bewilderment and angst.

Ki was looking into the eyes of the Illuminati. The excitement of his savors washing away most of his humbleness from before. He wanted to laugh in their faces and tell them how he'd beaten them, but he kept his mouth shut. The fight wasn't over yet. Giving Sheriff Worden Pruitt's data chip was a good start to the Zendolini's and Illuminati's fall, but their power will not be so easily tarnished. They were a hydra with many heads.

"This was finally worth it." He murmured to himself. "Finally I did something, I did something wort-"

The pistol cracked against Ki's skull and the last thing he saw was Uka Buka smiling over him.

***

Big shouldered brutes stalked the shadows of resident trees and heavy columned driveway gates. Flashes in the sky spotlighted the bouncing gorillas moving about in a covertish sort of way.

Boom! Blasts of fireworks blew up in the sky above the industrial block Ki was held up in. The Grunion closed in on the Dolini Pits, frequently making room for the armed force who slid through on the broken sidewalk. The Sheriff glanced back down at his blinking GPS dot on his phone and put his fist up to bring a halt to his company.

Ki had told Pines to tell Mokes his plan to burn down the Harmony Oil Rig, so Mokes would tell the Zendolinis, the Zendolinis would find Ki, and the Sheriff would find the Zendolinis breaking the law yet again. The proof was there, and anyone involved in tonight's kidnapping would be affiliated with the criminal actions on Pruitt's chip. It was bulletproof. Hopefully just like the vests on Worden's squad.

Deputy Stokely and a full swat team stood ready for the Zendolini siege. They had received Pruitt's data chip earlier that morning and held a warrant for Mr. Zendolini's arrest. The Grunion used fireworks as a diversion tactic so the Zendolini guards surrounding the industrial outpost would be bamboozled during the encroaching skybangs.

The Sheriff asked the Mayor for backup. She complied with force.

The Sheriff looked into the eyes of his team. All of them were professional marksmen; the bouncing gorillas playing rocket fire boom booms behind them were just the Grunion distraction team.

"Riddle them with rubber bullets and secure the area. Alright..." The Sheriff took a long deep breath.

"LET'S MOVE IN! Go, Go, GO!"

***

Tawa and Fish pulled up to Ki's mother's house to tell her his dire situation. S.O.S by Buppon played on the radio. A yellow bandana held back Tawa's dreaded black hair. She looked pained to tell a mother her child had been kidnapped by the mafia. The snowballing effect was certainly real for Ki right now, and they were in the middle of Summer. Another sign that climate change could alter more than just the weather.

After Fish turned off his truck engine, he sat there feeling the same way. Fish was glad Tawa volunteered to come along; it would have been terribly difficult to tell Leia alone. The love he had for Ki and his Mother weighed heavily on his tear ducts, and his palms slipped with nervous sweat.

They got out and let themselves in through the side gate. Usually, the flourishing alleyway of plants and trees brought comfort and natural ambiguity. However, this time, they felt an edge to the sprightly garden home. An edge that cut into all the living, making Tawa and Fish feel like they were on the brink of spilling into an endless void.

They continued their walk to the back and peered through the kitchen window, canopied by a jungle of plumeria trees and elephant leaves. A Japanese guy who looked like Ki was speaking woodenly to Leia.

Fish and Tawa looked at each other for only a moment, and then came sharp silver necklaces that crossed their throats.

"Inside now." A distorted English dialect ordered. They all went inside.

"Karera ga soto kara mite iru no o mitsukemashita." The woman said with a smooth and steady voice.

The man interrogating Leia responded back to the woman in black.

"Wakarimashita. Hoka ni dareka ga inai ka mōichido shūi o kakuninshitekudasai."

She nodded and was gone. Like a ghost ninja. Quick, silent, and scary.

Fish twinked.

"You don't look like her son. Why are you here?" The two burglars had a hard time with English, yet looking into the man's eyes, Fish could tell this was no robbery; those eyes were highly intelligent, like a wizard looking for lost treasure.

"Sit." He motioned them to sit next to Leia on the kitchen stools. He held no weapon but the ripped muscles around his flat mouth seemed like he could eat rocks.

Fish hugged Leia, and Tawa watched the man with stoic eyes.

"Leia here can't get a hold of her son. So I'm going to ask you. Get a hold of someone close to him and get him over here before midnight.

Alone. Or you all die and we vanish."

Fish started his text to Baggans.

There is a Bad Wizard Treasure Hunter and a Ghost Ninja at Leia's looking for Ki. They say they are with the Yakuza. Ki needs to come alone or everyone dies. Including me bro. So, yeah. You have till midnight.

If this was really going to be Fish's last text message, he wanted it to be lush with character.

The wizard read it, laughed and pressed send.

***

Baggans read the text from Fish, grabbed a bundle of fireworks from Smeagols backpack and ran down the block towards the Industrial building Worden's swat team had just raided. The team was already cuffing the Zendolini guards out front. The floodlights lit up tons of cops, but everyone seemed busy and distracted.

A broken window fifty yards to the left of the entrance hung halfway in a shadow. He needed to get this information to Ki.

He threw a burning bundle of fireworks to the right and slipped into the shadows. When the boom booms went off, scaring the shit out of everyone, Baggans hoisted himself up through the window, and an officer was there with their back turned. No Zendolini or Swat is going to stop me! He commanded himself.

He charged and rugby tackled the officer to the ground, cheek to cheek. "Sorry about this, I need to get to…" An electric charge went through him as another officer stun gunned Baggans to his knees. In his tense voltaic pain he struggled out the words. "Sheriff Worden, pleas-"

The Deputy and another Officer carried Baggans down to the den. The open hallways were riddled with bullet holes. There were armored officers either helping the wounded out of the building or patrolling and securing the arrested Zendolini mafioso. This place used to be an old wine barrel storage facility, made into an art gallery and presently converted into a Zendolini vehicle repair zone. Dump trucks and massive tractors lay dormant in the center quarter as hallways ran along its three-tiered perimeter with mostly vacant office rooms. They walked Baggans down a flight of stairs, and the scene got worse and worse.

More red covered the walls, and the stench of gunpowder, death and shit hung in the enclosed air. When Baggans saw Sheriff Worden ahead, deep in the basement, he tripped over a Zendolini body and fumbled over a heavy breathing officer with his face covered in blood. The Sheriff was standing over Mr. Zendolini's dead body while talking with Ki. Ki's cheek had a deep slash under his fresh black eye.

"Sheriff, this man rushed into the warehouse and assaulted an officer apparently looking for you."

"What the fuck Dave. Are you fucking kidding me? This is an intense warzone you bashed yourself into!"

Baggans looked around. He saw Brock sitting on the broken pieces of the poker table, head down and hands cuffed behind his back. Charlie glared at Baggans and was seated in the corner with two other Zendolini thugs. And directly to Baggans' left, the legs of a wooden chair were stuck in the drywall.

"I have urgent news for Ki."

"It can wait."

"Worden, this is life or death. Please."

The Sheriff grabbed Baggans and took him over to the couch where Ki was spectating. He then nodded to Officer Tenley to give them a minute to speak.

Ki broke his grin and angled closer to Baggans. "Whats up Bags?"

"It's… it's Leia. She is in trouble."

Ki flew up and threw down the patch holding his cheek flaps together.

"Where is she?"

"Is it the Illuminati assassins? They only escaped from here about 10 minutes ago!?" The Sheriff roused in awe.

"No, listen to me. Please. First, if Ki has anyone with him, Fish, Tawa and Leia all will die." They all shuffled around a little before accepting that Ki had to go alone, then gave back demanding eyes on who was endangering their people.

"Okay, Fish sent me a message saying, Yakuza have kidnapped them and are waiting for you. Shit I mean, you need to get over there by midnight or… Come on, we need to get you out of here!"

"Dave, you need to take some heat so I can get Ki upstairs and on his way." Baggans nodded repeatedly like that was the obvious solution.

"Deputy Tenley, keep this man with the Zendolinis; we will write him up later at the precinct. I need to talk with the Mayor."

"Yes Sir."

They left Baggans with Officer Tenley and Charlie practically growling under his teeth. Past the door, past the bodies, Ki began to sprint and the Sheriff quickly caught him by the shoulder and tried to explain their situation to him. Over the railing was a colossus tractor in the open warehouse.

"It's 11:01 Ki, you still have time, but you won't have time if we leave here in the wrong manner."

"What do you mean? You want to take one of those?" He pointed his elbow at the tractor and swiped at his nose.

Sheriff Worden, again, looked astounded by his teammate's imagination. "No mate, you have to dress up like me and take my truck. Park far away from your mom's house and walk there." As he was explaining, he was unbuttoning his jacket.

"Take deep breaths. Here, wrap this bandana adjacently over your eye. Come on, strip off your clothes, let's go."

Ki took off his shirt and started hustling the Sheriff's clothes on.

"Listen to me Ki. These Yakuza want something. If you delay them and somehow bring them to the park behind Leia's, I'll be waiting there by the lightning tree. They are killers Ki, so be careful."

Ki finished tying the bandana around his head and tightly strapped Worden's belt to his waist. The Sheriff had a couple dozen pounds on him.

"Here are my truck keys. Act like a cop. If anyone stops you, say you are picking something up for the Sheriff."

"Okay. Thanks Conner." Ki hugged the Sheriff in his chonies and skipped off. A minute later the Sheriff walked out of the Industrial building and to his lucky stars he caught the eye of Ms. Mayor Force.

"Sheriff, what in the world!" She moved her eyes down to his groin.

"And why in the seven hells do you have that!"

Gangsters

Ki regretted taking the backroads to his mother's house. Usually the route was much quicker cutting directly through the mountain that stood between the lowlands and beach cliffs. The unexpected problem was while taking the windy turns at reasonably high speeds Uka Buka was spinning like a tasmanian devil and Toko Tuki was jetting back and forth at Uka, trying to get the totem brain to flinch.

Ki and his one operable eye had to drive mostly blind because of this. The crunch of metal on metal followed him through the streets as the Sheriff's truck bashed into parked cars and street signs. It seemed he was in a much larger truck than he was used to. Thankfully for him, he grew up on these roads, so occasionally looking out of his driver-side window was just enough to make it home.

"Can't you guys go anywhere but here. Fuck. You're spirits, aren't ya!" Flustered Ki stuttered as both of the heads were babbling on the dashboard, blocking Ki's one eyed view once again and causing him to skid onto the curb. They stopped and watched his recovery like curious little puppies.

Ki's emotions flip flopped with the totem spirits. He hated that they made him feel like a lunatic, but sometimes he loved the power they gave him. The impulse to push. A hidden magic he had unlocked somehow, someway.

On the last road to home, he looked around the truck for a weapon. He reached to the rear window and grabbed Sheriff Worden's shotgun.

"Shells, where you at?" The truck pulled off to the side and Ki ramped up the volume on the Sheriff's playlist as he looked for shotgun shells. His spirit friends were calm and interested in Ki now, probably ready and anticipating the storm coming.

11:32. No shells, fuck it. My mom needs me, now!

The racking of the truck engine rattled and roared down the street.

"Let them know I'm coming. The fucks!

The truck hydraulics bounced him into Leia's driveway, and Ki jolted out and kicked Leia's front door open with the empty shotgun aimed before him.

"Ah, no no no." Said a man who held his Mother with a gilded knife to her throat.

"Put the gun down, close the door and relax. We are Sokuru and friends. We came for what Leia here stole from us!" A flash of anger ran through Sokuru and he pulled her head back with his fist wrapped in her blue streak of hair.

"Put that gun down boy. Now!" Sokuru's broken English order rang throughout the comfortable abode.

He had heard of this man before. The man who had betrayed his father. Ki saw the death in his eyes and finally threw the shotgun down. Fish and Tawa gave great sighs of relief.

"Whatever you want. We don't have it."

Then a blade slipped into the back of Ki's thigh.

Silence came as the blood spilled. Chaotic white noise of pain drummed in Ki's ears. The slap on his right ear rolled his eyes to the back of his head, and he was pushed forward, at least closer to his friends. Tuki dashed from Sokuru to the lady ninja again and again, as Uka Buka ballooned in size, enveloping the room. Watching with glee.

Just one second. One more second of breath was bliss. Why hasn't Ki been enjoying this pleasure his entire life? He took a big inhale and an even longer exhale, trying to release the pain from his leg. This night has beat the bloody fuck out of him. A black eye, flap of a cheek, busted skull, stabbed sciatic nerve, and ringing to the right ear drum.

Toko Tuki embodied the floorboards in front of Ki's face, and the bright, colorful feathers around its tiki face inspired Ki to a kneel.

The hooded slim figure deviously stalked into his sight and took her place behind Tawa and Fish.

"Now. You are the key, Ki. Heh. Your mother says you are the one who knows where the National Preservatory paperwork is. Hattori Honzo's Land Rights. Show us, or die in horror." His darkened statement fell out of his mouth casually.

Maybe the Illuminati would come and try to assassinate him as well. Then the Yakuza and the Illuminati might fight each other. Both of them imbued with an ancient arrogance of destroying any competitor that walked in their path.

Fish twinked in his shaken excitement and Ki saw a real wink from his mother. She never winked. Ever.

A small dagger pierced through her shoulder, "No tricks, Meinu…"

Ki winced as if the knife was penetrating through his skin, wincing for his Mother, wincing for what she meant for him to do. During these petrifyingly heavy moments, his whole life clicked in front of him. She knew this day would come and she prepared. She prepared her house, the garden, the shed, and she even prepared him, but it only clicked at this moment. He'd do whatever he could to save her. He needed to save her.

He realized now that his people were his world. While he's been trying to help save the actual planet, he's been missing the greatest planetary truth of all. The people, the love, the connection between family and friends was what he needed to live for. Without them the sunshine would seem faint. Toko Tuki was his spirit ward now, and he yearned for the gift of love instead of hate.

Toko Tuki raced to the backyard and through Leia's jungle. Happy to show Ki, what his whole life has led up to.

Ki's finger croned like a witch's wand. "Follow the path. The latch on the far wall, past the nightshade. It unlocks a secret doorway."

Sokuru nodded at his ghost ninja lady companion and she wisped out the window and to the shed. Within a couple minutes she was back, coming from the front door this time. Again sweeping the perimeter of their household. She quickly spoke some Japanese in Sokuru's ear.

Sokuru smiled and spoke, "Youu are going to open it, boy."

Ki limped back to the shed with the wicked little ghost ninja. She threw back her hood for awareness and Ki noticed her hair was in two cute black buns on top of her head. They walked around orchids, ferns and calla lilies to reach the back of the garden. The inanimate tiki faces watched their movements. Ki even thought of trying to summon Suga Duka for help, but he had already given into the depths of his eternal quest - Always do what your Mother tells you.

After thinking of the plus side, he reminded himself that these assassins were more deadly than he could have ever imagined. He thought of his father and what a badass he must have been to try and build another gang to rival the Yakuza.

With the power of his father, Ki opened the door into the shed, which was so far back into Leia's jungle that it was barely visible to the living room window. Ki could still make out most of Sokuru and Leia and then the heads of Tawa and Fish.

Pop. Broken nose. Biggest received punch in Ki's life. He fell back onto the gardening counter and closed his watering eyes. He felt the blood pouring down past his lips and the tears burning the open wound of his slashed cheek. The cute black ninja buns weren't as cute now.

He ripped off the bandana bandaging his cheek together in frustration. This was life or death. Pure and simple. No need for minor bandage repairs now. He wanted to be gross. He wanted to be a monster like his enemies. He wanted Uka Buka.

The ninja moved in very close to him like she wanted to make love to his deformed face. Her mouth parted slightly, and he caught a glimpse of a lisping tongue. Her fingers on one hand thrust into his pants and her breath puffed out hot aromas of marigolds. At the moment when he thought she was going to twist his balls over his dick, her other hand tore the skin flap off his cheek.

Ki kept from yelling, the shock went straight to his blazen eyes. More blood spilled and now funneled through his tooth gap and into his mouth. He felt the plops of blood drip onto his chest. Yet, she wanted more from him, so she stabbed him in the back of his thigh again with something sharp. Ki finally yelled out in pain, in horror. Sokuru was right, they were freaks and they were about to wreak terror to get what they wanted.

Toko Tuki swam to him in a blur and he reminisced about his life and all of its love. His first girlfriend Lexi. So beautiful… His brothers and sisters of the rugby club… And his mother… his Mother.

Then Uka Buka shoved Tuki out of the way and Uka Buka'd.

Rage swelled. Everything his father fought against as a Kiza, boiled inside him now. Maddened anger. Gangs that fucked the planet and delivered their furious wrath. Killing the best of our people. His friends… his family. The power and the strength going in the wrong direction! Ki gritted his teeth at the smiling Yakuza lady and pulled the lever down next to him. A dart from above the doorway shot out of a little hole in the wall and spiked into the back of her head. The silver dart stuck up between her hair buns. Ki dashed forward to catch her chin and hold her as if she were still alive. They stood there in a weird romantic embrace, a deformed monster and a dead ghost ninja. He took this moment to recollect and assess his enemy inside. Now the physical pain he endured was cured by the blood pouring down his face, like a fountain of relieved redemption.

Uka Buka gobble laughed and flew up and above the garden, only to look back at Ki in astonishment at what he had cleverly done. The spirit was amazed at Ki's ingenuity and continued to spin around the moonlit sky and laugh.

Sokuru barked, "Alisano?"

Within a minute Ki heard the sound he never wished to hear. The slight slink, slunk of a blade through flesh. Ki watched as Sokuru's samurai sword rose to his side, dripping with blood. Tawa and Fish were gone.

Charmed with glinting shattered glass, Sokuru broke out of the window, chopped all green life in his way and grabbed Ki's arm. He clasped Ki's hands together and smoothly slid his tantō knife through the middle of both of them. While Ki was shackled in his pain, Sokuru checked on Alisano, the true ghost of a ninja now, Ki focused on keeping his mind a little in reality. It was drifting into shock, delusion, and hysteria. His friends were just killed, half his face was ripped off and…

Sokuru put his thumb to Ki's blackened eye and pushed.

With his worst fear coming true of having his eye pushed into his socket, Ki went into an illusion. To survive he needed to embody the Tiki spirit. A face made of earth and wood. He needed to remember he was just a walking bag of bones and that bodily damage could not kill his spirit.

"We move to get the Honzo Preservation Paper Rights now. Or she die."

Feeling the mush of his eyeball still trying to roll around inside his skull, Ki puked, then responded, feeling inches from death.

"I buried it." His voice sounded strange to him. Like someone else's.

"It's at, park, in the nook of split lightning tree. I only ask for, to finish her quickly… if I take you." Death brought no desire for grammatical diligence.

Sokuru rebelliously growled, spit gurgling and teeth snarling.

"Take me now." He drop-kicked a wooden chair and tied a broken leg around Ki's stabbed leg as a splint.

"Let's go."

Good thing it was past midnight and no neighbors had to get involved. From far off in the lower city and along the coast, fireworks still popped off once every ten minutes. The sky was misty and wet, and the air was thick with death. Ki knew nothing of what Sokuru asked for, but he knew he had to keep tricking the bastard until the end. The park next to his house also seemed like a good place to...

They reached the park's ominous gate and Ki began to cry. He continued to hobble forth into the darkness, but his saddened tears overwhelmed his soul. The park was where he took Zoo Za'mara. In fact he never went to the park without her. She would have barked with all the commotion in the house. That furry princess, that little hero of a dog. His best friend. She would have... barked...

Through his one good eye his gooey tears blurred everything around him. His bloody fingers from the knife still stuck through his palms didn't help to wipe his tears away. Outlined in the blur was the three way split lightning tree. Lost in pain and anguish, the rustle of leaves slowly caught up to Ki. He rolled his shoulder up to clear the blur in his one good eye and saw Leia's movement. She gave a good uppercut to Sokuru, along with a quick attempt to break his kneecap, but he caught her with a roundhouse kick that knocked her out cold.

Ki watched, now he knew he must have been in shock. He watched his mother just get knocked out and he just stood there. His hands ached as they tried to clench. He relaxed and began to believe that she might be better off asleep. The night brought too many horrors.

Over the tree line that rested beyond the lightning tree a sliver of the moon positioned itself as a silver arching seat. Only a week ago during the El Nino storms, a bolt of lightning split this tree in three. Trunks splayed out in different directions as the bolt hit directly on center. One trunk lay in the brush leading towards the moon. Another trunk was on the border of the road, and the last trunk lay across, blocking the walking path.

A samurai sword slinging out of its sheath under a majestic moon would usually seem beautifully honorable to Ki. The courage it took to battle in close combat with the caution of being chopped in half.

However, in this moment, it pissed him off, an unworthy, dishonorable foe held the blade, the same blade that killed his innocent friends.

Sokuru hung his sword over Ki's aura of space.

"You have Asagaio's characteristics boy. Whatever had come between us long ago, there was once a time we were great friends."

Sokuru's body tightened and the air thickened around them. The idea of his father was like a blinding light, only there to remind him of what's been with him day after day. Too bad the Sun wasn't there to watch him die.

Ki felt too saddened to watch the blade come down to him, so instead, he watched Toko Tuki race to him with its too real of a tongue, as long as its wooden face, flap around.

"Toko Tuki, Toko Tuki!"

Competing with the mesmeric sound of a sword undone, a hatchet came somersaulting with the wind over the fallen trunk blocking the trail. A warcry followed, and the dull end of the steel collided with its flesh bond mark. Surprised, Sokuru turned on the torrid storm of paintballs fired at his crotch and was suddenly checked in the face with the entirety of the gun.

Pines! The Sheriff must have told him where I might be!

Pines tried to kick the sword out of Sokuru's hand, but instead he missed the hilt and the blade cut into his foot. It pained Ki to see his friend wounded so quickly. Where he should have been rewarded for his heroism, he too has joined a night of cripplation.

Already down on one knee, thigh bloodied and leg inoperable, Ki was in the perfect position to tackle Sokuru. To do so properly, he wanted to break free. The knife impaling his hands together jerked through his tendons, bones and skin. His arms pulled while his hands held no feeling, asleep and perhaps on a bloody vacation. The blade's final release left him filled with ecstatic freedom.

Ki's first move, after licking his lips and finding that half his upper lip was missing, was to pick up the liberated knife, the tanto, a japanese warrior's dagger. He tried to pick it up off the ground, but his fingers would not move.

His shoulder rolled up to wipe at his blurred eye to smear clear enough vision to see Sokuru's dark figure shaking off Pines' hit. Ki lunged with his one good thigh and put his shoulder right under Sokuru's butt cheek. The lift took Sokuru up in the air only then to be slammed back into the ground, hoping he'd bend him enough to break his back.

Sokuru, the old Yakuza gangster, turned in the air to lessen the impact of the fall. While he was briefly laid out, Pines jumped into the air and focused all his weight on the point of his elbow, and slammed it down on Sokuru's wrist. An ambiguous POP, POP echoed in the hollows of the lightning tree. The sword popped out of Sokuru's hand. The other audible pop was from Pines' shoulder dislocating.

As sprung as a monkey tossing shit, Sokuru knee'd Ki in his bloody cheek as he rolled backward, resolving onto his feet. Ki retreated a few butt bumps back, reassembling his mind swimming through the currents of pain.

Pines limped over to the samurai sword and had just enough time to swipe it into the brush. His disarming victory was quickly met with a powerful kick into his back, folding him across the fallen trunk that bordered the path. Sokuru ran up the fallen trunk that had timbered into the forest brush, looking for his sword or acquiring the high ground to survey the battlegrounds.

As if time slowed down, Ki watched the frame of reality that carried a strange assassin standing on a lightning-storm defeated tree and a sliver of a moon shining above. With a blink, Uka Buka serenely floated down from the starry sky, facing Ki as if flaunting himself. Slowly descending a little below the moon, two silver horns revealed themselves on top of Uka's blocky tiki planked face. Ki felt his bones chill and his sunken eye roll in the back of his skull. With a jolt Uka attached itself to Sokuru like a mask, finally together with its destined vessel, and seemingly giving Sokuru a larger than life struction. A dangerous villain now wicked with Uka Buka hatred and bloodthirst.

In Ki's stricken gaze, he looked at Uka Sokuru's first victim, Pines. However, Pines too, seemed larger than usual, swaggering from the fallen trunk with more life, more power.

Only able to see him from behind, the perimeter of his head was arrayed with colorful feathers. Ki's heart leapt an inch. Toko Tuki, the brotherhood spirit for Ki, now embodied Pines, his brother! An always loving character in Ki's imagination, now fought the mad creature of hate, Uka Buka. Two forces of nature that imbued themselves into this recent year of Ki's life. Another reassurance in Ki's lucid mind that nature was the true divinity.

Limp, crippled, bloody, and ragged as ever, Ki rose off his butt, charging himself with the moon and waiting for his moment to join the fight between his shoulder angel and shoulder demon.

Uka soared down from the trunk with his legs bent in an air crouch. Tuki moved toward the jumping, tongue slathering beast. Both of them with wounded arms, one a broken wrist, the other a dislocated shoulder, came together, bashing at each other like shield bearing Vikings. Their wounded sides were used as shields, and their good arms were used as axes, giving each other blow after blow.

Tuki Pines, being a loving friend his entire life, quickly began taking on more strikes and kicks than the Yakuza born hitman and blood hungry Uka Sokuru. It was time for Ki to get in the mix. He slinked forward and thought of his lost brother Fish, the Basher of the Smasher. *This is for you bro!*

He rushed in to meaningfully headbutt Uka, but was instantly met with a roundhouse kick right in Ki's bloodied cheek again, making Ki feel skeletal. Skin and flesh were just a barrier, bones had to be what kept him moving.

As Tuki Pines swung with a fist of fury, Ki felt even more empowered by his death-ridden skeleton body. He decided to use his bones, the hard parts of his body, Muay Thai style.

With his head still spinning from Uka's kick, Ki went in blindly with a big swinging elbow to the back of Uka's greasy black long mossed head.

Now both Tuki Pines and Ki bashed on the villain. It felt so good, like it was the foundation of life itself to bash on what was evil.

Uka ninja blocked multiple anticipated strikes and spun, screaming and splintering spittle all over Ki while grabbing his arm and breaking it in half with his shoulder.

There went the strength of his everlasting bones. He cried out, hazed by his gnarled body and unimaginable sequences of injuries. Black eye, stabbed thigh, broken nose, cheek torn off, stabbed thigh again, impaled hands, pushed in eye, a broken arm, a broken heart…

Tightening his calves to send power up through his body, Tuki Pines did all he could with his punches. Each swing inched closer and closer to a perished fate, and with a last bit of hope, Tuki craved immediate success and threw his entire body at Uka to move the monster away from Ki. Uka used Tuki's momentum to twist and throw him into the throne nook of the lightning tree's split core.

Ki stood. Broken. Enchanted by the beauty of the night. It was sad, it was miserable, but the action between the two spirits was magnificent. He gawked at what was either his total imagination or a spiritual truth that only he could see. The moon smiled at his pain as Uka did. At least the sky was happy.

Could thy vastest sky hold sentiment?
Doth the globe have reason to torment?
Possibly every happening is happiness?
Good or bad, it is bliss'ness.

Hate can have a wicked grin.
Chop up the helpless,
For the pleasure of Sin.
Hate silently grow'eth in Eden's Trellis.

Hate severs thy connection between elements.
Anger is the annoying squawk of danger.
Fear comprises hateful developments.
An angle on'wence known as thy Lone Ranger.

Collide with Darkness you may spark a light.
Fall into Darkness, you no longer exist in sight.

Uka Sokuru pulled back for a massive punch at bewildered Tuki, but Tuki Pines was a trickster and was giggling with blood between his lips before he counter-headbutted Uka Sokuru's fist as the punch headed for impact. Uka shook it off and went for a jab at Tuki's weak spot. The spot between the spirit and the body, his throat.

Before the collision, Ki wrapped his forearm around Uka's shoulder and yelled, "Love, Uka!" And Ki headbutted surprised Uka in the bridge of its nose. Face to Face. Finally… The smell of chipped fresh cut wood and blood meandered through the air.

Uka's face leaned far back and thrust in for its own headbutt, knocking Ki down to watch the clouds ride through the moonlit sky.

He tried to soak up as much love from the starry night as possible.

Hath thou drown in fright? There is might to overcome.
Hath bringth a relic of choice,

For it was previously loved in tomes undone.
Listen to the ambience of one another's voice.

Find the greatest feeling, which is love untold.
Words not hold truth as well as thy eyes.
Love comes from a teardrop in a twinkling sky.
Love resides in the act of remembrance.

Love is the ability to sacrifice till we die.
Love hath no connection with thy body.
Thy soul is thy bridle that directs goodness.
Goodness is thy saddle embroidered with t' power of love karate.

Ride the shadows of evil and your mark of love will shine.
I have lived a life in love,
For you my dear mother,
Let your planet's eye arise,

Over any other.

Ki's ears caught a slip slush and then a plop.

Leia came to his side after a beautiful moment of silence, "My dear boy, I'm so sorry."

Ki looked into his mother's eyes like they were the unseen universe, collapsed into a sphere on the peak of the tallest mountain. Peace, he thought. Peace is nice.

***

Leia helped her undead looking son sit up and embrace Pines. Toko Tuki lifted off his face with a shake and a happy little twirl, then vanished into the forest. Sokuru lay dead with the tanto dagger through his spine and neck. Uka Buka bashed into the dirt, repeating

Uka Buka, Uka BukA, UKA BUKA! Until Uka and the Earth were once again together as one, and vanished into her, leaving only a spiraled piece of bark behind.

"Pines?" Ki gave him a questioning thumbs up to see if he was okay, but his tendons were severed, so his hand really didn't work properly.

Pines had a long red feather on his shoulder that Leia picked off of him curiously.

"I'm better than you, that's for sure."

Sirens were heard out in the distance.

"Thank you Kavika. Thank you." Leia told Pines with watery eyes.

"Why?" Ki pointed his tired, mutilated face at the dead Yakuza in a nice loose-fitting Japanese parachute-style suit.

"There was a small bit of your father's story I left out…" Leia stared into the dark forest and decided that this was a better time than any to tell her son the full story.

"Your father and I visited the Ise-Shima National Forest every chance we got. It embroidered our relationship as well as briefed Asagaio with his next missions for saving the environment. In Ise-Shima lived a brilliant man who gifted Asagaio with a legacy. Hattori Hanzo was his name, your father's mentor. A most magical cape and grand piece of land on the Ise-Shima coast was his to pass down, and he and your father were twins in their beliefs. They worked together in diminishing the atrocious acts of the Whalers, and tried to create a new radical environmentalist organization that fought for the planet. If dangerous people could ban together for bad, dishonorable things, stupidly horrific things, then avenging empathetic people could ban together for good things.

"When the future seemed crystal clear and change was shifting under their toes, Sensei Honzo gave us Ise-Shima's Legacy and the rights to steward the land and take care of its surrounding waters… Unfortunately this was when Asagaio and Hattori Hanzo grew very bold and more reckless with their plans. They felt bulletproof, with a legacy as their shield and a Japanese forest as their castle. So eventually," Leia kicked the body on the ground.

"Sokuru found out their plan in overthrowing the Yakuza. And again, Honzo and Asaga were only trying to make it better, an organization to help the planet and fight against evil-doers. Yet Sokuru gathered a Yakuza force and quickly brought all of their rich ambitions to an end. Brought Asagaio to an end…" Leia bent down next to Ki and gently massaged his stabbed hands.

"You were a new beginning though Ki. The key to my escape. They were never supposed to find us here. Sokuru asked about the Stewardship documents that fateful night when your father died. He believed his reward for capturing the leader of the rebellion was the territory rights to this epic piece of land.

"How he found us in California 25 years later is… Sokuru must have learned of your exploits in the Earth Enforcers Association or a Yakuza gang member saw you in Jail."

Ki began thinking to himself. Or, Yakuza had connections with the Illuminati. Zendolini sent word out about a Japanese American kid doing exactly what his father died for, then the ninjas and assassins started booking flights.

Unable to tell if Ki was looking at her or even listening, Pines put his hand on Leia's knee and gave it a squeeze. A tear fell from Leia's face and she softly brushed her fingers over Ki's sunken eye socket.

"If your Father could see you now Ki. He'd be so proud of you." She looked at Pines and then back to Ki.

"And probably a little scared of you too." Ki cracked a relaxed grin and Leia and Pines giggled softly.

The sirens got closer and closer, right down the street from them now. The first patrol car arrived and flashlights beamed around haphazardly.

Later, while Ki was being loaded onto a stretcher, Sheriff Worden made his way over to him, "Ki. Oh. Are you alive?"

Ki blinked his one good eye and slightly opened his mouth. The morphine was just beginning to help with the pain and he felt like uttering any noise was unnecessary. He did enough tonight.

"Ki… the Zendolini gang is being arrested for criminal syndicate organization and murders. You also have to be charged with arson on the Harmony Oil Derrick. I mean if you live through the night…"

Ki blinked his one eye again, he didn't care. He should have been dead. He actually felt dead until…

His mother's voice sang to him, "Oh Ki! ZooZa is okay by the way. I gave her a load of CBD so she could sleep through the Fourth of July fireworks!" Leia said cheerily as if she was reading his mind.

The smile on Ki's face rivaled the moon's wicked curve, and he felt Toko Tuki's blessing of love as wind whooshed through his cheek and into his mouth.

Ahh fresh air and a new beginning.

Epilogue

Three and a half years later after the burning of Oil Derrick Harmony.

A large box waited for Ki La'dori when he got out of prison. For four years he was condemned for arson on Oil Derrick Harmony. Lucky for him, he was given one year off for helping the town's Mayor, Patricia Force, catch a concealed mob syndicate for multiple counts of murder, money laundering, fraud, and extortion. During his time behind bars, he received another six months off his sentence based on his ample behavior and ability to work with others, a characteristic originally unknown to Ki.

After his fight with Sokuru, the Yakuza gangster, the Orthopedic Surgeon went to work on him, but could only bring back movement in one of his hands. His right hand was now unable to close because his tendons were too severely severed. Making his offhand, the left, his new good hand.

Resting his elbows on his knees above a gifted departure box, Ki stared at his left palm, recently tattooed with a skull and crossbones emblem. The scar where Sokuru slid his tanto knife through both of Ki's hands as bladed manacles that represented one of the crossed bones on the skull.

He exhaled a long breath, relieved he was only a few minutes away from being released and free to be amongst his natural divinity.

His left hand opened the box and pulled out a backpack, clothes, nice cargo pants, an earth-toned buttoned-up shirt, a dark blue jacket, a basic hat, socks, and sneakers. He slid a phone and a wallet stacked with $3500.00 cash into his pockets, and there were two more last items at the bottom of the box that made him itch at his temple, an envelope and a worm-engraved staff with a polished triangular stone on top. The stone was smooth and had multiple quartz veins running around it.

The envelope clinked as he picked it up and delicately studied the concealed bulge. Using his limp hand as a base, he stuck his left hand into the envelope and came out with three rings around the first nubs of his fingers. One ring was charred and burnt black, another had an eastern mold resembling wind circlets, and the last ring was just a wooden knot. His elemental rings.

Ki was almost positive this care package had been from his mother, Leia La'dori, but this solidified it. He pulled out a letter with his mother's writing and read with his one good eye.

Ki,

Sorry I wasn't there to visit you, Ki. I'm dropping off your package and heading straight to Ise-Shima's National Forest. When you are released, come find me. To help you find my secret location, Suga Duka will be waiting for you. She will face an enshrined leap towards a rocky reunion of Sun, Moon, and Sea. I can't wait to see you. I love you!

Here is some light to shine upon you because you likely reside in the dark.

The E.E.A. has been 'terminated' due to its increased association with corporate development sabotage in the community. This is mostly your fault, but don't worry! The Earth Enforcers Association is just a name. All your friends are still active Environmentalists and are now 'covertly' working together.

Colin Richardson took over the reins of the Ellipsis Waste Industry. Pines and Vander are regulars at the shooting range, but other than that, they stay home with Zoo Za'mara and keep a low profile. After I sold our house, I moved all your stuff into Pines' garage, so maybe you'll need to visit them briefly before coming to Japan. Brock was released from all criminal charges binding him with his father's Mafia syndicate, and there's a rumor going around that he left with Mokes to the Big Island.

Baggans... after Tawa and Fish's funerals, Baggans figured he would start working a graveyard shift at the cemetery. He might even live there now as the night attendant. Pines told me he wanted to keep busy and be left alone. Maybe he feels closer to Fish there, or perhaps the graves are helping him grieve.

Ki, please don't get in any more trouble. When you get out, just come straight to Ise-Shima and straight to me. We will work everything out from here.

Safe journeys my boy.

Love, Mum

Ki got dressed, packed away his mother's gifts, and finally wrapped his good hand around the worm-engraved staff. The lights in the private meeting room slowly fluttered, blinking dimmer and dimmer, and then, within a second, the electric energy brightened so vibrantly it caused Ki to close his eye. Ki could only wait in shock for the pulsating energy to disperse throughout his body.

That feeling would have had Gandolf himself passing the pipe to study the magic within it. Still, the heavy stone bolted to the top made it feel more like a sturdy walking stick than a legendary wizard staff.

Ki's first step out in fresh air and away from the block would have been great in itself, but with the Toko Tuki's worm-engraved staff now working as Ki's new cane, he felt another tremor of electric frequency run through him. He gurgled with suffocating power and swiped his nose with his thumb. This feeling was definitely something new that he'd have to get used to.

It's been three and a half years since he's felt anything other than the cold cement floor and prison walls. He's mostly been alone and, yes, in the dark, as his mother said. The contrast of this natural environment overwhelmed him so much that he keeled over and puked in the dead grass twenty yards outside the prison, out in the middle of nowhere.

These waves of euphoria were so unknown to him. Blinding him with so much light, so much renewed power, the air he inhaled enlarged his heart with every gulp. A colorful tickle of love and happiness floated over his right shoulder, and there he was, just as his dreams depicted, his long-lost spirit of goodness and brotherhood.

Toko Tuki, at the forefront of a far-off treeline, grimacing a slight smile and looking cheeky as ever by staring straight ahead and not at Ki.

Ideas were interweaving themselves with the clean air circulating through his entirety. He pondered, resting his weight on his power cane. *A couple of stops before the Airport won't stir up too much trouble… Not with an eyepatch-wearing, cripple-limping, tiki-shouldering ex-convict. Right?*

Uka Buka was gone, and Toko Tuki was with him. Love, and only love, was with him now.

UKA BUKA